In Loving Memory of Erin

AN ISOLATED INCIDENT
ISBN: 978-1-912767-44-1

Published worldwide by Zertex Media Ltd.
This edition published in 2022.

4

www.jdkirk.com
www.zertexmedia.com

BOOKS BY J.D. KIRK

A Litter of Bones

Thicker Than Water

The Killing Code

Blood & Treachery

The Last Bloody Straw

A Whisper of Sorrows

The Big Man Upstairs

A Death Most Monumental

A Snowball's Chance in Hell

Ahead of the Game

An Isolated Incident

Colder Than the Grave

Come Hell or High Water

City of Scars

Here Lie the Dead

Northwind: A Robert Hoon Thriller

Southpaw: A Robert Hoon Thriller

Westward: A Robert Hoon Thriller

Eastgate: A Robert Hoon Thriller

CHAPTER ONE

IMPROBABLY, there was somebody at the door.

Way out here.

At this time of bloody night.

There had been no glow of headlights. No sound of an engine, nor of tyres coming sweeping up the makeshift driveway. No closing of car doors, no swishing of footsteps through the grass.

No sound at all, in fact.

Just the knock. Just a moment ago.

And again. There. Just now.

His wife's face registered the same concern that he felt. Or a fraction of it, anyway. She didn't know.

Not like he did.

"What on earth?" she muttered.

He silenced her with a look and a finger to his lips. His bones were suddenly heavy, and it took more effort than it should have to raise his hand to his mouth.

She flicked her gaze to the door that led off from the other end of the living room to where the kids slept soundly in the room next door. Her concern was that they'd be woken by the noise. It had been a long few days. They all needed some unbroken rest after the last few weeks.

His own concerns were somewhat more visceral.

The knocking came again. It was firm. Insistent. A knock that had no intention of going away. A knock that would only get louder.

A *crack* from the embers dying in the hearth made him tense. A whisper from his wife made him jump.

"Who's that at this time of night?"

"Well, I don't know, do I? What am I, bloody psychic?" he whispered back.

The curtains were drawn on all the windows, and the only light was the brooding red glow of the dying fire. There would have been no beacon for a stranded motorist to spot. No siren's call promising warmth and shelter to any travellers wandering lost on the hills.

Whoever was at the door had come here on purpose. *With* a purpose.

"Maybe they'll go away," his wife reasoned.

"Maybe," he said.

They wouldn't, he knew.

They should've kept moving. Should never have stayed here this long. But, she'd loved the place so much, and it was so remote and out of the way.

And he'd been so careful.

Hadn't he?

He was casting his mind back over everything he'd said and done outside the house—everyone he'd spoken to, every lie he'd told, and photo opportunity he'd politely declined—when the knock came again. Louder, this time, less patient.

"It might be someone hurt, or in trouble."

"It might be," he said. His gaze was fixed on the door. He could only see part of it from the armchair he'd claimed as his own back at the start of the week, and the darkness outside turned the frosted glass window to a square of charcoal black.

But he got an impression of something out there. Real or imagined, a shape loomed beyond the glass. Large. Imposing.

Inevitable.

Knock. Knock. Knock.

"You'd better answer it. They're not going to go away," she said.

His gaze unlocked itself from the door and went to his wife in the chair across from his. He almost swore at her. *What? You go and fucking answer it!* But, she was right. Anyone who came all this way out into the middle of nowhere to knock on a door at this time of night was not going to just give up.

The people who were after him would *never* give up. They'd hunt him to the ends of the earth, if it came to it.

Perhaps, they already had.

The poker scraped on the rough stone of the fireplace as he removed it from its hook. He'd been jabbing at the flames with it for most of the night, keeping the fire going as best he could, and the metal tip still radiated enough heat to burn anyone who found themselves on the other end of it.

And, of course, there was the damage it could do with a good hard whack.

He saw his wife's eyes flit to the makeshift weapon. She said nothing, but got to her feet and positioned herself in front of the door to the room where the girls were sleeping.

They could call the police, of course. Assuming the wind was blowing in the right direction for them to get a signal. But it would take them at least twenty minutes to get here at full pelt with lights flashing.

Add in the time to make the call, to explain, to give the address, and—

The knocking returned as a thumping fist that rattled the glass in the old doorframe. He jumped, his breath catching in his throat, his grip tightening on the limply held poker handle so that it sprang erect.

"Fuck," he whispered, and the word hung there in the fiery red murk.

He thought about the back door.

He thought about leaving her—leaving them—to face his mistakes.

But he couldn't do that. He couldn't.

Someone would almost certainly be waiting out the back, too.

The door shook. His wife hissed.

"Go and see who it is, Archie!"

The poker shook in his hand.

Out there in the darkness, a shape shifted behind the glass.

CHAPTER TWO

DRAT!

He'd sliced it. *Idiot!*

He kept his eyes fixed on the ball as it curved off to the right, and studiously ignored the gleeful remarks of this morning's companion.

"Look at it go! Water, water, water!"

There was a distant *ker-splunk* and a sound from behind him that was a cheer disguised as a commiseration.

"Aw, bad luck, Boyley-ma-boy! You'll no' be getting that one back without a wetsuit and snorkel."

Rufus Boyle scraped his vibrantly white top teeth across his bottom lip, bit down for a moment until the urge to swear had passed, then turned to his opponent and smiled.

"Ah well. Can't win 'em all, I suppose," he said, playing up his privately-educated Edinburgh twang just enough to remind the other man who his betters were.

"Seems like you can't win *any* this morning, can you?" his opponent replied, grinning like the proverbial idiot. He was a local man. Mid-fifties, so around Rufus's own age. Worked in the aluminium factory half a mile down the road. John, or Bob, or something equally as mundane.

The club had matched them up based on both ability and avail-ability. Rufus liked to play early, but not *too* early. Mid-morning worked best for his schedule, as it allowed him a leisurely breakfast —either in the downstairs snug, or out on the balcony on the rare occasions that the weather allowed—and an hour or two to get the day's business out of the way.

John, or Bob—Billy, maybe?—worked late shifts at the factory, so mid-morning was a good fit for him, too. And they were, though Rufus hated to admit it, well-matched opponents.

Handicap-wise. There, besides gender and approximate age, any and all similarities ended.

"How come you're doing so shite the day? Something on your mind, Boyley-ma-boy?"

Rufus detested the name the other man had given him, but had made a point of not letting on, in case his protests served as some sort of encouragement.

He'd much have preferred 'Rufus' or, ideally, 'Mr Boyle.' But *Boyley-ma-boy*? God Almighty. It was how John, or Bob, or whatever his name was always addressed him, and each time he did, it brought him one step closer to having his head caved in with a pitching wedge.

"I'm going to play again," Rufus stated, fishing another ball from the pocket of his gaudy tartan breeks and setting it on the tee at his feet.

"Of course. Go ahead," the other man said. "Just mind and write down the one-stroke penalty."

The sudden jerk of Rufus's hand knocked the ball off the tee and onto the grass. "I meant I'll just write off that last attempt entirely."

"I know you did. But it's a one-stroke penalty. Them's the rules, Boyley-ma-boy."

Rufus picked up the ball, squeezed it hard, then returned it to the tee where this time it remained.

"Fine. Yes. Fine. I didn't realise we were taking it *quite* so seriously, but fine. Whatever makes you happy," Rufus said, punctuating the sentence with an impressive array of passive-aggressive hand movements and facial expressions. "I mean, if it means that much to you..."

"Just playing to the rules," the other man said, and even

without looking, Rufus could picture his self-satisfied smirk. "You seemed to think it was so important on the ninth, when I—"

"I said I'll take the penalty," Rufus said.

The bastard was trying to get under his skin. That was it. Throw him off his game.

As if Rufus didn't already have enough to worry about.

His watch gave a buzz, warning him of an incoming call. He glanced at the display, muttered below his breath, then unzipped the side pocket of his golf bag and retrieved his phone. "Sorry, I have to take this. Business-related."

"Fire on, Boyley-ma-boy. No rest for the wicked."

"Quite, yes," Rufus said, stepping away with his finger hovering above the button that would answer the gently vibrating mobile.

In truth, he was quite grateful for the call. Ever since he'd mentioned to John, or Bob—Chris? Could it be Chris?—that his working day ended around ten in the morning, he'd been subjected to quite a lot of ribbing from the others at the club.

This largely took the form of him being called a lazy, workshy bastard, so there was a certain sense of satisfaction now that his leisure time was being interrupted due to a business matter at—he checked his watch again—nearly half past eleven.

Hopefully, once the other fellows at the club realised he was always on-call for business-related emergencies, they'd appreciate just how hard he truly worked.

He answered the phone and spoke in a slow, clear voice to the woman on the other end. "Good morning, Magda. I'm in the middle of something. Is there a problem?" he asked, not wasting any time. His cleaner wasn't ringing him up for a friendly chat, after all. She knew better than to do that these days.

"Mr Boyle. It is are you good morning, yes?" Magdalena replied in what could generously be described as 'broken' English, and more accurately as 'barely.'

"It *was*, Magda. What is problem? Why you calling?" he asked, simplifying the sentence structure and raising the volume of his voice, which was as close as he ever got to speaking any language that wasn't the Queen's English. "What you need?"

"Who the fuck are you talking to? Tarzan?" asked his golfing nemesis. Rufus already had his back to the man, but rolled his shoulders forward to further shield the conversation from his prying ears. Ears which, Rufus imagined, had not been cleaned behind in years.

"Is house, Mr Boyle. Guest House. Is no empty, I think. Is guest people still inside."

Rufus blinked. Magda was a fine cleaner, but holding a conversation with her could be like trying to carry water in a sieve. Not only was her grasp of the language tenuous at best, Rufus had also come to the conclusion that she was thick as pigshit.

Never exactly a winning combination.

Still, she was a hard worker, knew her way around a vacuum cleaner, and the one thing she had a worse understanding of than English was the minimum wage regulations.

"Was that a question, or are you telling me?" he asked.

"Pardon?"

"'Is guest people still inside,' you said. Was that a question, or are you saying they're still inside?"

"Still inside. I think. Curtains..." Magda hesitated, like she was replaying the word to check it was the right one. "...closed. All closed. Up. Down. Closed."

"They might have left them shut."

"Pardon?"

"I said... Nothing. Forget it. Have you looked?"

"Looked?"

Rufus removed the phone from his ear, pushed out his lower lip with his tongue to imply the woman on the other end of the line suffered some sort of disability, then swallowed back his rising irritation.

"Just knock. Check. They should have left."

"They should have left."

"I know. That's what I just said!"

The sound of a titanium driver striking a golf ball made him look back over his shoulder. The hissed, "Yes! Get in!" only served to further spoil his mood.

"Just knock on the door and go in," he instructed.

"I no like to go in if people inside."

"They won't be inside, Magda," Rufus snapped. "If they are,

then they bloody well shouldn't be. So knock, go in, and if they're in there, tell them to sling their hook."

The silence from the other end was riddled with confusion. Rufus sighed and rubbed his forehead with a gloved hand.

"Look, I'll hold on. Go in. If they're there, you can put me on speakerphone. I can talk to them."

"I... I should go in?"

"Yes! For Christ's sake, Magda. It's not hard. Go in. In you go. You go in. Understand?"

The sound changed on the line. A breeze blew. Birdsong echoed. A car door *thunked* shut.

"I go in. But I no like."

Rufus wanted to point out that he didn't particularly like having his morning golf game interrupted for the sake of some unopened curtains, but the linguistic gymnastics that would be required to get his point across would only frustrate him, so he elected to remain silent.

"You about done?" his opponent asked. "We'll have people wanting to play through if we don't get a shifty on, and I'm working at two."

Rufus held up a finger for silence. "Just... one moment."

He listened to Magda's breathless panting as she lugged her cleaning box up the incline to the guest house's front door. She was wheezing like an old racehorse on the way to the knacker's yard. Christ, don't tell him he'd have to start looking for a replacement. Cheap foreign labour was proving increasingly difficult to get.

"You there yet?" he asked, after what felt like an eternity of listening to her puff and pant.

"Soon. One minute more," she rasped.

Rufus rolled his eyes, gave an apologetic sort of wave to his golf partner, then turned away again.

"How far away did you park?" he asked. "Cornwall?"

"Pardon?"

"Nothing. Just hurry up. I'm in the middle of something important."

"Here now," Magda said, dropping the level of her voice.

"Why are you whispering? Don't whisper. Just knock once and go in. You're in the right," Rufus told her, then he simplified that all down before she could question it, and repeated only the, "Go in," part.

He heard her knocking. It was quiet and timid-sounding. If the guests were still asleep, it would do nothing to wake them.

"They no answer."

"Then go in, woman! You've got keys."

Rufus listened to the *clack* and the *creak* of the door being opened.

"It no locked," Magda told him, her voice barely audible now above the sounds of wind and birdsong. "I go in. I go in and—"

He heard her gasp.

He heard the *thump* of her phone hitting the floor, the rustle as it bounced and slid across the carpet.

He heard her babbling in her native tongue, the words themselves meaning nothing to him, but their increasingly hysterical tones telling him that something was seriously wrong.

And then, through a crackle of low-signal static, he heard her muffled screams.

CHAPTER THREE

DC TYLER NEISH had been married less than forty-eight hours, and was already halfway through the first official argument with his new wife.

They sat in Sinead's car outside the polis station on Burnett Road, windscreen wipers fighting a losing battle against the raging rain. He sat in the passenger seat, shoulders stooped and head down, like a child being reprimanded.

"No, it can't wait," Sinead told him, her voice all hard and sharp around the edges. "You need to tell him today. Your operation's on Thursday."

Tyler wobbled his weight from one arse cheek to the other. "Aye. No, I know, I just—"

The look she shot him was harsher still than her words had been. They'd been having this same conversation for almost a week now, and no amount of gentle encouragement and supportive words had helped spur him on.

Seeing him slouched there, she found herself softening again. She couldn't be annoyed with him. Not about this. Plenty of other things, aye, but not this.

She took his hand and wove her fingers between his. "I know it's scary, Ty. But they have to know. *He* has to know."

Tyler nodded, but didn't yet look up. "I know. I know, it's just..."

"It makes it all real?"

"Suppose. Maybe, aye. But not just that," he said. He met her gaze then, and the fear and uncertainty in his eyes almost brought tears to hers. "What if they start treating me differently? What if it's... you know, weird?"

"Weird how? They're not going to start ringing bells and shouting, 'Unclean!' or anything."

Tyler smiled at that. "Aye, but... they would, wouldn't they? Normally, I mean. If it was something less... serious."

Sinead blinked as she realised the root cause of her husband's hesitancy. "Wait... you're worried they *won't* rip the piss?"

"What? No!" Tyler considered this. "I mean, I don't know. Maybe. Aye. I just don't want it to be different, you know?"

"You do remember who we're talking about, yes?" Sinead said, smiling. "Do you really think that lot could stop taking the piss for five minutes if they tried?"

Tyler gazed ahead at the station. The movement of the rain on the windscreen made the building's walls shift and dance like the whole place was alive. A smirk tugged at one corner of his mouth.

"You could be right," he admitted. "And, I mean, it's not like we're not used to morbid stuff. We deal with death all the time, don't we?"

"We do," Sinead agreed, unclipping her seatbelt. "But you're having a bollock chopped off, you're no' dying." She gave his hand a squeeze, then nodded ahead at the shimmering station walls. "So, don't you think it's time we broke the news?"

DCI Jack Logan sat alone in his office, quietly making an arse of eating a bacon and fried egg roll. The egg was runnier than he'd been expecting, and the yolk had erupted out of the back of the roll on the first bite then splattered onto his desk.

Fortunately, this was far from his first bacon and fried egg rodeo, and he'd had the foresight to place the white paper bag the roll had come in directly in the splash zone, thereby saving his desk from the worst of the mess.

He couldn't say the same for his hands. Yolk, grease, and melting butter were slowly cascading along the lengths of his fingers, dripping in oily blobs whenever they met the fold of a knuckle.

Usually, he'd power through, then surreptitiously lick the worst of it off when no one was looking, but there was too much mess already. He was just one bite in, and his hands were so covered he didn't dare continue without first cleaning up.

He'd just set the roll down in the nest of the paper bag, and was contemplating what he could use to wipe his fingers when a gruff male voice came from the direction of the door.

"Fuck me, what have you been up to?" it demanded. "Fingering Casper the Friendly Ghost?"

Logan glowered at the man looming in the doorway, and for a moment the only sound was the irregular dripping of egg yolk on paper.

"Bob? What are you doing here?" he finally asked, giving his hands a wipe on the crumpled white bag. "I thought you'd catch fire if you ever set foot in the place again."

The former Detective Superintendent Bob Hoon gave a grunt that simultaneously acknowledged the joke and made it clear he didn't find it funny. "Aye, well, needs must," he said, giving nothing away. He pointed to the roll on the desk in front of Logan. "You going to eat the rest of that, by the way?"

"Yes. Of course I am," Logan replied. He gestured with glistening hands to the darkened Incident Room at Hoon's back. "Seriously, how did you get in?"

"How the fuck do you think I got in? A jetpack? I walked in the front door and up the stairs. Surely that's no' a stretch of even your limited fucking imagination, Jack?"

Hoon dropped into the chair across the desk from Logan, spread his legs wide, and began twisting from side to side until the metal and plastic *creaked* out a little rhythm.

Logan expressed his irritation with a tut and a sigh, then leaned forwards so his elbows rested on the desk. This put him directly above the remaining four-fifths of his roll, and the aroma of bacon and egg drew an impatient grumble from his stomach.

"Let me rephrase that question, then," he said. "*Why* did you get in? What do you want?"

"A favour."

The shock hit Logan like it was a physical thing, making him blink and draw back. "A favour?"

"You deaf, or is there a fucking echo in here?" Hoon asked. "Aye. A favour."

Logan drew air in slowly through his teeth and stared at his old boss like he was trying to read the man's mind—disturbing as that would almost certainly be.

"Are you in trouble?" Logan asked. "Because I can't help if you've got yourself arrested, or—"

"Fuck off!" Hoon interjected. "You think I'm a fucking scally or something? Believe me, if I was up to no good, you eggy-fingered fuckmuppets'd be the last to know about it. *Am I in fucking trouble?* Jesus."

"What, then?" Logan asked, keen to get back to his roll as soon as was humanly possible.

Hoon tapped his hands on the arm of the chair. His throat clenched and relaxed a few times, like a bird trying to regurgitate something large and unpleasant.

"I need a reference," he finally managed to say.

Not a line, not a crease of Logan's face moved.

"A reference?" he asked. "As in..."

"For a fucking job. Aye."

"A reference for a job?" Logan said, speaking the words slowly like they were the clue to some cryptic puzzle. "*You* want a reference for a *job*? From *me*?"

"Fuck me, Jack, it's no' that hard to grasp, is it? Surely even you can get that big fucking melon head around such a simple concept?" Hoon spat. He prodded himself in the chest. "I—me— require you, sat here in your sad, pokey wee office, to write me a job reference."

"Why?"

"Jesus fuck! So I can make it into a wee paper hat and wear it to parties. Why do you *think* I want a job reference, Jack? Put on your fucking thinking helmet for a minute if you have to, and mull that one over. I'll wait."

Logan scowled, annoyed more at himself than at Hoon. It had

been a pointless question, given that his roll was continuing to go cold on the desk in front of him.

"What's the job?"

"Never you fucking mind what the job is," Hoon told him, stabbing a finger against the scuffed surface of Logan's desk. "All I need is a few hundred words saying what a joy I am to work with, what a fucking honour it was for you to have me as a boss, and how your life is so utterly pointless without me in it that every morning when you wake up and remember you won't be working with me, you contemplate getting a razor and opening up your fucking wrists." He gave a wave of his hand. "I mean, it doesn't have to be word for word that, but you get the gist."

Logan nodded slowly. "Should I mention you getting fired and narrowly avoiding prosecution, or...?"

"Do you really want me to answer that?"

"And what do you mean 'without you in my life?' I swear to Christ, Bob, I see you more often now than I did when you worked here."

"Look, just shut up. You're like a wee granny up the back of the bus, giving it all *meh, meh, meh, meh* about the price of a fucking fish supper." He made a flapping mouth movement with one hand. "Are you going to write me a fucking reference or not?"

Logan gave a weary sigh, shot a glance down at his congealing breakfast, then returned his gaze to the man across the desk. Hoon was a few years older than Logan and lacked the DCI's height and imposing build.

He was ex-special forces, though, and while his time behind a desk or in a bottle during his latter years at the polis had padded out his middle and rounded off his chin, he'd spent the last several months sculpting it away again. Were it not for the thinning hair and perpetual scowl-lines etched as wrinkles into his face, he could've passed for a man half his age.

Well, maybe two-thirds.

He was a dangerous man. He'd always been a dangerous man. Logan didn't want him in his office any longer than was absolutely necessary.

Besides, he'd been the one to track down Tyler at the weekend, and avert a potential wedding disaster. Logan owed him something for that, if nothing else.

"If I say yes, will you leave?"

"You think I want to sit around here looking at your face any longer than I fucking have to?"

"Fine. When do you need it?"

Hoon checked his watch. "Half ten."

"What? Today?"

"Naw, Jack. Half ten on Christmas morning," Hoon sneered. "Of course today. Why else would I be gracing you with my presence if it wasn't urgent? Fuck's sake. Are you sure you're cut out for the polis, Jack?"

Logan held his hands up. "Fine. I'll do it in a minute. But you're not waiting here while I write it."

"Too fucking true I'm not," Hoon said, getting to his feet. He leaned over the desk, dipped a finger in a blob of egg yolk that lay cooling on the paper, then rubbed it on his gums like he was testing the purity. "Where's that from? Across the road?"

Logan regarded the fingerpint in the yolk blob for a few moments, then raised his head and glowered at his old boss. "Aye. That's right," he said. "Now, do us both a favour, Bob, and tell me where to send this reference, then piss off out of my office."

A business card was placed face down on the desk between them. "Email address is on there," Hoon said. "Needs to be there at half ten at the latest. At the fucking *latest*."

Logan reached for the card, but Hoon pinned it beneath an egg-stained finger. "Wait until I've gone," hc said, and for perhaps the first time Logan could recall, the words coming out of Hoon's mouth sounded more of a request than an instruction.

He leaned back in his chair and shrugged. "Right. Fine. I'll email it. Was that everything, or did you want to hurl some more abuse at me for a while?"

"Hurl abuse? You'll fucking know when I hurl abuse, Jack. I'll hurl it so hard it'll punch a hole right through that saggy-titted chest of yours. This is just friendly banter," Hoon said. He tapped the business card. "So. Half ten, aye? At the latest?"

"Half ten," Logan confirmed, reaching for his roll. "I'm sure you can see yourself out the same way you came in."

Hoon stopped in the doorway, fumbled with a couple of vowels and a consonant or two, then ejected a muted, "Cheers, Jack."

"No bother," Logan told him. "Good luck."

"Aye," Hoon said, but he didn't yet start moving.

"Was there something else, Bob?" Logan asked, his stomach mewling like an injured animal as he held the roll just inches from his lips.

"You spoken to Boy Band yet?"

Logan frowned. "Boy Band? Oh, you mean Tyler? About what?"

Hoon glanced back over his shoulder, then shook his head. "Nothing," he said. "Doesn't matter."

And with that, he was gone.

CHAPTER FOUR

THERE WAS some commotion when Tyler and Sinead crossed the reception of Burnett Road Station, making for the stairs. Five or six uniformed officers were escorting someone off the premises through a side door, while a dozen others stood ready to jump in and lend a hand if things started to escalate.

Quite ironic, Sinead thought as they started up the steps, given that there was very little that would escalate a situation more effectively than twelve Uniforms blundering in with good intentions and swinging batons.

"Wonder what that was about," Tyler mused, his feet *thacking* on the hard steps as he plodded his way up them.

"Probably just some nutter," Sinead said, shrugging the question off. "I swear, this place attracts them like moths."

Tyler smiled. "You talking about the staff, or...?"

"Aye. Us lot are the worst of all," she said, keeping the conversation light.

She could see the worry written across his face, and the way each step seemed to take more effort than the one before. His mind might have accepted what had to be done, but his body was doing its best to put a stop to it.

"Just another day," he'd pleaded that morning. "We can tell them tomorrow. Another day won't hurt."

And, in a way, he was right. There would be no real harm in

holding back the news until tomorrow. It was Monday, and his operation wasn't until Thursday. Given the circumstances, they'd understand why the request for time off was coming at such short notice.

But she'd spent the first day of her married life watching her husband stressing about telling them the news. The thought of it was eating him up worse than any cancer ever could. He had to tell them. Today. For his sake.

They continued to speak about nothing whatsoever until they reached the Incident Room and found it mostly in darkness. The only light filtered out through the gaps in the blinds on Logan's office windows.

He was in, then.

Of course, he was.

"You OK?" Sinead asked, putting a hand on Tyler's back and rubbing it. "You want me to come in?"

"Eh... I don't..." Tyler inhaled, then breathed out in short stages, like he was battling labour pains. Once his lungs were empty, he shook his head. "No. It's fine. I can do it."

"Because I can. If you want me to. I can come in."

"No. Thanks, but... I sort of... I think I should probably just..."

She rubbed his back again, letting him know that no explanation was needed. "I'll be right out here," she told him, then she packed him off with a kiss to the cheek, and watched him go shuffling into the light.

"WHAT THE HELL are you doing here?" asked Logan. "I thought you were meant to be enjoying the first few days of married bliss?"

"Eh, aye, boss. That was the plan, right enough," Tyler confirmed. "But, well... something came up."

"Jesus Christ, son, she's no' kicked you out already, has she? What did you do?"

"What? No. No, nothing like that, boss," Tyler said.

The lad was very subtly rocking his weight from one foot to the other, Logan noted, while picking at the skin around his thumbs with the forefingers of each hand.

"What is it, Tyler?" Logan asked.

"Eh..." Tyler glanced back into the darkened Incident Room, closed the door, then faced front again, all smiles. "Mind if I have a seat, boss?"

Logan indicated the chair opposite with a nod, then scrunched up the paper bag that had been spread out on his desk, swept quite a large number of crumbs onto the floor, and waited for Tyler to spit it out.

"Something kicking off downstairs when were we coming in," the DC remarked. "Someone getting dragged outside."

Logan gave a satisfied little chuckle at that. "Aye? Good stuff. It was Hoon."

"Hoon?"

"Aye. He came to see me. I called downstairs once he'd left. Wanted to make sure he made it all the way outside."

Logan would usually have expected Tyler to see the funny side, but his face had fallen at the mention of the former Detective Superintendent's name.

"What did he want?"

"Job reference, would you believe?" Logan said. He reached across the table, picked up the business card, and flipped it over.

The first thing he saw was the logo of the supermarket chain, *Tesco*. The next thing he saw was a name: 'Gavin Howden - Junior Manager'.

Logan spent a few seconds imagining how a *Tesco* junior manager called Gavin would cope with the mighty Bob Hoon. He tried to enjoy the thought of his old boss stacking shelves or working the checkouts, but to his great annoyance found that he could take no pleasure from it.

"A job reference? Was that it?" Tyler asked.

Logan set the card down next to his computer keyboard, glanced at the clock to check the time, then turned his attention back to the DC. "Aye. Actually, no. He asked about you."

Tyler's smile was so thin it bordered on being transparent. "Me, boss? What did he say?"

Logan unfastened the top button of his shirt and loosened his tie. He'd been given quite the talking to by Detective Superintendent Mitchell when he'd returned to Inverness following their last case, and it had been agreed that he would 'make more of an effort.'

So far, this had extended to him arriving at work with his shirt fully buttoned and his tie straight. His record for keeping them that way was a shade under three hours, and two of those had been spent in an operational meeting with the Assistant Chief Constable.

"Not a lot. Just asked if I'd talked to you," Logan replied. He interlocked his fingers and leaned forward, eager with anticipation. "So, I thought to myself, 'Talked about what?' And now, here you are. So, what is it you want to talk to me about, Tyler?"

Tyler squirmed like a worm on a hook. He rubbed a finger across the edge of Logan's desk like he was checking for chips in the wood. "Aye. Well. No. Aye. I mean... there was something, boss. That I wanted to talk about. To you, I mean."

Logan dipped his head forward, urging him to continue.

"Like, I mean, it's not that I *want* to. Nobody wants to talk about stuff like... But, well, I suppose it's sort of... There's no getting away from it, is there?"

"I have no idea what you're talking about, son," Logan pointed out. "There's no getting away from what?"

"The thing I wanted to talk about. You know? Like the... what is it they say? The elephant in the room," Tyler said.

He was sweating now. Beads of perspiration were giving his forehead the same sheen as Logan's greasy, post-bacon-and-egg-roll fingers.

"I think an elephant in the room refers to something that everyone is aware of, but nobody's mentioning," Logan said. "That's the opposite of what we've got here. Because, again, I don't have a clue what you're talking about. What's wrong, Tyler? Spit it out, son."

Tyler drummed on the desk with both hands, clicked his tongue against the roof of his mouth so it made a loud *tock* sound, then nodded.

"Aye. Best way. I'll just say it."

Logan waited.

And waited.

"Did you mean out loud, or...?"

"What? No. Aye." Tyler took a breath so deep he almost swelled up like a toad. "See, the thing is, boss—"

The phone sitting between them on the desk rang. Tyler's eyes went to it. Logan's did not.

"The thing is...?" the DCI urged.

"The, eh, the thing is..." Tyler shifted his weight around like he'd forgotten how to sit. "The thing is that..."

His eyes were drawn back to the insistently purring phone. Logan lifted the handset without looking, then set it down again.

"The thing is...?"

Tyler opened his mouth, closed it, then took another run-up at what he was attempting to say.

"The thing is, boss... Remember the accident I was—"

Another burst of ringing from the phone cut the sentence short. This time, Logan picked up the receiver, slammed it down, then took it off the hook.

"Continue," he said, still holding eye contact with the younger detective.

Tyler raised an unsteady finger and pointed to the phone. "Are you sure you shouldn't...?"

"It can wait. What is it you want to tell me, son? I'm on the edge of my bloody seat here."

"Right. Aye. Sorry, boss." Tyler cleared his throat, smoothed down the front of his shirt, sat up a little straighter, then began to speak.

He made it all of three words when the Incident Room was flooded with light, and a stern female voice demanded, "Is he in?"

"He's, um, he's in a meeting," both men heard Sinead say, but the quiet thunder of approaching footsteps made them both turn their attention to the door just as it was thrown open to reveal a small black woman who somehow gave the impression she was three times her physical size.

"Answer your phone when I call you, Detective Chief Inspector," Detective Superintendent Mitchell said in a tone that made it very clear that he would not enjoy the consequences of ignoring this request.

"I was in a meeting," Logan told her. He pointed to Tyler, as if presenting evidence.

Tyler, who was closer to the DSup and so more directly in the line of fire, smiled apologetically and gave a little wave, and was immensely grateful that she chose to ignore both these actions.

"Yes, well, I'm sure it can wait," Mitchell said. "And, even if it can't, it'll have to. You've had a shout. A bad one. Two adults, two kids. Home invasion, by the looks of things. That's the local take on it, anyway."

"Jesus. Where?"

"South of Fort William."

"Again? We just got back from there," Logan remarked.

"I'm well aware of that. I swear, they must be putting something in the water down there," Mitchell said. "I want you on the road within the hour. This has the potential to go very public very quickly. I want it contained and dealt with."

"Aye. We'll get right on it, Ma'am," Logan said.

"Make sure you do. Within the hour," Mitchell reiterated. She pointed to his phone. "Now, put that back on the hook. And for goodness' sake, Jack, straighten your bloody tie."

The door swung closed as she left. Logan listened to her retreating footsteps until he reckoned she was safely out of earshot, then returned his attention to Tyler.

"You were saying?"

A look of surprise faltered its way across Tyler's face. He blinked, gave a curious sort of half smile, then jerked a thumb back over his shoulder. "I was just going to say that me and Sinead have decided to cancel our days off this week, boss," he announced. "And just as well, too. By the sounds of things, you're going to need all the help you can get!"

CHAPTER FIVE

MITCHELL HAD CALLED IT 'A BAD ONE.'

Christ. Talk about an understatement.

There were four of them, just like she'd said. Two adults, two kids.

Hands and feet bound with coils of gaffer tape. Mouths sealed shut with strips of the same. Blood pooling on the carpet beneath their huddled bodies.

Logan had arrived first, hitting the outskirts of Fort William while the rest of the team were still getting themselves organised back in Inverness. He'd even beaten Geoff Palmer and his army of white paper suits, and he stood alone in a stranger's front room now.

Just him and the dead.

The room was nice, assuming that you could overlook the corpses. It was simple and unfussy, with faintly grey walls and a few tartan trimmings, and the way it balanced style and easiness of cleaning clearly marked it as a short-term holiday rental.

Some of the touches—the plump cushions, the rustic oak table, the reclining armchair by the fireplace—indicated a room designed to look cosy. Right now, though, it was cold. Bitingly so. The ashes in the hearth told him a fire had burned itself out, and the lack of any discernible traces of heat from the embers suggested it had happened at least a day ago.

The Uniforms guarding the scene had given him what little information they had when he arrived. The family had been staying for a week, and were due to check out first thing that morning.

The cleaner had turned up to find the curtains closed and the front door unlocked. She came in, freaked out, then ran off, and was currently hyperventilating into a cup of tea at the small polis station in Glencoe Village. Her boss—the house's owner—had been on the phone to her at the time of the discovery, and had called 999 once he'd realised what the hell was happening.

There was no sign of forced entry. The windows were all intact, and Logan had noticed no damage to the door or frame. If the door had been unlocked, someone could have just walked in. Or, they could've knocked, waited for someone to answer, and talked their way inside.

Logan retreated into the hallway. There was a small, spindly-legged table against the wall across from the door. A vase stood upright, a visitor guest book undisturbed. A struggle was unlikely, then.

He made his way back into the living room, the plastic coverings on his feet crinkling as he walked. He still hadn't turned his attention to the bodies beyond a cursory glance. He would, of course, but not quite yet. It was easier to remain objectively detached when he hadn't yet seen their faces. Seeing the terror in a dead child's eyes made logic and reasoning a much bigger ask.

The *who* and the *why* could wait. Best to focus on the *how* for the moment, and let the rest follow on from there.

Four people were a lot for one intruder to manage, especially when half of them were frightened kids, and the other half—presumably—were protective parents. There were a lot of unpredictable elements in that equation. A big risk for one person on their own, unless they knew exactly what they were doing.

The kids were wearing pyjamas. The woman had been wrapped in her dressing gown, although it now hung off her shoulders, revealing nightwear that erred on the side of practical, but left a little bit of leeway for the fun stuff.

It had been late, then. Under cover of darkness, probably. The kids might well have been asleep upstairs, which again implied that there had been more than one intruder. Too many moving parts for someone flying solo.

It was possible that this was the work of some lone opportunistic amateur, of course, but if it was then, Christ, they'd struck it lucky. They'd managed to get the kids downstairs, successfully secure all four members of a terrified family, kill them all, then make a clean getaway with whatever they'd managed to get their hands on.

There were no signs of struggling—no furniture moved, or pictures knocked off-kilter. Two wine glasses sat undisturbed on the coffee table, dried dregs staining the bottom. Take out the bodies and the blood, and you'd never know anything had happened here.

Logan gave the room another once-over, keeping to the edges and touching nothing.

Finally, when there was nowhere else to look, his gaze settled on the bodies on the floor.

They had been back to back, he thought. Parents and children, bunched together, their wrists bound behind them. He wondered if they'd interlocked fingers and squeezed hands. Had the adults tried to offer some silent comfort as the children sobbed behind the tape?

They were both girls, the kids. One around thirteen, maybe, the other closer to eight or nine. Both guesses, though, and possibly far off the mark. They had the same mousey blonde hair. Skinny wee things. There was no mistaking the family resemblance.

The mother's hair may well have been the same colour once, but it was now a nut-brown, with a line of grey at the roots where the dye-job had begun to grow out. Like with the kids, it was hard to pin her age down with any real accuracy, but Logan would put her in her mid-forties.

She was on the heavier side, and the way she'd fallen had caused one of her breasts to slip out of the vest top she wore beneath the dressing gown. It hung sideways so it was touching the floor and partially squashed beneath her armpit.

Logan didn't know the woman, but he wanted to cover her up. To save her this final indignity.

But, he couldn't give her that. Not yet. Not until she'd been measured, and pored over, and photographed from every conceivable angle. Not until a dozen or more strangers had been in and seen her lying there in all her shame and glory.

He muttered a near-silent apology, and turned his attention to the fourth victim. Male. A good bit older. Balding and grey, with a paunch of a stomach and a Rolodex of extra chins. Although, to be fair to him, the angle of his head probably wasn't doing him any favours on that front.

Something about the man's face stopped Logan in his tracks. There was something familiar about him, like he'd met him somewhere before.

He kept his distance, but squatted down to give himself a better viewing angle. The tape across his mouth and his wide-eyed look of terror were conspiring to make it difficult to identify him, but recognition was nagging away at the DCI. He knew this man. He knew him. He did.

The front door opened, just as something in Logan's brain went *click*.

"Jesus!" he ejected, standing up.

"Not quite," said a voice at Logan's back. It was not the nasal tone of Geoff Palmer, which he'd been bracing himself for, but an Irish twang that came miraculously close to bringing a smile to his face, despite the circumstances. "Although, sure, I bet I'd look deadly in a crown of thorns."

Logan pointed down at the man on the floor as the pathologist, Shona Maguire, stepped up beside him. He felt her tense and heard her give a little gasp—a rare reaction from a woman for whom death was just another day at the office.

"You OK?" he asked her.

Shona swallowed something down, then gave a single nod. "Fine. You?"

"Had better mornings," Logan said.

"You know who did it yet?"

"Still working on it," Logan said. "Expecting a breakthrough any moment."

"Good to know. Probably don't need me, then."

"No, but since you're here, you might as well have a look."

The whole exchange was delivered earnestly, and with straight faces. It was a pantomime, of sorts—a step away from grim reality for a moment or two. An escape from the horrors of the here and the now.

But they could never escape it for long.

Logan pointed down to the man at their feet. "Check it out. Recognise him?"

Shona bent and studied the victim's face. "No," she said, straightening again.

"Aye, you do!" Logan insisted.

Shona bent over again. This time, she spent a little more time looking over the dead man's features.

"I don't."

"You bloody do!" Logan insisted.

"I bloody don't."

"*Neeps and Tatties!*"

Shona stood upright, an eyebrow raised. "Sorry, what?"

"*Neeps and Tatties,*" Logan said again. He cupped a hand to his mouth and pretended to shout. "Where's the Haggis?"

Shona slouched her weight onto one hip and regarded the DCI like he'd lost his fucking mind. "I have no idea what you're talking about."

Logan gave an impatient sigh. "*Neeps and Tatties.* The 80s comedians. Off the telly." He stabbed a finger down at the dead man. "That right there, Dr Maguire, is the one and only Archie Tatties himself!"

"So, you didn't tell him?"

Tyler paused midway through folding a shirt into his case, then confirmed that no, as far as he could remember, he hadn't.

"What do you mean, 'as far as you remember?'" Sinead asked, shoving her own clothes into a holdall with far less care and attention than her husband.

"It was... there was a lot happening," Tyler explained. "I was about to—I was literally about to say the words—and then Mitchell came in, and..."

"And you didn't."

Tyler flinched at that. "And I didn't."

"And now, somehow, we're both working the week that you're meant to be having your operation? Just so I'm clear."

There was some puffing out of cheeks at that point. "Aye. I'm no' quite sure how that happened, right enough," he admitted.

And then, contrary to all his expectations, Sinead erupted in laughter, gave him a kiss, and told him he was a bloody idiot.

He was unable to mount any sort of counterargument to this, and instead followed her out to the car, placed his bag in the boot, and clambered into the passenger seat beside her.

"But you'll tell him today, though, yeah?" she said, starting the engine.

Tyler confirmed that he would. Of course he would!

And then he spent the two-hour journey racked with guilt over the first lie of his married life.

CHAPTER SIX

"SHE'S TAKING her bloody time in there," Geoff Palmer complained, not for the first time since he'd arrived. "What's the hold-up? Is she doing the PM on the living room floor or something?"

"She's just doing her job properly, Geoff," Logan said. He didn't turn to look at the Scene of Crime team leader. He wasn't worth the neck movement.

"Doing her job slowly, more like. It's bloody freezing out here," Geoff grumbled.

"Maybe go and sit in your van," Logan suggested, and he did his best to keep the hopeful note from his voice.

Palmer tutted and gestured to the eight or nine white-suited figures currently picking their way with great care around the edges of the driveway, gazes fixed on the grass. "Can't, can I? I've got to supervise this lot."

He didn't seem to be doing much supervising, Logan thought, but he chose not to say anything for fear of encouraging further conversation.

"It's freezing out here, though," Geoff pointed out once again. He shivered, presumably for emphasis. "It's alright for you, you can put on a big coat. You think this shit is windproof?" He tugged on the wrist of his paper suit, then thrust his arm in Logan's direction. "Have a feel of that."

Logan stared at the offered fabric sample. "I'll take your word for it," he said, then he returned his attention to the house.

It was the sort of house that popped up on postcards—a quaint little stone cottage with whitewashed walls and three little windows in the roof to let light into the converted loft space. Local Uniform had checked up there when they'd first secured the house, then retreated outside to avoid contaminating the scene any further.

They were learning, he was pleased to note.

An old outbuilding at the back of the house was apparently locked, though the door appeared rotten enough that a stern look might be enough to knock it off its hinges. Between the buildings, a wooden frame had been built, and two swings had been hung from it. Judging by their condition, they were a much newer addition—a couple of years old, maybe less.

The house was fine—nothing too fancy—but the location? Well, that was something else entirely.

Logan had always had a fondness for Glen Coe. There were a couple of points on the journey up the road from Glasgow that he always looked forward to. One of these was just north of Crianlarich, as you crested the hill and were presented with miles of open space ending in distant, snow-capped peaks.

The second was here, where mountains and river met, and the sky always matched the colour of your mood.

Today was no different. The house stood at the foot of the middlemost mountain of the *Three Sisters*, one of the area's most recognisable natural landmarks. Brooding black clouds had taken root above the rocky peaks, casting them and the gullies between them into deep pools of shadow.

Although the clock was ticking towards lunchtime, a morning mist clung to the grass around the cottage, covering it in a feathery blanket of white, and Logan half expected to hear the howl of a werewolf echoing from far off in the distance.

Polis vehicles had taken over the Three Sisters car park that lay back up the track, at the edge of the A82. Uniformed constables were directing traffic—a process which largely involved shaking their heads and making irate gestures at any drivers who started to slow down and indicate they were turning in.

The car park was usually jam-packed with tourist vehicles even this early in the season, so there was quite a lot of head-shaking going on, as well as the odd shouted instruction to, "Keep moving."

You'd have thought the wall of flashing blue lights and the cordon tape would've been enough of an indicator that the car park wasn't currently open for business, but if Logan had learned anything about the general public over the years it was that half of them were idiots, half of them were chancers, and neither side was good at taking a telling.

Logan had been expecting Sinead and Tyler to show up by now, but there was no sign yet. Traffic was moving slowly in both directions, thanks to an endless parade of rubbernecking bastards, so chances were they were just running late.

Plus, if past experience was anything to go by, Sinead would likely have had to stop multiple times to allow Tyler to throw up at the side of the road.

After a bit of persuasion, Detective Superintendent Mitchell had relented and allowed DI Forde to leave the Inverness station and set up base in Fort William for the second time in as many weeks. Ben's health was still a concern to everyone but the DI himself, who insisted he was in the best shape of his life, despite his newfound dependency on heart pills and throat sprays.

Hamza should be driving him down, once they'd picked up Dave Davidson, who would be handling Exhibits and providing support in the office.

None of the buggers were here now, though, and despite his distaste for gossip, Logan was itching to talk about the man on the floor in the living room.

"She's still not out," Palmer said, sighing heavily to make his displeasure clear.

"I can see that, Geoff," Logan replied. He tutted, annoyed at himself for even considering what he was about to do, then swivelled to face the other man. "Here, you remember Neeps and Tatties?"

Surrounded by its elasticated paper hood, the perfect circle of Geoff Palmer's face that was currently visible stared blankly back at the DCI.

"What, the vegetables?"

"No. The comedians. Off the telly," Logan said. *"Where's the haggis?"*

"Oh. Them. God. Aye," said Geoff, brightening. "They were good, weren't they? That was proper comedy. None of that 'woke' rubbish that you get now."

Logan gave a non-committal shrug. He'd been maybe five or six years old when the Neeps and Tatties double-act was in its prime, and their broad slapstick and catchphrase-based routines had seemed hilarious at the time. He had a nagging suspicion though, that were any of it to be viewed through more sophisticated eyes, it would be revealed to be a right old bag of shite.

"Why do you ask?" Geoff wondered.

Logan gestured to the house. "One of the victims is Archie Tatties."

"Bollocks it is! Seriously?" Geoff retorted, almost choking on his disbelief. *"The* Archie Tatties?"

"Certainly looks like him," Logan confirmed.

Palmer tutted. "Doesn't mean it's him. There's probably hundreds of people that look like Archie Tatties. Thousands."

Logan raised a quizzical eyebrow.

"Well, OK, maybe not thousands..." Palmer admitted, then he spat out a, "Finally!" as a masked-up Shona appeared in the cottage doorway, her disposable gloves and apron both flecked with spots of blood.

Logan set off to meet her, while Palmer rounded up the troops.

She was shaken, he could tell by the way she looked to the sky and blew out the air she'd been holding in for too long.

He couldn't blame her. However familiar you were with death, however comfortable you thought you'd become with it, it still had the power to catch you off guard. To floor you with a sneaky gut-punch out of nowhere.

And kids would hit you hardest of all.

"You alright?"

Shona smiled weakly. "Had better mornings," she replied.

"You need a minute, or...?"

"I need a coffee. Preferably an Irish one," Shona told him.

Logan glanced back at Palmer and his squad. They were now

marching up the driveway, Palmer's wee legs scurrying along as he struggled to make sure he was leading the way.

"This lot are going to be a while yet," the DCI said. "Everything seems under control here. I'll buy you that coffee and you can fill me in."

"Deal," Shona said. They stepped in opposite directions, letting Palmer's crew flow between them like a river, and watched until the last of the paper suits had vanished inside.

"Give me a minute. I'll meet you at the car," Logan said, handing her his keys. "There's a pub just up the road. We can go there."

Shona took the keys, tapped her forehead in salute, then set off to find Logan's Beamer in amongst all the other vehicles currently clogging up the car park.

Logan watched her go, then entered the house and sidled over to the living room door. He could hear the *clack* of cameras from every room, and the creaking of floorboards overhead. There were three members of the forensics team standing over the bodies, one taking pictures while the other two—Palmer and a woman Logan vaguely recognised from past crime scenes—contemplated the family on the floor.

The woman's exposed breast had been neatly tucked out of sight, Logan noted. He gave a nod too subtle for anyone else to see.

The coffee was definitely on him.

"Well, I'll be a monkey's uncle," Palmer remarked, placing his hands on his hips. "That dour-faced bastard was right. If that isn't Archie Tatties, I'll eat my bloody hat."

CHAPTER SEVEN

GAVIN HOWDEN, Junior Manager of the Eastfield Way Tesco superstore, smiled sympathetically and clicked 'refresh' on his email. He nodded to the man opposite while they both waited for the ancient laptop to *clunk* and *whirr* its way through its calculations, then peered at the screen over the rim of his round-framed glasses, and gave a shake of his head.

"Still nothing, I'm afraid."

On the other side of a piece of furniture that could generously be described as a desk, and more accurately as 'some bits of a table,' Bob Hoon shook his head too, only somewhat more emphatically.

"No, he was going to send it."

"Well... he hasn't, I'm afraid."

"Bollocks. Check again," Hoon barked with enough authority that the interviewer got halfway through another refresh before remembering who was supposed to be in charge here.

"It doesn't matter," Gavin said.

"Oh, it fucking matters, son. Believe me," Hoon spat. "Useless bastard. Aye, no' you. Him, I mean."

Gavin had not held his Junior Manager position long. He hadn't held *any* job position long, in fact, having left school just over eighteen months before. He'd rapidly risen up the ranks, though, thanks partly to his work ethic and positive attitude, but mostly through having a dad who was the area manager.

He had conducted eleven staff interviews since moving into management. Being a weasely little bastard who enjoyed wielding power over others, he'd thoroughly enjoyed most of them. He'd particularly enjoyed interviewing young women, and girls around his age. They'd all seemed suitably impressed when he'd regaled them of his meteoric rise to the top

He'd make Store Manager within the next two years, he'd told them, and from there the sky was the limit.

This interview, however, was proving less enjoyable. He'd opened with his usual speech about hard work and commitment, but the surly older applicant had all but laughed in his face, then tapped his wrist where a watch should have been and urged him to, "Crack on."

Despite his rush to get the interview underway, the applicant seemed reluctant to answer any questions, and appeared to be relying almost exclusively on a reference someone was supposedly sending that, as of yet, had not appeared in Gavin's inbox.

"Maybe we could just press on without it," Gavin suggested, straightening his spectacles. "I'm sure it'll turn up."

Hoon gave the lad the sort of look usually reserved for a daud of dog shite on a nice new carpet, then grunted. "Fine. Aye. Fire away."

Gavin smiled, sensing more familiar ground on the horizon. He still had a nagging uncomfortable feeling in the pit of his stomach, though. He'd been given interview training by the company and knew all about open questions, relaxing small-talk, and why failing to plan was planning to fail.

But, he suspected that whoever had prepared the training hadn't encountered an applicant quite like—he checked his notes—Robert Hoon.

"So, you were in the police?" Gavin asked, scanning his list of questions. "What was that like?"

"Which bit?" Hoon asked.

Gavin checked his notes again—a pointless gesture, as he knew he had no follow-up question prepared.

"Well... all of it?"

Hoon shrugged. "Right, well, five years being spat at by jakeys, a decade or so chasing paedos and rapists, then a lot of fucking paperwork with the occasional serial killer to break the monotony. So, you know, a right barrel of laughs, overall." His eyes narrowed. "How old are you, by the way?"

"Twenty," Gavin replied. "Well, twenty next month. The fifteenth."

"I don't need the details, son, I'm no' going to send you a card," Hoon told him. "Nineteen, then? Fucking hell."

"We try not to use that sort of language in the workplace. And we make a point of not discriminating by age," Gavin said. He looked down at his page and added, "Unfortunately," below his breath.

"That reference arrived yet?" Hoon asked.

Gavin glanced at the screen and shook his head. He jumped when Hoon thumped a fist down on the table and ejected a, "Fuck's sake!"

"It's... it's not a problem. Honestly," Gavin said. "Just try to, you know, relax. I know interviews can be stressful—they're a lot of pressure, so—"

"Pressure?" Hoon snorted. "Sitting in a pokey wee room being quizzed by a Value Range Walter the Softy out of the fucking *Beano*? Believe me, son, I've enjoyed farts with more pressure behind them."

Gavin self-consciously adjusted his glasses again. "I must ask you to stop swearing," he said, skilfully avoiding eye contact.

"Who's actually in charge here, by the way?" Hoon asked. "No' you, surely?"

"I'm Junior Manager."

"Aye, emphasis on the 'junior.' Who's the big boss, though? What about her I saw on the way in? Hefty lassie. Face like a bag of tits."

Gavin's brow furrowed and his lips moved silently for a few seconds. "Sandra?" he said. "No, she's Deputy Night Fill Assistant Supervisor."

"Jesus Christ. And that's a job, is it?" Hoon asked, then he tutted and tapped the sheet of paper Gavin still clutched in one hand. "Forget it. Go on."

The Junior Manager stared blankly, like he had no idea what the other man was talking about, then he remembered where he was and what he was doing. He checked his next question, before reading it out loud in his best managerial voice. "Why did you leave the police?"

"What's that got to do with anything?" Hoon demanded.

Gavin had expected the interview to go off the rails again, just not quite so soon. He blinked several times in quick succession, like something in his brain was doing a reboot. "Well, it's just a question I have to ask."

"Why?"

"Well, because..." the interviewer began, but he went no further. *Because that's what they told me in the training*, suddenly didn't feel like an answer that would satisfy the man asking the question.

"Let's just say we had a difference of opinion," Hoon said, sparing the younger man the effort of finding an acceptable explanation. "And leave it at that."

Gavin smiled and made a quick note. "Works for me!" he said, relieved to be moving on. "Why do you think you're suited for a customer services role?"

"You tell me," Hoon said, which prompted a confused smile from the Junior Manager.

"You're... you're meant to tell me," he explained. "That's sort of the point."

Hoon rolled his eyes. "Right, well, my sunny disposition. How about that?" he asked. "And I fucking love dealing with people. Can't get enough of the dead-eyed, cow-brained, graspy-handed, self-serving pricks. The more the fucking merrier. That answer your question?"

Gavin wrote a note made up exclusively of question marks, then replaced the lid on his pen, crossed his hands on the desk and smiled graciously.

"Well, I think I've got everything we need," he said, thrusting a hand across the desk. "Somebody will be in touch."

Hoon ignored the hand. "When?" he asked.

"Once we've made a decision."

"Which will be when?"

Gavin withdrew the offer of a handshake and stood up, signalling the interview was over.

"When we're ready. Please, I have other appointments, if you could just..." He looked pointedly at the door. "Please. We'll be in touch."

Hoon leaned back in his chair, ran his lips across his teeth, then nodded. "Aye. Fine. Thanks for your time," he said. "You know who I worry about, though?"

The Junior Manager didn't quite know how to respond to the question beyond a puzzled, "What? I mean, no. Who?"

"Sandra."

"Sandra?"

"Aye."

Gavin shot another look at the door. "Why are you worried about Sandra?"

"I'm worried about what she might do," Hoon said. "When she finds out what you called her."

Confusion formed lines on a face for which wrinkles were a distant, far-off concern. "Called her?"

"Aye. Don't pretend you don't remember," Hoon said. "You said she'd a face like a bag of tits."

Gavin's mouth dropped open. "What? No, I didn't. You said that."

"Whoa, whoa, whoa, what?" Hoon said. "I did nothing of the bloody kind."

"You did!" Gavin protested. "You said 'the fat one with the face like a bag of tits.'"

Hoon's eyes became two wide circles of innocence. "There are three women out there, son. You're the one who pointed the finger at poor Sandra. How the fuck would I even know her name, if you didn't say it? Or that she's the fucking Night Fill Junior Champion, or whatever it was you said she did? Why would I know that if you didn't tell me?"

His chair legs groaned on the thin carpet tiles as he stood up. Physically, Gavin was an inch or two taller, but in terms of sheer presence, Hoon filled the whole room.

"You think she'll put in a complaint?" he asked. "I would. I mean... face like a bag of tits. What sort of misogynistic arsehole of a boss says that about a woman working under him? I smell a fucking tribunal, son, I won't lie."

Gavin swallowed. He was sweating now, grey patches spreading around the armpits of his cheap white shirt. "They won't... Nobody will believe you."

"Oh really?" Hoon asked. "I'm a decorated Detective Superintendent of Police, son. You're a semi-inflated foetus in a clip-on tie." He winked. "Will we go and see whose word they take, will we?"

He gave the Junior Manager a few moments to consider his options, then suggested—firmly, but not unkindly—that he might want to sit down.

"I... I can't put you in Customer Services," the ashen-faced Gavin said, once his arse was firmly back in his chair. "I just... I can't."

"Sandra!" Hoon called, and every muscle in Gavin's body visibly tensed at the same time.

"Shh! Don't!" he urged, firing a panicky look at the door. "I'm not saying you can't have a job, I'm just saying not Customer Services."

"What then?" Hoon asked.

Gavin cleared his throat. He smiled, but it was a pitiful thing that only barely hung in place. "How do you feel," he began, "about security...?"

CHAPTER EIGHT

LOGAN WAS STANDING at the bar at the Clachaig Inn when a series of rapid-fire text messages arrived, making some disparaging remarks about his weight, penis size, sexuality, and parentage. Though not necessarily in that order.

"Oh, shite," he muttered, as two coffees were set on a tray before him.

"Sorry?" asked the barman.

"Hm? Oh, nothing," Logan replied. "Just something I forgot to do." He set a banknote down and picked up the tray. "Keep the change."

Logan had spent a few weeks waiting tables back in his teenage years, but if he'd learned any lessons during that time, none of them had stuck. By the time he arrived at the table where Shona was sitting, both mugs were noticeably less full than when they'd started, and a puddle of hot dark liquid was swishing around on the tray.

"Sorry, might have spilled some," he admitted, setting the tray down.

"Some?" said Shona, plucking a sugar sachet from the puddle before it could be completely dissolved.

"No' really my strong point," Logan said, pulling out one end of a wooden bench and sitting across the table from the pathologist.

"What, carrying stuff over short distances?" Shona teased. "I assumed that fell under the heading of basic motor functions."

"Aye, well, you know what they say about assumptions," Logan said, picking up his mug and giving the bottom a wipe on a partially sodden napkin.

They were tucked into the far corner of the inn, as far as possible from the handful of morning drinkers who sat in twos and threes, or stood gathered by the pool table. It was a climbers' pub, and the bad weather and poor visibility on the hills meant the climbers had nowhere better to be.

"It's nice," Shona said, indicating the pub with a tilt of her mug. She paid particular attention to the assortment of malt whiskies on the wall behind the bar. "Just wish I A, wasn't driving, and B, didn't have to go cut up four human corpses."

"Coffee's no' bad, though," Logan said. He shrugged. "What's left of it, anyway."

Shona smiled, clinked her mug against his, then took a sip. It was good, she agreed, then she stared into empty space for a few seconds, her mind drifting off to somewhere far away.

Or maybe just trying to.

"You alright?" Logan asked her, for the third time that morning. "It was pretty rough back there."

"It was," Shona admitted. "Kids get to you a bit, don't they?"

"They do," Logan agreed. "But then... we think we can deal with death because we see it so often, but it can still mess you up from time to time."

Shona shook her head. "Wasn't the death bit," she said. "Like you say, I'm well used to that. Wouldn't get very far in this job if the sight of a few dead bodies gave me the heebie-jeebies."

Logan wrapped his hands around his mug, letting the warmth seep into the muscles. "What was it, then?"

"It's what happened before they died," Shona said. "How scared they must've been. All of them, but the kids especially. Tied up like that. Helpless. Afraid. God, you can't begin to imagine, can you?"

While Logan actually did have first-hand experience of being in a very similar situation to the one the pathologist had just described, he shook his head. "No," he said. "You can't imagine."

She lingered in that faraway place a while longer, until the *clack* of colliding pool balls dragged her out of it.

"Right, so. Down to business," she said, locking eyes with Logan across the table. "So, they're dead, obviously. All four of them are very much dead, and have been for a couple of days, I'd say, but that's a very rough estimate at the moment."

"Any idea yet on cause of death?" Logan asked. "There was a lot of blood."

"Again, this is preliminary, but initial indications are that they were all stabbed in the chest, almost certainly while tied up."

"What sort of size knife are we looking at?"

"Sort of..." Shona spotted a jar on the table filled with cutlery wrapped in paper napkins. She pulled out a set, discarded the fork and spoon, then presented Logan with the round-ended knife. "About that length, I'd say, based on the width of the wounds. Only much sharper, obviously. You're not getting that thing through even a child's sternum. Not without a run-up."

She realised that a couple of the men over by the pool table had turned their way while she spoke that last sentence, and dropped the volume of her voice so they couldn't hear.

"The adult male was stabbed repeatedly—ten, maybe fifteen times—the others just two to three times each."

"Is that all? Lucky them," Logan remarked. "All sounds a bit sloppy."

"Yes and no," Shona replied. "Can't say they were the cleanest kills I've ever seen, but whoever did it at least knew where the hearts all were."

Logan frowned. "Surely everyone knows where the heart is?"

"You'd be surprised. Most people reckon it's much further left than it actually is. But, the killer knew *exactly* where it was. At least one of each victim's wounds was directly centred on the heart. And I mean *directly* centred on it. From what I can gather from the outside, anyway. I'll have to open them all up to confirm."

"Could've just got lucky," Logan suggested.

"Once or twice, maybe. Or with the adult male, when it was more frenzied. But four times? Seems like more than luck. He—or she, I suppose, I don't want you accusing me of throwing assumptions around—had a solid understanding of exactly where the heart sits in the chest, I'm sure of it. He might be from a medical background."

"Or she," Logan added.

"Or she, yes. Sorry." Shona wrinkled her nose. "Unlikely to be a woman though, isn't it? I mean, I'd have thought."

"Why?" Logan asked.

"I mean... really. How many women carry out home invasions? Statistically, how likely is it?"

The answer to that, Logan had to admit, was a resounding, "Not very." But, he wasn't ruling anything out quite yet.

He took a drink of his coffee, swished it through his teeth, then swallowed. "Course, maybe he or she knew where to put the knife because they have prior experience with this sort of thing. It might not be the first time they've killed."

"You're thinking serial killer?"

Logan shook his head. "I'm thinking a professional." He picked up one of the beer mats from the table and turned it over in his hand, fiddling as he thought. "Although, why someone would order a hit on Archie Tatties is anyone's guess."

"I'm still none the wiser about who that is, incidentally," Shona told him. "Was it a Scottish thing, or am I just too young, maybe?"

She smirked at that last remark, and Logan was reminded that there were a good six or seven years between them, with him on the wrong end.

"You know Cannon and Ball? Or... the other ones. Little and Large. You know them?"

"I am aware of their body of work," Shona confirmed. "Unfortunately."

"Right, well, Neeps and Tatties were like the Scottish equivalent of that lot."

"Ah. Hence why I've never heard a word about them," Shona said. "I'm assuming they didn't make it across the Irish Sea?"

"No, they did. They were bloody everywhere for a while," Logan insisted. "They started in the pubs and clubs in Glasgow, but they became huge. Toured the world. Did the Royal Variety Show. Got their own comedy series on the telly. Everything. They did the lot."

"Oh, so a bit like *Mrs Brown's Boys*?"

"Eh, aye," Logan said, a little unconvincingly. "I suppose a bit like that, aye."

Shona took a sip of coffee while she contemplated this. "No wonder someone wanted him dead," she remarked, then she set her almost empty mug down. "When was all this?"

Logan blew out his cheeks. "Maybe... eighty-two, eighty-three, eighty-four-ish."

"Right, so I was *negative one years old*," Shona said. "At a minimum. Or a maximum, I suppose, depending on which way you're counting."

"Aye, well, you have my sympathies," Logan told her. "You missed some classic comedy."

"I'm sure I'll somehow find a way to struggle on," the pathologist replied. "What happened? How come they stopped? Or did everyone just suddenly realise they were shite?"

"It might've been that right enough. But, eh... I can't actually remember," Logan admitted. "Think maybe there was some sort of falling out between them."

"And what have they been doing since then?"

"I have no idea," Logan said. He drained the rest of his coffee in one big gulp. "But I've got a horrible bloody feeling I'm going to have to find out."

TODAY WAS DI Ben Forde's lucky day. Moira Corson, the po-faced guardian of the Fort William Police Station front desk—and, by extension, the one with control of the buzzer that opened the door to the rest of the station—was nowhere to be seen when he entered the building. Instead, a young female constable stood behind the glass screen and met him, DS Hamza Khaled, and the uniformed Constable David Davidson with a warm and welcoming smile.

"Hello!" Ben called from halfway across the reception. "The dragon on her tea break, is she?"

The smile faltered. "Sorry?"

"The dragon. Moira. She's usually here," Ben said, coming to a stop at the waist-high counter. He peered past the young constable into the office behind her. "What's she doing, counting her gold?"

"Is that no' leprechauns?" asked Dave.

"Dragons sleep on a bed of gold," Ben said, shooting a slightly disappointed look at the man in the wheelchair. A flicker of doubt crossed his face, though, and he turned back to the constable behind the glass with a questioning, "Right?"

"I... don't know," the young officer replied. "Were you looking for Moira?"

"No. God, no! Trying to avoid her, if anything," Ben said, lowering his voice to a stage whisper. He stole another look through the door of the office. "She through there, is she?"

"No. She's off today, actually," the constable told him.

"Oh! Right! That's a relief, then," Ben said. "Well, you'd better sign us in, then! I'm DI Forde, this is—"

"I know, sir. You can go right through."

Ben hesitated. "Oh. Good. Right through?" he asked.

"I'll buzz you in."

"Right." Ben nodded. "You don't need us to fill out any forms, or anything?"

"No, sir."

"Don't need to sign anything, or...?" Ben prompted. "It's just, usually there's a bit of back and forth. And, well, Moira's a bit of a pain in the arse about it all, and then she eventually gives in and..." He glanced at the door beside them which led into the station proper. "We can... We can just go through?"

A button was pressed. A buzzer sounded. A lock disengaged.

"That's right, sir," the junior officer said. "No paperwork necessary. We've got it all from last time, and I can check you in."

"Nice one. Thanks!" Hamza said, already heading for the door. Dave Davidson rocked onto the back wheels of his wheelchair and spun himself around to follow, leaving Ben hovering around at the counter.

"Aye. Aye, nice one," he said. "Thank you, Constable..."

"Elliot, sir. Carrie Elliot."

"Good. Good, good," Ben said. He tapped his hands on the counter, glanced once more at the office door, then smiled. "Thanks, Carrie. Much easier this way. Without all the..." He pointed between them a few times, simulating the usual back and forth, then nodded. "Right, then."

He made it three steps towards the door, then doubled back.

"Everything alright, sir?"

"Aye. Aye, I was just... So we can get ourselves prepared. Is she back in tomorrow? The dragon, I mean."

"I'm, eh, I'm afraid not, sir, no."

"Right. Right. On holiday, is she? Off burning some village to the ground somewhere, is she?"

"She's... Well, she's on the sick."

Ben's face fell. "Oh. Oh. Right. I didn't mean... I was just..." He cleared his throat. "Well, if you're talking to her, give her our best. If, you know, you think that's appropriate."

Across the counter, the constable smiled. "I'll get the message passed on, sir," she said. "I'm sure someone will probably be speaking to her at some point."

"Right. Good. Thanks," Ben said. He played another drumbeat on the counter, glanced down at the pen attached to it by a chain, and the spot where a small pile of unnecessary paperwork would usually be sitting, then gave a nod. "I'll just... I'll go through, then."

He made it two steps this time, before doubling back.

"Sorry," he began, "what exactly do you mean by 'someone will *probably* be speaking to her at *some point?*'"

CHAPTER NINE

By the time Logan and Shona arrived back at the Three Sisters car park, Tyler and Sinead were waiting. He didn't notice them at first, as Sinead's car was dwarfed by the assortment of other polis vehicles crammed into the limited amount of available space. It was only a shrill whistle and a hollered, "Over here, boss," that eventually drew them to the DCI's attention.

Shona said her goodbyes to Logan, gave the two Detective Constables a smile and a wave, then headed for her car. She had a long day of deeply unpleasant work ahead, and delaying it would only make things worse.

Logan waved her off, watched until her car had disappeared around the first bend in the road, then went striding over to where Sinead and Tyler waited by the footpath that led past the house.

There was a bit of cutting across the grass required to get from the path to the building itself, but the alternative was the bumpy, uneven driveway that went all the way to the house's front door. Driving up there posed a greater risk of contaminating the crime scene, not to mention of knackering your bloody suspension.

"You finally made it, then," Logan remarked, joining them at the start of the path.

"Aye, sorry we took a bit longer than suspected," said Sinead.

"He sick?" Logan asked, indicating Tyler with a jerk of his thumb.

Tyler's eyes went wide. "Sick, boss? I'm not sick. Who told you I was sick?"

"He means were you carsick?" Sinead mumbled, and Tyler bit down on his lip to stop himself saying any more, leaving Sinead to explain. "No, it was mostly just traffic, sir. And we had to get stuff sorted for Harris tonight, so we were a bit late setting off."

"It's fine. You're here now," Logan told them. He gave Tyler a slightly quizzical once up and down, then set off along the path at a full clip, forcing them to hurry to keep up.

"What's the situation, boss? We're hearing home invasion gone wrong."

"Looks that way," Logan said. "But too early to make a call. Here's a shocker for you, though. One of the victims is Archie Tatties." This drew nothing but blank looks. "Neeps and Tatties. 'Where's the haggis?'"

"You had a stroke, boss?" Tyler asked.

"For the love of Christ, I'm surrounded by bloody infants," Logan grunted, further picking up the pace. "Where the hell's DI Forde when you need him?"

"As far as I know, he's headed—"

"Rhetorical question," Logan told him, then he stepped off the path and picked his way across the bogs and through the heather until he arrived in the vicinity of the cottage.

The place didn't have a garden, as such. Yes, the ground had been cleared a bit around the building, the marshier bits filled in, and then all covered over with dirt, and sand, and limestone gravel. But it wasn't a garden. Not by a longshot.

Still, why would you need a garden out here? It wasn't like you had a shortage of nice things to look at.

"That's a big hill," Tyler remarked, indicating the peak rising up behind the house.

"Aye, nothing gets past you, does it, son?" Logan said. He indicated their surroundings with the twirl of a finger. "There's actually a few of them, if you look hard enough. See how many you can find."

Paper suits were filing out of the house now, carrying cameras, and notebooks, and sealed plastic bags. Logan could hear Geoff Palmer giving orders, urging his underlings to get a shifty on so they could get back up the road in time for a late lunch.

There were four ambulances waiting in the driveway, one for each victim. The bodies were still inside, then. Otherwise, they'd already be making the journey north so that Shona could do her stuff.

"It's grim in there," Logan warned the younger officers. "Got a couple of kids involved. You don't have to come in if you don't want to. It's not necessary."

Sinead and Tyler swapped looks. Neither look was particularly excited by the prospect, but they were both in agreement.

"We'll come in, boss. Got to be done, doesn't it?"

"Aye, well," Logan replied. "Don't say that you weren't warned."

THE SIGHT of the bodies was bad, but the warning from Logan had done its job, and the tableau of horror that both Detective Constables had been bracing themselves for had been much, *much* worse.

There was something almost serene about the scene, now that Palmer's team had cleared out. The family had all been together at the end, though whether that had been a comfort or a source of further pain, Logan wouldn't like to guess.

They were beyond pain now, though. That was how he wanted to be able to look at it. That was where he wanted his mind to go.

It never did.

Instead, it focused on the lives cut short. The indignities they'd gone through. The loss of futures that would now never be. This way of thinking about their deaths offered very little in the way of consolation, but then he wasn't here to make peace with any of this, he was here to catch the bastard who'd done it.

That was when he would finally take his comfort. And not a minute before.

"They must've been terrified," Sinead remarked.

"Aye," Logan agreed. Even with the tape on their mouths, and the light gone from behind their eyes, you could see the fear written all over their faces.

"Looks like a home invasion right enough," Tyler said, and the usual chirp wasn't there in his words. "Anything taken?"

"We don't know yet," Logan replied. "That's what we're here to find out. You two pick rooms down here, take a look, see if anything jumps out." He noticed Tyler's gaze go flitting to the doors. "Any*thing*, Tyler, no' any*one*. House is empty, we've checked."

"What?" Tyler chuckled, a little too forcefully. "Wasn't worried about that, boss."

Logan chose not to argue. He instead left the DCs to it and headed for the steep wooden stairs that led up to the converted attic above. It wasn't a full staircase, but wasn't quite a ladder, either. It was some hybrid of the two, neither one thing nor the other, and Logan's height and girth meant some clumsy, undignified scrambling was needed to get him through the hole at the top.

The upstairs was one big bedroom, with an en-suite bathroom down at the south-facing end, and a large fitted wardrobe on the wall opposite. The room was built into the roof space, and three Velux windows faced out towards the road from one sloping wall, and three more faced the mountains behind on the other.

The ceiling was a single thin strip, maybe three or four feet wide. It was lower than normal, too, and the sense that the whole place was pressing in on him meant Logan kept his head tucked into his shoulders as he turned to survey the rest of the room.

It had been painted in a pebble grey, with glossy white skirtings and wall-fitted lights. Because of the apex of the roof, and the angle of the walls, the lights pointed at the carpet like spotlights at a stage floor. They were all currently on, lending some much-needed support to the weak grey daylight that meandered listlessly in through the windows.

There wasn't much in the way of furniture. A double bed—queen size, maybe—took centre stage, with small wooden bedside tables standing guard at either side of the headboard. The bed had been made to a standard roughly on par with Logan's own. The quilt had been flattened out so it roughly covered most of the sheet below, and the pillows were more or less in the position you might expect to find them. No more than a few seconds had been invested in making it, and the fitted sheet looked perilously close to pinging free from at least two corners.

The bed was a divan type with a base that went all the way to the floor, leaving no room to stash anything beneath it, and reducing the number of places he needed to bother searching.

A dressing table with a large mirror mounted on top stood on the same gable end as the built-in wardrobe, taking advantage of one of the two walls that didn't dramatically slope towards the centre of the room.

The surface of the dressing table itself was a masterclass in chaos. The contents of a makeup bag lay scattered across it—lipsticks, mascaras, blushers, and half a dozen things Logan could only guess the purpose of. There were several varieties of each, mixed in with a series of metal implements that were designed either for personal grooming or torture purposes, and very possibly both.

All fairly standard so far, but the dressing table was just getting started. There were two TV remote controls on there, half-hidden amongst the makeup. A small plastic wallet pinned beneath a tub of face and neck cream held four train tickets for the Mallaig to Fort William line, all scribbled on to show they'd been used. There was a receipt in the wallet, too, for a taxi journey totalling almost thirty quid. Presumably from the train station to here.

The tickets and the receipt were all dated from a week before, coinciding with what the house's owner had said was the family's arrival date.

When he'd first arrived, Logan had assumed that the kids would have been sleeping upstairs, but this was not a children's room, even if one of the children was a teenager. The adults had slept up here, which would've made it less difficult for a single invader to keep everyone under control. Still not easy, but definitely less of a challenge.

Logan looked out through one of the small square windows at the ragged wild land of Glen Coe. It was, he thought, a strange place to visit without a car. It only really made sense if you were looking for complete and total isolation.

Or maybe, he thought, just a place to hide.

The mish-mash of items on the dressing table went on and on:

talcum powder, a light-up yo-yo, an almost empty family-size bag of *Maltesers*, a cheerful-looking rubber duck, and two pairs of black socks rolled together into individual balls.

Several items had rolled off the edges of the cluttered surface and now lay on the floor. He saw a few lipsticks down there, along with a couple of brushes, and something that was either intended for curling eyelashes, or removing eyes.

Poking around on the dressing table top, he found a wooden box beneath a trashy tabloid magazine peddling tales of bereavement and betrayal. It contained several necklaces of silver and gold, a couple of brooches, and a tiny bracelet that would be hard-pushed to fit a child.

Logan had no idea of the value of any of it, but he'd be surprised if the average home invader did, either.

So, why was it still here?

Maybe they hadn't noticed it. It had been hidden, after all, although he suspected more by accident than design.

Maybe they hadn't bothered to check up here. There was something about the way the items lay on the floor that made him doubt that, though. He couldn't say why, exactly, but he felt like they'd been knocked off in a hurry, like someone had bumped into the dressing table, scattering the stuff onto the floor.

It could have been the kids, of course, or the parents themselves. But, some niggling little voice told him there was something wrong up here. Something the reasoned part of his mind was yet to pick up on.

He turned and surveyed the room again, and almost stepped into the empty abyss of the hole in the floor.

"Jesus," he muttered, catching his balance just in the nick of time. "Bloody death trap, that."

"You alright, boss?" called a voice from down below.

"Aye, fine. You get anything yet?"

"Nothing out of place in the kitchen, boss, no. All looks pretty normal."

Sinead's voice came from a little farther away. "Nothing in the kids' room, either," she said.

"Keep looking," Logan instructed.

Tyler's voice was suddenly loud and clear as he appeared at the bottom of the steps. "What's it like up there, boss? Anything exciting?"

Logan shrugged and shook his head. "No' particularly."

"There's an outbuilding out back. Want me to go take a look?"

"Be careful," Logan told him. "Palmer's team have been over it, but still. Go canny."

"Always do, boss," Tyler replied, then Logan heard the creaking of the front door and the whistling of the wind as the younger officer headed outside.

With one last glance around the room, Logan manoeuvred himself to the head of the staircase, and clambered down it backwards, like he was descending a ladder.

When his head was about level with the floor, he stopped, a shadow on the carpet catching his eye. He squinted at it for a few moments, then the stairs groaned in complaint as he made his way back up them again.

Dropping onto his hands and knees, Logan studied the spot where the shadow had fallen. There was a rectangular indent in the pile of the carpet, roughly the size of a playing card. He traced a gloved fingertip across it, then twisted so the side of his head was almost flat against the floor, and immediately spotted a second indent about two feet away.

From there, it was easy to find two more, four feet from the first set of imprints.

He almost overlooked a fifth, slap bang in the middle, but spotted it as he stood up and blocked the light from one of the windows.

Something had been on that spot, although it was impossible to tell when. The fibres of the carpet had at least partially sprung back up, suggesting that the object had been removed a while ago. Or, if it had been taken away recently, it hadn't been there long enough to leave much of a mark.

Logan considered the depressions in the carpet. It had been something with five feet—one at each corner, and one more in the middle for extra support.

Something heavy, then.

Not the right shape for an armchair. Far too small for a couch. A table? In a bedroom? Unlikely.

He quickly checked the feet of the dressing table. Four. Far too narrow. It wasn't that, then.

So, what?

An idea had just begun to form when Logan heard voices out front. The angle of the windows gave a fantastic view of the mountains and sky, but made it impossible to see what was happening closer to home.

He didn't have to wait long to find out what was going on, though, as the front door opened and Tyler's voice came rising up the stairs again.

"You there, boss?"

"I am," Logan said, turning down the two or three far more sarcastic answers that had immediately sprung to mind, on account of there being company present. "What's the matter?"

"Got someone here to see you, boss," Tyler called up to him.

"Tell him it's urgent," a second voice said from close-by outside.

"He says it's urgent."

Logan took out his phone, squatted, and snapped a photograph of the indents in the carpet. He checked the screen, making sure the marks could be seen, then tucked the mobile away in a coat pocket.

"Fine," he said, standing. He stood by the hole in the floor and looked down at Tyler waiting at the bottom. "Tell him I'll be right with him."

CHAPTER TEN

"I WAS THINKING I might head down the road now, sir. That alright with you?"

DI Forde looked up from the mug of tea he'd been staring into, blinked once, then gave DS Khaled a nod. "Hm? Oh. Aye. Good idea. In fact..." He fished around on his desk until he found his reading glasses, balanced them on the edge of his nose, then studied his phone screen. "Why don't you head to the polis station down in Glencoe? Cleaner who found the body's there. She's apparently keen to get home."

"I can do that," Hamza confirmed.

Ben wrote down the details from the text, then tore the page from his pad and handed it to the DS. "Good lad. When you're down there, I'll check in with Scene of Crime, see what Palmer's got to report."

"Rather you than me," Hamza replied.

It was safe to say that none of the team really clicked with Geoff Palmer. In fact, it wasn't a stretch to say that they all actively disliked the man. Nor was it a stretch to assume that they were not alone in this. Palmer was not an easy man to get on with. Not in a professional capacity, at least. None of the team had suffered the misfortune of having to socialise with him away from work, so they couldn't say what he was like off-duty, but they could all hazard a bloody good guess.

"What? Oh, yes. Never a pleasure," Ben said.

Hamza started to move away from the desk, then stopped. "Are... are you alright, sir?"

"Fine, son."

"Right. It's just, you seem... a bit distracted."

Ben smiled and sat up a little straighter in his chair. "Just deep in thought."

Dave Davidson shouted over from his desk by the door. "First time for everything."

"Oi! Watch the bloody cheek, you!" Ben warned him, but it was, like most things the DI did, good-natured. He turned back to Hamza. "Off you get down the road. I'd maybe give Tyler or Sinead a ring, let them know you're on the way and that you're dealing with the cleaner."

Hamza started to move again. Again, he faltered almost immediately.

"Tyler and Sinead? Are they not meant to be off?"

"Meant to be, aye," Ben confirmed. "Cancelled it, though, and came in."

"Oh," said Hamza. He turned and looked at the desks the DCs usually sat at when they were stationed in Fort William, like some explanation might be written there. "How come?"

Ben shrugged. "Beats me, son. By the sounds of things, though, it's a good thing they did. Going by what Jack's told me, we're going to need all the help we can get."

RUFUS BOYLE WAS a man who had a bob or two. It was written all over him, from his herringbone tweed plus fours to his matching flat cap and bodywarmer. It was there in his body language, and in the way he spoke, too. He had that tone shared by true toffs everywhere—the one that said that no matter what experience you might have, or what position you'd reached, they somehow knew better than you did thanks to lineage and bank balance alone.

He was in his fifties, with the ruddy complexion of someone who spent a lot of time outdoors. Probably shooting, or fly fishing, or hunting the working class for sport.

Suffice to say, Logan had not taken to him. It wasn't the over-priced outerwear, the upper-class lilt, or even the way one finger appeared to be permanently fixed in an angry pointing gesture. Those things, irritating as they were, the DCI could have looked past.

It was the things he had said, and the tone in which he'd said them, that had made Logan grind his back teeth together, and fight to resist squashing the toffee-nosed wee prick into his own makeshift driveway.

"It's my property. You hear? My property. No one else's," he said. "I have a right to go inside. You can't stop me. I mean it, you can't stop me."

This was the fourth time that the bastard had insisted he could go inside. No amount of reasoning, or calm explanation as to why he couldn't had thus far proven to be a deterrent, so Logan decided it was time for a different approach.

"I can think of ten ways I could stop you, sir, just off the top of my head," he replied. His mouth was curved in such a way that it might almost, under different lighting conditions, be considered a smile. "Why don't you pick a number, and we'll see what happens?"

Rufus Boyle was not a particularly clever man. Most of his wealth had been inherited, and the rest had come as a result of sound financial advice.

But, while he wasn't especially intelligent, he was a survivor. He knew danger when he saw it, and right now alarm bells were ringing.

Not wishing to show weakness—he didn't get where he was today by being bullied, or not since those nine years of boarding school, at least—he made a show of sighing dramatically and rolling his eyes, then quietly aborted his quest to get inside.

"What am I meant to tell the other guests?" he demanded. He shot daggers at the front door of the cottage like he was about to challenge the whole building to a square go. "They're arriving at three."

"Forgive me for being so blunt, Mr Boyle," Logan said. "But I really don't give two shites what you tell them. Just make sure they don't turn up, because I'd imagine I'll be somewhat more forthright and less tactful with them than you will, should they arrive here."

Boyle chewed his tongue and crossed his hands behind his back, like he was fighting to keep them under control. "I'll have to refund them. Everything. Not just the deposit, the whole fee. Who's going to reimburse me for that? You?" He released a hand long enough to gesture at the Uniforms milling around in the car park. "Them? If not, then who? Because someone better had. Why should my business suffer because—"

Logan didn't notice his feet closing the gap between himself and the other man. Nor did he notice his arm raising, not until he had a handful of Boyle's shirt bunched between his fingers and the tweed-wearing posho bastard was folding in on himself in fear.

"I'm only going to say this once, Mr Boyle," he growled. "I, and my fellow officers, have no interest in how much money you're losing here. We don't give a damn about you or your business. We're here for two reasons—to find out who killed this family, and to make sure they spend the rest of their lives rotting in a jail cell. Anything that proves to be an obstacle to that—anything that compromises our ability to do these things—I will tear to pieces with my bare hands, and take immense fucking pleasure in doing so."

He tightened his grip, drawing a little yelp of distress from the quivering Rufus.

"Is that understood?" the DCI demanded, lips drawing back to show teeth and spit and fury.

"Sir?" Sinead's voice came from the doorway of the house behind them. "Is, eh, is everything alright?"

"Everything's just peachy, Detective Constable," Logan said, neither releasing his grip nor breaking eye contact with Boyle. "DC Neish is checking the outbuilding. Maybe go and give him a hand, eh?"

"You sure, I... eh...?"

"Sinead. Go help Tyler. That's an order." He jerked an arm up, momentarily raising Rufus off the ground. Then, with a scowl of distaste, he released his grip, sending the other man stumbling backwards. "Mr Boyle and I are going to have a nice little chat somewhere more private."

Sinead found Tyler standing at one of the outbuilding's grime-encrusted windows, trying to peer in through several years' worth of compacted muck

"See anything?" she asked.

"Just... junk, I think," Tyler replied. "Door's locked. Padlock's old, too. Doesn't look like it's been touched in a while." He turned away from the glass. "Boss get that guy alright?"

"Aye. He was roughing him up when I left them," Sinead said.

Tyler raised his eyebrows, but otherwise didn't skip a beat. "Fair enough."

"He can be quite hard work."

Tyler shot a wary look back in the direction of the house. "Well, aye, but don't let him hear you saying that, for God's sake."

Sinead shook her head. "The other guy. Rufus. Everyone round here knows him. He makes sure of that. Gets himself in the local paper every couple of weeks for something or other."

"Oh. Right. Aye," Tyler said. He gave a little cough. "Maybe don't mention to the boss that I thought you were talking about him."

Sinead mimed zipping her lips closed, and Tyler sighed with relief. "I knew I liked you," he said. "Maybe we should get married? I'm game, if you are?"

She smiled back at him. "The last proposal was better," she said.

They both sat on what was left of the low wall that ran between the house and the outbuilding. It was an old drystane dyke that had succumbed to gravity and the elements. Quite some time ago, too, judging by the covering of moss on the fallen rocks and boulders.

For a while, they just sat there in silence, watching the activity further along the path. The wind was getting colder, and so they shuffled together for warmth and for comfort.

"You said anything to him yet?" Sinead asked.

Tyler had been waiting for the question. Dreading its arrival.

"Not yet," he admitted.

"You need to say something. The operation's on Thursday."

Tyler nodded. Looked down. Swallowed.

"Don't," Sinead said. "Don't even think about saying it."

"I just thought... I mean, I know it needs doing. Of course. ASAP."

"Good," Sinead said, trying to end the sentence there.

"But... would a week make any difference? I mean, really?"

"Yes."

Tyler plucked a long blade of grass from the ground in front of him and twisted it into a knot. "Aye, but... would it?"

Sinead shuffled a little away from him and turned so her knees were pointed in his direction. "So... what? You're saying you want to put it off? The operation?"

"Just for a few days," Tyler said. "You know, given what we're dealing with here... This case, is... I'd hate to leave them in the lurch."

"Jesus, Ty."

"I'm just saying..."

"What? What are you saying?" Sinead demanded. "That you'll get your cancer treated in a week? In a fortnight? Some day down the road? Your appointment is in three days. They rushed it through. And you want to push it back?"

"Just for a few days," Tyler said, with even less conviction than last time. "Just... I just don't want to let the boss down."

Sinead stood up. "Oh, right," she said, and the wind that blew around them felt colder still. "Well, lucky him."

THE 'SOMEWHERE MORE PRIVATE' was not as bad as Rufus had been bracing himself for. But then, he'd been half-expecting the detective to drag him into the wilderness and execute him, so most things were an improvement on that.

Still, his life had started to flash before his eyes as he was led to Logan's car. He'd instinctively felt in his pocket for his phone—he had 999 on speed-dial, just in case—but what was he going to do, call the police? The place was heaving with them, and the brute in the overcoat was apparently the one in charge.

Was this what he paid his taxes for? To be manhandled by

some fascist with a badge? It was one thing to do it to other people —lesser people—but he had standing. He was *important*. This sort of thing simply shouldn't be allowed.

"Get in," Logan had instructed, opening the passenger door of his BMW. For the first time ever, he almost wished he still had his old Fiesta, so he could clunk the bastard's head against the top of the door frame as he helped him duck inside.

"Where are you taking me?" Rufus asked, but most of the brash and bluster was gone.

Logan hadn't answered, and had instead just glowered until Rufus had buckled and climbed in.

A few seconds later, the DCI had jumped into the driver's seat. So far, though, he'd made no move to start the car, and had instead just rubbed his hands together to warm them, and made a few remarks about the cold.

"I think maybe we got off on the wrong foot, Mr Boyle," Logan began. "I'm sure you'll appreciate with a case like this, it's something of a stressful time."

"Yes, well, for you and me both," Rufus said, finding some of that earlier attitude. He stopped short of complaining about the money he was losing, though, which was probably just as well.

"Aye. For everyone," Logan said. "But mostly for the family in that house. Anything we're going through now, is a fraction of what they faced. There were children. You know?"

Rufus nodded. It was slow, and sad, and deliberate, like he wanted his sympathy to be noted. "Two of them. Yes. I saw it on the booking. And they're...? They're all...?"

"They are, yes."

Rufus shuddered. "Oh, how ghastly."

"Aye, you can say that again," Logan confirmed.

"What happened? Do you know?"

"Not yet. These things take time, as I'm sure you'll appreciate. We want to build a picture of the family's movements so we can start working the whole thing out. I'm hoping you can help us with that, Mr Boyle."

Rufus ran a hand down the front of his shirt, smoothing out the creases Logan's clenched fist had put there. "Oh, you want my help now, do you?" he asked. A subtle shift in the detective's body language made him quickly follow up with, "Of course, I'll give you any assistance that I can."

"I'm very glad to hear that, Mr Boyle."

Rufus flinched and drew back when the detective shoved a hand into the inside pocket of his coat, and Logan could practically hear the word 'gun' shrieking around inside the other man's head.

Instead of a firearm, Logan produced a battered notebook and a chewed stub of a pencil, then angled himself so he could fix Boyle with one of his better, most intimidating glares.

"Right then," he said, turning to a blank page. "Let's begin."

CHAPTER ELEVEN

Magdalena Nowak was having the worst day of her life. And, considering what many of the other days had been like, that was really quite an achievement.

It had started poorly—the bad weather made her joints ache, and she'd struggled to get out of bed. She'd forgotten to put the bin out the night before, too, so the kitchen had practically hummed with the smell of rotting fruit and cat food when she'd staggered through at five o'clock, eyes welded shut with the debris of a long and sleepless night.

Her car, which had been threatening to give up the ghost for a while now, had coughed and spluttered for a full five minutes before it had accepted that she wasn't going to give up, and reluctantly wheezed into life. Its days were numbered, though, and those numbers were likely single digits. What she'd do when it died, she had no idea, and she'd tried very hard not to think about it when she'd set off on the high road from Kinlochleven, headed for her first job of the day.

She was a businesswoman. Technically. In the sense that she was a self-employed cleaner with a handful of clients who she suspected all had people to put the bins out for them, and a selection of fully functioning motor vehicles from which to choose.

Apparently, it was seen as a good thing to be your own boss.

The few friends that she had were all so excited for her when she'd announced that she was starting her own cleaning business.

Her own view was somewhat less positive. There was no holiday pay, for one thing. No sick pay, either. In a job, she'd at least have money coming in every month without fail, and wouldn't spend half her time chasing up her regular clients for payments that were often weeks overdue.

And then there was tax. She should probably look into that at some point. It seemed quite complicated, though, and no one had come looking for payments in the three years since she'd started up, so she felt it best just to keep her head down and hope this state of affairs continued.

From that poor start, the day had gone rapidly downhill when she'd entered Mr Boyle's holiday rental and found... what she'd found in the living room.

She couldn't bring herself to say the words out loud. She couldn't express quite what she'd felt when she'd seen what lay there on the floor—not in English, and probably not in Polish, either. There were no words for what she'd felt. Not in any language.

Hamza offered her the box of tissues that the sergeant at the Glencoe station had dug out of a cupboard. The box had been bashed around and squashed down at some point so the corners had all ruptured, but there was still a good supply of tissues in it, albeit far fewer now, than there had been when the shellshocked cleaner had first arrived.

"Take your time, Magda," Hamza said. They were sat across from one another on mismatched chairs in a room that served a variety of purposes, and lent itself well to none of them. It was part interview room, part office, part canteen, and a couple of pillows and a blanket tucked away in a corner suggested it was sometimes part sleeping quarters, too. "Take your time, there's no rush."

Hamza gave her an encouraging smile, then stopped talking and tried to tune his ears in readiness for her reply. Her English straddled the line between 'poor' and 'incomprehensible,' and he'd had to ask her to repeat herself several times already in what had been a short and thus far largely unproductive conversation.

His Aberdonian accent wasn't exactly making it a barrel of

laughs from her point of view, he had quickly realised, and her reply to most of his questions had been to stare blankly at him for several seconds before bursting into tears.

He was starting to understand how she felt.

"There is am dead. On floor. Yes? Four." She held up the corresponding number of fingers. "Four?"

"That's four, yes," Hamza confirmed.

She stared at his mouth, concentrating. "Again?"

"I just said... Nothing. Forget it. Go on."

Magda shook her head, still fixated on his mouth like she was reading his lips. "I no... Sorry. Sorry, I no..."

Hamza waved his hands, crossing them over as he tried to dismiss her concerns. "You don't have to be sorry. You have nothing to be sorry for," he said, speaking so slowly he almost lost the thread of what he was saying halfway through. "Just tell me what happened at the house."

There was a short delay as she tried to process, decipher, and translate what he'd said, then tears sprang to her eyes again.

"I no know! How is... how am...? I no know what is happen!"

"No, I'm not asking you to solve the case," Hamza said, but the words came out far too quickly for the woman to follow, and the look that bounced back at him was a tangle of fear and confusion. "I was just..."

This was getting neither of them anywhere, he decided. At this rate, the poor woman would never get home.

"Wait there. One second," Hamza said, gesturing for her to stay put as he got to his feet.

He crossed to the door, opened it, and leaned through into the station's reception area, where the on-duty sergeant was typing on a battered old laptop.

"Getting anywhere?" the sergeant asked.

"Not really, no," Hamza admitted. "I don't suppose you know anyone who speaks Polish, do you?"

"Well... she does, doesn't she?"

Hamza gave the other man a second, hoping he'd figure out his error on his own.

When he didn't, the DS continued. "I meant to translate," he explained. "Someone who can speak Polish and English."

"Oh. Right, aye. Gotcha." The sergeant leaned back in his chair. He hooked a finger over his bottom lip as he contemplated the question, and pulled like a fish on a hook. "Do you know," he said, after some thought. "I might know just the man."

LOGAN, Tyler, and Sinead stood in respectful silence in the drizzling rain, as four stretchers were loaded into four ambulances, and four members of the same family began their separate journeys north.

Only once the vehicles had turned off the bog-mottled driveway and onto the main road did the detectives' conversation resume.

Something had happened between them. Logan could sense it the moment he'd met up with them again. An argument of some kind. He could see it in their movements, and hear it in their voices, if not in the actual words they used. They were trying to hide it from him. He was grateful for that. The last thing he wanted to get involved in was some sort of lovers' tiff.

"Aye, so, nothing in the outbuilding as far as we could tell, boss," Tyler said. "Looks like it hasn't been used in a while. Padlock seems to be untouched, and there's no other way in or out."

Logan nodded, then lowered himself onto one of the two swings that hung from the wooden frame at the side of the house. "Aye. The owner said as much. Palmer and his lot had a check around the outside and went over the door, and they don't reckon anyone's been inside it, either."

"You find anything upstairs, sir?" Sinead asked.

"No. Aye. I mean... maybe. There's an imprint on the carpet."

"Of what, boss?"

"I don't know. Bit of furniture. Five legs, or maybe feet."

"You think something's been taken out of the room?" Sinead asked.

"Maybe. Wouldn't be easy with that bloody hatch, though," Logan said. "Could be old—might have been done months ago, in which case it's irrelevant—or it might be recent. In which case, it isn't."

"The owner know anything about it?" Sinead asked.

"No. Not that he was letting on, anyway."

Tyler and Sinead both looked off in the direction Rufus Boyle had gone in his beaten-up old Land Rover after Logan had finished questioning him. "You suspect him, boss?"

"I suspect everyone, son," Logan replied. He swung back a few inches, much to the dismay of the supporting chains, and stared at the ground beneath his feet, lost in thought. A drip of rain formed at the tip of his nose, wobbled briefly, then fell with a *plop* into a puddle below.

Tyler and Sinead swapped looks, neither one quite sure what to say, or whether to even say anything at all.

"He says he didn't know who Archie Tatties is, either," Logan eventually stated. "The owner, I mean. Boyle. Mind you, he was probably out bloody... grouse shooting or something back then. No' sitting home eating fish fingers in front of the telly."

The DCI stood up, and the entire frame of the swings gave an audible sigh of relief. He stole another look at the house, turned to regard the assembled Uniforms who were all trying to look busy while doing precisely fuck all, then ran a hand down his face, wiping away the worst of the rainwater.

"Right, let's head back up the road," he said. "Get a cup of tea and a *JJ's* inside us, and see where we're at."

"Sounds like a plan, boss," Tyler said.

"There's still the cleaner in the station at Glencoe," Sinead said, and Logan groaned.

"Shite. Forgot about her." He sighed. "Right, well, you two head up the road, I'd better go and talk to her."

"No, it's fine. I was going to say, Hamza's there already," Sinead continued. "He's talking to her."

Logan's demeanour lightened. Not by much, but a little. "Nice one. That's good," he said. "How's he getting on, do we know?"

"Haven't heard yet, boss," Tyler said. He shrugged. "But I'm sure he's doing fine."

HAMZA SAT at one end of the table, his head moving from side to side like he was watching a particularly fast-paced tennis match. Judging by the expression on his face, though, he had no idea who was winning the match, or even what the rules were.

The man who had been brought in to translate was what the sergeant had referred to as, "A local toerag," and while his English was good, it wasn't half as clear as the visible contempt he'd shown for both officers when he'd come strolling into the station.

He was in his mid-twenties, Hamza guessed, with hair that had been bleached to silvery white some weeks before, and now showed black at the roots. He wore a bright blue and orange track-suit, and an assortment of jewellery that he'd apparently selected based on levels of chunkiness alone.

Hamza wasn't sure what sort of look the man had been going for, but he presumed the one that he'd arrived at—a young Jimmy Savile—was probably not it.

Still, conversation was flowing freely between the newcomer and the witness now. All Hamza needed was for some of it to start filtering in his direction, and his plan would have paid off perfectly.

"What's she saying?" he asked, after a particularly lengthy burst of Polish from the cleaner.

The tracksuited toerag—Jakub—held a hand up for silence, and continued to nod along to whatever Magda was telling him. It was traumatising, whatever it was, as the cleaner had emptied out the box of tissues now, and was making a solid dent in the station's supply of toilet roll.

Jakub replied to the woman in Polish, then reached across the table and gave her hand a squeeze. It was a small show of kindness, but it was genuine. It bumped the man up in Hamza's estimation by a point or two, although he still remained comfortably below the five-point mark.

"Right. So, what do you want to know?" Jakub finally asked, turning his attention to the DS.

Hamza clicked the top of his pen and positioned the point on his pad. "Everything."

"Everything?" Jakub asked, suddenly doubtful. His accent was a strange blend of Polish and teuchter, suggesting he'd grown up in the Highlands. "She said a lot of stuff."

"Aye. I noticed. And I need you to tell me what it was."

"Yes, but... all of it?"

"All of it," Hamza confirmed.

Jakub blew a jet of air out through both nostrils, clicked his tongue against the roof of his mouth, and rolled his eyes all at the same time. "Fine. Everything," he said. "You ready?"

Hamza nodded. "Ready."

"First, she asked how my mother is."

Hamza's pen started to move, then stopped after a swirl or two.

"Then, she asked how I was doing, and told me the last time she'd seen me I had been ten or eleven, and doesn't time fly? Personally, I think she's thinking of my little brother, but it didn't feel like the right time to correct her." Jakub leaned an elbow on the table and supported his head on a hand. "Then, she asked if I had a girlfriend, and I said no, and she said she was surprised. Handsome young man like me? The girls round here must be blind."

With his free hand, Jakob gestured at Hamza's pad. "You're not writing any of this down. You said you wanted everything. I'm giving you everything."

That point or two that Jakub had earned from the hand squeeze were mentally subtracted again before Hamza replied.

"Fine. Tell me everything relating to what happened today at the house," he said.

"Right. Yes. I thought you'd see sense," Jakub replied. He flicked his gaze to the notepad again. "Ready this time?"

"Just get on with it."

"Right," Jakub said, lifting his head from his hand and sitting up straight. "Then I shall begin."

CHAPTER TWELVE

THE TEAM RECONVENED around a couple of desks and a few square sausage rolls in the Incident Room. Entering the building was a joyously swift and painless process with no Moira Corson to contend with, and for once the rolls were still piping hot when they started tucking in.

There was no shop talk during the three or four minutes it took them to devour the food. Instead, they reminisced on the wedding at the weekend, complimented the bride and groom on a fine day out, and ripped pure pish out of the speeches.

They discussed Honeymoon plans. The newlyweds had decided to put it on hold until the school summer holidays and take Harris away, they said, though they didn't seem entirely convinced.

Logan mostly just watched and listened while the others did the talking. He watched Sinead and Tyler, in particular. Sinead had touched Tyler's hand at several points during the conversation. Not romantically, Logan thought, more supportive.

The lad had nearly bottled it on Saturday. Done a runner. That hadn't made sense to Logan. Aye, Tyler was an idiot, but no' *that* much of an idiot. He was loved-up—ridiculously so. He'd been desperate to get married, probably worried that Sinead would come to her senses.

He'd seemed out of sorts a bit on the stag night, too. It had turned into quite a subdued affair, and it was only the injection of some karaoke—and, in particular, Logan's roof-raising rendition of Elvis Presley's *The Wonder of You*—that had finally got the party started.

When the rolls were all eaten, Logan scrunched up his paper bag and filed all those thoughts away. He'd come back to them later, but for now, they had more pressing matters to attend to.

"Right, then," he began, tossing the ball of paper into the waste paper basket beside the desk. "Sinead, you're on Big Board duty. I'll go over what we got at the house, and what the landlord said, then Hamza, you can fill us in on how things went with the—"

"Knock knock!"

They all turned as one to see Chief Inspector Alisdair Lyle—better known to most of the polis by his nickname, 'Praying Mantits'—poking his head around the door. He had a big smile on his face that he thought made him appear approachable, but instead gave him the look of a simpleton.

Not a sound was made from those seated around the table, but Logan could physically sense the collective groan.

"Not interrupting anything important, am I?" Mantits asked, stepping fully into the room.

"No, just a quadruple homicide investigation, Alisdair," Logan retorted. "What can I do for you?"

"Ha! Yes, quite!" Mantits ejected. He wagged a finger, shook his head gleefully, and then turned to the rest of the table. "He must keep you on your toes, eh? With the banter." Mantits threw a few quick jabs at thin air and made some corresponding punching sound effects with his mouth. "He's relentless, isn't he?"

The Chief Inspector let out a long, happy sigh, then clapped a hand on the seated DCI's shoulder. "Jack Logan," he said, with a wistful air that suggested he was either going to burst into tears or burst into song. Or, if they were very lucky, just burst in general.

He did none of the above. Instead, he did a straight-arm point to the scrunched-up paper bags on the table, said, "JJ's," more as a statement than a question, before finally yawning and stretching when he couldn't think of anything else to say.

"Was there anything in particular you were after, Alisdair?" Logan asked.

Mantits shook his head. "No. No, nothing really. Just thought

I'd pop in and say hello. It's been so long since we saw each other! How long's it been? Must've been oooh... a week?"

He laughed at that. Nobody else around the table joined in, although Dave Davidson had his head down and was trying very hard *not* to laugh, but probably not for reasons the Chief Inspector would have liked.

"Right, well, enough fun," the Chief Inspector declared, despite the fact that he was the only one apparently having any. He prodded a finger on Logan's desk. "Back to work, you lot." He mimed cracking a whip, complete with appropriate sound effect, then grinned expectantly, like a performer waiting for his applause, before concluding that none was likely to be forthcoming.

Instead, he let out another happy sigh, patted Logan on the same shoulder as last time, clicked his fingers once or twice, and shambled for the door.

The door had just swung closed behind him when Dave's contained laughter escaped as some loud snorting and a series of violent shoulder shakes.

"What the hell was that about?" Sinead asked.

"I think... I think he might fancy you, boss," Tyler remarked. "Did anyone else get that vibe off him?"

"Now that you mention it..." Hamza said.

Ben rolled back his chair and got to his feet, drawing Logan's attention.

"What's up?" the DCI asked.

"Eh, nothing. I'll just... I need to ask Mantits something."

They all watched the DI go hurrying out of the room, and heard the low murmur of conversation from somewhere along the corridor. Ben was keeping his voice down, so Logan clapped his hands and stood up, affording his old friend a measure of privacy.

"Right, Sinead, Big Board. Tyler, check the inbox in case anything's come in from up the road."

The door opened again and Ben returned. He took his seat without a word, wrote something in his notepad, then picked up his tea and turned to face the board.

"Everything alright?" asked Logan.

Ben raised his mug as if in toast. "Everything's grand, Jack," he said, though his thin-lipped smile did nothing to sell it. "Everything's just grand."

SHONA MAGUIRE SAT in her office scoffing a pulled pork flavour *Pot Noodle*, and contemplating her life choices. Four bags lay on four tables in the room next door. Four lives cut short in four brutal acts of violence.

This was not particularly unusual, of course. Lives cut short in brutal acts of violence were her bread and butter. To be blunt about it, lives cut short in brutal acts of violence had paid her mortgage for the last six years.

But today had felt different. Children always did, of course. Those deaths were harder to process, more difficult to understand.

She always understood them on the biological level, of course. That bit was easy, relatively speaking. She never failed to figure out *how* they died.

It was the *why* that always eluded her. Even when it had all been figured out, even when it had all been explained to her, she could never see it. Not really. The reasons given—money, power, revenge—were never enough to make her understand.

Maybe it wasn't the *why* that was the problem, then, she thought. Maybe it was the *what*. What sort of person could do these things to a child? What sort of world were they living in when this sort of thing could happen?

She slurped down another forkful of sauce-sodden noodles, and shot a look at the swing doors leading to the mortuary. There were no windows, and yet she could somehow see them clearly. Not just the bags, all zipped up and labelled, but the bodies themselves, cocooned inside. The parents. The children.

She found herself imagining for the fifth or sixth time that day what they must have gone through, what they must have felt, and the raw horror of it turned her stomach.

Her *Pot Noodle* clacked down on her desk, barely half-finished. She glared at it accusingly, as if it had betrayed her somehow. She had been relying on it to delay her. Every second gobbling down those limited edition flavoured noodles was a second not standing over those children, not cutting into their flesh, not weighing and measuring their component parts.

But the thought of what that family had endured had soured everything. She couldn't face another bite. Not now, not ever.

Well, OK, that was going a bit far. She still had a *Bombay Bad Boy* tucked away in the bottom drawer of her desk, and there was no way in hell she was letting that go to waste.

But for now, at least, eating was off the cards.

She slid down off her stool, crossed to the sink, and spent far longer than usual scrubbing up. Then, she made a stop at the PPE box, and broke her personal best for Most Time Spent Putting on Gloves.

That done, she put a hand on the door plate, but couldn't quite summon the energy to push. Not yet. Not quite.

She was talking herself into it when the main office door opened behind her. A tall, angular man stood there, his grey pallor and sunken cheeks making him look for all the world like one of Shona's former patients.

"I heard what happened," he said, his voice like the crunching of dry leaves. "And I thought you might like a hand..."

CHAPTER THIRTEEN

THE BIG BOARD was filling up with scribbled *Post-Its*, as Sinead hurriedly jotted down the key points from Logan's recounting of the morning's events.

She thought of this as the 'Brainstorming Stage' where her job was to get as much information slapped onto the board as possible, which could then be picked apart, honed, and refined as the investigation developed.

So far, Logan had mostly focused on the where and the when of the family's visit, which he'd gleaned from his interview (and near punch up) with Rufus Boyle.

They had arrived one week ago—Monday evening—having booked online just a day previously. They'd tried to book an extra week, Rufus had told Logan, but there were other guests due in, and while the family had offered more than double the usual rates, the owner had held firm, being more concerned with his Airbnb review score and Superhost status than some short term financial gain.

Usually, given how out of the way the house was, guests tended to drive, but the family had said they were coming by train, and had asked Rufus to arrange a taxi to pick them up, which he had done.

Logan presented the train tickets and taxi receipt in an evidence bag, and confirmed that they corroborated the owner's story.

"Did he meet them in person?" asked Ben.

"Apparently not, no."

Hamza's head raised from where he had been looking at his notes. "He said that? He didn't make contact?" he asked. "Because the cleaner, Magdalena, she told me he always goes to meet new guests when they arrive. She was sure he'd have popped in to see them."

"Aye? He was adamant he hadn't been to visit," Logan said. "Worth us double-checking, though. If he's lying about that, no saying what else he's lying about."

Sinead started writing on an orange *Post-It*. "But at the moment he's claiming no face to face contact at all?"

"That's his story at the moment," Logan replied, and Sinead slapped a note saying as much onto the Big Board.

There was still a lot they didn't know, the DCI explained, although this early in the investigation nobody had been expecting it to be any other way. Cause of death was almost certainly the stabbings, and he had Sinead make particular note of the accuracy with which the wounds had been inflicted.

Time of death was still up in the air, and they'd need Shona to give them a clearer indication. Two or three nights ago, maybe, but no point putting it on the board until they had something more concrete.

He mentioned the indents on the bedroom carpet. He'd asked the cottage owner about them, but he'd been none the wiser. Sometimes, guests took the TV upstairs, he'd said, and he'd been visibly annoyed at the thought of it. Maybe it was that?

Logan had gone back inside to check the TV and the unit it stood on in the living room, but neither had come close to matching the marks on the floor.

"You said it might have been months old, though, didn't you, boss?"

Logan confirmed that, aye, that might well have been the case. It probably was, in fact, given that all the available evidence disproved the theory he'd come up with for what the indents were.

"How do you mean?" asked Ben. "What are they?"

"Could be wrong, but... it's a bedroom," Logan said. "So, I'm thinking travel cot. One of them collapsible ones."

There was some general murmuring of agreement that this made sense.

"But we've got four train tickets, and the booking was for four people only, two adults, two kids. I also did a quick Google search of Mr Tatties. He's got three kids of his own, all adults. He remarried a couple of years back, and his new wife has two girls."

"The two in the house," Sinead reasoned.

"Aye. No other kids. Certainly none young enough to be in a cot," Logan said. "I asked the owner if he's had families with babies staying recently, and he reckons about three in the past couple of months."

"That's probably it, then," said Tyler.

Logan nodded. "Aye. That's probably it," he agreed.

"Wait, wait, wait. Hold on just a minute," said Ben. "Mr Tatties?"

Logan frowned, then glanced from Ben to Hamza and Dave. "Shite. Did we not say? The victim. One of them, I mean. He's Archie Tatties."

While neither Hamza nor Dave's expression flickered so much as an iota, Ben's face practically spasmed in shock. "What, as in Neeps and Tatties?"

"Aye."

"As in..." Ben cupped a hand at the side of his mouth, "... 'Where's the haggis?' That Archie Tatties?"

"The very same."

The DI leaned back in his chair. "Bloody Nora!"

"Eh... who's Archie Tatties when he's at home?" asked Hamza.

Ben sat forward again. "What? Archie Tatties. Neeps and Tatties. 'Where's the haggis?'"

Hamza looked between both his superior officers. "Aye, you're just... You're just saying the same things again."

"We don't know who you're talking about, boss," Tyler said, lending his sergeant some backup.

"Aye, you do!" Ben insisted. He cupped his hands around his mouth again and inhaled. Sinead butted in before he had a chance to start bellowing.

"Saying, 'Where's the haggis?' again isn't going to help, sir," she said.

"Here. I've Googled them," Dave announced, holding up his phone to show a photograph of two men dressed in shiny black suits.

It looked like some sort of promotional image, although quite what it was meant to be promoting was any bugger's guess.

One of the men—a skinny fella with a face like a startled tortoise—held a couple of turnips in front of him like they were women's breasts. The other, much heavier-set man with a thick moustache and a head of permed hair, had fashioned his own makeshift tits from a couple of small potatoes, and was enviously side-eyeing his much more impressively endowed partner, who was grinning down the lens of the camera like both their lives depended on it.

"What were they, bawdy greengrocers?" Hamza asked.

"Comedians it says here," Dave replied. "Back in the eighties."

"Before our time," Tyler said. "That explains why we've never heard of them."

"Before your time? It was just in the eighties, how can that be before your..." Ben fell silent as he counted in his head, then his face took on something of a haunted look. "Jesus Christ," he muttered, once he'd finished doing his sums. "Aye, a bit before your time, right enough."

"We're surrounded by bloody children," Logan added, having run through the same mental calculations as Ben and similarly found himself on the wrong side of the answer.

"Aye, well it's their loss," Ben said, grasping for some sliver of consolation. "Neeps and Tatties were comedy bloody gold. Very much the Francie and Josie of their day."

"Who?" said everyone in the room under forty.

Ben rolled his eyes and sighed. "Doesn't matter. Just... forget your Cannon and Ball, or your Little and Large, or your Morecambe and... Well, no, they were no Morecambe and Wise, obviously, but they were better than most of the shite doing the rounds at the time."

"What's the 'Where's the haggis?' about?" Tyler asked.

"That was their catchphrase," Ben said, chuckling at the memory. "They'd come on and say, 'Hello, we're Neeps and Tatties!' and the audience would shout back, 'Where's the haggis?'

because neeps and tatties are usually served with haggis, you know? So, then..." He wiped a tear from his eye. "Aw, this was good... they'd lob handfuls of haggis into the crowd. Just great big handfuls of it, just chucked it right into the audience. Pelted them with it, so they did."

The younger officers all contemplated this for a few moments.

"Jesus," Tyler eventually muttered, speaking on behalf of all of them.

"They did the Royal Variety Show one year—mind, Jack?" Ben continued, his enthusiasm for the subject only growing as the memories came rushing back. "Fired the haggis out of gold cannons. Aye, no' real gold, like. Painted."

"Real haggis, though?" asked Sinead, her face frozen in a sort of rictus of horror.

"Oh aye, very much so," Ben confirmed. "Very much so." When the DC expressed her concern for any vegetarians in the crowd, Ben quickly waved the notion away. "No, it's fine. That wasn't really a thing back then. Just hippies and weirdoes, and they didn't let them anywhere near the Royal Family. Not in them days. Just in case."

He smiled fondly and looked over at the window like he could see one of their performances playing out there.

"Neeps and Tatties," he said, the words coming out as a wistful whisper. "Went over to America at one point. Tried to crack the market over there."

"And did they?" asked Dave.

"Christ, no. No. The Americans didn't get it. They've no' got the same sophisticated sense of humour as us," Ben said, and the younger officers' eyes were all drawn back to the two gurning men pretending vegetables were tits on Dave's phone. "Lost a lot of money, I seem to recall. Think that's what led to them splitting. Shame. Just flew too close to the sun, I suppose. Wonder what they're up to these days?"

"Well... most recently, fifty percent of them were getting stabbed repeatedly in the chest," Logan said.

Ben frowned for a moment like he was failing to grasp the punchline of a joke, then gave himself a shake. "Oh, aye. Shite. Sorry, got a bit sidetracked there. Forgot how we got onto the subject." He blew out his cheeks. "So, Archie Tatties is dead. You know what that means, don't you?"

"No reunion tour?" Dave guessed.

"It means we'll have the press crawling all over the case," Logan said.

The junior officers all looked highly sceptical. "He's not exactly a household name, boss," Tyler pointed out. "Once upon a time, maybe..."

"Aye, but most tabloid readers aren't out of bloody school like you lot. They'll remember Archie Tatties, all right. Family of tourists killed in a holiday home invasion is headline news on its own. Throw in a minor celebrity and the bastards will be foaming at the mouths to get themselves an exclusive."

"We taking bets on the headlines?" Dave asked. "Fiver on 'Highland Holiday Home Horror.'"

"Missing the celebrity angle," said Hamza. "More like... 'Tattie Planted in Highland Holiday Home Horror.'"

"'Nobody Killed in Highland Holiday Home Horror,'" Tyler suggested. When this was met with confused looks, he clarified. "Because, you know, he's a bit of a nobody these days."

Logan's voice trampled all over the rest of the conversation. "This is all great fun, of course," he said, in a tone that very much said the opposite. "But, I'm sure you don't need reminding that we've got four corpses cooling up the road in Raigmore right now—two of which are young girls—and that the bastard or bastards who put them there is still roaming free."

"Sorry, boss," Tyler said, beating the others to it by half a second.

Logan dismissed their apologies with a shake of his head. He couldn't be angry at them. It was how they coped. It was how they always coped. At the end of the day, it was a job. Let it become your life, and you'd lose yourself to it. You'd lose everything.

Christ knew, he had.

So, you laughed, and you joked, and you hoped that it didn't get to you. Prayed that it didn't start gnawing at you, eating you up from within.

It was an unspoken agreement among all polis everywhere, Logan thought. If you laughed, and you joked—all of you, together

—then the system worked. A shared delusion was created, that this was all normal, this was all fine. You laughed, and you joked, and the demons were kept at bay.

For a while, anyway.

"'Tatties has had his Chips,'" Logan suggested, and there were smiles all round. Relief, mostly. The system was still working. Shields were still raised. Logan checked his watch. "I need to get up the road shortly for the PM," he announced, then he pointed to Hamza and jabbed a thumb at the Big Board. "But before I do, DS Khaled, tell us what you've got."

CHAPTER FOURTEEN

Two hours later, Logan entered the Pathology Department at Raigmore Hospital, and found a cadaver sitting propped up at Shona's desk.

"Jesus," he ejected, then the man at the desk tilted his head upwards, and Logan realised that despite appearances he was, in fact, somehow still clinging to life.

Dr Albert Rickett—better known as Ricketts to anyone he'd worked with in the past twenty years—sat back in the chair. Something creaked, but Logan couldn't decide if it was the wooden seat, or the old man himself.

"Ah. Detective Chief Inspector Logan," Ricketts intoned, raising one feathery white eyebrow. The way he'd said it, Logan thought, suggested the man should be stroking a white cat, while subtly reaching for the switch that would drop the DCI into a tank of hungry piranhas.

"Albert," Logan said, giving the older man a curt nod. "Thought you'd retired? Again. After that whole failure to recognise a murder victim when you saw one thing with the Snowman case."

"Iceman," the pathologist corrected. "And yes, I did. I have. Mostly. I'm just lending a hand. Big case. Lot to get through. Thought I'd chip in."

"Very noble of you."

Ricketts shrugged, and Logan would have sworn he heard the bones in his shoulders rattling together. "It was this or painting," he said, then he tapped the side of his head with a finger that was all knuckles. "Important to keep the brain active."

"Aye. Fair enough," Logan said, keen to get this part of his day wrapped up quickly.

Ricketts had apparently been thinking the same thing, and there were a few more creaks and groans as he turned and indicated the swing doors on the far wall. "Dr Maguire is just finishing up now," he said. "She's been expecting you."

Mr Bond, Logan added silently, then he thanked the old man, got himself masked and gloved up at the PPE station, and pushed through into the unwelcoming cold of the mortuary.

Shona was studying something purple and wobbly on a set of scales when he entered, and Logan briefly contemplated pulling a crisp about-turn and walking straight out again. He forced his size thirteens to stand their ground, though, despite the sickly stench that permeated the room and made a mockery of his paper mask.

"Oh, hello!" Shona called over to him. "You're earlier than I thought. I'm still elbow deep." She adjusted the scales a little, and the purple thing wobbled like half-set jelly.

Logan swallowed. "So I see."

"Want to wait out in the office? I'll be about another hour here," Shona said. Despite her mask, he saw her smiling. "I mean, you're welcome to stay..."

"No, no, you're fine," Logan said. "Far be it from me to get in your way."

He'd seen enough bodies not to be too put-out by their contents, but he didn't share Shona's fondness or fascination for all the more grisly parts of the post-mortem process. Still, he didn't much fancy sitting out there with Ricketts for an hour, either.

Fortunately, he had a third option, although it was arguably even less pleasant a prospect than the other two.

"I'll shoot off and be back in an hour or so," he said, stealing a quick timecheck from the clock on the mortuary wall. "I, eh, I think I owe someone an apology."

Bob Hoon stood in his hallway, shiny with sweat and reeking of booze, his face a masterclass in utter contempt.

"Well, well, well, if it isn't McFuckface Forget-Me-Not," he spat, giving the detective on his doorstep a slow, deliberate look up and down. "Here to fucking gloat, are we?"

"No, Bob, I—"

"Cracking reference you sent, by the way. Fucking Grade A, ten out of ten. Glowing it was. Bring a tear to a fucking glass eye, so it would," Hoon said, then he rattled his knuckles on the side of his head like he was knocking on a door. "Wait. No. Hold on a fucking minute. No, it wasn't, because you didn't take your maw's clunge-smelling finger out of your fat, useless arse long enough to write me one. Did you?"

"Sorry, Bob. No. I meant to, but we got a shout. Family of four. Home invasion."

"Oh, and I suppose that's more fucking important, is it?"

"Well... aye."

Hoon tutted, but offered no counterargument. "Fine. Fuck's sake. Fine," he said. "Didn't need your help, anyway. Got the job on my own. A better one, actually."

Logan managed a thin smile. "Great. When do you start?"

"Whenever I like. Manager seems pretty open to me doing whatever I want."

"Right. Right. And that's... at Tesco?"

Hoon's face flashed red. For once, it was not due to rage. Or not *solely* due to rage, at least.

"Aye. It's in security, though, so..." He gestured down at the creased tracksuit bottoms and food-stained t-shirt he wore. "Thought I'd better get my arse back into shape."

Given that Hoon was several years older than Logan, his shape was already pretty impressive. His time behind a desk on the force had led to him becoming a little doughy around the edges, but since he'd been given his cards he'd started sculpting it all away again, thinning out the lean bits, and bulking up the rest.

Hoon gave Logan another appraising look. "Take it you gave up on the whole fucking notion?"

"What notion?"

"Getting fit. Losing weight."

It was Logan's turn to look down at himself. "I did," he protested. "I'm about the right weight now."

"The right weight?" Hoon snorted. "For what, a fucking bungalow?" He threw a punch, stopping it just short of Logan's stomach before the DCI could even react. "You're all tits and arse, son. And no' in a fucking good way, either. You need to get yourself a training partner." He gestured back over his shoulder. "Come on. I've got the weights out."

"Eh, another time, maybe," Logan said. "Still got that home invasion to sort out."

"Oh. Right. Aye," Hoon said. He sniffed hard, draining his sinuses, then spat their gelatinous contents out past Logan into the front garden. "Well, again, thanks for fucking nothing, Jack. Remind me next time you need my help for anything to tell you to ram it up your arse."

"That's fair," Logan conceded. "Good luck with the job, Bob."

"Aye. Well," Hoon grunted. "Good luck with..."

Logan nodded. "Cheers," he said, turning away. "I'll leave you to it."

"You spoken to Spandau Ballet yet?" Hoon asked.

Logan stopped and turned back. "You mean Tyler?"

Hoon scowled and shrugged, indicating he had no interest in getting on first-name terms with the man. "You spoken to him?"

"About what?" Logan asked.

"That'll be a 'no' then," Hoon muttered. He caught the edge of his door and started to close it. "I'd have a word with him."

"About what?" Logan asked again.

"Not my fucking place to say, Jack," Hoon said, and then the door closed between them with a firm, definitive *click.*

Down in Fort William, most of the team were deep in research mode. Phone calls were being made, conversations were being had, and leads were being followed up. A pile of Post-Its— still small, but getting larger—was growing on Sinead's desk, as Tyler, Ben, and even Dave secured new nuggets of information and scribbled them down for her to process.

Three miles away, on the strip of road that separated Fort William train station from the local *Morrison's* supermarket, DS Khaled sat in the middle row of a stationary seven-seater taxi, listening to the boom of the driver's voice from up front.

"Yeah, so, Monday, it was. But you knew that already, didn't you? It was you what told me that," the driver said, talking to Hamza via the rearview mirror.

He was in his late thirties, Hamza estimated, but had been cursed with early-onset male pattern baldness and had tried to disguise it by shaving his head almost all the way to the bone. He was in better shape than might be expected of someone who spent ten to twelve hours a day sitting down, and who subsisted on a diet that largely consisted of whatever the local petrol stations had left on their shelves at three o'clock in the morning.

His voice was unnecessarily loud, like it had adapted to having to be heard over the sound of an engine, and had never quite figured out how to reset itself.

"Monday. Evening, I think. Not sure of the time, exactly. They'll have it written down at the office, I'm sure. Evening, though. Definitely evening, because I'd been home for a kip in the afternoon," the driver explained. "Normally, I'd hang about here to see who wanted to go where, but I knew I had this job booked in, so I nipped home and put my feet up for a while."

"Right, so—" Hamza began, but the driver interrupted him.

"Wait, wait, they were off the Mallaig train, weren't they? So, they'd have been in about twenty to eight." He nodded. "Yeah, yeah. That's about right. I'm sure that's when it was booked for. Think it was running a few minutes late, mind you—no bloody change there. But about twenty to eight. Monday. That's it."

The driver tapped both hands on his steering wheel like a little victory drum beat, then met Hamza's eyes in the mirror and nodded for him to continue.

"OK, Mr... Sorry, I don't think I got your name," the DS said.

There was some grunting and wheezing as the driver turned himself around enough to offer up a handshake. "Sorry, yeah. Hill. Pete Hill," he said. "I'll give you a minute to get the jokes out of the way."

Hamza blinked. "Jokes?"

"Yeah. Pete Hill. *Peat* hill. Like, as in... a hill of peat."

"Oh."

"Like peat the muck. The... soily stuff."

"Right, aye," Hamza said. Pete gazed back at him with such a look of expectation that Hamza felt compelled to give a little chuckle. "It's good."

"Easy for you to say," Pete said, his expression becoming pained. "Try going through primary and secondary school with a name like Pete Hill. Relentless, those kids were."

"I can imagine."

"'Check you oot, you fat fuck!'" Pete said, imitating the cry of some unnamed tormentor. "'Your maw's fanny smells like shite!'" He shook his head. "Vicious, they were."

Hamza hesitated. "Right. I thought... I thought you meant they made fun of your name."

"Well, maybe not as such, but that was definitely the root of it," the driver said. "Call a child 'Pete Hill' and you're painting a bloody target on their backs, aren't you? That's why I joined the army, so I could learn to kick shit out of the little fuckers." He tightened his grip on the steering wheel. "Course, they were brutal there, an' all."

"Eh, aye, I can imagine," Hamza said. "Couldn't you have gone with 'Peter?'"

It was Pete's turn to miss a beat. "What?"

"Couldn't you have used 'Peter' instead of 'Pete?'"

The driver turned and faced forward again. For several seconds, he just stared ahead at the bus station that stood tucked in at the side of the supermarket.

"Fuck," he mumbled, after some thought. Then, he gave himself a shake and went back to addressing Hamza via the mirror. "Anyway, your man sure saw the funny side. Cracked him up it did. Pete Hill. He was firing them out, the jokes. Jokes about holding twenty times my own body weight in water, about capturing and storing carbon dioxide, about drying me out and throwing me on a fire! I tell you this much, he knew a lot about the uses for peat. More than most, anyway. More than me, even, and I thought I'd heard them all over the years. He was relentless, though. Relentless."

Hamza had a nagging feeling that this interview was starting to slip away from him, so he shunted it back on track with a question.

"This is the car you took them in, yes?"

"It is. They needed something roomy. Had quite a bit of luggage with them, so this was ideal," Pete said. "This'll carry pretty much anything. I can get my bike in. Fishing rods. Furniture. You name it. I've had a fridge freezer in here once. One of them big American ones. With the ice dispenser on the front. It wasn't turned on at the time, obviously—I mean, where would you plug it in? But still, it fit in with the seats down. The back ones fold right into the floor. Flat, so you wouldn't know they were there. Makes a difference."

Hamza grasped at the thread of the conversation and clung tightly to it. "You took them from here to the house in Glen Coe? Any stops along the way?"

"Aborted starts, more like," Pete said. He indicated the supermarket ahead of them. "The wife popped in there with the kids. Your man waited here. Right where you're sitting now, actually. I didn't recognise him at first. He had sunglasses on, you see? And I thought, 'Oh, hello. He's someone.' Because who wears sunglasses at twenty to eight in the evening in Fort William? I thought, 'Either he's blind, or he's someone.' And then, once I'd got speaking to him a bit, it clicked who he was. I'd seen him perform, see? In the Gulf. They did a special for the troops. Fucking awful, it was, but that's another story. Absolute shit. We were all livid. We were meant to be getting Kim Wilde."

Hamza tried to cut in and reroute the conversation, but Pete steered it back on his own.

"Anyway, I said to him, I said, 'Here, you're him, aren't you?' and he denied it at first, but then he admitted it in the end, when I shouted to him... you'll like this... I shouted to him, 'Where's the haggis?' He owned up quick smart then, I can tell you."

"How did he seem?" Hamza asked.

"Not like on the telly, but then you wouldn't be, would you? He was still funny, though. Full of jokes. Full of fun. We were getting along like a house on fire by the time his wife came back with the little 'uns and a trolley full of shopping. Chatting away like old friends, so we were. I got out and loaded the bags into the car. They'd just dumped all the other stuff in the back, so I had to move it all around. It's a big car, I told them, but it's not the fucking TARDIS. Archie liked that one, so I told him he could have it. For his act, like. He seemed pleased at that. So, anyway, once it was all moved around and the shopping was loaded up in the boot, the five of them jumped in and I took them down the road."

"OK, so from there, you..." Hamza stopped. Frowned. Met Pete's reflected gaze in the mirror. "Wait," he said. "Five?"

CHAPTER FIFTEEN

LOGAN SAT in the coffee shop just inside the entrance of Raigmore Hospital, enjoying a ham sandwich. Well, technically he wasn't so much *enjoying* as *tolerating it*. It was getting later in the day, and the pieces had been sat out since morning. This, combined with a lack of butter for presumably health-related reasons, meant the bread had reached near sandpaper levels of dryness.

The ham itself was fine, though. He picked idly at it while he waited for his cardboard cup of tea to drop a degree or two below scalding, so he could finally take a sip.

The car park, as usual, had been a bloody nightmare. Had Ben been here, everyone within earshot would've been subjected to his rant about city centre shop and office workers using the car park "like a bloody park and ride!" and thereby reducing the number of spaces available to actual visitors to the hospital.

Logan had heard it so often now he could practically recite it word for word. And, as he watched the five-fifteen bus pull in at the stop and a dozen men and women in business clobber come swarming out, he had to concede that the DI had a point.

His tea had almost fallen to a temperature where it wouldn't melt his lips off when his phone buzzed on the table. Ben's name appeared, and for a moment Logan wondered if the old bugger had somehow read his thoughts, and was calling to complain about the parking situation all over again.

"Benjamin," he said, tapping the screen and bringing the mobile to his ear. "What's up?"

"Where are you?" Ben asked. "You on the way back down the road yet?"

"Not yet, no. Still waiting to go in and get the PM results. Why, what's up?"

"Hamza's been..." Ben began, then he switched tracks. "So, you're still at the hospital?"

"Aye," said Logan, sensing what was coming next.

"You get parked alright?"

"Fine," Logan lied. "Straight in."

"Well, that's a bloody first!" Ben retorted, then he forced himself to get back on topic. "Anyway, Hamza was out talking to a..." There was the sound of a page being turned. "...Pete Hill."

A single line on Logan's forehead became a little more defined. "Hamza was talking to a peat hill?"

"No' a peat hill. I don't mean a hill of bloody peat. Why would he be...? *Pete Hill*. That's his name. The taxi driver who picked up the victims from the station."

"Oh, right. Aye," Logan said. "Thought you'd finally lost your marbles there. And? What happened?"

Ben drew in a breath. "You were right, Jack. There were five of them came off the train," the DI said. "Two adults, two kids..."

"And a baby," Logan concluded. "Jesus."

"Looks like we're no' just dealing with a homicide now," Ben said. "We can throw in kidnapping, too."

"God. Right, we need to—"

"We're on it, Jack," Ben assured him. "We're on it right now. You just get done up there, then get down the road, and we'll hopefully have more for you by then."

Logan groaned. This complicated things. Which was actually quite impressive, considering what they'd already been dealing with

"Right. I'll be as quick as I can," Logan said, then he hung up, took a swig of his tea. The, "Fuck!" he ejected when it all but blistered his tongue earned him dirty looks from one end of the coffee shop to the other.

Ten minutes and a few big glugs of cold water later, a masked and gloved Logan stood in Shona Maguire's office, watching her peeling off her blood-mottled PPE.

Ricketts was sitting at her computer, a skeletal finger circling above the keyboard before pouncing on a letter every few seconds in what was the most frustrating display of typing Logan had ever seen.

"What a day," Shona remarked, snapping off her gloves and disposing of them in one of her coloured bins.

"You OK?" Logan asked, and he caught a brief flick of Ricketts' eyes in his direction.

"Yeah, fine. Bit... you know. Few sleepless nights ahead, I'm sure. But fine."

Logan had a near overwhelming urge to put his arms around her, but the ghostly presence of Albert Rickett made him err on the side of professionalism.

"If it's any consolation, I doubt any of us are going to be getting much sleep, either," he told her.

"Developments?" Shona asked.

"Could say that," Logan replied. "Let's just say the case just got a whole lot bigger."

Shona gave a low whistle. "Bigger than four victims and a minor TV celebrity?"

"Aye. Turns out there were five of them at the house," Logan said.

"Oh. Right. So... the fifth is the killer?"

"The fifth is a baby. Whereabouts currently unknown."

Shona's eyelids fluttered like someone had thrown a punch that just stopped short. "Oh. God. That's... God."

"Like I say, not much sleep for us tonight."

The gravelly voice of Ricketts cut in on the conversation. "You should try. A good night's rest is vital for a reasoned mind. You're doing nobody any favours if you stay awake. A man in your position needs to be alert, Detective Chief Inspector. Alert, and aware."

Logan considered the bag of skin and bones in the chair, then arranged his features into something that might be mistaken as a moment of appreciation to the untrained eye.

"Thanks for the advice, Albert," he said. "I'll keep it in mind."

Ricketts nodded solemnly, then resumed his series of prodded attacks on the keyboard.

A single look passed from the detective to the pathologist that managed to ask several questions, while simultaneously suggesting they should go somewhere else to talk further.

Shona, amazingly enough, managed to pick up on all of this, and summoned Logan through to the room next door with a wave of a hand and a, "Want to come through and we'll go over everything?"

It was only when they were enclosed in the much colder area of the mortuary, and the doors had swung closed behind them, that Logan vocalised what his eyes had already said.

"What a creepy bastard that man is," he whispered. "What was all that about?"

"He means well," Shona said. "He's just a bit..."

"Hammer House of Horror?"

"Old-fashioned."

Logan shot a glance back at the doors, like he thought he might catch Ricketts peering through the narrow gap where they didn't quite meet in the middle. "I tell you, if we ever get victims turning up with all the blood drained out of them via two wee holes in their neck, I know whose door I'm knocking on first."

He saw the four sheets that covered the four mounds—each one smaller than the one before—and he fell silent. Despite the chill of the refrigerated air, he felt stiflingly warm, and gave a tug on his tie to loosen it further than it already was, in the hope it cooled him down.

"OK, so the good news," Shona began, with a faux enthusiasm that fooled neither Logan nor herself. "Three-quarters of them didn't suffer. Not physically, at least. Not for long. They were all stabbed in the right ventricle. Directly. Bang on, every time."

"That's unusual?"

"Very. They'd have passed out almost immediately, and brain death would've occurred in maybe three to five minutes. But the accuracy, though... That's the impressive part."

"What about the other stab wounds?" Logan asked. "There were a fair few of them. Sure the direct hit wasn't just luck?"

Shona shook her head. "I think the other wounds were done after, probably to hide the fact they knew what they were doing. On everyone but the male, at least. His was different. I think—and Geoff might be able to shed some more insight on this with blood splatter—but I think that he was stabbed around the rest of the chest first, then the heart last. Like whoever did it wanted to hurt him. Make him suffer for a while."

"So, it could have been a personal grudge, rather than a random attack?"

"I'll let you be the one to figure out the motive," Shona said. "But the wounds were certainly inflicted in a different pattern, there were far more of them, and they were done with more force, so go ahead and make of that what you will."

Logan filed the information away, then moved on through his list of questions. "How accurate can you be on time of death?"

"I can tell you it wasn't within the last thirty-six hours," Shona replied. "Rigor mortis has gone, and there are some early signs of bloating, so I'd say we're looking at three days. Stomach contents show the last meal they ate was fairly substantial, so if you want my opinion—and you do, obviously—I'd put time of death at between..." Her lips moved as she counted below her breath. "... seven o'clock and eleven o'clock on Thursday evening."

Logan made a mental note of this, too, although he knew the report would be in the email inbox by the time he was back down the road. The time fit with the home invasion theory, as they were generally carried out later in the day when witnesses were fewer and farther between.

Of course, given the remoteness of the house, witnesses would have been thin on the ground at any time of day.

"I think my initial estimate about the knife used was a bit off," Shona said. "Longer than I thought. Pretty thin, though. Blade's about twenty centimetres long, maybe a little more. It has a triangular prong down near the handle around three centimetres wide. That's the widest part."

Logan drew a mental picture of the weapon in his head. "Fish knife? Like... for filleting?"

Shona clicked her fingers and pointed at the detective. "That's the conclusion I came to. I Googled some pictures, and it fits the wound pattern."

"Hardly designed for puncturing a human chest, is it?"

"No, but there's no reason it wouldn't," Shona said. "Given enough force." She pointed to the largest of the sheet-covered shapes. "There's something else about your man, too. Mr Tattie."

"Tatties," Logan corrected.

"Right. Sorry. How could I have got that wrong?"

"His real name's..." Logan's eyes narrowed as he struggled to recall. "...something else," he said, when it became apparent that nothing was coming back to him anytime soon. "They'll have it down the road by now."

"No need. I Googled him, too. It's Sutherland. Archibald Sutherland."

"That's him, aye. What did you find?"

"Cancer," Shona said. "A whole big pile of it, in fact. Lung, mostly, but it's spread to his liver and one of his kidneys, too. I pulled his medical records, and he was aware. Got official diagnosis just over a month ago."

"Was he on any treatment?"

Shona shook her head. "He was offered chemo and radiotherapy, but declined both. It would've bought him an extra month or two, at most, and that time likely wouldn't have been pleasant."

Logan regarded the vaguely man-shaped mound on the table. "So, he knew the clock was ticking, then."

"Maybe that's why they took the trip. One last holiday, sort of thing," Shona suggested.

"Aye. Maybe," Logan said, although there was no conviction behind it. He looked up at the clock, then double-checked it against his watch. "I'd better get going. Long night ahead, like I say."

"I'll get the report typed up and sent over," Shona said. She anticipated Logan's next question, and worked quickly to set his mind at ease. "Don't worry, I'll be the one typing it, not Albert."

"Thank Christ for that," Logan remarked. "We'd be waiting weeks at the rate that old bastard pokes the keys."

A smile passed between them. Something else, too.

"I, eh, I had a good night. On Saturday. The wedding, I mean,"

Shona said. "We should definitely do it again. Ourselves, I mean." Panic flashed across her face. "I don't mean... I don't mean a wedding, I just meant a night out. Pub. Or... restaurant. We've been talking about it for how long now?"

"A long time," Logan conceded.

"We should definitely... At some point."

"We should. We definitely should," Logan agreed. "At some point."

Shona smiled. Nodded. Did something unusual with her hands that she couldn't quite offer any explanation for. "Yes. Definitely at some point."

There was an awkward moment during which neither of them quite knew what to say or do. There was a moment of half-contact that wasn't quite a hug, but was somewhere in that vicinity, then Logan said his goodbyes and headed out through the swing doors.

Shona exhaled, admonished herself with a low mutter, then straightened suddenly when one of the doors swung open again.

"Fuck it," Logan announced. "Assuming that both of us aren't up to our necks in all this, what are you up to next Friday?"

CHAPTER SIXTEEN

It took Logan seventy minutes to make the drive from Inverness to Fort William, three minutes to get from the car park to the Incident Room, and then a further twenty seconds to fly off the handle.

"What do you mean you've got no idea?" he demanded, glaring at the two DCs and the DS like a hawk deciding which unsuspecting field mouse to swoop down on. "How the hell can we have no idea?"

"It's... We just can't find any record, sir," Hamza said, putting himself in the firing line. "We managed to speak to both families—liaisons are with them now offering support—and neither of them knew anything about a baby. It wasn't theirs. Not unless Mrs Sutherland gave birth in secret."

Sutherland. That was it. Archie Tatties' real name. *Archibald Sutherland.*

"And given that her ex-husband and her sister both saw her regularly, we reckon we can rule that out," Sinead explained.

"Did you check with Missing Persons?"

"Nothing about any babies going missing, boss," Tyler said. "Nothing outstanding, anyway."

"So... where the fuck did it come from?" Logan asked. "The taxi driver's *sure* there was a baby?"

"He was adamant," Hamza said. "Couldn't say if it was a boy

or a girl, but he reckoned it was very young. A few weeks, maybe, although he only got a quick look. Said they had a pram and a travel cot, too. The wee one slept the whole way down the road, apparently. Didn't make a cheep."

"He's sure it was alive, though?"

Hamza and the others were taken aback by the question. "Well... she took it into Morrison's, so... yes? I think so. I can double-check with him, but I'm pretty sure he would've said something if he thought it was dead."

"Aye, but check anyway. Might not have occurred to him," Logan said.

"Why would they be lugging a dead baby around, boss?" Tyler asked.

"Could've been taking it out there to bury it," Sinead suggested, paling at the thought of it.

"Aye, but if it was dead, why would you take the pram and cot, too?" Tyler asked. "They'd be a right pain in the arse to carry around on public transport, especially if you didn't need them. I mean, the pram, maybe—they could've pushed it around and said the wee one was sleeping—but why drag the cot around if you're not going to use it?"

Logan shed his coat and dumped it on the back of a chair. "Let's check with the taxi driver. Chances are the wean was just sleeping, like he says, but let's rule out any other possibilities, then I think we need another recap. Got a few new bits of info to share." He looked around at the empty chair by DI Forde's desk. "Where's Ben?"

"We, eh, we don't know, sir," Sinead admitted. "He said he had something to do, and that he'd be back in an hour."

"When was this?"

"Ten... fifteen minutes ago, maybe?" said Sinead.

"And he didn't tell you what it was?"

"No, sir," Sinead replied. "But, from the way he was acting, it looked like it was something important."

Ben didn't like hospitals. *But then, does anyone?* he wondered, as he made his way along the Combined Assessment corridor at the Belford, following the directions the nurse at the entrance had given him.

She'd been surprised when he'd asked where to find Moira Corson. He was, she told him, her first visitor.

"Of the day?" Ben had asked, although he already knew the answer.

She was propped up on the bed farthest from the door when Ben entered, her head turned away so she could look out of the large window at the garden beyond. The days were stretching, and there was still a couple of hours of light left despite the near ever-present covering of cloud.

Two of the other three beds had women lying in them. Both had visitors—two at one, three at the other. They were all chatting away, harking back to happier times, and making plans for when the patient was eventually discharged.

Moira lay in silence, looking out at the world, but separated from it by the glass, and her reflection in it.

"Alright, you malingering auld bugger?"

Her face didn't change. Not the side Ben could see, at least. She turned away from the window, and the effort it took made Ben wince behind his plastered-on smile.

There was a pull on the right side of her face from when the stroke had struck. Her mouth had a noticeable downturn at that corner, blighting her features with what looked like a grimace of distaste. More so than usual, even, which was saying something.

"What are you doing here?" she asked, and Ben was pleasantly surprised to hear only the faintest slurring of her words.

"I heard what happened," the DI replied. "Thought I'd pop in and see how you were doing."

Her eyes swivelled in their sockets as she looked him up and down. "Why?"

"Well, because I'm nice like that," Ben said.

One half of Moira's face scowled. The rest did its best to join in, but didn't pack nearly the same punch. "I don't need anyone's pity."

"Good bloody job, because you'll no' be getting any from me," Ben told her. He sat the supermarket carrier bag he'd been carrying on the chair beside the bed, then produced a small bunch of flowers from inside. "I brought you these."

Moira eyed the bouquet with suspicion. "What for?"

"Just... because that's what people do, isn't it? When they're visiting someone in hospital. They bring flowers."

"I've got nowhere to put them," Moira said with a sniff.

Ben's eyes fell on a cardboard pee bottle hanging at the bottom of the empty bed. He unhooked it, shoved the flowers inside, then set it on Moira's bedside table. Due to the design of the bottle, the flowers stuck out at a shallow angle, so they were more lying down than standing upright. Undeterred, Ben presented it with a, "Ta-daa!" then reached back into the bag.

"Got you these, too," he said, holding up an orange bottle and a yellow and red cardboard box. "Bottle of Lucozade and some tea cakes. Aye, *Tunnock's*. None of your cheap rubbish."

"I can't stand Lucozade, so you can take that away with you," Moira told him. She shot a fleeting look at the box, rolled her eyes, then begrudgingly gave him permission to leave the tea cakes.

"You want one now?" Ben asked. "I'm sure I can find us a cup of tea."

"I'm fine for now, thank you," Moira curtly replied, much to Ben's disappointment. He eyed the box of tea cakes longingly, then set it down on the bedside table beside his makeshift vase. "Aye, well, if you change your mind, I can always open them up for you."

"I'll be quite alright," Moira said. She turned her head and went back to looking out of the window. Ben returned the *Lucozade* to the bag and had just picked it up when Moira spoke again. "You can sit down if you must. Man your age, legs must be getting past it."

Ben chuckled and pulled out the chair. "Aye, no' half," he said. There was a *whuff* of air as he dropped his weight down onto the padded vinyl seat. "Mind you, reckon I'd beat you in an arm wrestle."

Moira turned her head on her pillow and glowered at him. "What?"

"Depending on the arm, I mean," Ben said. He indicated her right arm, which lay limply on top of the bedcovers. "I'd be in with a shot against that one. The other one? Anyone's game."

Moira continued to glare at him for what seemed like forever. The voices of the other patients and visitors continued to ring out in the chilly silence.

And then, she let out an exhalation—a single ejection of air—that might, under intense forensic examination, reveal itself to be a laugh.

"Just you go ahead and keep telling yourself that," she said, her stare losing some of its intensity. "What on earth are you doing here, anyway?"

"I told you, I thought I'd pop in and—"

"Here in Fort William, I mean," Moira spat, like only an idiot would have failed to realise this. "I thought you lot were all away back to Inverness? I thought we'd got rid of you?"

"Oh. Aye, we were," Ben said. "But we're back again."

"God, what now?" Moira asked.

"Home invasion in Glen Coe," Ben said. "Nasty business. Tourists. A family." He lowered his voice. "Mind Archie Tatties? Off the telly?"

"Couldn't abide him," Moira said, the flaring of her nostrils confirming her opinion. "Awful unfunny shite."

"Aye. Well. It was him," Ben told her. "I probably shouldn't have said, we're trying to keep it—"

Moira had more pressing concerns than the identity of the victim. "You get checked in properly at the desk?"

"Eh? Oh. Sure. Aye."

"*Properly* properly, I mean?"

"I'm telling you, aye. We did. Some young constable did it," Ben said.

"Filled out all the paperwork? Signed the forms?"

"Yes, Moira, we did," Ben said, but a badly timed swallow gave the game away.

"You're telling me lies," the woman in the bed scolded.

"I'm no'! We filled everything in properly, just the way you'd have wanted," Ben said, then he quickly changed the subject before she could question him further on it. "Everyone's asking for you, by the way."

Moira stared straight up at the ceiling. "Now I *know* you're lying. Why are you even here, anyway?"

Ben hesitated. "Which one do you mean this time? Here in Fort William, or here in the hospital?"

"*Here* here. What are you visiting me for? Why are you bringing me..." She gestured with her good arm. "This rubbish?"

Ben didn't rush out an answer. Not right away. Instead, he gave it the consideration it deserved because, quite frankly, he wasn't sure why he *had* come to visit the crotchety old bastard.

"The, eh, the constable on the desk told me what happened. About your... About the stroke," he said. "And she mentioned that she thought your husband had passed away last year..."

Moira recoiled, aghast. "So, what? You thought you'd try moving in on me? Is that it? Thought you'd try and take advantage?"

"What? No!" Ben spluttered, drawing glances from the other occupants of the room. "Christ, no! No, nothing like... No! That's not what..." He shook his head with considerable force, then reaffixed the smile that had fallen away. "I just... I know what it's like, that's all. To be on your own. And at a time like this, I just thought maybe you could do with a friendly ear. A bit of company for half an hour. That's all. I can go, though, if you like."

"I think that would be best, don't you?"

Ben tapped the flats of his hands on the wooden arms of the chair. "Eh, aye. Aye. OK. If that's what you want," he said. There was some *creaking* as he pushed himself up off the seat. "I hope you feel better soon, Moira. I can't speak for anyone else—because, I'll be honest, most of them think you're a right pain in the arse, and I don't think you can really blame them for that—but I missed seeing you on the desk today. The place isn't the same without you."

He picked up the bag with the *Lucozade* in it, and visibly struggled to fight back a grin.

"It's arguably better, I'll give you, but it's definitely no' the same," he teased. "You take care now."

He had just turned away when Moira's answer came. "Detective Inspector Forde," she said.

"Yes, Moira?"

Her eyes crept to the red and yellow box on the bedside table. "Maybe now would be a good time for that cup of tea."

Ben sat the bag on the floor and rubbed his hands together with glee. "Now you're talking my language," he told her. "But please, call me Ben."

CHAPTER SEVENTEEN

Ben caught the warning looks from Hamza and Tyler just moments before the shouting started.

"Christ, the wanderer returns! Wonders will never bloody cease!" Logan barked. He'd been standing over by the Big Board, discussing with Sinead what needed to go up there, but was now marching between the desks to intercept the DI. "Where the hell have you been?"

Hamza and Tyler both looked down at their work, trying very hard to pretend they weren't there. Dave Davidson, who had until a moment ago been logging the evidence bags sent down the road by Geoff Palmer's team, sat back in his wheelchair and prepared himself for a show.

He was in for a disappointment.

Ben removed his jacket and draped it over his arm before replying. "I had something I had to do," he said, his voice several decibels lower than Logan's.

"Something to do? During a key stage in an investigation?" the DCI snapped. "Well, I hope it was bloody important!"

"It was, actually," Ben confirmed, standing his ground. "Very much so."

Logan huffed and blustered for a few moments, making noises that sounded like words, but weren't. Then, his hackles fell and he accepted with a grunt, that this approach was unlikely to get him anywhere.

"Aye, well. Fair enough," he said. If Ben said it was important, then it was. He'd known the older man long enough to have learned that lesson many times over. "We were just going to have a catch-up, then call it a night. Want to come back fresh tomorrow."

"Sounds good," Ben said. Then, with a wink at Tyler, he followed Logan over to the board, and wheeled his chair out from under his desk to give him a better view.

"Right, gather round," Logan boomed. The others, hearing all that unreleased anger in the DCI's voice, hurriedly moved to join Ben in the semi-circle around the board.

Logan gave a very short introduction that consisted mostly of, "Sinead, you do the talking, will you?" and then he perched on the edge of a desk with his arms folded while the DC got herself organised.

Sinead hadn't yet had time to properly update the board, so was working from several different notes on a selection of pads, and a handful of documents that had dropped into the inbox during the past few hours that they'd printed out.

The first minute or so showed off her full repertoire of *ums* and *ahs* as she tried to get things into some semblance of order, then she decided just to pick a page from the pile and start from there.

"Right, so, the family," she began. "We've got details. Archie Sutherland, sixty-four. Former TV comedian who, as we know, went by the name 'Archie Tatties'. He now runs—or ran—a small video production company based in Girvan. Doing well, based on what we got from Companies House." Sinead looked down at her paperwork, then passed the top sheet to Ben, who sat nearest to where she stood. "Very well, actually."

"Bloody hell," Ben remarked. "He made all that through wedding videos?"

Tyler leaned over to read the page, spent a few seconds scanning it, then ejected a, "Jesus Christ!" when he found last year's turnover. "What do they produce, Lord of the Rings?"

"Wedding videos, mostly, and some corporate stuff."

The page was offered across to Hamza, who reacted in similar disbelief to the figures. "No way you make that from wedding videos," he said.

"You obviously haven't seen the price of a bloody wedding video recently," Tyler muttered, and he winced at the thought of the bill he still had to pay.

Logan took the printout and whistled through his teeth. "He'd have to be filming every bloody wedding in the Central Belt to hit those numbers," the DCI said.

"Corporate stuff seems to be where most of their focus is," Sinead said. "Going by the website, anyway. I've emailed the link."

"What about the rest of the family?" asked Ben.

"Right, yeah. Donna Sutherland, Archie's wife. Aged forty-six. They've been married for three years, met at a charity thing she was doing PR for a year before that. Bit of a whirlwind romance, it seems. The two younger victims—the girls—they're hers from a previous marriage."

"The father been informed yet?" Logan asked.

"We're trying to get hold of him. He's working with Doctors Without Borders in Libya at the moment. Someone is tracking him down."

"Sounds like we can rule him out as a suspect, at least," Hamza said.

"Aye," Logan confirmed. "Pretty solid that, as alibis go."

It was usually a decent shout, too, in situations like this—the father. There were few things more dangerous than a scorned man, and fewer still that would sink as low. Logan had attended too many cases where a jilted husband had taken his own life and those of his children, in some ultimate act of revenge.

One case. That was how many he'd attended.

One too many.

"She's from the east coast, originally. Near Fife," Sinead continued. "But she and the kids moved into Archie's house shortly before the wedding."

"In Girvan?" Logan asked.

"Aye. Same address as the business."

Logan looked down at the page again, and that number with all its zeroes. "So... this is run from his house?"

"Aye, but I pulled it up on Google Maps," Sinead said. "It's a pretty big place."

"Still..."

"You think it's dodgy?" Ben asked.

Logan tore his eyes from the number on the printout. "If not, I'm in the wrong line of work," he replied, then he waved the page for Sinead to continue.

"The girls were Alexis and Elizabeth. Aged thirteen and ten. Their surname's Moir. They stuck with their dad's name."

"But the wife changed hers?" Tyler asked, and the others couldn't miss the little barbs at the edges of the words. "When they got married, I mean, the wife took his surname? Like, you know, is traditional?"

Sinead angled the page she was holding up a little, as if fashioning it into a shield. "Yes," she said, accompanying the response with a very deliberate look. "Presumably she didn't have professional considerations to take into account."

"Wait," Logan interjected. "You're no' taking his surname?"

Sinead shifted her weight from foot to foot. "Is now really the time to talk about that?" she wondered aloud.

"Thank Christ," Logan said, sighing with relief. "Two DC Neishes in the same office and working the same cases was going to be a bloody nightmare."

"Aye, that's a relief, right enough," Ben said. "I was getting a headache just thinking about it."

Tyler tutted and sat back in his chair. Sinead's expression softened, but he wasn't looking, so failed to catch it.

"Anyway," she said, going back to her paperwork. "We still don't have any idea whose baby they had with them, or where it came from. They travelled across from Skye, though, and we're not sure what they were doing there yet. We're waiting on bank statements to try to trace their movements before they got on the ferry. Should get them through during the night, or early tomorrow morning. In the meantime, Uniform is phoning around guest houses and hotels to see if we can find out where they stayed."

"Checked the taxi companies?" Ben asked. "On Skye, I mean. They had a lot of luggage and no car. They didn't walk it down to the ferry."

Sinead clicked the button on a pen and scribbled a note. "I'll get Uniform to check," she said, then she glanced at her watch. "I've got an interview shortly with the ticket collector who was on duty the day the Sutherlands travelled down from Mallaig. He's coming in on the late train from Glasgow. Gets in around half ten. I'm hoping he can confirm they had the baby with them the whole way."

"There were only four tickets," Logan recalled. "At the house. There were four train tickets."

"Kids that age travel free," Hamza said. "They don't need a ticket."

"You sure?" Logan asked.

"Unless they've changed the rules in the last year or two, aye," Hamza confirmed. "I think they have to be, like, four or something before they need to get a ticket."

"Check that, will you?" Logan said, and Sinead added it to her list.

With that done, the DC continued her rundown of the family. Archie had two previous wives, one living, one dead. The dead one, Julie, had been his first, and had died in a car accident while driving to meet him after a pub gig back when he was just starting out.

He'd met his second wife, Alison, on the set of *Neeps and Tatties: With all the Trimmings*, their 1984 festive special which had won the Christmas Day ratings war, albeit exclusively in the STV region of Western Scotland. She'd been working as an assistant in the makeup department, was ten years his junior, and had been heavily pregnant when they'd walked up the aisle in September of the following year.

They went on to have three sons, all now in their thirties, before divorcing in 2003 due to Archie's alleged infidelity.

Fortunately for Mr Tatties, he'd been as good as broke at the time of the divorce, and Alison had walked away with nothing but the keys to a Nissan Micra, and a part share in a poky wee flat in the East End of Glasgow, back in the days before redevelopment had started to drive up property prices.

The news had been broken to the families. Cursory interviews had been carried out over the phone, with a promise to follow-up in more detail later. They were quickly ruled out as suspects, though —Archie's sons all lived abroad, and his ex-wife had been staying with the youngest in Australia for the better part of three months. All pretty solid, as alibis went.

With the family backstory all wrapped up, Sinead gladly surrendered the floor to Logan, who rattled his way through the report that Shona had sent. Between that, and the one Geoff Palmer had emailed over, they were able to build up a bit of a picture of what had happened on the night the family had died.

They'd eaten dinner, probably around six. It was possible they'd played one of the battered board games that were kept in a cupboard in the house, as the box was on the shelf of the coffee table, and their fingerprints were all over the pieces.

The kids had polished off some cookies and milk, then gone through to the bedroom at the back of the house and climbed into the two single beds. Archie and Donna had poured themselves some wine, set the fire roaring, and then...

"Someone turned up," Logan said. "Either the door was unlocked, they had a key, or they just knocked and were let in. No sign of forced entry, anyway."

"Do we know if there's anything missing from the house, boss?" Tyler asked.

"What, apart from a human child, you mean?" Logan retorted.

"Eh, aye. Apart from that, I mean?"

"Not that we know of. But we don't know what they had with them, so it's hard to say. We need to focus on that baby, though. That's the key."

"I checked with Pete Hill. The taxi driver. The wee one was definitely alive. He could hear it breathing when he was helping load up the luggage," Hamza said.

"Right, well that's good news, at least," Logan said.

"CID and Uniform have the feelers out, trying to figure out where they got it," said Hamza. "But it's hard to know where to start."

"Well, they didn't conjure the bloody thing out of thin air. It came from somewhere, which means it went somewhere, too. Whoever has that wean knows what happened. We find it, we find our killer. It's that simple."

Nobody argued. When he was certain they weren't going to, Logan continued.

"Sinead, I want you to be the main point of contact on the baby. Everyone working on it reports to you, and you report to the rest of us. We all need to be in the loop on this, but you're taking lead and staying on it, however long it takes."

An uncertain look passed between Sinead and Tyler. He nodded, encouraging her to say yes. Logan had already moved on, though, her acceptance of the order taken for granted.

"Tyler, you're coming with me. We're heading down the road. Tonight."

Tyler sat up straighter at the mention of his name. "Eh, down the road, boss?" He studiously avoided Sinead's gaze. "For how long?"

"For as long as it takes," Logan retorted. "Why, you got something else planned for this week?"

From the corner of his eye, Tyler could see Sinead trying to shift herself into his line of sight. He didn't dare look her way, though, especially given what he was about to say.

"No. Nothing planned."

Logan regarded him for a moment or two, then nodded. "Right. Good. That's settled, then. Archie Tatties' old comedy partner lives just south of Glasgow. Billy Neeps. We're going to have a word with him, and scope out Archie's production company, too." He wafted the page around. "Something doesn't feel right there."

"In what way, boss?" Tyler asked, still doing everything he could to avoid meeting Sinead's eye.

Logan checked the company income report again, having almost convinced himself he must have misunderstood it last time.

He hadn't. He'd read it correctly. All seven figures of it.

"Based on how much money he's bringing in, I can't help but think that Mr Tatties was in business with some very dangerous people."

CHAPTER EIGHTEEN

BRUNO CAPELLI UNDERSTOOD that the corners were important. You could sweep and mop the rest of the floor as much as you liked, but miss the corners beneath the shelves and fridges, and that was where the eyes went. He didn't care if you could eat your dinner off the rest of the floor—neglect the corners, and the place would never look clean.

Of course, to properly do them justice he had to get right down on his hands and knees and set about them with the dustpan and brush. His daughter had bought him a wee hand hoover, but the battery never lasted, and even fully charged the suction power was nothing to write home about.

You knew where you were with the dustpan and brush, though. Yes, usually it was on your throbbing knees, cursing the aches and pains of old age, but it got the job done better than any modern gadgets ever would.

Bruno had just finished sweeping out the corner where the tinned goods met the porn mags, and was admiringly appraising his work when he heard the bell *ba-ring* above the door.

The toilet roll shelf lent him enough support to clamber back to his feet, and he went hobbling down the aisle towards the front counter before any bugger could have it away on their toes with the box of *Creme Eggs* he had sat there.

They were bloody gannets for the *Creme Eggs*, the shoplifters around here. He'd lost three boxes over the weekend alone, and had taken to emptying most of the contents into a bag behind the counter, and leaving just a few of the foil-wrapped chocolate eggs out on display.

And these were no ordinary eggs. After some sticky-fingered bastard had pinched the third box, Bruno had selected four eggs from the new box, and tipped the rest into a carrier bag.

Then, he'd carefully unwrapped the foil of each *Creme Egg* in turn, placed the eggs fully into his mouth one at a time, before rewrapping them and placing them in the box on the counter. If anyone tried to buy one, he substituted it for one of the eggs from the bag. If anyone stole one—and there were just two left in the box the last time he'd checked—then hell mend them.

They'd probably never know their contraband had spent ten seconds in the mouth of an elderly Italian shopkeeper, of course. But he would, and he took some amount of satisfaction from it.

"Hello, hi, I am coming," Bruno called, announcing his presence to any would-be thieves while he hurpled along the narrow aisle. "I will be right with you."

"No rush, Bruno. We've got all the time in the world," came the reply, and the shopkeeper froze between the cat food and the clingfilm.

"We don't really, Uncle Frankie," another voice said. "We've still got to go see—"

"Paco?"

"Aye, Uncle Frankie?"

"Gonnae shut the fuck up?"

The voices were similar. Local accents, almost indistinguishable from each other, although one was notably younger than the other. Bruno knew those voices well. Every shop owner within a two-mile radius did.

There were three of them today, he noted. That did not bode well.

There was all five and a half feet of Frankie himself, with his slicked-back hair and thin moustache, and a crackle of danger in the air around him. He was in his mid-thirties, but with the teeth of a man twice his age, and the swagger of a man half of it. A scar curved upwards from one corner of his mouth, giving him a permanent half-smirk. It had been there for as long as Bruno had known him, yet still looked red and raw, and wept a milky white fluid in the summer months.

"You should see the other guy," Frankie joked, whenever the scar was mentioned.

That was impossible, of course. No one had seen the man responsible in years. No one would see him ever again.

Frankie's nephew, Paco, was tall and skinny, with a mop of ginger hair that wasn't yet committing itself to any sort of style. He carried a clipboard like a prop, holding it balanced on one arm while he fiddled idly with a well-chewed ballpoint pen.

There was no air of danger hanging around Paco. Everyone around here knew that he was nothing without Frankie. Were his uncle not around, Paco wouldn't so much melt into the background as go running towards it, crying and insisting he was sorry. Insisting he'd had to do those things, that he'd been a victim of Frankie's just like everyone else.

And yet, Bruno had watched Paco sniggering away as Frankie had done his stuff. He'd seen the glee in the boy's eyes when a till had been emptied, or a window had been smashed, or a finger had been broken.

Frankie was a bully, yes, but most folks Bruno knew hated Paco more. At least Frankie was up-front about what he was, and what he'd done.

And what he very well might do again.

The third man was someone new. He was so large that he must have ducked to get through the door. His skin, which was almost the colour of coal, seemed to absorb the glow of the shop's fluorescent lights, making the whole place seem darker.

His face was so blankly impassive he might well have been sleeping, were it not for the fact that he was slowly cracking each of his knuckles in turn, like he was limbering his fingers for something nasty.

"Frankie," Bruno said. An attempt to keep the fear from his voice failed during take-off. The other men couldn't fail to notice.

"Mr Capelli!" Frankie cried, holding his hands out wide. "C'mere you. Get in here."

Bruno didn't move. Not at first. Not until Frankie made beckoning motions with both hands, and the grin on his face became something dangerous. Only then did he shuffle closer. Only then did he let the other man pull him in close for a hug.

Sweat, and cigarette smoke, and overly expensive cologne assaulted Bruno's nostrils until he almost gagged.

"Oi!" Frankie yelped, jumping back with a look of horror in his eyes. "Did you just touch my arse there?"

Bruno blinked. "Sorry?"

"Did he just touch my arse?" Frankie asked the other men in the shop.

"I think he might've, aye, Uncle Frankie," Paco said, the words accompanied by a little cackle of glee.

"No, I did not touch... I did not."

Frankie's face fell. He stepped in closer, and it felt to Bruno like the air was humming between them. When he spoke, Frankie's voice was empty of everything human. No inflection. No emotion. Just letters and words. "Aye, you did. You just touched my arse, you dirty old fuck."

"I—"

"If you try to tell me you didn't, I'll put your face through that fucking window," Frankie warned.

His voice may have been lacking emotion, but his eyes made up for it. They were glaring twin beams of pure rage up at the shop-keeper. Had they bulged any further, they'd surely have burst in their sockets.

And then, a smile spread across the smaller man's face. A laugh cracked out of him like a whip, making Bruno flinch.

"I'm fucking noising you up, Bruno!" he jeered. He turned to his companions. "See his fucking face there? Totally shiteing himself!"

"Classic, Uncle Frankie! Totally classic! A belter! Pure magic! Totally—"

"Alright, alright, we get the fucking point," Frankie snapped.

He pointed to a fridge next to the counter, and the big man stopped cracking his knuckles long enough to fetch a four-pack of *Stella*. Frankie held eye contact with Bruno as he took an offered can, cracked the ring-pull, then slaked his thirst with four big gulps and finished with a burp so loud he'd be talking about it for days.

"Don't mind, do you, Bruno?" he asked, giving the half-empty can a shake. "Thirsty business, this."

Bruno shook his head. What other choice did he have? "It is fine."

"Where are my manners? You want one yourself?" Frankie asked.

The old man shook his head. "No," he said, but he refused to add the, "thank you."

"All the more for me, then," Frankie said. He was still staring at the shopkeeper, and didn't seem to have blinked in well over a minute. "Budge there doesn't drink on duty, and Paco's teetotal. Doesn't drink at all. Tell him how no'."

"Kills brain cells," Paco explained.

Frankie grinned. "Kills fucking brain cells. And he should know, he's got two Highers, or fucking... O-Levels, or whatever they're called these days. Brains of the family, so he is." He sniffed, snorted, then spat a wad of something green and chunky onto the floor. "Don't know where he gets it, mind, his ma's as thick as shit."

"Frankie, I..." Bruno began, but a finger to his lips stopped him.

"Shh. Hush, now. I'm talking," Frankie said.

He pressed his finger harder until the old man had no choice but to pull back, then finished the last of his lager with a couple of big swigs.

"See, a little birdie tells me you've been complaining about the quality of the customer service you've been receiving from your old pal, Frankie. That right, Bruno? You unhappy with the quality of my customer service?"

"No, Frankie, I..."

"How much does Mr Capelli here still owe us, Paco?"

The answer came in the following breath. "Nine and a half, Uncle Frankie."

Frankie touched a finger to his ear. "Hear that, Bruno? Nine and a half. Nine and a half thousand smackeroonies. That is a lot of fucking money, is it no'?"

"It is, Uncle Frankie."

"I wasn't asking you," Frankie replied. His eyes were still locked on Bruno's. He still hadn't blinked. Not once. "You want to pay me that back the now, Bruno?"

Bruno couldn't. Of course, he couldn't. Not even close.

"No, thought not," Frankie said.

Bruno flinched when a hand moved suddenly towards his face. Then, with a smirk, Frankie wiped something off the old man's shoulder.

"So, here's what we're going to do. You're going to fork up this week's instalment, we'll add on, say... five percent to make up for the damage my good reputation has taken thanks to shooting off your big fucking mouth, and we'll call it a night at that."

His hand clamped down on Bruno's shoulder. His smile was an insidious thing that slithered across his pock-marked face, curving both his moustache and his scar.

"What do you say?"

Bruno tried to swallow back the word, but it came out on its own. It had been held back too long, for too many months, for too many years.

"N-no."

The hand became a dead weight on the old man's shoulder. Frankie's mouth continued to smile, but his eyes stopped lending it their support.

"Sorry, Bruno, for a horrible fucking moment there, I thought you said..." Frankie shook his head. His fingers became pincers, and Bruno felt the bones in his shoulder creak. "Tell me I didn't just hear what I thought I heard, Bruno. Tell me you didn't just say—"

"No," Bruno said, with more conviction this time. "I have... I have paid you back many times over. Many times. I cannot afford to continue. I wish... I want to retire. I cannot keep paying. I can't. I... I won't. I just... I won't."

There was silence then, like the whole world was holding its breath. What was left of Frankie's smile had gone now. He blinked. Finally, he blinked.

The hand was removed from Bruno's shoulder. Frankie took a step back and then, to the old man's surprise, he clapped.

"Bravo, Bruno. Fucking bravo. That was some speech. Was that no' some fucking speech?"

"That was some speech, Uncle Frankie."

"That was some fucking speech! Proper moving stuff. Powerful. And, it was high time you stood up and got that off your chest, Bruno. High fucking time!"

He plucked a *Creme Egg* from the almost empty box on the counter. "Don't mind if I do," he said.

Over by the door, Paco turned the sign from 'Open' to 'Closed.' Frankie unwrapped the egg, the crinkling of the foil deafeningly loud in the silence of the shop. He bit the top off the chocolate, licked the trailing fondant from his lips, then raised the *Creme Egg* as if proposing a toast.

"Budge," he said. He finished chewing, then swallowed. "Fuck this prick up."

CHAPTER NINETEEN

"Is it just me, or is there a weird smell in your car, boss?" asked Tyler, as Logan clipped on his seatbelt and started the engine.

"Both," the DCI said, the word ejected alongside an indignant grunt.

Tyler turned to him, his nostrils narrowing like his nose was putting itself into shutdown. "How d'you mean?"

"There's a weird smell that you bloody well caused," Logan said, punching the gearstick into reverse and pulling away from the station. He saw the blank look on the DC's face. "When you threw up."

"When did I throw up?"

"After your crash," Logan said.

They hung a left at the roundabout, and the Beamer accelerated smoothly away. Tyler watched the lights of Fort William Police Station go sliding past. For a moment, he thought he saw Sinead standing at one of the windows, but they were already too far away for him to say for sure.

"Oh. Right. Did I throw up? I don't remember. Shite. Sorry, boss. Think I was a bit dazed at the time," Tyler said.

"Aye, you can say that again," Logan agreed. "On the drive to the hospital you kept calling me Brian."

"Brian?" Tyler asked. His brow creased as he flipped through some mental Rolodex. "I don't even know anyone called Brian." He moved around in his seat, trying to get himself comfortable for the long journey ahead. "Brian May, I suppose, but I doubt I was getting you mixed up with him."

They had made the turn onto the southbound A82 before Tyler finally found a good position. It was only then that the previous few moments of conversation properly hit him.

"Wait, so that smell is sick?" he asked, the colour draining from his face like a tap had been turned on. "That's old puke I'm smelling?"

"No! Jesus, what do you think I did, just leave it?" Logan retorted. "What sort of clarty bastard do you take me for?"

"So, why am I still smelling it?" Tyler asked. He jabbed at the button on his door that should open the window, but the glass refused to budge. "And why's that not working?" he demanded, his presses becoming more and more frantic.

"Jesus Christ, son, a minute in and you're already a pain in the arse," Logan said. He flicked a switch on his own window controls that allowed Tyler's button to do its job. The DC practically shoved his head out through the hole where the glass had been, and gulped in big lungfuls of air.

"You're smelling the cleaning stuff," Logan insisted.

"I don't know, boss, it smells a bit pukey to me."

"Aye, well, it's not. It's bloody... *Dettol*. Or *Vanish*, or whatever they used."

Tyler angled his head away from the window just enough to side-eye the man in the driver's seat. "They?"

"Aye. The valet people. You think I was cleaning it up? No bloody chance," Logan said. "Which reminds me, you owe me twenty-five quid."

"If I was you, I'd be asking for your money back, boss, because that's still honking."

"It's the cleaning stuff," Logan insisted. He sniffed the air a few times. "Although it is a bit pukey, right enough, now that you mention it."

"Jesus!" Tyler groaned, forcing his head further out of the open window. "The smell of spew turns my stomach."

"It's your own bloody spew!"

"How's that better?" Tyler yelped.

"God Almighty. Think about something else," Logan said. They were heading out of town now, but were still just one or two percent of the way into the journey. There was no way he could tolerate a perpetually vomiting Tyler for the next two and a half hours.

"Like what?" Tyler asked, his desperation apparent in his voice. "I can't think of anything but puke now."

"I talked to Hoon," Logan said. He heard Tyler gulp—possibly swallowing back the urge to throw up, but just as possibly something else. "He asked if I'd spoken to you."

"Spoken to me? About what?"

"You tell me."

The wind whipped at Tyler's hair as the BMW hugged the lines of the road. It was a futile gesture, though, the sheer amount of product in his hair stubbornly resisting the worst that Mother Nature might throw at it.

"I don't know, boss," the DC said.

"Aye, you do," Logan insisted. "I can tell when you're lying, son. You know how?"

"How?"

"Because you're shite at it," Logan said. "There's something going on. If you don't want to tell me, then fine. If it's none of my business, that's no bother. But don't lie to me. Alright?"

The wind, having given up trying to affect Tyler's hair, went for his eyes, instead. Tears streamed from them, before being whisked off his cheeks.

"I told you, boss. It's nothing. There's nothing to worry about." Tyler closed his eyes and let the flowing air wash over him. "Everything is absolutely fine."

SINEAD STOOD on the platform at Fort William train station, watching the 18:23 from Glasgow arriving.

It had started its journey almost four hours ago as four carriages, then split apart at Crianlarich so half the train could head to Oban and the other half could continue to Fort William, then west to Mallaig.

It was a journey that Sinead knew well. The train had always been her preferred means of travelling to and from Glasgow, whether it was for shopping, or gigs, or visiting friends from school. She'd spent more hours than she could recall just watching the world through the train windows, as hills and glens became high-rises and office blocks, or vice versa.

On almost every trip, she'd planned to spend a big chunk of the journey sleeping. Thanks in part to the view out of those windows, she was yet to manage it once.

The train stopped with some hisses and clacks, and Sinead stepped aside as a smattering of passengers disembarked. She recognised most of them as locals, and swapped a few nods and smiles with those she was most familiar with.

There were only a couple of passengers left in the closest carriage, both seated separately, and both swiping frantically at their phones, enjoying the few minutes of network coverage before the train continued on and they lost the signal again.

A man in a *Scotrail* uniform leaned out of the open doorway, looked in both directions, then spotted Sinead as she walked towards him.

"Hi. Are you... the policewoman?" he asked.

"Detective Constable Sinead... Bell," she said, hesitating in her introduction just long enough for it to be noticeable, but only if you were paying attention.

The ticket collector was still standing just inside the train, giving him a considerable height advantage over Sinead. He peered down at her, though the expression he wore was hard to read.

"How old even are you?" he asked, then a little widening of his eyes suggested that he'd meant to keep that thought to himself. "Sorry, I just mean... You're younger than I expected."

"It's fine," Sinead said. "I was told you'd have a few minutes?"

The ticket collector checked his watch. "Not really. We're running late. Meant to be making up time. We really need to get off."

"It won't take long."

"Aye, but... We've got to stick to the timetable."

Sinead grinned. "That'd be a first," she said, but the joke was not well received.

"Yeah, well, all the more reason not to hang around here blethering."

Sinead looked past him into the train, then back through the station to where she'd parked the car out front. "What about if I jump on, we have a chat, and you drop me at Banavie?" she suggested.

The ticket collector mulled this over. "It's two-sixty for an adult to Banavie," he said. "If it was up to me, obviously, I'd let you on for free, but—"

"Deal," Sinead said. She fished in her pocket, produced the exact change, then stepped aboard. "Now, what can you tell me about Archie Tatties?"

IT WAS HALF-PAST MIDNIGHT, and Logan was feeling the pull of his hotel room's minibar. It was rare that they got put up anywhere expensive enough to boast such an extravagance, and he could feel it calling to him from behind the cupboard door, luring him in with its siren call.

Tomorrow, once admin had time to find somewhere else—somewhere cheaper—he and Tyler would have to relocate. No more waterfall shower. No more king-size bed with fancy sheets.

No more minibar.

It had been a long, stressful journey. Tyler hadn't talked about whatever the big secret was, but he'd made up for it by talking about anything and everything else until finally, Logan had announced that they both had something to contribute to the journey, and that Tyler's contribution should be silence.

And then, there had been the pitstops. All those snatches of time spent waiting with the engine running while Tyler hurled into a bush in yet another layby. Still, at least it wasn't into the front footwell this time, so that was an improvement.

Logan didn't remember how he'd got there, but he was squatting in front of the minibar now, staring at its tantalising glass frontage. It was jammed full. Enough to keep him going half the night, if he was so inclined.

He stood up. Turned away.

No. He couldn't disappoint them. He couldn't disappoint himself.

He turned back. Knelt.

But, no one would know.

And he wouldn't be the one paying for it, which was a bonus.

And no one would know.

"Fuck it," he said, then he pushed down the guilt, pulled open the minibar door, and reached inside.

TEN MINUTES LATER, Logan had already polished off the *Pringles* and the little bag of pretzel things, and was now just waiting for the kettle to boil so he could get ripped into the *Kit Kat*. It was a tiny plastic hotel kettle, and had been heating up for what felt like quite some time. Judging by the sound it was making, it was a long way from the finish line, too.

There had been two cups on the tray alongside the kettle, both roughly the size of a thimble. Combined, they might be able to hold a good gulp's worth. There was a teabag waiting in both so they'd be ready for action in the unlikely event that the water in the kettle ever reached boiling point.

Logan tore the corner of the *Kit-Kat* wrapper, teasing himself with it. He could feel his guilt rising—he was still technically supposed to be on his health kick, particularly after the decadence of the wedding weekend—and was hoping he could get at least some of the chocolate down him before it rose too far.

A knock came at the door just as the kettle reached the home straight.

"Boss? You awake?"

Shite!

Logan grabbed up the empty packets from the room's desk/dressing table and bundled them into the bin. This, he realised, only drew attention to them, which was the precise opposite of what he'd been going for.

The knocking came again. "Boss?"

"Aye, I'm coming," Logan said. He grabbed the bin and shoved it into the bathroom on his way to open the door.

Tyler stood in the long, narrow hallway, dressed in what Logan assumed were pyjamas of some sort. They were made up of a pair of grey shorts and a matching grey t-shirt. A large bright red face grinned out from the front.

"What the fuck are you wearing?" was Logan's first question. "Is that a Muppet?"

Tyler looked down at his PJs. "Eh, aye. It's Elmo, boss. Sinead got me them."

"What, when you were nine?"

Tyler frowned. "I didn't know her when I was nine."

"No, I know, it was... Forget it," Logan said. "What's up?"

The DC looked past him. Given that Logan filled most of the doorway, this took some effort. "Might be best if I come in for this, boss, if you don't mind. Not really a conversation I want to have out here."

Aha! Here we go, Logan thought. *The bottom of it approaches.*

He retreated into the room, and Tyler followed. The kettle clicked off, and the DC nodded when he spotted the two cups, each with a teabag inside.

"Don't mind if I do, boss. Cheers," he said. He pointed to the partially unwrapped *Kit Kat.* "If there's biscuits on the go..."

"You've got your own bloody Kit-Kat," Logan protested, then he relented with a grunt and a wave of a hand. "Fine. You can have half. But just half, mind! Don't try any funny stuff."

Tyler took care of biscuit unwrapping and distribution duties while Logan made the tea in silence. Only when they were sat down—Tyler on the desk chair, Logan on the foot of the bed—did the conversation start.

And even then, it took a bit of prompting.

"Well? To what do I owe the pleasure?" Logan asked, then he bit the end off one of the *Kit Kat* fingers and chewed while he waited for a response.

"I, eh, just got off the phone to Sinead, boss," Tyler began.

"And?"

"And, she has a bit of news for us."

Logan swallowed his bite of biscuit. "News?" he asked. "What do you mean?"

"About the case."

Somewhere in Logan's brain, a lever was pulled, and tracks were switched. "Oh. Right. Is that what you're here for? I thought... Nothing. Go on. What did she find out?"

"I think we know what's missing from the house. Besides the mystery baby, I mean," Tyler began. "See, the ticket collector on the train from Mallaig says he saw Archie and his family struggling with the pram, travel cot, and all that stuff, and started helping them on by picking up their bags."

"They definitely had the baby on the train, then?"

"Aye, boss," Tyler confirmed. "But it was one of the bags that the ticket fella said was most interesting."

Logan took a sip of his tea. "Oh?"

"Heavy as hell, he said. Like... a holdall. A blue holdall, he thinks. Weighed a tonne."

"Could be anything," Logan said.

"It was bulging, he says. So the zip was burst open a bit, and he could see inside."

Logan waited. "Are you dragging this out on purpose?" he asked when Tyler didn't volunteer anything else. "We don't need the big pauses for dramatic effect, son. What was in it?"

"Money, boss."

"Money?"

"A *lot* of money. He couldn't even guess how much, but a lot. Archie got a bit shirty when he realised he'd clocked it, and grabbed the bag off him, pronto."

Logan stood up and started to pace around the room. He might as well make the most of that, too. It was unlikely that tomorrow's room would have much in the way of pacing space.

"So, we've got a bag of money and the mystery baby both missing from the house."

"And everything that goes along with a baby, boss, aye. There's literally not a trace of the wee one having been in the house, except them marks on the carpet. And even them, we're not sure of."

"Why would he have a big bag of money?" Logan wondered. He answered himself before Tyler could offer a reply. "Nothing good, anyway. You don't cart holdalls full of cash around if it's legit."

"Maybe he was buying the baby," Tyler suggested. "Or selling it."

"Then why would he have the baby and the cash at the same time?"

Tyler shrugged. This made Elmo's eyes widen like he'd just become very excited by something. "Alright, then... maybe he was going to pay someone to take the wee one off his hands? Like, not selling it, but giving it to someone, and giving them the money to look after it, too."

Logan stopped pacing and stood contemplating this.

"That's... a possibility," he conceded, then he shook his head. "But it's one of several. Personally, I think it's more likely that Archie stole both the baby and the money from someone who came and took them back."

"I think my idea's simpler," Tyler said.

"These things are rarely simple, son."

"Well, no," Tyler conceded. "But they don't always have to be complicated, do they?"

Logan looked doubtful, but chose not to argue. "It's good that you're coming up with ideas. Keep it up."

Tyler's face took on the same expression as the one on his t-shirt. "Aye? Cheers, boss!"

"Your theory doesn't explain who killed them," Logan told him. "But, we'll keep it in mind."

"Right, aye. Good," Tyler said, then he bounded to his feet. "I'll leave you to it, then. Just thought you'd want to know."

Logan met the younger man's eye. "Was that it?" he asked. "There was nothing else you wanted to say?"

Tyler folded his arms. He made a show of thinking that was presumably meant to appear casual, but came over as anything but. "Eh... No. No, don't think so, boss." His mouth curved upwards unconvincingly. "Think that's everything."

"You sure? Nothing you want to get off your chest?"

"Well..." Tyler shifted his weight from one foot to the other. "There was one thing I wanted to ask, boss."

Logan took a seat on the bed.

Here we go.

"Fire on, son."

"It was just..." Tyler drew in a breath, then it tumbled out with the rest of the sentence. "Can I have your Pringles?"

Logan resisted the urge to glance at the empty slot in the mini-bar. "My what?"

"Your Pringles. I've already eaten mine, and I'm bloody starving," Tyler said. "And I know you're on your diet, so..."

"It's no' a diet," Logan objected. "It's a healthy eating..." *Christ, what had Shona called it?* "...regime. Or bloody... I don't know. But it's no' a diet."

Tyler blinked very slowly. "Right," he said, dragging the word out a little longer than was strictly necessary. "Well, whatever, do you mind if I have your Pringles?"

"I didn't get any," Logan lied. "There was just the Kit Kat."

"Oh. Was there?" Tyler took a quick shifty through the glass of the fridge and saw that the dookets for the food were, indeed, all empty. "That's a shame. You should complain, or they might charge you."

"Aye. I will," Logan said. He stood again and began ushering the younger detective to the door. "Well, if that's everything, we'd better get some rest."

"Right, boss. Sure thing," Tyler said, heading for the door. To Logan's dismay, the DC hung a left at the bathroom. "Mind if I just nip for a pee first, though? I'll never make it all the way down to my room in the lift."

"Well, I—"

It was too late. Tyler closed the bathroom door between them, leaving Logan trapped outside.

"Click the light on, will you, boss?"

Logan sighed and flicked the switch on the wall by the door. An extractor fan whirred into life.

"Here, boss?" the voice from the other side of the door called.

Logan closed his eyes. "Yes, Tyler?"

"I think I found your Pringles."

CHAPTER TWENTY

BILLY PINNOCK, the artist formerly known as 'Neeps,' muttered under his breath as a stupidly small screw fell onto the magnetic pad on the worktop, failed to stick, then went bouncing away onto the shop floor.

It was, he knew, very likely the last he'd see of it until it went tinging up the tube of the Hoover a week or two from now. He could get down on his hands and knees and hunt for it, of course, but he had boxes of the things for exactly this sort of occasion, and his knees weren't what they used to be.

His knees weren't even what they used to be back in the days that he'd first started saying, "My knees aren't what they used to be." He'd give anything for those knees these days, never mind the knees he had originally.

He removed the next screw and sighed as it, too, was lost to the floor.

"Fifteen ninety-nine," he said, shooting a dirty look at the magnetic pad. "Biggest waste of money I've ever made."

That wasn't true, of course. Not by a long shot.

An electronic bell chimed, and the front door of the shop opened, letting in the morning sun and all the accompanying noise that came with it. The shop stood on Kilmarnock Road, just a few feet south of the official marked limits of the City of Glasgow, so it fell under the jurisdiction of East Renfrewshire Council.

The location was... fine. The shop was one of five in a little sort of strip mall thing, with a Chinese takeaway at one end, and a funeral director at the other. Billy's place was slap bang in the middle, sandwiched between a beautician's and, ironically, a sandwich shop.

Would he have preferred to be in the middle of Glasgow, with all its passing trade? Definitely. He'd be an idiot not to.

Did he want to pay the rent on such a location? Maybe.

Could he?

Could he fuck.

He carefully set the mobile phone he was working on down in the plastic tub he'd taken it from, closed the lid, then tucked it away under the counter. He'd learned that lesson in his first week of business. It didn't matter if a phone had been reduced to its component parts, if some bugger saw an opportunity to grab it and run, they would.

Only when he was sure the device was out of snatching reach did he look properly at the two men who had entered the shop. He recognised them right away. Not their faces—not them individually —but what they were. Billy could practically smell the authority coming off them.

Or, off one of them, anyway. The younger one, not so much.

"Bloody hell. You haven't changed a bit," the older of the two men announced. "You're Billy Neeps."

"Ha! No. Well, yes. Well, not for a long time," Billy said. He stood up. His glasses, which he'd pushed up onto his head while he worked on the fiddly close-up stuff, fell and landed on his nose with a mildly amusing *thunk*.

It hadn't been deliberate. He hadn't meant for it to happen. Things like that just happened on their own to Billy Neeps.

Whether it was his trousers splitting at precisely the wrong moment, his shoes inexplicably developing a high-pitched squeak that only appeared during funerals, or that time he'd found himself hurtling down Douglas Street on a carelessly placed skateboard, Billy was tormented by that sort of thing on a daily basis. It was a curse of some kind, he was sure of it. If there was a god of unintentional slapstick, Billy often thought he must have done something to really get on his tits.

"Sorry, you are?" he asked.

The older and much larger of the men produced a wallet with an ID card inside. "My name's Detective Chief Inspector Jack Logan," he said, confirming what had already been quite a firm suspicion on Billy's part. "Do you mind if we take up half an hour of your time, Mr Pinnock?"

"Uh, well..."

"It's quite important. I'm afraid we've got some bad news to give you."

Billy started to sit, but stopped himself in the nick of time. He checked behind him. Sure enough, his chair had rolled away when he stood up. That was a close one.

"Oh, dear. That's a shame," he said, pulling the chair back into position beneath him. He managed to lower himself onto it without any embarrassing incidents. "Then, of course. Please... go ahead."

"It might be best if we maybe go somewhere more private," the policeman suggested. "Or at least lock the door?"

"You can if you like," Billy said. "But nobody comes in, anyway. You're the first drop-in I've had in weeks." He fished out his keys and placed them on the counter between them. "But, by all means, go ahead. Just... just... What is this all about?"

The DCI picked up the keys, considered them, then set them back down again. "Tell me, Mr Pinnock," he said. "When was the last time you saw Archie Sutherland?"

BACK UP THE road in Fort William, Hamza was trying to figure out where the money had come from. This had involved several thus far fruitless calls to various banking officials, none of whom had been of any help whatsoever.

"We're going to have to kick this one up the chain I think, sir," he announced, slamming down the phone after arguing with yet another complete and utter banker. "They are 'not prepared to give out any information at this time.'"

"Might need to get a warrant," Sinead suggested.

They both waited for Ben to respond. He eventually picked up on the silence and gave a little start. "Oh. Aye. Aye, hoof it up to the high heid yins and let them sort it out. Might as well get them working for their money." He yawned and rolled his head around, stretching his neck muscles. "What else have we got going on this morning?"

"Donna Sutherland's sister is coming over from Glenrothes to do the formal identification at some point early today," Sinead said. "I don't know if you want one of us there, or..."

"We'll get someone up in Inverness to go in with her. No point one of us driving up, only to have to come back down again an hour later."

Dave Davidson called over from his desk. "I can phone up and get that sorted, if you want?" he suggested. "Doing naff all else."

"Aye. Do that. But then we'll put you to work," Ben replied. "We still don't know how long the family was on Skye, and what they were doing while they were there. We need to trace their movements. Find out where the journey started, see if they had the baby with them the whole time." He turned to Hamza. "Still nothing turned up from Missing Persons?"

"Not a cheep, no. Nobody's reported any lost babies."

"And it definitely wasn't their own?" Ben asked. "We're sure about that?"

"Sure as we can be, sir," Sinead said. "Unless it was some sort of overnight pregnancy, I don't see how it could've been Donna's."

"Could it have been his, though?" Hamza wondered. "To another woman, I mean?"

"That's possible, I suppose," Sinead conceded. "It could explain why nobody has reported it missing."

"Talk to family and friends," Ben instructed. "See if any of them have any ideas who the wee one might belong to. Jack's right, we find the baby, and we find who killed the family."

He looked to the window, and to the hills beyond. Snow still dotted the top of Ben Nevis, even this close to summer. He shivered at the sight of it, and at the thought of something else.

"I just hope the poor wee thing's alright."

CHAPTER TWENTY-ONE

BILLY NEEPS HAD ALWAYS BEEN the quiet one. The straight man. The patsy. Archie Tatties had been the one making the jokes, but Billy had been the one the audience inevitably laughed at.

At. Not with.

Here, in his shop almost four decades later, it wasn't hard to see why.

There was just... something about him. An aura. Or a pheromone he gave off, maybe. Whatever it was, it fostered in Logan—a man who despised bullies—an urge to flush the man's head down the nearest available toilet.

He had a face that cried out for a custard pie. The thick lenses of his black-rimmed glasses exaggerated his eyes so they looked cartoonishly huge. They were fixed firmly on Logan as the DCI spoke—too firmly, in fact. It was like Billy had read a book on how to make a good impression, and abandoned it halfway through the chapter on making eye contact.

It would've almost been unnerving, were Billy not five-foot-five with shoes on, and about nine and a half stone soaking wet.

The shop was much like any other mobile phone repair shop Logan had ever been in. The outside was an affront to taste and design, with frontage so bright yellow it could probably be seen from space. The main sign above the shop, and the three other smaller signs that filled the glass of the windows and doors, all had pictures of mobile phones on them. Even Logan could tell they were at least five years out of date now, which probably rendered them obsolete.

As they'd approached the shop, he'd wondered what unique affliction the owners of mobile phone repair shops had that left them unable to choose a decent typeface for their signs. Logan was no expert on such matters—not by a long shot—but even he could tell that none of the four different fonts used in the sign of Billy's shop looked in any way professional or pleasing to the eye.

Inside, the walls were lined with gaudy phone and tablet cases of every conceivable size, colour, and shape. The only thing they had in common, in fact, was the 'Made in China' stickers affixed to the plastic wrapper of each one.

Well, that and the fact that no bugger was buying them.

Cardboard cups from the sandwich shop next door stood around Billy's workspace like pawns on a chessboard. The aroma of coffee permeated the place, though it at least masked the smell of damp that occasionally wafted through from a small back room that was half-hidden by a bead curtain.

"So, you say the last time you saw Archie was in December of last year?" Logan asked.

He was well aware that this was the answer that Billy had given just moments before, but he was buying time for Tyler to finish hunting his pockets for his notebook.

"That's right. He came in here. To the shop."

"Got it," Tyler announced, finally tracking down the missing pad. "Carry on, boss. I'll just... Shite. Have you got a pen?"

Logan fished a plastic promotional pen from a jar on the counter. "Do you mind?" he asked Billy, then he passed it back when the shopkeeper shook his head.

"Cheers!" Tyler said, before a look from Logan made him shut up and get writing.

"Did he come to see you often?" Logan asked the man behind the counter.

Billy picked up a coffee cup, gave it a shake to check the fill level, then placed it down on the counter again. "Not often, no.

That was the first time he'd been in here, in fact. Ever. To be honest, I'm not even sure he knew it was my shop. He'd dropped his phone. Smashed the screen. Needed a replacement."

"And did you fix it?" Logan asked.

"Yes. It took a couple of days because I had to wait for the screen to come in, but I fixed it. iPhone 11. Good phone. I'm an Android man myself, but you can't fault the Apple build."

"So, he came back in for it once you'd fixed it?"

Billy shook his head. "No. He had me send it on. Never bloody paid me, either."

"You sent it to his home?"

"To an office address. His production company. He made... videos. Weddings, maybe? I'm not sure what. Doing well, by the sounds of things," he said, and he tried very hard to keep the note of bitterness from his voice.

"Aye, we heard about that," Logan said, taking note of the tone. "Did you keep in touch? Before he came in to get his phone fixed, I mean. Have you kept in contact over the years?"

There was a blowing out of cheeks and a shrug of slender shoulders. Something about the movements came very close to making Logan laugh, although he'd be damned if he could explain why. "Sometimes. Not often. But yes. From time to time."

"I'd heard you'd had a falling out. That was why the act stopped."

"God, yes. Huge," Billy confirmed. "It was awful. It got really quite acrimonious for a while."

"But you made up?"

"Not really, no."

"Oh. So, what happened to get you talking again?"

Billy gave another shrug, and this time pulled a face that could only be described as 'comically befuddled.'

"Thirty-odd years, I suppose. The mellowing that comes with old age. The perspective it brings. We were young men, then, full of fire. Archie was determined we were going to crack America. I thought we should play it safe here, but he was all big talk about Vegas. And Hollywood, of all the bloody places."

He drummed his fingers on the counter and looked around at the shop, as if only just seeing it properly for the first time.

"And now look at me. Failed comedian. Failed teacher. Failing shopkeeper." He clucked his tongue against the roof of his mouth. "We lost a lot of money with that American Dream tour. Almost everything, in fact."

Tyler jumped in before Logan could continue. "Sorry, you were a teacher?"

"For about a year before we started, and five or six years after it all went tits up. It was a nightmare the second time around, though," Billy said, his lips drawing back in distaste. "Kids had seen the shows then, you see? Couldn't go anywhere without one of the little bastards throwing haggis at me. One time, they filled all my desk drawers with it. Filled it right to the top. And I... I knew then that I couldn't continue. I just couldn't. You can't, can you? Go on? Not when your drawers are being filled with haggis."

"The American tour—was that what caused the break-up?" Logan asked.

"Yes. No. I mean... yes. That was the final straw, but things hadn't exactly been rosy before then. Not for a while. There's a lot of pressure, you know? Being at that level of fame."

There was a sound from Tyler. Not quite a laugh, but not *not* a laugh, either. Billy glowered at the much younger man, his face becoming something cold and stern. "We were, you know? At that level of fame. A lot of people dismiss us as a novelty act now, but they forget we did the Royal Variety Show. And not just once, either. Three times. Once for the Queen herself. *And* we went head to head with the Terry & June Christmas Day Special, and nearly won. And that was on the BBC. In some parts of Scotland, we did win. And this was when Terry & June was at its peak, not towards the end."

Billy's face had been completely taken over by a scowl now, and the words were gushing out of him like some sort of blockage had worked itself free.

"And people nowadays, they go, 'Yeah, but you were no Cannon and Ball, were you?'" He raised a finger to some imagined figure in the shop doorway. "Fuck off! *Cannon and Ball?* I could tell you a thing or two about Cannon and Ball. Believe me. I could tell you things that'd turn your hair grey." His tongue flicked out, like he was ejecting something distasteful. "Fucking Cannon and Ball."

It appeared to occur to him then that perhaps he'd said too much, and he wound his neck back in. With a shaking hand, he took a sip of his coffee before continuing.

"That sort of fame's a lot of pressure, like I say. The cracks were there before America. That just hammered a chisel into them." He gave himself a shake, and a sound rang out like a fart asking a question—a parp of surprise that rose in inflection at the end. Billy's face fell. His eyes, which were already impossibly wide, somehow grew another ten percent. "That was the chair. That wasn't me. That was the chair." He bounced up and down on it and said, "See?" despite the fact that the sound didn't come again.

Logan was decent enough to gloss straight over it. "And you haven't heard from Archie since December?"

"Got a card at Christmas. We've always sent them, even those years when we weren't talking. We put a pound note in them. Been swapping the same two for decades now." He looked at Tyler again. "The pound note was a callback to a little skit we did for the telly, where..." He sighed, recognising the indifference on the younger man's face. "Actually, doesn't matter."

"And that was the last you heard from him?" Logan asked.

"Yes. Why?" Billy asked. He adjusted his glasses on his nose. For reasons Logan couldn't quite grasp, this involved him contorting the rest of his face into a grimace. "What's happened? Is he alright?"

"I'm afraid not, Mr Pinnock," Logan said, and both detectives scrutinised his reaction. "I'm afraid Archie Sutherland has been murdered."

Billy's eyelids fluttered like someone had thrown sand in his eyes. His body froze, and Logan half expected him to topple sideways off his chair in comically exaggerated shock.

Instead, he cleared his throat, swallowed, then replied in a voice so quiet it was barely a whisper. "Sorry, he's been...?"

"We believe there was a home invasion at a holiday cottage Archie was staying at. He and his family were all found dead."

Behind the counter, Billy sunk further into his chair. "Found...?

You mean they were...? They were *killed*? Oh, God. Archie. Oh, God! Where? When? In Spain? He had a house in Spain. Is that where...?" His hand flew to his mouth, missed slightly, and knocked his glasses squint. "Oh, God, Archie. Oh, those poor girls."

"I'm very sorry to be the bearer of such bad news," Logan said. "In answer to your question, not in Spain, no. Here. Up in the Highlands."

"The Highlands? What was he doing in the Highlands?" Billy frowned, almost absent-mindedly. "He never took holidays in this country. Never. 'It's either pissing down, or it's midges,' he used to say. That was why he bought the place in Spain, so he could get away from Scotland. There's no way he'd take himself out there to the middle of nowhere. Not on purpose."

"Well—"

"Wait, sorry, sorry," Billy interjected. "You're *sure* he's dead? It's definitely him?"

"There's still to be a formal identification made. His sister-in-law is coming up later today to make it official, but yes," Logan confirmed. "It's definitely him."

"And it was... So, the attack. The home invasion. Was it...? Do you know who did it?"

"We're looking into it," Logan said.

"Was it... random, do you think? Wrong time, wrong place, or...?"

"At this stage, we can't be sure. That's why we're talking to people who knew the family, to see if we can figure out who might have had reason to kill them. Did Archie have any enemies?"

The chair let rip with another parp as Billy leaned back. This time, he didn't seem to notice. "I mean... he never saw eye to the eye with the Krankies," he fretted. "But then, who did?" He chewed on a knuckle for a moment, then spat it out and shook his head. "No. Ian and Janette wouldn't do something like this. They couldn't. Not at their age."

Logan agreed that this was probably something of a stretch.

"Anyone else you can think of who might have wanted to kill him?" he asked. "Besides the Krankies, I mean. Anyone he had any business dealings with that might have gone sour?"

Billy claimed to know nothing about any of that stuff. Most of Archie's current life was a mystery to him.

"We didn't meet up often, but when we did we spoke about the old days, for the most part. People we worked with who went on to do well. Archie always hated that. Even people he didn't know. He much preferred a good downfall," Billy explained, and that sourness crept in again. "When Barrowman got *Doctor Who*, he was spitting teeth."

Tyler looked up from his pad. "Do you want me to put John Barrowman off *Doctor Who* down as a suspect, boss?"

"That won't be necessary, Detective Constable," Logan replied in the very next breath. He pressed harder on the wide-eyed man across the counter. "So, there's nobody else you can think of? Nobody you think it's worth us having a word with?"

"Well, I mean—" Billy bit his lip. Shook his head. Looked away. "No, it's... I doubt... No."

"We're no' asking you to tell us who the killer is, Mr Pinnock. Just anyone you can think of who had... let's say a *fraught* relationship with Archie."

Billy puffed up his cheeks and blew out slowly as he reached for a block of *Post-It* notes and one of his complimentary pens. "I sat with Archie at Gerard Kelly's funeral. Rest his soul," he said, studiously writing out a name. "This man gave Archie dirty looks the whole way through the service, and called him some *very* unkind things at the wake. And I mean the worst words there are. I guarantee, whatever you're thinking of, it was worse than that."

"I've got a pretty wide-ranging vocabulary, Mr Pinnock," Logan assured him. "Whatever it was, I imagine I've heard worse."

Billy revealed a few of the words that had been hurled Archie's way. Logan *had* heard worse, but not often, and only from one man.

"Aye, that seems harsh, right enough," he confirmed, then he picked up the note and read the name. Then, he read it again. And once more, while his brain tried to process what it was seeing. "And this is a person's name, is it?"

"Yes. Not his given name, obviously. I don't think that would be allowed. But that's the name he goes by."

Logan passed the note back to Tyler, and did his best to ignore the muttered, "Fucking hell."

"And where will I find this gentleman?"

Billy pushed his glasses higher on the bridge of his nose, and the magnifying effect doubled the size of his eyes. When he spoke, it was in the sort of hushed tone usually reserved exclusively for the phrase, 'Don't go near Castle Dracula."

"Oh," he said, "finding him shouldn't be too hard."

CHAPTER TWENTY-TWO

A SOUND EMERGED from Hamza that was quite unexpected. It was like a laugh with a question mark, or a cheer of confusion. It was not a sound he was aware of having ever made before, and he immediately swore an oath to himself that he'd never make it again.

It had done its job, though, and drawn the attention of Ben, Sinead, and Dave. They all looked over as excitement propelled Hamza up onto his feet.

"What's happened, son? Have the lottery syndicate numbers come up, or something?"

"Afraid not, sir," Hamza said, his Doric twang becoming stronger as his pulse quickened. "But I've found something. Archie Sutherland and his family were in Inverness the week before last."

Sinead scooted her chair over. "What? How do you...? Oh! Is this on Facebook?"

"Aye. On one of the Inverness community groups," Hamza said.

"And what's the story?" Ben asked. "What are they saying?"

"Not saying much, sir," Hamza replied. "But there's a picture. Someone took a photo of the family at the train station. Looks like they were just arriving. They've got their bags, and..." He squinted at the screen. "Does that look like a blue holdall to you?"

Sinead confirmed that it did. "Bulging, too, like the ticket collector said. Looks like they were lugging the money around then, at least." She indicated the rest of the picture. "But not the baby."

"What?" Ben asked, hurrying over to join the younger officers at Hamza's computer.

Sure enough, there was a slightly off-kilter picture on the screen that looked like it had probably been taken in secret. Archie and Donna Sutherland were in the process of filing through the platform turnstiles, the two girls right behind them.

There was no baby, no pram, and no travel cot. They had arrived in Inverness *sans infant*.

"Any other pictures?" Ben asked.

Hamza rolled his mouse wheel, scrolling down the post to the comments. "No, sir. The fella who took the photo says he used to be a big fan, and tried to get Archie to pose for a selfie, but he was having none of it. Says he was quite abrupt with him."

"Can you get onto him? The fella who took the photo?" Ben asked. He gestured vaguely at the computer with both hands. "On this thing, I mean? Can we track him down?"

"I could send him a message," Hamza said.

"Good. Find out when he took the photo. Day and time. Talk to him and find out if there's anything else he can tell us. Did anyone meet them off the train? Did they get in a taxi? That sort of thing. Get as much information off him as you can. Let's get building up that picture. We've had a lucky break here, so let's make the most of it. But go canny. We don't want it getting out yet that he's dead. The press don't seem to have picked up on it yet, and I'd like to keep it that way for as long as possible."

"I'll be suitably vague," Hamza said.

"Good lad," Ben said. He checked his watch, then picked up his jacket. "Right, man the fort, will you, Sergeant? I need to nip out for a bit. Anything urgent comes in, give me a ring."

"You're, eh, you're going out, sir?" Sinead asked.

"There a problem with that, Detective Constable?"

"No, sir. No, not at all. Just... if DCI Logan asks, where should we say you are?"

Ben wrestled his arms into his sleeves, zipped the jacket closed, then took his car keys from his pocket. "Out," he said, then he winked, pushed open the Incident Room door, and left them all to it.

"Want me to follow him?" asked Dave, once the DI was out of earshot.

Sinead smiled. "Eh, no. You're fine. Cheers, though."

"Thank God for that," Dave said. "You ever tried chasing a car in a wheelchair? Let me tell you, no' as much fun as it sounds."

"No, I'll bet," Sinead remarked. Her gaze lingered on the door for a moment, then she headed back to her desk, picked up her pen, and got to work.

THERE WAS nothing about the outside of *Honey B's* that marked it as a gay bar. Anyone passing through Glasgow's Merchant City area would likely assume it was just another trendy pub aimed at the young and successful.

Step through the doors, though, and there was no mistaking the theme. Everything from the purple-pink padding of the booth seats, to the sparkling butterfly-patterned tiling on the walls marked it out as more... flamboyant than most of the other pubs in the vicinity. An enormous length of rainbow-coloured ribbon that meandered between the chandeliers on the ceiling was just the icing on the cake.

Logan felt a sense of unease creeping up on him as he strode towards the bar. Not because of the gay thing—where people chose to put their various bits and pieces had never been any concern of his—but because this was everything he had always hated in a pub.

A pub, as far as he was concerned, was where you went to feel thoroughly miserable in the company of people you could temporarily tolerate. They were like churches, in some ways—a place to go for some quiet respite, and to reflect on the awfulness of the world that lurked out there beyond the heavy front doors.

A good pub had comfy chairs, quiet and inoffensive background music, a well-curated selection of whiskies, and in his more recent years, some half-decent coffee. He could tolerate a bandit, or even a quiz machine if it came to it, but a jukebox was an extravagance too far, because most people had no musical taste whatsoever.

A good pub was drab. It was depressing. It consoled you while you were inside, and made you feel all the better for having left it.

This place was the opposite of that. It was all gaudy colours, flashing neons, and there were old American Diner style jukeboxes on the tables in every booth. There was a small stage up against the back wall, too, complete with spotlights, PA system, and—unless he was very much mistaken—a karaoke machine.

Logan briefly flashed back to another karaoke machine, and to a spirited, if tuneless, turn as Elvis Presley, then he shuddered and walked more quickly until he reached the bar.

There were at least two hundred bottles of spirits on the wall behind the bar, each on its own little shelf. Logan could identify maybe three of them. Which, considering his previous expertise in the field of alcoholic beverages, really said something.

He wasn't sure *what* it said, exactly, but definitely something.

"Doesn't look like there's anyone around, boss," Tyler remarked as they stood waiting at the bar. "Through the back, maybe?"

There was a groan from the floor on the other side of the bar. Both detectives leaned over lager taps until they saw a woman lying there, one hand over her eyes.

"We're just open," she muttered. "Why are you here already?"

"Eh... Are you alright?" Tyler asked.

"Do I look like I'm alright?"

"Do you need help?"

"Do I look like I need help?"

Tyler decided to defer the rest of the conversation to Logan, and passed it to him with a nod and a shrug.

"I'm Detective Chief Inspector Jack Logan. This is my colleague, DC Tyler Neish."

Down on the floor, the woman whipped her hand away from her face, and stared up at the men in shock.

"Oh. Shit," she hissed, then she scrambled to her feet using the sink below the bar for support. She jumped to her feet, smoothed down her *Honey B's* t-shirt, then managed to arrange her face into something that was somewhere within the same postcode as a smile. "Sorry, I thought you were punters."

"Are you alright?" Logan asked, his eyes creeping down to the floor where she'd been lying, as if in search of an explanation.

"What? Oh. Yeah. Just hungover. Late night. Couple of the regular guys got hitched, and we threw a big bash for them. Didn't get cleaned up until after four."

"A wedding? Nice one. I got married on Saturday," Tyler announced, before quickly adding: "Aye, but not... To my wife, I mean. My woman wife. Not, like, to a fella. Not that there's anything wrong with that. It's good. It's great! More power to them. To you. Unless... are you? Or are you not...?"

"I am, aye."

"Right. Good," Tyler said, floundering. To his horror, he found himself giving her a double thumbs up. "Well done."

Logan regarded the DC for a second or two. "Your '*woman wife?*'" he muttered, then he turned back to the barmaid. "Can I maybe get him a lemonade, and he can go sit quietly in the corner?"

The barmaid reached for a glass, but Logan raised a hand to stop her.

"It's fine. I'm joking. I can't let him out of my sight. He'll only wander off," he said. "We won't take up much of your time...?"

"Katie."

"Nice to meet you, Katie. Like I say, we won't take up a lot of your time. We were just hoping you might be able to point us in the direction of someone." He nodded to Tyler, who slid Billy Neeps' note across the bar without a word. "I believe he's a regular here?"

The barmaid glanced at the note without picking it up. "She," she corrected.

"Sorry?"

"When she uses that name, she's she. Not he." There was a furtiveness to her now. Her eyes flitted between the detectives, then once to the front door, like she was sizing up her chances of a clean getaway. "What's it about? Is she in trouble?"

"Not that we know of," Logan said. "We just think that he— sorry, *she* might be able to help us with something." He could sense the barmaid's reluctance, and offered what he hoped would be a reassuring smile. "We just want to talk, that's all."

"Just talk? You promise? You're not going to arrest her?"

"We have absolutely no reason to. We just want her help. That's all."

There was a *skoosh* as the barmaid blasted some *Irn Bru* from a mixer tap into a half-pint glass. She knocked back a gulp like it was Dutch courage, then took a pen from the pocket on the front of her t-shirt.

"Fine. This is her address. But for Christ's sake, don't tell her I gave it to you," she said, scribbling on the note Tyler had placed on the bar. "Or I swear, she'll fucking kill me."

CHAPTER TWENTY-THREE

THE ADDRESS the barmaid had given them was a ground floor flat in one of the nicer sandstone tenements in Dennistoun. Tyler had paled at the thought of it, Dennistoun being one of those places whose reputation preceded it all the way to the Highlands, and likely much further still.

The area had been on the up since the Commonwealth Games regeneration project, though, and was barely recognisable as the place that had earned its then well-deserved reputation.

There were more students around now, and a few trendier pubs and restaurants had opened up to accommodate them, giving the place a more vibrant, livelier atmosphere.

It had been lively enough back in the day, of course, but for very different reasons. To say it had 'had its problems' with Class A drug misuse would be understating the issue. And, of course, where the junkies went, the dealers followed.

They were still knocking around now, of course, though far fewer in number. The dealers were less visible now, too, and unless you got a big old pile of smack off them on tick, they were unlikely to cause you any problems.

Logan stood on the front step of a block of flats, a finger resting on the bottom button of the intercom system. He regarded DC Neish, whose eyes were fixed on the door like he was accusing it of spilling his pint. At the same time, he had his weight on the balls of his feet, and his body half-turned from the door as if he was about to make a run for it.

"You alright, son?" Logan asked.

"Hm? Oh. Aye, boss. Just preparing myself."

"For what, a bear attack?"

Tyler took note of his body language, then adjusted the positions of his arms and legs, in an attempt to appear more relaxed. This had the precise opposite effect to the one intended.

"No, just... Not sure what to expect, boss. I'm just being alert, and all that."

Logan grunted. "First time for everything, I suppose," he said, then he jabbed the button and heard the intercom ring through the window over on their left.

A set of red Venetian blinds parted momentarily in the middle. Logan caught a glimpse of an eye peering out at them, then the blinds fell back into place again.

There was a crackle from the intercom, then silence.

Logan hesitated, waiting for the person on the other end to speak. When they didn't, he took the lead. "Uh, hello?"

Nothing.

"Can you hear—?"

A buzzer sounded and the door's locking mechanism gave a *clunk*. Logan pushed it open before it secured itself again, and led Tyler into the close. Like the rest of Dennistoun, the close was an improvement on those of even a few years previously.

There was nobody lying dead with a needle in their arm, for one thing. Although, this had probably been quite rare a thing to come across back then, too, for anyone not involved in the frontline emergency services.

Still, the place was far better than Logan had been expecting. It had been freshly painted within the last few months, he'd guess, including the metal handrail of the steps that led up to the flats above.

The door on their left looked reasonably new, too. The fact that the owner had gone for style over security said as much about the changes to the Dennistoun area as anything else the detectives had seen that day.

It opened as they approached it, but just far enough for a chain to catch and the same eye that had peered out at them through the blinds to appear in the gap.

"Phone thing's not working," rasped a voice from inside.

It was a smoker's voice, and a sixty-a-day one at that. The accent had been rough once, but the edges had been smoothed down over the years. They were all still there, though, if you knew where to look and how to listen.

The eye studied them. "You're with the police?"

"What makes you say that?" Logan asked.

"Because of your faces, and the way you dress. And everything else about you. It's, like, could you *be* any more obvious?"

"Aye, well, you got us," Logan conceded.

As he stepped closer, the head of a small, yappy dog emerged near the bottom of the door and began barking furiously. It was one of those wee boggle-eyed bastards, little more than a rat with big ideas, but its sudden appearance made Tyler jump back and hiss out a, "Jesus!"

"Mulan! Will you cut that shit out?" the voice on the other side of the door cried. There was a hint of an American twang to it, too, Logan noted. Nowhere specific, and very likely an affectation rather than anything that had actually been picked up overseas. As accents went, it was as much of a mongrel as the dog was, and equally as pleasing on the ears.

"Can I just check? Are you..." Logan hesitated and stole the briefest of glances at his notebook. He'd taken it out on the way up the path so that he'd have the name to hand. He wasn't sure why. It wasn't that it was an easy name to forget. "...Fellatio McFudd?"

There was a smile in the voice when it replied. "Sometimes. Not right now, but maybe if you play your cards right."

"Do you mind if we come in?" Logan asked, holding his warrant card up to the door. "We think you might be able to help us with something."

"Is it your fashion sense?" the owner of the eye asked, shouting to be heard above the high-pitched *yipping* of the mutt. "Because, sweetheart, I'd say you're way beyond help on that front."

"It's regarding a case we're working on," Logan said. "We're hoping you might be able to give us some background information on one of the people involved."

The eye regarded them with suspicion, then eventually relented with an emphatic sigh. "Fine."

The door closed. A chain rattled. Logan heard Tyler take a deep breath, as if he was preparing for a long swim underwater.

When the door opened again, it revealed a bald black man in a pair of jeans so tight they could only have been sewn on, and a baggy orange jumper that hung off one bare shoulder.

The dog came racing out, its high-pitched barking echoing around the close. It went for Logan first, then evidently thought better of it, and set its sights on Tyler instead. He danced back a few steps as it growled and snarled at his shoes, its eyes sticking out so far they were facing in opposite directions.

"Eh, nice dog you've got," he said.

"She's a selfish, self-absorbed little asshole," the animal's owner replied, then he glowered down at the thing with a look of utter contempt. "Jesus, Mulan, I swear to God!"

Mulan's barking did not abate when Logan and Tyler entered the flat. Far from it. This invasion of its territory only served to drive the thing even more demented, and by the time they had been led along the narrow hallway and into the living room it had barked itself hoarse.

It wheezed out a few more objections when the door was closed behind them, then slumped away in defeat upon realising that nobody was going to be leaving anytime soon.

The living room had been themed in reds and blacks, from the paint on the walls and ceiling, to the slanted checkerboard carpet that made Tyler feel like the whole room was leaning away from him.

Most of the furniture was black, with bursts of red appearing in the form of vases, or well-filled ashtrays, or other little contrasting accessories.

It was presumably some sort of style statement, Logan thought. Although, beyond 'I like red and black,' he had no idea what that statement might be.

The couch they'd been invited to sit on looked more comfortable than it actually was. It was made of some sort of plasticky fake leather material, and it crinkled beneath them as they tried to find a way of sitting that wouldn't eventually see them sliding off onto the floor.

Although, given how thick the pile on the carpet was, the floor might have been a better choice.

The room—the whole flat, in fact—was stale with the smell of cigarette smoke. It hung in the air, floating around at head height, drifting like long strings of cloud.

"I'm assuming Fellatio is a stage name, then?" Logan asked.

"I can see why they made you a detective. Yes, that is correct. Ms McFudd is my alter ego," the man in the baggy jumper replied, with a theatrical bow. "You may call me Hank. Hank Wanamaker."

It was as fake a name as the other one, Logan reckoned, but he chose not to question it for the moment.

"Good to meet you, Mr Wanamaker," he said.

He introduced himself and Tyler, received a slightly snidey, "Charmed, I'm sure," for his trouble, then got down to business.

"Tell me, Hank... Can I call you Hank?"

"You can call me whatever you like," he replied. It was the sort of line Logan would've expected to be delivered with a smile and a wink, but instead, there was a flatness to it. A resignation of some kind, like the man was reciting lines he'd long ago grown tired of.

Logan smiled. "Right. Hank, then," he said. "Tell me, Hank, when was the last time you saw Archie Sutherland?"

An eye twitched. A beat was skipped.

"Who?"

"Archie Sutherland. Maybe you know him better as Archie Tatties? Most people do."

"Oh," Hank replied, in a tone that strongly implied a silent, "That piece of shit," at the end. "Tatties? I don't know. A while."

"Can you be more precise?" Logan asked.

Hank's mouth tightened, like he was sucking all the plaque off his teeth. "June twenty-sixth last year. Eleven-twenty-two. In the morning."

"That's very specific," Logan said.

"Yes, well, you don't forget the time someone stabs you in the back, do you?" Hank spat. "Should've seen it coming, of course. Not like he hasn't done it, like, fifty times before."

Logan checked to make sure that Tyler was writing, and

instead found him locked in some sort of staring contest with the dog that now sat in the corner. He gave the DC a nudge with his elbow, and waited until he'd fished out his notepad before continuing with his questions.

"What happened?"

"The fucker undercut me. Again," Hank said. He lit a cigarette and took a long draw on it, as if recalling the memory first required a steadying of the nerves. "Panto auditions. We were both up for the dame."

"Panto? At the King's?" asked Logan.

Hank almost choked on his cigarette. "Fuck off, *at the King's!* Elaine C. Smith has got that fucker sewn up. I swear, you'll have to prise that role from the bitch's cold, dead hands." He sucked on the cigarette so hard the tip almost spluttered fully into flame. "I mean, a woman playing the dame? Just who the hell does she think she is?"

"Is it no' always a woman?" Tyler asked, looking up from his pad.

A look passed between Logan and the owner of the flat.

"What?" the DCI asked, the couch crinkling as he turned.

"The dame. In pantos. Widow Twankey, or whatever?" It was clear from Tyler's expression that he was realising he should have kept his mouth shut, but it was too late now. The damage was already done. "Were they not...? Are they not women?"

"Oh, I like him," Hank said, pointing with his cigarette. "He's a keeper, that one."

Over in the corner, Mulan voiced her disagreement with a couple of shrill barks, but then lay down and curled up in the huff when nobody paid her any notice.

"No, not the King's. Pavilion," Hank continued. "It was... fuck, I don't remember. *Cinderella*, let's say. They all blur into one. We were both up for the dame. Some fella from *River City* was playing Buttons. I'd heard through the grapevine that I was getting it. Grant Stott knew the director, and he'd tipped me the wink."

"Who's Grant Stott?" Logan asked.

"I think he's John Leslie's brother, boss."

Logan appeared none the wiser. "Who's John Leslie?"

"Off the telly. Blue Peter presenter turned alleged sex pest," Tyler said.

"Oh, aye. Him," Logan said, dimly recalling the man in question.

"So, anyhoo, I get called into the Pavilion to talk to the casting director," Hank continued. "I'm skipping in there like I'm in a *Bodyform* advert. I'm bloody... I'm dancing. I'm literally dancing, thinking I've got this one in the bag, but... oh-ho. Who's this coming out grinning like the cat who got the fucking cream?"

"Archie Sutherland?" Logan guessed.

"Archie bastard Tatties. In the flesh," Hank confirmed, his face twisting in distaste at the thought of it. "And you know what he says? As he's passing? You know what the cheeky fucker says? 'Better luck next time, darling.'" His jaw dropped, the words still shocking him all these months later. "'Better luck next time,' he says. 'Darling,' he calls me. Can you believe the fucking nerve?"

Hank inhaled the last half-inch of his cigarette in one big suck, then stubbed it out in a red glass ashtray.

"It's a good job for him Fellatio wasn't around. She'd have put the slimy little toad in his place. *Better luck fucking next time.* She'd have given him 'darling.' She'd have shoved his 'darling' right up his shitter. Sideways, and wrapped in barbed wire."

"I thought you were... Are you not Fellatio?" Tyler asked. He shot a worried look at his notes. "Because that's what I've written down."

"Sometimes. But I wasn't then, not right at that moment," Hank offered by way of explanation. "If she'd been there, though, she'd have sorted the little weasel out. Talk to her like that? She'd have ended him. I swear to God, she'd have fucking ended him. It's a miracle she hasn't done it long before now, in fact. Lord knows he's been asking for it for years. What she wouldn't give to get her hands around that little bastard's throat. She'd wring his bloody neck."

Logan noted how Hank's hands trembled as he took another cigarette from a pack. There was no sound but the rasping of the lighter while he lit up, then he steadied himself with a nicotine fix, blew a smoke ring, and turned back to the detectives.

"So, anyway, old Tatties," he said. "What about the vile little shit? What's he done?"

"He hasn't done anything," Logan said. "I'm afraid Mr Sutherland's been murdered."

Hank froze with the butt of the cigarette resting against his bottom lip. His eyes searched the faces of the two men on his couch, like he was waiting for a punchline that was never going to come.

"Oh, I see," he said, and his natural accent came through loud and clear. "Well, eh, in that case..." He flashed a worried smile. "Any chance we can strike all that stuff I just said off the record?"

CHAPTER TWENTY-FOUR

"You're back," Moira said with a roll of her eyes and a grimace of distaste. "Why are you back?"

"Thought I'd bring you a wee magazine to read," Ben said, holding up a copy of the one he'd chosen from the dozens of near-identical offerings on a rack at the supermarket.

"Why?" Moira demanded. She was propped up in bed, but slouching a little to the right. The railing at her side would stop her from falling out, but she didn't exactly look comfortable, Ben thought.

"We'll call it professional courtesy," the DI replied. He put the magazine on the bed, then put his hands on his hips as he considered her. "That's a hell of a position you've got yourself into there. Do you want me to get one of the nurses to give you a shift?"

"Away you go," Moira retorted. "Have they no' got enough to do without heaving me about? They'll get to me when they get to me."

"Right, well, how's about you let me?" Ben began, moving in closer to adjust her. A warning look stopped him in his tracks.

"Don't you bloody dare lay a finger on me, Detective Inspector," she told him. "I'm quite capable of sorting myself, thank you very much!"

Ben held his hands up in surrender. "Right, aye. Sorry. Just thought I'd try and help."

"I don't need or want your help," Moira told him. She wriggled in the bed, her weakened arm not yet capable of heaving her back into position on its own.

"You sure you don't want a hand?" Ben asked, after several seconds of grunting and shuffling from the woman in the bed. "I could just..."

"You can do nothing of the bloody kind. Just... Hold that pillow so it doesn't move."

Ben obliged. He caught the corner of the top pillow and kept it from being dragged up the bed by Moira's shoulder. She was a thrawn bugger, right enough.

"That you?" he asked, once she'd managed to get herself into a marginally more comfortable-looking position.

Her reply was brief, and short of breath. "Aye." Her chest heaved, and her eyes closed over as the effort caught up with her and made her head spin.

Ben picked up the magazine and took a seat. "You had lunch yet?" he asked.

Moira shook her head, still recovering from her ordeal.

"What are you having today? Something nice?"

"I highly doubt it," she managed, her breathing coming back under control.

Ben chuckled. "You mean they've no' got Gordon Ramsay down in the kitchen whipping up something special for you?"

"God, I hope not," Moira muttered, finally opening her eyes. They swam for a moment, finding focus. "Can't stand that man."

"Better than yon other one, though. Oliver something."

"Jamie Oliver?" Moira suggested, her lips drawing back in disgust at the very thought of him.

"That's him!" Ben said. "He did a telly thing in Inverness a good few years back. Some big thing with the Highland Council. There was a big event for it. Provost was there, and a few of us had to go along. We all got lined up and he came down the line shaking hands like he was the bloody Queen. What was it Hoon called him again? 'Smarmy do-gooding mockney wanker,' I think it was." The DI gave another chuckle. "You should've seen the poor lad's bloody face. None of us knew where to look."

Moira closed her eyes again, and this time there was a suggestion of a smile. "Aye, I'd like to have seen that," she said, revelling in the thought of the TV chef's misery.

"Anyway. This magazine, I bought. You seen it before? It's called 'Love It, exclamation mark,'" Ben announced. This drew another distasteful look from the woman in the bed.

"Doesn't sound like my cup of tea."

"You say that now, but check out these headlines," Ben said. He put on his reading glasses. "Now, keep in mind these are on the front cover of a magazine that's called 'Love It!' That's important," he said, then he cleared his throat and began to read. "'He dressed me up in his dead sister's clothes for sex.'"

Moira blinked her eyes open. "He what?"

"He dressed her up in his dead sister's clothes for sex. That's all it says. I have no more information to give you than that at the present time. Not until we look inside," Ben said. "But... *Love It*! 'He dressed me up in his dead sister's clothes for sex.'"

"Love It!" Moira said, getting in on the joke. "Is there more?"

"Oh, you'd better believe there's more, lassie," Ben said. "I'm working from the worst to the best here. We're just getting started. Brace yourself. Are you braced?"

"I'm braced."

"You don't look like you're—"

"Just get bloody on with it!"

"Right. OK. Here we go," Ben said. He cleared his throat again. "Love It! Remember. Here we go. 'They stole my son and drained his blood.'"

Moira let out a cackle at that. "Love It!"

Ben laughed, too, although he sounded much less like a fairy-tale witch when he did it. "Who in the name of the wee man thought that was an appropriate title for this sort of thing?" he wondered aloud. "I mean, there's a wee story at the bottom here—'Help! My husband's poisoned me!' Christ, woman, don't write into a magazine about it, call a bloody ambulance!"

"She'll have been dead before it saw print," Moira remarked.

"There's a lesson there for all of us," Ben said. "Christ knows what it is, mind you." He indicated the magazine with a nod. "Want me to carry on?"

Moira tutted. "Well, no," she said, scowling. "But, I suppose, since you're here..."

Ben got himself comfortable in the chair at the side of the bed. "Right, then," he said, searching for the next headline. "Where were we?"

SINEAD STARED AT HER SCREEN, her brow furrowed and her fingers pressed to her temples like she was attempting telekinesis. She'd read the same piece of text on the same document six or seven times now, and was still none the wiser as to what it actually said.

"You alright?"

The voice beside her snapped her back to the here and now. She felt the meaning of the sentence she'd been attempting to decipher slipping away again as she turned to find Hamza watching her in concern.

"What's up?" he asked.

"Nothing. No, it's... Nothing," Sinead told him. "Just wondering how Tyler's getting on. Tyler and the boss, I mean. How they're getting on."

"Worried about how Tyler's going to cope in the big bad city?" Hamza laughed.

"No, not... Something like that."

"They'll be fine," Hamza assured her. "The DCI won't let anything happen to him. No saying he won't throttle Tyler himself, of course, but he won't let anything else happen."

Sinead forced a smile and backed it up with a brief nod. "Aye. You're right. Worrying about nothing," she said, then she steered the conversation onto a subject less fraught with pitfalls than Tyler's current wellbeing. "Been looking over this statement you got from the cleaner."

Hamza scooted his chair a little closer so he could see the screen. "What about it?"

"I was just reading the bit where she says that Rufus Boyle usually goes to visit anyone renting his house."

"She did," Hamza confirmed. "But he says he didn't this time. I called to double-check, and he's insistent he didn't go. Thought he'd give them their privacy."

"Right. Fair enough. It's just... bit weird that, isn't it?" Sinead said. "I mean, it's part of his usual routine. It's not like he's got a hundred-and-one other things to do. And I don't imagine it's every day he has a celebrity come to stay."

"He said he was away on the day they arrived and didn't get back until late."

"And that checks out?"

"Yeah. Long weekend playing golf. Gleneagles. Flash bastard. Got back on Tuesday morning."

"They were there for a week. He didn't find ten minutes to pop in at any point during that time?"

"So he says."

Sinead put her hands behind her head and leaned back in her chair.

"You don't believe him?" Hamza asked.

"I don't know. Maybe. I mean, it's not out of the question," Sinead said. "Just... I remember him. From when I was in Uniform down here, I mean. Right nosy bastard. Thought he was a bit of a local celebrity himself. Always getting involved in everything. Hosting events, lending his support to candidates at elections, doing talks at the schools..."

"Talks about what?"

Sinead shrugged. "Business, mostly. How to be successful. He came to the high school to talk to my class in fifth year, actually. It was basically about how to get rich. Annoyingly, he missed off the first and most crucial step in his process."

"And what was that?"

"Be the only child of wealthy parents," Sinead said, and they shared a smile at that. "You know he got in touch after my parents died and asked if I wanted him to say a few words at the funeral?"

"Did they know him?"

"No," Sinead said. "He just thought, since he was one of the local 'worthies,' that I might want him... How did he put it? 'Lending the event a bit of gravitas.'"

"Shut up! He did not!"

"He bloody did," Sinead confirmed. "Needless to say, I politely declined his generous offer."

Hamza's eyes narrowed. "How politely?"

"Not very, if I'm honest," Sinead admitted. "It was quite impolitely, actually." She shook her head and sat forward again. "My point is, he's a man who likes to get his face seen. Does it surprise me that he turns up at the door to introduce himself every time he has new guests? No. Does it surprise me that he *didn't* this time? Yes. From what I know of him, that's completely out of character."

"Maybe we should bring him in," Hamza said. "I'd have to run it by DI Forde first, but might be worth having a word with him."

"I think you're right," Sinead said. "Like Logan says, if he's lying about this, there's no saying what else he's lying about."

Hamza rolled over to his desk again and reached for the phone. "Want to sit in, if we get the go-ahead?"

"Aye," Sinead said, relieved to have something to take her mind off Tyler, even if only temporarily. "Why not?"

CHAPTER TWENTY-FIVE

TYLER SAT on the couch beside Logan, both of them ever so slowly sliding towards the floor. They'd fallen into sync with their push-backs now, and every few minutes would simultaneously readjust their positions to stop themselves oozing off the cushion and onto the carpet.

It had been a full ten minutes since Hank had left the room to 'powder his nose,' and both detectives were starting to get agitated. It had barely been a fortnight since another witness had clambered through a downstairs window and made a run for it to avoid answering questions, and were it not for the clattering and thumping coming from the room next door, Tyler would've assumed this one had made a break for freedom, too.

"What's taking him so long, do you think?" the DC whispered, earning himself a low growl from the dog. She was no longer curled up in the corner, and had instead set herself up on his lap, where she huffed and sighed every time he stopped patting her head.

Logan had a very good idea of why the owner of the flat was taking such a long time to return. He had become upset upon hearing what had happened to Archie and his family, although the sympathies were aimed more at his wife and kids than at Archie himself.

The questioning hadn't been particularly probing, despite Hank having, moments before, expressed his desire to kill the victim. Logan had simply enquired about when Hank had last been in any sort of contact with Archie, and what his movements had been over the course of the previous week.

It had been enough to send Hank into what he described as 'a right tizzy,' though, and Logan hadn't objected when he asked if he could leave the room for the aforementioned nose powdering.

He wasn't going to come back, the DCI knew. Not the version of him that had left, at least.

There was a screech of triumph as the living room door was thrown wide. A figure that was all dress, hair, and fingernails came striding in on heels so high they probably came with a safety net.

"Holy fuck!" Tyler caught himself ejecting, and the dozing dog in his lap growled at him again in her sleep.

"Bitches and gentlefolks, Ms Fellatio McFudd has entered the building!" the towering drag act boomed.

The movements were nothing like Hank's. His had been quicker, smaller, more furtive. His alter ego's were none of those things. While Hank had scurried out of the room, Fellatio didn't walk back in so much as sweep. Her hands and arms moved constantly, weaving slowly through the air like two snakes having the last dance of the evening.

Hank had plastered enough makeup on to change not just his complexion but his skin tone. He was still black, but Fellatio's face was paler, with more of an orangey hue. Long blonde eyelashes and bright yellow lipstick added a level of grotesqueness that was only heightened by the talon-like fingernails painted in a rainbow of sunshine shades.

"Y'alright, gents?" she asked, and the accent was suddenly from somewhere in the east end of London. "Making yourself comfortable, are we? Room for a small one in the middle?"

She winked salaciously, licked her lips, then started to sit before either detective could move. They managed to part just in time to save the dog getting squashed, or any inappropriate knee-sitting incidents.

"This is cosy, isn't it?" Fellatio grinned. Despite the other transformations, the teeth were the same stained yellow as before. "A right little *ménage à trois* we've got going on here, don't we?"

She reached for the cigarette pack on the coffee table, lit one, then took a draw on it. She held it differently, Logan noticed. Where Hank had seemed embarrassed by his smoking habit, Fellatio relished it.

"Now, a little birdie tells me you've got some questions about that role-stealing bastard, Archie Tatties. Gone and got himself done in, I'm hearing." Fellatio sat back so she could check out both detectives just by turning her head. Her gaze lingered on Tyler, who was now laser-focused on patting the dog like the fate of the world depended on it. "That right, lover?" she asked him. "Someone's gone and done in poor Archie Tatties?"

"That's right, miss," Logan confirmed, playing along. There was no point in not. He didn't care if it was Hank Wanamaker, Fellatio McFudd, or the bloody Tooth Fairy who answered his questions, just as long as some bugger did. "We were hoping you might be able to shed some light on—"

"You seen his films?" Fellatio asked. "What his company makes?"

"You mean the wedding videos and corporate stuff?" Logan asked.

Fellatio's laugh was a shrill, irritating thing, like fingernails being dragged down a blackboard. Even the dog protested with a raising of its head and a low, exasperated *whuff*.

"Oh yeah. 'Wedding videos,'" the drag queen said, making the quotation marks in the air with her clawed fingers. "I don't think so. You know what they call him on the estates? Tatties? Know what they call him?"

"What estates?" Logan asked, but Fellatio brushed the question off.

"'The Filther King.' That's what they call him. You know, like 'The Fisher King' but for filth? On account of them films he makes."

"You mean porn?" asked Tyler, before he could stop himself.

Fellatio turned her gaze on him again, and fluttered her terrifying eyelashes. "And what would a nice young man like you know about a naughty thing like that?" she asked, her voice dropping into a husky whisper.

"Archie was making pornography?" Logan said. "That would certainly help to explain his company's income."

"Doing well, was he? *Bastard!*" Fellatio puffed on her cigarette, then blew it out through her teeth. "Course, you go into business with that lot, and there's always plenty of money floating around, I suppose. Blood money, you ask me. I'd want no part of it, myself." She put a hand on Tyler's leg and he tensed as she pressed her nails into his thigh. "I can think of a few parts of you I wouldn't mind getting my hands on, though..."

"And what people would that be?" Logan asked, drawing Fellatio's attention again.

When she turned to him there was a flash of panic on her painted face, and her hair *swished* as she gave her head a hurried shake.

"Oh, you know? Just... people. Nobody in particular. I wouldn't know any of their names. I just mean..." She looked over to the window, as if worried someone might be standing out there, listening in. When she spoke, her voice was less Fellatio and more Hank. "Well, an industry like that. Making that sort of thing. You're going to get mixed up in it, aren't you? You're going to be rubbing shoulders with some right horrible bastards."

"It's not an industry without its share of unpleasant characters," Logan agreed.

"Especially the stuff he was making. Foul stuff. Really nasty. And believe me, I'm an open-minded girl," Fellatio said. Tyler whimpered as a nail was dragged up the inside of his thigh. "You might say I'm as open-minded as they come," she purred, slipping fully back into character.

"Are we talking underage?" Logan pressed.

"Oh. No. I mean, I don't think so. No. Everyone consenting. So he said, anyway, and he's a horrible slimy little fucker, but I don't think he'd be involved in anything *that* bad. But, it was all very... full-on, shall we say?"

"And he was definitely in partnership with someone?" Logan pressed.

"Yes. I mean, so I heard. I'm not the bitch's publicist, but yes. They handled distribution, I believe. He did the production. I got the impression that they also put up some of the initial money for equipment."

"You mean like cameras and that?" Tyler asked.

Fellatio smirked. "Among other things."

"Where did you hear all this?" Logan asked.

"From the great big gob of the man himself. He wasn't exactly shy about it," Fellatio said. She scratched the top of her head while she thought, making her wig shift around on her scalp. "Must've been Gerard Kelly's funeral. God rest him. We all had a few drinks afterwards, much to my shame. I couldn't stand the fucker, even then. Yeah, Tatties, I mean, not Gerard Kelly. Gerard Kelly—now *that* was a gentleman. But, Tatties had a few drinks—we all did by that point—and he got onto talking about it. Offered to get me involved in a film. Said there were people who'd pay good money to see that sort of thing." She tightened her talons on Tyler's leg again, and the DC was grateful for the dog blocking access to his crotch.

"And did you agree?" Logan asked. "Did you appear in one of his films?"

Fellatio rounded on him. "Did I fuck. I told the creepy little shit what I thought of him, in no uncertain bloody terms. I don't mind being an exhibitionist, but I'm not putting it all out there on video for the whole bloody world to see." She sniffed a very manly sniff. "Mind you, he did say it was a lucrative business. Said he'd done very well out of it. Financially."

Aye, no' half, Logan thought, thinking back to the digits on that statement of accounts.

"And he didn't say who he was in business with?" the DCI asked. "He didn't mention a name?"

Fellatio said nothing as she leaned forward and stubbed out her cigarette.

"Please think," Logan urged. "It could be important."

"He never mentioned a name, no." Fellatio glanced furtively around the room, presumably on the off-chance that some interloper had managed to sneak in without triggering the dog-shaped intruder alarm. "But," she whispered, once she was sure the coast was clear. "I may have been privy to a rumour or two..."

DAVE DAVIDSON WAS BORED. Cataclysmically bored, in fact.

His main role—his only role, officially—was to log the bags of evidence in and out, so they could be tracked throughout the investigation, and an important job it was, too.

It became substantially less important when there was no new physical evidence coming in, and nobody was showing any interest in checking any of it out. The last bit of excitement had been when Archie and Donna Sutherland's phones were being sent up the road to the tech bods to try to access, and he'd had to get a couple of signatures.

That had been yesterday.

Most of today had been spent double and triple-checking everything was recorded correctly, then playing some *Minesweeper* on the computer. He had only rediscovered the game recently, having last played it on a school computer when he was eight or nine. He was better at it now, although considering he hadn't understood what the hell he was meant to be doing back then, this came as no real surprise.

Christ, he was bored.

He'd made the phone call to Inverness to request that someone up there meet with Donna Sutherland's sister for the formal identification of the bodies. Someone from CID was going to handle it. They'd also find out where the sister was at the time of the attack, and generally have a good root around in her life to find out if she had any connection to the case beyond the one afforded to her by genetics.

That had been ages ago.

DI Forde was usually good at giving him tasks to do, but he'd cleared off out of the office, leaving Hamza to run the Incident Room.

Now, though, Sinead was laying out info on the Big Board, and Hamza was on his phone, chasing up such-and-such, or following through on whatever.

And that was fine. They had their jobs, and he had his. He wasn't part of the team. Not really. It was more like he was in their orbit, circling them as they worked the case.

He'd like to have thought of himself as a sidekick—the Robin to their Batman—but he was kidding himself. He was the Alfred to their Batman. Less than that, even. He was the guy who changed the oil on the Batmobile. Important, yes, but there were a million mechanics in Gotham City who could do the job just as well.

Dave spent some time thinking about Batman, as plastic hands crept at a glacial pace around the clock.

He liked Batman.

Five minutes later, he got himself blown to bits on another game of *Minesweeper*.

He checked his box of Exhibits.

No change.

God. He had to get away from his desk.

He wheeled himself backwards, then rolled across the Incident Room, steering himself between the other desks until he reached the Big Board. Sinead looked back at him and smiled.

"Alright?"

"Yeah, just thought I'd come check the board out," Dave said. "Good to know where we're up to."

"Your guess is as good as mine," came the reply, as Sinead finished pinning up seven index cards in a row across the top. "Just setting out what we know of the timeline."

Dave scanned the cards. Several of them were blank. Most of them, in fact. "Is that when he was seen in Inverness?" he asked, pointing to the card second from the left, which had the words 'Family at Railway Station' written at the top and highlighted in yellow pen.

Sinead confirmed that it was. The person who had shared the photo on social media had asked a lot of questions when Hamza had got in touch, but had ultimately been eager to help. They were able to pinpoint the date to the Wednesday of the week before the attack—eight days prior to the family's deaths. They had come in on a train around lunchtime, but Scotrail was still to provide CCTV from the station cameras that would verify this, and hopefully show their next movements.

"Want me to chase them up?" Dave asked.

"It's fine. Hamza's on it," Sinead said.

Dave hid his disappointment behind a thumbs up. He would've enjoyed shouting at Scotrail. They didn't, in his humble opinion, get shouted at nearly enough.

"Anything else I can do?" he asked. "I could phone the taxi companies and see if anyone remembers picking them up."

"Already done," Sinead replied, pinning up another card. "We've been in touch with all of them, but nobody remembers having them in their cars. So, we're hoping the footage from the station will give us a company name. That's if they even got in a taxi, of course. They might have walked somewhere, or got on a bus."

"With two kids and a big bag of readies? Bold."

Sinead regarded the note she'd been writing for a moment, then nodded. "Aye, I suppose it would be pretty reckless. And the money would've been heavy. Too heavy to carry far. They must've got in a taxi, or maybe been picked up by someone."

"Or stayed in the hotel at the station."

Sinead's pen jerked, extending the line of a letter on her index card. "What?"

"The hotel. What's it called? The Royal Highland, is it?" Dave said. "It's right there in the square. Like, five seconds' walk from the station entrance." He shrugged. "They could've stayed there. That's what I'd have done."

Sinead looked at the board, then down at the card she had just messed up. "Aye," she said, after some thought. "Aye, that's... That's not a bad shout."

"Want me to give them a ring?" Dave offered. "I'm at a bit of a loose end, anyway, so... I mean, obviously if you'd rather do it yourself..."

"Aye. I mean, no. I mean... would you mind? We're meant to be interviewing Rufus Boyle in a minute."

Dave grinned. "Believe me," he said. "I'm all over it."

CHAPTER TWENTY-SIX

"Please, call me 'Mr Boyle.'"

Rufus sat on one side of the interview table, his arms spread wide like Jesus in the painting of the Last Supper, but with a look on his face like he'd just found out he was footing the bill.

Across the table, Sinead summoned the closest thing she could to a smile, given the circumstances, and nodded her understanding.

"Sorry for the informality, Mr Boyle. We appreciate you coming in."

"I already spoke on the phone to some Aberdonian man. I told him everything."

"That would be me," said Hamza.

Rufus blinked, taken aback. "Oh. Yes, I mean... OK." He looked Hamza up and down. "You're not what I expected."

"What did you expect?" the DS asked.

"I don't know, I just... Not..." Rufus cleared his throat, brought his hands together like he was about to lead them in prayer, then nodded at them both in turn. "Anyway. What was it you wanted to talk to me about?"

"I'm sure you can probably hazard a guess, Mr Boyle."

"I mean... I'm assuming it's something to do with the awful business at the house? Mr Sutherland, and his family?"

"That'd be a pretty safe bet," Hamza confirmed. "You've told us twice now, Mr Boyle, that you didn't visit the house at any point during Mr Sutherland's stay, and that you didn't meet the family face to face."

"That's correct," Rufus confirmed. "I didn't."

"But you usually do pop in and meet guests in person," Sinead said. "Just not this time. Why was that?"

Rufus turned to her, his eyes narrowing. "Do I... I know you, don't I? You're local, aren't you? Sharon? Chantelle?"

"Sinead."

Rufus slapped the table. "Sinead!"

"But you can call me Detective Constable Bell," Sinead told him, and Hamza had to fight the urge to give her a fist bump under the table. "And I'd appreciate it if you answered my question. You didn't go and see Archie and his family. Why?"

"I was away. Golfing," Rufus explained.

"All week?" Sinead asked, though she already knew the answer. She was determined to make this difficult for him, not just for his offer of 'adding a bit of gravitas' to her parents' funeral by speaking at it, but for all those years of school visits where he'd bored the arse off everyone in the class.

Rufus sighed pointedly, like this whole thing was a big waste of his time. "No. As I already explained on the phone, I was away for a long weekend. Got back very late on Monday night."

Hamza tapped the closed folder of notes sitting on the desk in front of him. There was very little in the folder relating to the man being interviewed, but *he* didn't know that. "Hold on, you told me you got back on Tuesday morning."

Rufus dismissed this with a shrug. "Fine. Tuesday morning, then."

"What do you mean, 'Fine,' Mr Boyle?" Sinead asked. "Either it was Monday night or it was Tuesday morning."

"*Or* it was shortly after midnight, so both could apply. Which it was. I got in around twelve-fifteen. Which, yes, technically is Tuesday morning, but could also be considered Monday night."

"I assume you have someone who can verify this?" Sinead asked.

"The golfing weekend or the arrival home time?"

"Both."

Rufus gave a little roll of his eyes. "Golf weekend, yes. Dozens of people, in fact. And photographic evidence. They'll also be able to verify when I left, and my wife can confirm what time I arrived home. I'm sure all your Big Brother cameras on the A9 will be able to show me driving up the road, too. Range Rover. Silver. Can't miss it."

He spoke the words like a taunt. *Range Rover.* 'You'll never be able to afford one,' his tone implied. 'But I can. Aren't I marvellous?'

"That just leaves Tuesday through to Sunday," Sinead said, ignoring the obvious jibe.

Rufus frowned. "Sorry?"

"To explain your whereabouts."

"Why on Earth would I do that?" Rufus asked, his nostrils flaring like the very thought appalled him.

"Because we're asking you to, Mr Boyle," Hamza said. "To help us with our investigation."

"It's none of your business," Rufus replied. "I can assure you that I didn't go to the house. I didn't speak to Mr Sutherland or any member of his family, and I certainly didn't kill them. Everything else is none of your concern."

He was right, annoyingly. They had nothing on him other than a second-hand insight into his usual routine—third-hand, if you counted the translator—and some personal experience of what a dick he was. Neither was grounds for arrest, and if he hadn't already done so, Rufus would reach that same conclusion soon.

This was getting them nowhere.

Time for a risky play.

"You say you didn't go to the house, Mr Boyle," Hamza said, channelling his inner Jack Logan. "But we both know that's not true, don't we?"

Boyle frowned and opened his mouth to reply, but Hamza raised a hand, calling for silence.

"Before you say anything, I want you to think very hard about your answer," Hamza warned him. "*Very* hard. And remember that this interview is being recorded, and that anything you say is admis-

sible in court. Similarly, anything *we* say in follow-up to your statement..." He gave the folder a meaningful tap. "...anything that
contradicts what you've told us, will also be heard in court."

Sinead saw the play that Hamza was making, so interlaced her
fingers and leaned forward in perfect synch with the DS.

"What Detective Sergeant Khaled is saying, Mr Boyle, is that
you might want to start telling us the truth, before you make things
any worse for yourself."

Rufus's eyes flitted between them. He swallowed so hard that
he practically said the word, 'Gulp.'

"But I... I mean..." He scratched himself. Tilted his head back,
like he was trying to get away from them. "I honestly didn't," he
insisted. "Honestly!

Both detectives adopted the sort of expressions found on the
faces of parents who *weren't angry, just disappointed*.

And also a bit angry.

Neither of them said a word. Both of them—Sinead in particular—enjoyed how visibly uncomfortable this made the man across
from them.

"Oh! Wait! Actually, I forgot something!" Rufus announced.
"There was one night that I thought about going in to say hello. I
was passing by, and I considered popping in. I was coming back
from the cinema. The new one. In town. They're showing old
Bond movies. A new one each night of the week. But I didn't.
Swing by the house, I mean. I didn't go in. I swear."

"Why not?" Hamza asked.

"I could see they had guests," Rufus replied.

"Guests?" Sinead asked. "How do you know?"

"There was a car out front," Rufus said.

"A car? What kind of car?" DS Khaled pressed.

"I don't know. I have to confess, it's not an area of expertise.
Not that type of car, anyway. Small. Black, or... dark blue, maybe.
It was on the drive. So, I thought I should probably leave them
to it."

Sinead scribbled a note. "And what night was this?"

Rufus blew out his cheeks. "Now you're asking. It was
Goldfinger, so what's that? Fourth one?"

"Third," Sinead said. Her dad had been a fan. He'd subjected her to all of them, more than once.

"Wednesday, then," Rufus said.

"Time?"

Rufus checked his watch, like it might somehow show him the time back then, rather than the time right now. "I'm not sure," he admitted. "Later. Maybe... half-eight? Quarter to nine? Around then."

Hamza waited until Sinead had jotted this down before continuing. "And you didn't think to mention this before because...?"

Rufus blinked. "Because I... I mean..." He cleared his throat, shook his head, then said a firm, "No," to no one in particular.

Then, he sat upright and straightened his shoulders, his tone shifting into something clipped and condescending. "I'm *very* sorry, but I'm a rather busy man, and I'm dealing with a lot at the moment. Mostly, the discovery of four dead bodies in my house, and the ongoing headache of having to cancel and refund multiple future guests because apparently nobody is able to tell me when I'll be able to open up again. You'll forgive me if *briefly seeing a parked car* didn't rank high on my list of recent memorable moments."

He checked his watch for a second time, nodded like he'd just received the answer to a question that had been bothering him, and tapped his hands on the table.

"I'm afraid I have other appointments today, so we'll have to call this to a close," he told them.

"We still have questions, Mr Boyle," Sinead said.

"We all have questions, *dear*," he said. "But, if you want me to answer any more, you can explain your reasoning to my solicitor, and he can arrange a convenient time and place." He looked from one detective to the other and smiled patronisingly. "Sound good?"

It didn't 'sound good.' Not even close.

But they had nothing to hold him on, and they were left with no choice.

"If that's your final decision, Mr Boyle..." Hamza began.

"It is."

"Then, we'll terminate the interview now," the DS concluded.

Sinead leaned back in her chair, arms folded. "But don't leave town," she said. "Will you, *dear*?"

ONCE RUFUS BOYLE had retired to the comfort and safety of his Range Rover, Hamza and Sinead stood in the corridor outside the interview room, their backs against the wall.

"At one point in there, I thought you were going to take a swing at him," Hamza said.

"Just one?" Sinead replied. "You obviously weren't paying attention." She turned to the senior officer. "He is a dick, isn't he? It's not just me?"

"It's not just you," Hamza confirmed. "Entitled knob. World's full of them, unfortunately."

"Aye. I've met most of them," Sinead said. She gestured to the door Rufus had been escorted out through. "Think he's telling the truth?"

"About not going to the house or seeing the car?"

"Either. Both."

Hamza shrugged. "I don't necessarily think he isn't."

Sinead, to her immense disappointment, was forced to agree. "If he's lying about going to see them, then he's the killer. And, much as I'd love to personally manhandle him into a jail cell, I don't think he is. I don't think he'd kill someone. He's more likely to pay someone else to do it." She perked up at that thought. "Maybe he paid someone!"

Hamza shook his head. "Doubt it. He hasn't got much of an alibi for Thursday. Boss asked him."

Sinead's eyes narrowed. "What difference does that...?" she began, then she nodded and let the sentence fall away. If you were paying someone to commit a quadruple homicide, you'd make sure your alibi was cast iron. Ideally, you'd be on live TV somewhere. In another country. At the very least, though, you'd make sure you couldn't be connected to the deaths.

"I don't see a motive, either," Hamza said. "I don't think 'being a dick' is enough of a driving force."

Sinead sighed. "No. I suppose not."

"Still, the car's a new bit of info," Hamza said. "Potentially useful."

"Aye. Could be," Sinead said, a little distant. She checked her phone screen, frowned at it, then put it back in her pocket.

"No word from Tyler?"

"Hmm? Oh, no. Sorry. Nothing."

Hamza pushed himself away from the wall with a foot. "He'll be fine," he assured her. "You know what the boss is like. He's probably working the poor bugger's fingers to the bone."

CHAPTER TWENTY-SEVEN

THE SECOND PUB of the day was much more Logan's style. To describe *The Pig & Bicycle* as 'bleak' would've been to massively overhype it. It had been a traditional working man's pub in the 60s and 70s, then a place where the unemployed came to drown their sorrows after the big lay-offs on the Clyde during the 80s.

Various owners had taken the place on over the years, and attempts had been made to gentrify and modernise it. Most had failed.

The only one that had stuck was the bar menu that had been introduced somewhere around 1988—a menu which had not, to the best of Logan's knowledge, been altered since.

The pub had actually found itself in keeping with a few newer places recently, due entirely to the cyclical nature of fashion and design. Just a stone's throw away, other pubs were spending tens of thousands to recreate the authentic feel of places such as this one, bringing in expensive distressed wooden flooring, and sourcing original brass fittings from specialist dealers.

The Pig, as it was most commonly known—marginally ahead of 'that shitehole on the corner'—had all these features baked in. On top of those, it added red leather seating patched up with silver tape, a dartboard with a bulge around the treble twenty, and the heady aroma of old men's piss.

It was, Logan thought, the perfect pub.

"How's your Chicken Kiev?" he asked, through a mouthful of overcooked beef that was refusing to allow itself to be swallowed.

Tyler looked up from pushing a rock-sized mound of something brown and crispy around his plate with a fork. "Don't know, boss. Can't get into it," he replied. "Think if I ask they'll give me a chisel?"

Logan looked past the DC to where the tattooed barman stood flicking through a copy of *The Daily Star*.

"Aye, but I'd be worried where they might shove it," he replied.

"Thought you said the food in here was good?"

"I did say that," Logan admitted. He moved the gristly ball of beef to the other side of his mouth, in case the teeth there had more luck. "In hindsight, my memory might've been playing tricks on me." He tapped the edge of Tyler's plate with a knife. "Still, eat all that and there's a *Wall's Viennetta* with your name on it, son. My shout."

Tyler smiled. "You're too generous, boss," he said.

The front door opened. Logan's head didn't move, but his eyes shifted to check out the shifty-looking younger lad who came striding in. He had trouble written all over him. But then, so did the eight or nine other punters in the place.

Logan followed the newcomer by watching his reflection in the big dirty mirror behind the bar, then turned his attention back to his lunch when the man ordered a drink.

"And you like this pub?" Tyler asked. There was a heavy note of scepticism to the question, like a ten-year-old asking if Santa is really *really* real. "I mean, you actually like it. Not in an ironic sort of way?"

"How do you like a pub in an ironic way?" Logan asked. He grunted and gestured around with a fork. "And aye. I like it. It's not fancy."

Tyler agreed that 'fancy' was not a word that was ever likely to be applied to the establishment.

"It's a proper pub. It's honest."

Across the table, the DC almost choked on his half-pint of non-brand cola. "Honest? This place?" he said, dropping his voice to a whisper. "I could lob this Chicken Kiev in any direction and hit a crook in here, boss. Mind you, I'd better not. I'd probably kill him with it."

"Aye, but there's an honesty in that, too. It's no' saying, 'Just you leave your wallet on the table and it'll be there when you get back from the toilet.' It's saying, 'We will not think twice about robbing you blind.'" He grimaced as he forced down the blob of stringy meat. "That's honest, too, in its own way. A place like this might smash you in the face with a claw hammer, but it won't stab you in the back."

"That's... comforting, I suppose."

Logan took a sip of something that had laughably been described as 'fresh lemonade' but tasted more like the gas had gone on the *Schweppes* tap.

"The same doesn't apply to the punters, mind," he pointed out. "They'll stab you in the back without a second thought."

Tyler scanned the bar. "That doesn't come as a surprise."

What did come as a surprise—both to Tyler, and, if the DCI were honest, himself—was Logan pronging his fork through another bit of the beef that swam in the grey sludge on his plate, and then shoving the meat in his mouth. He chewed quickly before he could overthink it, and distracted himself from the texture by moving the conversation on.

"Any idea why we're here?" he asked.

Tyler looked down at his plate. "Am I being punished for something, boss?"

Logan shook his head. "When I'm punishing you for something, you'll know about it," he said. "One of those names Ms McFudd gave us—Shuggie Cowan..." He made a circling motion with his knife. "...owns this place. That's him sitting in the far corner. Don't look."

Tyler had already started to look, so continued sweeping his gaze up towards the ceiling, where it lingered for an unnaturally long time on an utterly unremarkable light fitting. He nodded once, like he was giving the thing his approval, then turned his attention back to his meal.

"Don't think he saw me, boss," he muttered.

He hadn't exactly seen the man in the corner, but he'd managed to get an impression of him. He was half-hidden behind a pillar at the table furthest from the door. He was older, Tyler thought. There had been a suggestion of grey as his eyes had flitted past, anyway. Not a small man either, he reckoned, but he resisted the urge to double-check.

"Is he, like, a gangster or something?"

Logan raised his knife and fork up and down, like he was weighing them in his hands. "Aye. Or something. Or he was. Supposedly on the straight and narrow now, but... we'll see."

"We going to talk to him?"

Something in the ball of meat went *crunch*. Logan ignored it and continued chewing. "Maybe, aye. Eventually. For now, I'm just enjoying my lunch."

"I find that very hard to believe, boss," Tyler said, and he jabbed at his Chicken Kiev like he might be able to surprise it and catch it with its defences down. No such luck.

Although, given how much difficulty Logan was having with the chewing and swallowing process, being unable to even cut into his own lunch might turn out to be for the best.

"What did you think of Billy Neeps?"

Tyler looked up from his ongoing battle with his lunch. "Eh... fine. Seemed alright."

"Nothing strike you as weird?" Logan pressed.

"Weird? I mean... he was a bit odd, right enough, but nothing in particular, boss. How come?"

Logan ground something between his teeth, then shuddered. "I didn't like his reaction to us being there. It felt off."

"In what way, boss?"

"Well, I mean the two of us turn up at your shop, tell you we're from the polis... I don't know about you, but my first reaction is concern. Has something happened to my wife?"

Tyler frowned. "Your wife?" he asked, then the penny dropped. "Oh. Billy's wife. You're Billy. Right."

"I wonder if there's been an accident. I ask the question, at least. It's the first thing that crosses my mind," Logan said. "Unless I'm already expecting a visit."

"You think Billy might be involved?" Tyler asked.

Logan made a non-committal grunt. "I don't know."

"How would he even know where to find Archie though, boss? Seems to me like he was in hiding."

Logan conceded the point. "Aye. There's that, right enough. But someone knew where to find him." He hacked through another piece of meat and shoved it in his mouth. "Shona's PM for Archie was interesting," Logan announced out of the blue. "Did you read it?"

Tyler drew his head into his shoulders, bracing himself. "Eh, was I meant to, boss?"

"Well, ideally you'd have at least had a glance at the bloody thing, given that you're investigating his murder, but I didn't specifically tell you to, if that's what you mean?"

Across the table, Tyler relaxed. "Good stuff. Then no, I haven't had a chance to look yet. What's interesting about it?"

The meat in Logan's mouth was going nowhere. This bite, if anything, was more determined to hang on than the first one had been. He trapped it between his back teeth and bit down, then momentarily froze when something went *pop*.

"You alright, boss?"

Logan glanced at his napkin, considered disposing of the contents of his mouth, then decided that he was no coward, and battled on with it.

"Fine. So, Archie's post-mortem."

"Stabbed?"

"Aye. We knew that, though. You know what we didn't know?" Logan asked. He let the question hang there for a moment, before answering it himself. "He had cancer."

Tyler picked up a beermat between thumb and forefinger and tapped it lightly on the edge of his plate. "Aye?"

"So it seems. Bad, too. Was going to do its worst before too much longer," Logan explained.

"What, like, kill him you mean?"

Logan nodded, moved the partially masticated ball of meat-mush around in his mouth, then continued. "Silly bugger was refusing treatment, would you believe?"

"So... what? They could've cured him?"

"No. Don't think so. He was way too far gone for that," Logan replied. "Left it too late to get checked. Kept putting it off. So the medical records say, anyway." He shook his head. "Daft bastard."

Tyler turned the beer mat over. He looked at the writing on the back, but didn't read it. "I suppose... maybe he was just, you know, scared. Or whatever."

"Lot of bloody good being scared did him," Logan said. "He was already a dead man walking when he got to Glen Coe. Getting murdered just sped the process up. It might've been the best thing for him, in fact. Probably no' for the rest of the family, obviously, but for him."

Tyler frowned. "How do you work that one out?"

"Well, it's not a nice way to go, is it? Cancer," Logan said. "Can be a bloody horrible thing. Bastard of a disease. No rhyme nor reason to it."

"No. Suppose not."

"Amazing what they can do these days, mind you," Logan said. "All the new treatments they've got. Makes a big difference."

Tyler folded the beer mat in half, then folded it in the opposite direction. Logan used a mouthful of flat lemonade to coerce the lump of grey meat down his gullet.

"Which one is it?" he asked, once he'd forced it down.

The bending of the beer mat stopped. It took a second for the frown to fully develop on Tyler's face. "Boss?"

Logan pointed with the end of his knife at the table. Were someone to draw a straight line through the wood from the cutlery's tip, it would stop roughly in the same neck of the woods as Tyler's testicles.

"Which bollock?"

Tyler looked down at his crotch, then back to the DCI. "I don't know what..." He turned the beer mat over again, then chewed on his bottom lip before replying. "How did you know? Did Hoon tell you?"

"No."

Tyler's face fell. "Not Sinead? I asked her not—"

"Nobody told me, Tyler. I'm a Detective Chief Inspector of the bloody polis. They don't give that out in boxes of cornflakes, you know?" He tapped the side of his head. "I figured it out."

Tyler stared back at him in amazement. "How?"

"Lots of wee things. You getting cold feet at the wedding was a big billboard that something was wrong, but there were signs before then, too. Little things."

"Like what?"

Logan shoved a chunk of carrot in his mouth. At least, he hoped it was carrot. It looked like a carrot, but the taste and texture were far removed from what he'd been expecting.

"Nothing major," he said, once the shock of the maybe-carrot had passed. "The way you and Sinead have both been staring off into space for half the day, then giving each other reassuring wee smiles all through the other half. The way you try so hard to act normal, but forget to tell your hands."

Tyler stopped turning the beer mat over and over, and set it down on the table.

"Little things like that," Logan said. "It's the right one, isn't it?"

Across the table, the DC gawped. "How the fu—? How do you know that?"

Logan shrugged. "Because you touch it about three hundred times a day," he said. "That was also one of those wee clues I mentioned, by the way."

Tyler sat back, and his rickety chair made a chorus of creaks. "That's... I'm impressed, boss."

"Like I say, I'm no' a detective for nothing, son," Logan replied. He swallowed the slimy carrot-thing and shuddered. "Also, you nodded off in the car on the way down the road last night, and you talk in your sleep. So that was a helpful pointer, too."

That earned a laugh from the Detective Constable. He took a moment to process all this, and cast his eye across the pub to a boar's head mounted on the wall above an old bicycle wheel. The pig was a moth-eaten, threadbare old thing with one tusk missing. Judging by the look on its face, it was not impressed by its current predicament. You could hardly blame it, he supposed.

"Meant to be getting the operation on Thursday," he said.

"What do you mean 'meant to be?'" Logan asked.

"No, I am, boss. I am. I'm getting it done," Tyler replied. "I'm just..." He stared down at his plate like it was suddenly the most interesting thing in all the world. "I don't know."

"You're scared."

"Scared?!" Tyler snorted. "No! I'm not scared, boss, I'm just..." He sighed, the charade collapsing. "I suppose I am, aye."

"It's understandable," Logan said. "It's a big thing. The operation, I mean, no' your bollock."

"That's pretty sizeable," Tyler insisted. He drummed his fingers on the table. "I don't know what I'm scared *of*, exactly. Not the operation itself. It's called an orco...something or other. But it's not that I'm worried about. And while I'm not over the moon about having one ball—"

"Never did Hitler any harm," Logan pointed out.

"True. And it's not the end of the world. I'll still have one. Talking to the doctors, they don't see any reason why we won't be able to have kids. Assuming, you know, that it all goes OK." He tapped his fork on the edge of his plate. "It's just... what if it doesn't? What if they find out it's spread? What if they open me up, take one look, then tell me I'm a dead man?"

"That'd be a hell of a bedside manner," Logan remarked. "And it's 'orchiectomy.'"

Tyler looked up. "What? Oh, aye, the operation. Aye, that's it. How do you...?"

"My, eh, my brother had it done," Logan replied.

"Your brother, boss? I didn't know you even had a..." Tyler's voice trailed off when he saw the answer written between the lines of Logan's expression. "Oh."

"He was older than me. It was a long time ago. Treatments weren't as good then as they are now," Logan told him. "But the big problem was that he'd left it far too long. He'd put off going in. For months. Because we do that, don't we? Men. We're silly bastards with this stuff."

He hovered his fork above his plate, searching for its next victim among the gristle and slime. Suddenly, though, he didn't have the stomach for it, and so he set the cutlery down and pushed the plate off to the side of the table, out of his immediate line of sight.

"With Andy, it had spread. Because he'd delayed going in for so long. It had taken root in the lymph nodes, then started on a kidney. Got a good hold," Logan explained. "They can do a lot about that now, I think, but back then... no' so much."

"Shite. I'm, eh, I'm sorry to hear that, boss," Tyler said. "I don't... I'm just... I'm really sorry to hear that."

Logan nodded. "Thanks. It is what it is, I suppose."

"They've, eh, they reckon they've caught mine early. It was the scan I got after the crash that showed something up. They ran a couple more tests, and... bingo. But they say they've caught it early on. So, you know, that's good."

"Aye. It is," Logan confirmed. "It's very good." He checked his watch. "We'll get you off on the next train up the road. You're getting that operation."

"Come on, boss, you need me down here," Tyler protested, but he was given short shrift.

"I'm sure I'll find some way to cope without you, painful as that will no doubt be. You'll get up that road to the Fort tonight, then Sinead can take you up to Inverness. No arguments. I want you back on your feet and fighting fit. I need you on the ball."

Tyler smiled. "Good one, boss."

"And I don't want you busting a nut to get back," Logan continued.

"How long did it take you to think them up?" the DC asked.

"Half the bloody night," Logan admitted. "I tried to come up with a third—something about hitting the sack, maybe—but I couldn't get it to work."

"Points for effort though, boss. And the Hitler one was good."

"Cheers." Logan raised his glass and they *chinked* them across the table. "You're going to be alright, Tyler. You're too much of a jammy bastard for this to—"

A shadow fell across the detectives. Quite a large shadow, at that. They both slowly raised their gazes to find three man-shaped sacks of testosterone towering over them. The men had been poured into black trousers and white shirts, with black ties pulled tightly in an attempt to keep their necks from bursting out of their collars.

"Yous polis?" asked the one at the front, in a tone that suggested the answer to that question had better be a resounding, "No." Or, preferably, "No, sir."

He looked almost identical to the other two—same sloping fore-head, same blubbery-lipped scowl—but Logan reckoned if you cut him open and counted the rings he'd turn out to be a few years older than the other two.

Logan didn't see the worried glance from Tyler, but he felt its sting. "Who's asking?" he said.

This caused some visible confusion among the men, until the man standing back and to the left finally formulated a response. "*We* are," he said.

"No, I can see that, pal," Logan said. The words were friendly, but the tone was not. "I mean who are you three, exactly?"

It was the man at the front who replied. "Just answer the question. You polis?"

Logan's gaze switched from the one on the left to the one in the middle. "What's with the conversation jumping around? You three sharing a brain or something here?" he asked, then he pointed to the guy on the right. "When does he get a shot?"

"Seth!"

All eyes but Logan's went to the corner, where the pub's owner had a hand raised. Some signal passed between him and the three brutes. When the frontmost member of the group spoke again, it was in a less confrontational tone. "Are you Logan?" he asked.

"That I am," the DCI replied. "Your boss want to see me, does he?"

He stood up suddenly, and the men took a step back like they really were one collective entity. Their movements weren't quick, though. There was no flinching, or clenching of fists. These were not men who were easily intimidated.

"Jack Logan. You brass-necked bastard," said the man half-hidden in the corner. His voice was not loud, but it carried across the now almost-silent pub. "You've got some bloody nerve coming in here."

"Aye, well, you know me, Shuggie. Always turning up where I'm no' welcome," Logan replied. He turned back to Tyler. "Off you go, son. Get your stuff and get on that train."

Tyler blinked. "What? No, I can't... I'm not just going to leave you here, boss."

"Aye, you are," Logan insisted.

At the table in the corner, the old man gave a dry chuckle that became a cough. "No, he's no'," he said, once the wheezing had subsided. "Seth, how about you and the boys take Mr Logan's friend there upstairs and keep him entertained for a while?" He leaned out from behind the pillar, revealing a grin, a gold tooth, and a scar in the shape of a swastika. "Jack and I have a *lot* of catching up to do."

CHAPTER TWENTY-EIGHT

BEN RETURNED to the Incident Room to find a fully updated Big Board, and a raft of new developments.

The car was on there—black or dark blue, small, Wednesday evening between half-eight and nine. It was a nice juicy addition, but it had been overshadowed almost immediately by Dave's discovery.

His hunch had proven correct. After getting off the train, Archie Sutherland and his family had walked the few dozen yards to the entrance of the Royal Highland Hotel, and collected the keys for the room they'd booked earlier that morning.

Four of them had checked in on Wednesday afternoon.

When they'd left the following Monday, five of them had checked out.

Hamza pointed to the chain of index cards that made up the timeline on the board. "Somewhere between them arriving on Wednesday and the early hours of Saturday evening, they acquired a baby," he said.

"Why Saturday morning?" asked Ben, rolling up the sleeves of his shirt.

"Cleaners came in just after eight on Saturday. Family had 'Do Not Disturb' signs up all week, but they must've forgot to put it out on Saturday. Archie chased the cleaner out, sharpish, but not before she saw Donna Sutherland holding the baby," Hamza explained. "She reported it to her supervisor, but the hotel doesn't charge extra for kids that age, so they never followed up on it."

"And they didn't think that was weird? Them producing a wean out of thin air?"

"You've clearly never worked in the hospitality sector," Dave said. "Shite like that happens all the time. I used to work in a hotel, years back, and you got some right oddballs staying. I mind I had to bring a pillow up to some guy in his room one time, and when he came to the door I saw he had a goat in there with him."

"A goat?" said Sinead. "What, in his room?"

"Aye. In his room. A full-grown adult goat. I clocked it right away, and he obviously saw me clocking it, because he says... and I'll never forget this... He says, 'It's nothing weird. We're just friends.'" Dave's grin almost cut his face completely in half. "Nothing weird! They were just friends! *Friends!* Him and a fucking goat!" He laughed, shook his head in disbelief, then pointed to the card on the board. "Babies turning up out of the blue is nothing. That's an average day. I'm not surprised that it didn't flag anything up."

Ben stood before the board, his hands on his hips, and followed the progression of the case so far. "They don't have any idea where the family was heading next?" he asked.

"They asked at reception for a bus timetable to Skye," Sinead revealed. "Dave volunteered to phone around, and we're pretty sure they went on the eight-forty-five bus, arriving in Portree just after noon."

"You checked with hotels on Skye?"

"We've gone through most of them between us, sir," Sinead said. "But haven't got a hit yet. Lot of Airbnbs and self-catering accommodation up that way, though, which could make it more difficult."

"Are we getting anywhere accessing the phones yet?" Ben asked.

"Not so far, sir, no. Nothing back from the tech team, anyway," Hamza said. "I can double-check, but they're usually pretty good at keeping us posted."

"Have we tried tracking movements via the network?"

"Got a request in, but it's slow-going. I think we're going to need to get a warrant this time."

"Signal's a nightmare on Skye, too," Sinead said. "It's mostly blackspots. There's no saying we'll get anything useful, even if they do give us the details."

"Fair point, aye," Ben agreed. He indicated a couple of blank cards to the right of the timeline. "And this is *our* blackspot. We know they left Inverness on Sunday morning and arrived on Skye Sunday afternoon." He jumped the blank cards and went to the next one marked with Sinead's careful handwriting. "We know they got the ferry on Monday—eight days later—then the train down here, and a taxi out to the house in Glen Coe. A few days later, they're all dead." He rapped his knuckles on one of the gaps in the timeline. "This middle bit's bothering me, though. Why were they on Skye with a big bag of money and a mystery baby?"

"No idea about why they were there, or about the money, sir," Sinead said. "But we might have something on the baby."

Ben wheeled around so quickly he had to lean on the desk to stop his head spinning. "You do? How? What have we got?"

It was Hamza who answered. "Pete Hill, the taxi driver who took them out to the house, he reckoned the baby couldn't be more than a couple of weeks old."

"Which would fit in with the timeline of Archie getting his hands on it," Sinead continued. "If it was two weeks old when they were in Fort William, and the cleaner saw them with it nine days earlier..."

"It would've been practically a newborn," Ben concluded. "Shite. Have you—?"

"Already spoken to the maternity unit at Raigmore, sir," Sinead confirmed. "We've got the details of all the women who gave birth there that week." She stepped past him and pinned a list to the board. Quite a long list, he noted. "All forty-seven of them."

"Forty-seven? Christ, was there a power cut nine months ago, or something?" Ben asked. He rolled his head around on his shoulders, stretching out the stiffness in his neck, then he fished his wallet from his jacket pocket. "Right, who's on the phones, and who's going out to J.J.'s to get the bacon rolls?"

IT HAD BEEN a long time since Logan had last sat across a table from Shuggie Cowan. It was not an experience he had missed.

A lot had changed between those days and now, of course. Both men were older for one thing. Maybe wiser, although they'd have to wait for time to tell.

Age had delivered Cowan the kicking that Logan himself had longed to give the bastard so many times over the years. He had not taken well to his later years. He'd been a boxer in his prime. A heavyweight, with emphasis on the first part. There had been very few men in Glasgow willing to stand toe to toe with him either in the ring or out of it, and fewer still willing—or indeed able—to try twice.

A couple of decades of high time and good living had softened him physically, though, so the bulk of his muscles was now simply bulk and nothing more. He was still a man who could do you a lot of damage, Logan reckoned, but mostly by falling on you, and there was no saying he'd be able to get back up without the help of a trained first-aider.

And, of course, he was still a man who could do you a lot of damage via his close network of younger, fitter, stronger bastards. Loyal men without an off-switch.

Some things never changed.

He'd protested Tyler being taken away initially. Then, when it was clear that they would be taking him regardless, he'd switched to assuring the DC that everything was going to be OK. And it was. Definitely. Nothing to worry about.

He hoped.

"Nice scar you've got yourself there, Shuggie," Logan said. He sat across the table from the older man, after it was made clear that, one way or another, he wasn't going to be allowed to remain standing. "Never pegged you as being in with the neo-nazis. Always had you down as a bastard of the free-range variety."

One of Cowan's fingertips brushed lightly across the scar. One of his eyebrows gave a twitch. "Not through choice. Got you to thank for it, in fact."

"How do you figure that one out?"

"Got it last time I was in the nick. The time a certain someone not a million miles away from where I'm sitting played a hand in putting me there."

"That's terrible, Shuggie. Really sorry to hear that," Logan said, although the way he said it suggested otherwise. "You can probably get some compo for that. Maybe try one of those 'no win, no fee' places? '*Have you been branded by a Nazi while in the jail? Call us now.*' These ambulance chasers are a dime a dozen nowadays."

"You haven't lost your sense of humour, I see," Cowan said, sounding like a man who'd had his own surgically removed. "Everything was quickly dealt with, thank you for asking."

Logan regarded the scar. It looked deep and would've been painful. He almost felt sorry for the idiot who'd done it.

"Aye, I can imagine," he said, then he looked at the pub around them.

The other punters had been ushered out, leaving just Logan, Cowan, and the man behind the bar. He was a big fella, and looked more than capable of handling himself in a scrap. You had to be in a place like this, which wasn't so much a *dive* as an *already fully submerged*.

But the barman was just that, Logan thought. A barman. Not a bodyguard. He was standing behind the bar, still flicking through his newspaper, paying the other two men no heed whatsoever. If Logan had made a grab for Cowan, there was no way he could get to them in time to intervene.

"Getting awfully trusting in your old age, Shuggie," the DCI said. "Was a time you wouldn't even contemplate sitting down with me without a couple of heavies on standby."

"Aye," Cowan admitted. "Was a time. But times change, Jack. We're all on our own evolutionary journeys. Like... butterflies."

Logan raised an eyebrow. "Butterflies?"

"Well, some of us are butterflies. Some of us are moths. The principle's the same, though," Cowan said. "The only thing constant in life is change. The only thing set in stone is that nothing is set in stone."

"Jesus. Where'd you pick that up? Tibet?"

"The Big Hoose. You meet some enlightened characters while being detained at Her Majesty's pleasure. Plenty not so enlightened too, of course, but there are an odd few nuggets of gold among the shite."

"So, you're a changed man then, are you?"

Cowan held his hands out as if presenting himself as evidence, like the detective just had to look at him to see the answer to that question for himself.

Logan wasn't buying it. Shuggie might have mellowed a bit with age, but this was not a man who would ever slip quietly into his twilight years. He'd earned a fearsome reputation as a teenager while clawing his way free of a broken home, junkie parents, and a speech impediment that had earned him the nickname 'BaBam.' This—the word 'Bam' with a suggestion of a stutter at the start—was what had passed for clever wordplay among some of Glasgow's finest hardmen and headcases at the time.

The name didn't stick for long. It turned out that Shuggie was sensitive about his stammer, and reacted swiftly and violently should he suspect anyone of taking the piss out of him for it.

Within a year of its first use, nobody called Shuggie 'BaBam.' Instead, they mostly addressed him as 'Mr Cowan,' or 'Sir,' or 'Please, no' the face!'

The man had a list of charges that would fill a phone book. Only two had ever led to convictions, and he'd been in and out of the jail in less than six months each time. He knew people. And, to those people he didn't know, he was good at making it clear that he could get to know things about them quickly, like how many kids they had, and where they went to school.

There was a myth about old Glasgow gangsters. Old gangsters the world over, in fact. It went something like this:

They were a different sort, back then. Treated people with respect. Never harmed the old folks or the weans, only people who were asking for it. The streets were safer with them around, if anything. Kept the scallywags away.

There was a nugget of truth in it somewhere, but it was predominantly a load of old shite. Just because crime was organised didn't mean it wasn't crime. When drugs started flooding into cities, crime rates went up. More grannies got mugged, more houses got burgled, more shops got turned over. Funnily enough, firing a load of smack into the veins of a city like Glasgow didn't turn it into some crime-free Utopia. Far bloody from it.

"You're looking old, Jack," said Cowan. "I thought all that mountain air was meant to do you good?"

"It was that lunch I just ate. Aged me ten years," Logan retorted.

"I'll be sure to pass your compliments to the microwave."

Logan sniffed. "You've been keeping track, then?"

"Of course. I'm retired, Jack, I'm not dead. Not yet. You've been keeping busy up there," Cowan said. "Dealt with Petrie properly, I hear. Long overdue, if you ask me. I did offer to have that little problem taken care of for you way back when. Seems like it could've saved you a lot of trouble."

"Aye, well. I'm no' here to talk about Owen Petrie," Logan said.

"Then to what do I owe the displeasure?"

"Your name came up," the detective told him.

"I'm assuming you don't mean in casual conversation?"

"In connection to a case."

Cowan gave a whistle, drawing the attention of the barman. "What are you drinking, Jack? You still on the hard stuff?"

"No."

"Pint, then?"

"I'm fine."

Cowan looked him up and down. For the first time since Logan had sat down, there was a hint of a smile on the older man's face. "Butterflies. Eh, Jack? How things change." He raised his voice to the man behind the bar. "Couple of coffees, Tam."

"Right you are, Mr Cowan," the barman replied, then he found a couple of reasonably clean-looking mugs, and set to work.

"You do drink coffee, yes?" Cowan asked, turning back to the DCI. "Not eliminated all vices, have we?"

"Coffee's grand," Logan said, then a thump from upstairs drew his eyes to the yellowing ceiling.

"Relax, Jack," the older man said. "No harm's going to come to anyone, if everyone just keeps the heid."

There was a sound like two hard things hitting sharply together, then a derisory cheer from a voice that wasn't Tyler's.

Right then, the barman set two mugs and a cracked cafetière of coffee down on the table between them.

"Besides," Cowan said, reaching for a mug. "Sounds to me as if they're all getting along like a house on fire."

A FEW MINUTES prior to the *thump* and the *clack* and the spontaneous cheering, Tyler shuffled past a foul-smelling bathroom with his breath held, then was guided with a shove into what he guessed was a large room.

He couldn't say why he guessed that, exactly. The windows were heavily shuttered and there was no light except the dim glow seeping in from the stairwell, so he couldn't see more than a foot or two in front of him.

But something about the air in the place, maybe, or the sound of their footsteps told him it was one big upstairs space that stretched all the way from the front of the pub to the back.

He was 'encouraged' forwards. Something large loomed in the shadows ahead of him, but he only got a suggestion of a shape before the door closed behind his three chaperones, and the room was dragged deep down into the dark.

"Right then, polisman," a voice growled behind him, and Tyler's heart began trying to climb its way up out of his throat. "We're all going to play a little game."

CHAPTER TWENTY-NINE

LOGAN STIRRED HIS COFFEE, waiting for the answer to his question. In truth, Cowan's eyes had already answered it for him—he was good at keeping his expression measured, but the eyes gave him away—but Logan wanted to hear if the rest of him said the same thing.

"Aye. Of course the name means something to me. Show me someone our age from this part of the world who says they haven't heard of Archie Tatties and I'll show you a liar," the old man said.

Logan stirred. Watched. Waited.

"And, in recent years, prior to my retirement, he and I were in business together."

The spoon stopped swirling around in the cup. Logan tapped it twice on the rim, then set it down on the metal tray with a *clank*.

"Aye, I'd heard that might be the case," he said. "What sort of business were you in, if you don't mind me asking?"

Across the table, Cowan tore open a sachet of brown sugar and poured it into his coffee. "I'm sure you're well aware, Jack."

"Humour me."

"As you wish," Cowan said, shaking the last few grains from the sachet. He reached for another and repeated the process. "We were in the adult entertainment industry."

"You mean the porn business?"

Cowan appeared genuinely offended by the comment. "No,

Jack. The adult entertainment industry. We weren't just tits and shagging like all these internet bastards. We told stories."

"Aye, but... stories about tits and shagging, though?"

"The shagging was secondary. On our stuff, the plot was king. We didn't make pornos, Jack, we made fucking *magic*."

"With heavy emphasis on the first part of that phrase, I'd imagine," Logan said.

Cowan scowled, but then bit down on his lip, physically stopping himself from sniping back. Clearly, the remarks had touched a nerve and threatened some sort of artistic illusion the old man had built around himself.

"So, he's dead, is he?" Cowan asked, changing the subject. "I mean, I'm assuming that's why you're here?"

"That's some assumption to make, Shuggie."

"Not really. You're still MIT, aren't you? If his kids had been kidnapped he'd have already been on the phone to me about it."

"Asking if you'd taken them?" Logan guessed.

Cowan exhaled sharply through both nostrils, like a bull contemplating a charge. "Asking for money to pay the ransom, more like. Archie was a funny guy, and an artist in many respects, but he had fuck all knack when it came to managing a budget." He opened another pack of sugar—the fourth now, Logan thought—and dumped it into his mug. "What happened?"

"He was stabbed. Wife and kids, too."

"What? Jesus. Not Donna and the girls?" Cowan asked. He sounded shocked, but it was hard to tell quite how genuine the reaction was. "Are they...?"

"Afraid so, aye," Logan confirmed. "Someone tied them all up and killed them, one by one. What sort of twisted bastard would do something like that, do you think?"

"I take it this was the part where my name came up?" Shuggie guessed. "I can assure you, Jack, I had nothing to do with any of that. Archie was a business partner, but he was also a friend. We made good money for each other over the years. It was a good thing we had going. Even if it hadn't been, as for thinking I'd hurt his wife and kids. That's not my style, Jack."

He took a sip of his coffee, grimaced at the taste, then picked up another couple of sugar sachets and began tipping them into the mug.

"Oh, I don't know if I'd say that, Shuggie," Logan said. "I'm sure you've threatened to do damage to many's a wean over the years."

"Threatened, aye. Done? No. Cowards and animals go after weans, Jack. I don't consider myself to be either."

Logan brought his coffee to his mouth, caught the smell of it, then sat the cup back on the table without comment.

"He had a big bag of money with him," he revealed, watching carefully to see what the response would be.

"Money? What, cash, you mean? How much?"

"We don't know. Whoever killed them took it."

Cowan frowned. "Then how do you know...?"

"Taxi driver and train ticket collector both saw it," Logan said. "We've also got a photo of Archie with the bag. Blue holdall. Mean anything to you?"

Cowan shook his head. It was too definite a movement, Logan thought, too sure of itself. "No. Not a thing, I'm afraid."

"He didn't... Oh, I don't know, let's just say, for example, steal that money off you and promptly fuck off with it, then?"

"Ah. So, that's where we're at, is it?" Cowan asked. "You think I had him done in."

"Did you?"

Cowan idly tapped a fingernail on the table, contemplating his response.

"It's no' a difficult question, Shuggie," Logan prompted.

"Tam?"

Over by the bar, Tam raised his head from his newspaper. "Aye?

"Gonnae fuck off for five minutes?" Cowan said. "Take a walk around the block or something."

Tam folded the newspaper closed and tucked it in at the side of the coffee machine without saying a word. Neither of the men at the table took their eyes off each other as the barman took his jacket from a peg, pulled it on, and headed outside via the pub's back door.

Cowan waited for the door to thud closed before speaking again. "You mind if I smoke, Jack?"

Logan indicated that he didn't care with a shrug and a shake of his head.

"You're not going to grass me up, are you? Bloody smoking ban. Meddling, that's what it is. Nothing but meddling."

He took out a packet of cigarettes, flipped open the top, and offered them across the table.

"No, thanks."

"Quit that, too, did you?" said Cowan, raising both eyebrows. "You're a man of some willpower, Jack."

"Sometimes."

Cowan lit a cigarette with a battered old *Zippo* lighter, drew in a lungful of smoke, then let his head flop back while he took a moment to enjoy it. He exhaled upwards, then spent a few seconds watching the undulating patterns of the smoke.

"Meddling bastards are killing this industry. I mean, look at me. Normally, I can't even have a fag in my own fucking pub!" Cowan said. He chuckled. "Mind you, I said that to an American fella last week, and he was *very* confused. Over there, 'fag' means—"

"Did you kill Archie?" Logan asked, cleaving a line through the bullshit.

"Why would I?"

"You're not answering my question, Shuggie."

Across the table, Cowan smirked, then took another draw of his cigarette. "No. I suppose I'm not, at that," he admitted. "Fine. You want answers? Fine. No. I didn't kill Archie. I had no reason to kill Archie. I *liked* Archie. Like I told you, he and I did very well out of our business association, and he was a funny guy. Aye, not like when he was on the telly, *actually* funny. Sharp sense of humour."

He took a gulp of coffee and another lungful of smoke before carrying on.

"Do you know he was offered a show? A one-off special for Hogmanay this year. On the BBC this time, too, not STV. Neeps and Tatties were meant to be ringing in the New Year. He was hoping it might lead to a series." The older man shrugged. "I thought their stuff might be a bit... broad for modern audiences, but, 'Look at *Mrs Brown's Boys*,' he said. 'People love that shite.' And he had a point. They do. For some reason."

Logan frowned. "He was going back on the telly?"

"Forty-five-minute special, aye," Cowan confirmed.

"Did Billy Neeps know?"

"I should fucking hope so, aye. They both signed on for it."

"He didn't mention it," Logan remarked. "Don't suppose you know who Archie was talking to at the BBC?"

Cowan snorted. "I was his business partner, Jack, not his agent. So, no. I've got no idea. Billy'll know, though, I'm sure."

Logan nodded, then took a sip of his coffee and waited. Shuggie hadn't sent the barman away for no reason. There was information coming. Something Cowan couldn't risk getting out into the public domain.

"The fact of the matter is, Jack," Cowan began, and from the way he side-eyed the front door, Logan knew that this was it. "I haven't worked with Archie in a year or more now. I... offloaded my business interests. All of them, apart from this place, and a couple of bookies. I'm too old to be throwing my weight around these days, and the adult entertainment market has... well, it's changed. And not for the better."

"You sold your share of the business?" Logan asked. "To who?"

"My nephew."

"Nephew?" Logan's brow furrowed as he mentally ran through what he knew of Cowan's family tree. Shuggie didn't have kids of his own, but there was a sister, right enough. Maybe two. Neither one had ever been in any bother, though, as far as Logan could remember.

"Frankie. His name's Frankie. He's... ambitious. Full of big ideas."

"Let me guess, Shuggie. 'He's a good kid, just misguided.' Is that what you're going to tell me?"

Cowan took another draw on his cigarette. Logan couldn't help but notice the shake as he raised it to his mouth.

"Christ, no. Frankie is... I don't want to say one-of-a-kind, because he isn't. He's a dime a bloody dozen. Wee guy with an attitude problem and a temper on a hair-trigger. Sure you've seen plenty of them in your time."

He had. Of course, he had. Far too many of the gobby little bastards.

"Except with Frankie, there's no off switch," Cowan continued. "He's always been the same. Got expelled from God knows how many schools for fighting. And when I say 'fighting,' I mean life-changing injuries type of fighting."

"How come I've never heard of him?" Logan asked. "If he's such a bad bastard, why has he never come up before now?"

"He's young. And he's smarter than he looks. After he eventually got kicked out of school, I got him a job. Aye, perfectly legitimate, working in a corner shop I had. I kept an eye on him, which kept his maw happy, and everything was golden. For a while, anyway."

Cowan sat back nursing his coffee, the smoke from his cigarette encircling his head like a halo. "He was... what? Sixteen? Seventeen, maybe? Something like that. Anyway, about a week after he starts, I start getting complaints."

"From customers?" Logan asked.

The other man shook his head. "From some of the other lads I had working for me. Big lads. Serious. Not your average shop staff, shall we say?"

"What were they saying?"

"That he made them uneasy," Cowan replied. "Can you imagine? Skinny wee teenager, and he's making these big bastards nervous. And these were not lads who spooked easily. Far from it. But, to his credit, he kept the head screwed on straight, and did his job. Kept asking to get involved in my... other interests, but I kept him out of it. His maw, my sister, she'd have done her nut if he'd got messed up in anything *less than legal*. I'd have never heard the end of it."

Cowan looked around for an ashtray, remembered that he wasn't going to find one, and stubbed the cigarette out on the table-top. He lit a second before continuing.

"Then, she goes and fucks off with some new fella she met in Spain. He's twenty years younger than her. More. Right slimy bastard, he was, but she thinks it's love and moves over there. Six months later, boat accident kills them both."

"I'm sorry to hear that," Logan said. "How did your nephew take it?"

"He, eh... he saw it," Shuggie replied, choosing his words with care. "He was there with them on the boat. When it happened. He'd gone over to visit for a few days. He hadn't been keen, but we'd talked him into it. Be nice to get a bit of sunshine, see his maw." Cowan waved a hand, and a zig-zag of smoke followed it. "They found him clinging to the upturned boat. The... hull, is it? Found him there, brought him in. The other two...they were never found."

"You think Frankie did it," Logan said. It was a statement, not a question.

Shuggie regarded him across the table, and his eyes said something very different to the words that came out of his mouth.

"I wouldn't know. But, I do know that things changed after that. Once he got back. He started pushing more and more to get involved with the business—the bigger business, I mean, not the shop. Eventually, God help me, I agreed."

"And now he's running the show?" Logan asked.

"Not all of it, no. He took over my share of the production company, but I'd already shut most of my other interests down."

Logan laughed drily. "Sure you did, Shuggie."

"I don't really give two shites if you believe me, Jack," Cowan bit back. "I'm trying to help you out here. Frankie took over the por —the *adult entertainment* stuff, and that was meant to be that. He's a lad with big ideas, like I say, but anything he does beyond that didn't come from me. That's all him."

There was something buried in the lines of Shuggie's face. Logan had sat across tables from the man dozens of times before, in pubs like these and in polis stations, and he'd never seen what he was seeing now.

Fear.

"You're scared of him, too. Aren't you?"

"Am I fuck," Cowan spat back. He *harrumphed* a bit and shifted around on his chair. "I'm... troubled by him. He's... I don't know what he is. I've done some things in my time, Jack—Christ, you know that more than most—and I built up quite the reputation, but Frankie?" He shook his head. "Frankie's something else."

"And how did Archie take it?" Logan asked. "Having to work with this... something else?"

Across the table, Cowan shifted uncomfortably on his rickety chair. "Aye, well," he said, shooting another look at the door to make sure it was still closed. "Not great. They didn't exactly hit it off right away. See, Archie... Archie's a gentleman. The girls—the actresses, I mean—he sees them right. You get a lot of lecherous bastards in the adult entertainment business. Folks who think they've got a right to *sample the talent*, if you know what I mean?"

"Well, it's no' exactly a cryptic metaphor, Shuggie. I can imagine that sort of thing probably goes on a lot, aye."

"Aye, well Archie wasn't like that. Not one bit. Archie was like a father to some of those girls. And I know how that sounds, before you start—what sort of father films his daughter getting pumped on all fours?—but I mean it. He looked out for them, treated them fair and square. He cared about them. Cared *for* them. It's an exploitative business by its very nature, but Archie made sure none of our girls ever felt they were being taken advantage of. They had a problem, they came to him, and either he sorted it, or—depending on the nature of said problem—I had it dealt with. Those girls... Those *young women* were like family."

Logan could see where this was going. "I take it Frankie doesn't share that level of consideration?"

"You can say that again," Cowan muttered. "He and Archie clashed heads from the start. And if there's one man you don't clash heads with, it's Frankie. Not if you want to hang onto it, anyway."

"Sounds like he and I should have a word," Logan reasoned. "Where will I find him?"

Cowan laughed. "I'm not telling you that. In fact, I didn't tell you any of this."

Logan blinked, barely able to believe what he was hearing. "You are, aren't you? Shuggie Cowan's actually afraid of someone."

Across the table, Shuggie's smile was a thin, joyless thing. "Let's just say, I don't need the drama," he replied. "I'm sure your old colleagues in Dalmarnock will be able to point you in the right direction. Even that useless shower's bound to have noticed him by now."

"I wouldn't count on it," Logan remarked. "But I'll check." He glanced at his watch, then up to the ceiling. It had all gone very quiet up there now. Worryingly so.

"Don't let me keep you, Jack," Cowan said. "Lovely as it's been to catch up, I'm more than happy for you to get up and go, anytime you like."

"Far be it from me to outstay my welcome, Shuggie," Logan said, but he made no move to go anywhere yet. "I'm going to need one more thing from you, though."

Cowan let out a single, "Ha!" at that. "Are you indeed?" he asked. "And what might that be, exactly?"

"I'll need details of the women who've appeared in your films."

"No. Absolutely not," Cowan said. "I won't compromise their privacy."

It was Logan's turn to laugh, although his managed to be even more brief than Shuggie's. "You weren't worried about compromising their privacy when you were filming them getting pumped by some big lad from Cowdenbeath."

Cowan frowned. "We don't have anyone working with us from Cowdenbeath."

"Or wherever the fuck they're from," Logan said. "I just meant your privacy concerns soon go out the window when there's money to be made."

Cowan stabbed a finger onto the tabletop. "They use fake names. We never shared any identifying details, unless they instructed us to in writing, and only then with a witness present. Archie protected our girls. We both did."

Logan leaned forward in his chair. "Aye, see, that's what's got me thinking, Shuggie. That's what's got the old noggin ticking away. Archie looking out for those women. That's got me wondering."

Cowan took another draw on his cigarette and peered at Logan through the haze of smoke. "About what?"

"Archie and his family, they weren't just lugging a big bag of money around with them," Logan said, paying close attention to the older man's reaction. "They had something else with them, too..."

CHAPTER THIRTY

LOGAN OPENED the door at the top of the stairs to find Tyler bent awkwardly over a table, as a man with a big stick stood glowering behind him.

There was a jerk of an arm, a *thack* of balls smashing together, and then a cheer of glee as the black ball bounced once in the jaws of the pocket, then flopped down into the workings of the pool table.

"Yes!" Tyler cried, raising his cue triumphantly above his head like some sort of wizard's staff.

The man with the other cue cleared his throat, drawing Tyler's attention to the white ball. It was lazily rolling back along the table, trundling closer and closer to the pocket closest to where he stood.

"Don't you dare," Tyler groaned, his gaze creeping along after the ball.

There was a *thunk* as it tumbled into the pocket. Tyler's arms, which had remained raised, fell to his sides. A hand large enough to crush his head patted him on the shoulder.

"Better luck next time, wee man," his opponent told him. "Good game, but hard luck at the end there."

Another of the men pointed to where Logan stood in the doorway. "Looks like your dad's here to pick you up."

"Eh? Oh! Alright, boss?" Tyler called over. He took a sip from a can of *Irn Bru*. The proper stuff, too, none of your knock-offs up here. "That us ready to go, is it?"

Logan hadn't quite known what to expect when he'd come up the stairs to collect the DC. It was safe to say, though, that it had not been this.

"Aye. That's us," he confirmed. "You, eh... You alright?"

"Grand, boss. We've just been playing pool," Tyler said, indicating the table like he thought Logan might not have noticed it. "There's another bar up here, too. They gave me free juice!"

"Don't forget your crisps," one of the men said, tossing Tyler a bag of *Quavers*.

Tyler caught it, then gave a thumbs-up. "Nice one. Cheers, Marty!" he said. "I'm starving after that horrible bloody Chicken Kiev."

The atmosphere in the room changed in an instant. For a moment, the only sound was the creaking of a floorboard beneath Tyler's feet, then Marty, the man who had thrown the crisps, emerged from behind the bar.

"What?" he asked.

"The Chicken Kiev I had for lunch," Tyler said, oblivious to the change in tone. "Or that I *didn't* have for lunch, I mean! It was completely inedible."

"I made that," Marty said. He stood there, looming. Not over Tyler, specifically, just doing a general sort of loom that made what had, until then, been quite a large room seem significantly smaller. "I do the cooking at lunch."

Tyler swallowed. A number of times, in fact. "Did you?" he asked, but the words came out embarrassingly high, so he cleared his throat and tried again, this time too low, if anything. "Did you?"

Marty was just drawing himself up to his full terrifying height when the first crack in his act appeared, and a smirk proved impossible to hold back. "Nah, no' really," he said. "And you're right, it's shite. We don't touch any of it."

"Oh, thank God," Tyler wheezed.

"Got you there though, eh?" Marty laughed. "You were shiteing yourself."

Tyler tried to dismiss this suggestion while not outright contradicting it, in case this led to them kicking the living shit out of him.

They'd been surprisingly nice lads so far, but he didn't want to push his luck.

"Don't forget your jacket," said another of the men, indicating where Tyler had draped it across a table before they'd started playing pool.

"Oh, aye. Nearly forgot that there!" Tyler said. He picked the jacket up, performed a complex juggling act as he pulled it on while still clutching his *Quavers*, then waved enthusiastically to the other men. "Thanks again, lads. I had a great time."

"Cheers, Tyler."

"Awrabest, wee man."

"Catch you later, eh?"

Logan held the door open as the DC trotted through, beaming from ear to ear. He shot a series of suspicious looks at the shower of scary-looking bastards clustered around the pool table, then let the door swing closed between them.

"I'll be honest, boss, I was a bit worried when they took me up here," Tyler said, leading the way down the stairs. "But they're a great bunch of lads. Cheating bastards at pool, like, but nice enough."

"Aye, well, I'm glad you had a good time," Logan said, feeling very much like he should be carrying a party bag with a slice of birthday cake in it.

"You'd have been proud of me, though, boss. I think I might've managed to get some info out of them, too," Tyler added, with a tap to the side of his nose. "But subtly, I mean. Proper James Bond stuff."

"This should be good," Logan muttered, mostly to himself. Then, raising his voice, "What did you find out?"

They reached the bottom of the stairs. Tyler glanced at the double swing doors that led into the bar proper, and then to his left, to where the outer doors were currently bolted shut.

"Brace yourself, boss. This'll blow things wide open," Tyler whispered. "It turns out that Archie had a new partner in the porn business. A right bad bastard he is, too."

Logan raised his eyebrows and shoved his hands into the pockets of his coat. "Well now," he said, rocking back on his heels. "Is that a fact?"

SINEAD HAD JUST HUNG up her desk phone when her mobile rang. She snatched it up from her desk, swiped quickly on the green icon below the picture of Tyler, and spun her chair so she was facing away from the others.

"Ty? Where are you? Are you OK?"

"I'm fine," Tyler told her. "I'm, eh... The boss is making me get the train up the road in a bit. We... had that chat that I've been putting off."

Sinead relaxed into her chair. Later, she'd swear she actually felt some of the weight leaving her shoulders. "Good. That's... great. How did he take it?"

"Better than expected. He was pretty good about it, actually."

"What did you expect? A bollocking?" Sinead asked, then she winced. "Sorry, bad choice of words. Was he shocked? When you told him?"

There was a pause from the other end of the line. "I'm not sure 'shocked' is the right word," Tyler said. "But, anyway, I'm supposed to get in after ten. The boss says we're to head up the road, but I thought maybe we should hang on until the—"

"We're heading up the road," Sinead told him. "We can have the day at home tomorrow, then..." She caught the puzzled look from Hamza who, like Ben and Dave, was currently engaged in conversation with someone on his own phone. That didn't, apparently, stop him overhearing Sinead's. "...we can talk about it later."

"Aye, we'll figure it out," Tyler said.

"Right. Good. And... you're OK?"

"I'm fine," Tyler assured her. "Feel a bit guilty leaving him down here on his own, though. But, I'm actually phoning with a bit of news."

Sinead reached for her notepad. "Go on."

"We got a list of names of the women who appeared in Archie's porn films."

Logan's voice came muffled from somewhere in the background. "The hell's this 'we?' You buggered about playing pool."

"Naw, it was definitely a collective effort, boss," Tyler insisted, and Sinead smiled. His voice was lighter. More relaxed. More Tyler.

There was a rustling and a thumping from the other end of the line. "Here, give me the phone," Logan said. "You sit there and eat your *Quavers*. Hello?"

"Hello, sir," Sinead said.

"How you doing?" Logan asked, and Sinead knew that it wasn't being asked out of politeness. DCI Jack Logan was many things, but 'polite' was rarely one of them.

"I'm... OK, sir. Thanks. You?"

"My head's spinning with this gobshite, but otherwise grand, aye. I'm sending him up on the next train. I'm assuming you're OK to deal with everything from there?"

"I am."

"Good. I'll phone Mitchell, fill her in. You can talk to Ben yourself, explain why you're heading up the road, or I can do it. Up to you."

Sinead looked across to where DI Forde sat with his phone to his ear, one finger stabbing away at the numbers on the keypad. "I can tell him."

"Right. OK. You do that, then. And if there's anything you two need..."

"I know, sir," Sinead said. "You don't need to say it."

Logan grunted. "Good. I should hope not," he said, then his tone changed as he became all business. "Right, you ready for this list?"

Sinead clicked the top of her pen, extending the nib. "Ready when you are, sir," she said, and Logan began to reel off a list of Archie's 'starlets.'

He was spelling out the fourth one when Sinead stopped him. "Hang on, hang on," she said, her pen stopping halfway through the first name. "Jazmin? Not McAllister, is it?"

Somewhere between Glasgow and Fort William, a beat was skipped. "Aye. How'd you know that?" Logan asked.

"I think... I think that's her. I think this is it, sir!"

"What do you mean?" Logan asked.

"Jazmin McAllister's on our other list."

"What other list?"

Sinead spun in her chair to face the printout on her desk. It was her share of the call-sheet they'd divided up between them.

"It can't be a coincidence," she muttered. "No way. That's got to be connected."

"Sinead!" Logan snapped. "What the hell are you banging on about? What other list?"

The DC picked up the printout and scanned it until she found what she was looking for. There, second from the bottom, was the name that Logan had just given her.

Jazmin McAllister.

"The list we got from Raigmore. From the Maternity Unit," Sinead explained into the phone. "Jazmin McAllister's on it, sir," she continued, her excitement at the find rising. "Jazmin McAllister had a baby two weeks ago!"

LOGAN'S BMW sat in the taxi rank by the door of Queen Street Station, much to the annoyance of the drivers of the actual taxis vying for space.

There had been some honking of horns when he'd pulled in, and a couple of the bolder drivers had come over to challenge him. A quick flash of the warrant card and one of his less palatable looks, however, had soon sent them back to their cabs.

They were still visibly seething, though, some of their glares so intense Logan was convinced they'd be putting dings in the Beamer's paintwork.

"Right, you fit?" Logan asked, as Tyler scrunched up his empty crisp bag. "Train's in ten minutes. You need to go and get a ticket."

"Or... how about this, boss?" Tyler began, summoning the smile he generally reserved for trying to charm old ladies into making statements.

"No," Logan said, shutting him down. "You're getting on that train and going home."

"Aye, but listen, boss. I was thinking," Tyler said, pressing on regardless. "What if I just stayed tonight, and got the early train tomorrow? I could be in the Fort by lunchtime."

"Or you could be there in four hours," Logan said. He unclipped Tyler's seatbelt for him. "Come on, fuck off."

"I don't like the thought of you going to talk to this Frankie guy on your own," Tyler said. "You should have someone with you, in case things get out of hand."

"And you think you're going to be of help in that situation, do you?" Logan asked.

"Maybe. Aye! I mean, better than you being on your own," Tyler insisted.

"You know they've got polis in Glasgow, aye?" replied the DCI. "You know it's no' just you and me?"

There was a knock at the window. An irate taxi driver—presumably a recent arrival—demanded to know what the hell they thought they were playing at, until Logan held up his warrant card and indicated with a jab of a thumb that he should return to his car.

When Logan turned back, the smile had gone from Tyler's face, his attempt at charm having fallen on deaf ears.

"Look, son, it's best all round if you—"

"I'm scared, boss," Tyler said. He needn't have bothered saying the words. It was all there in his eyes.

Logan sighed. "Aye. I'll bet. But you'll be fine, Tyler."

He nodded. It wasn't a nod of agreement, though, more like he was trying to convince himself. "I know, boss. I just..."

He looked past Logan to the station entrance, where a *Big Issue* seller was stamping his feet to keep warm, and cracking jokes that were roundly ignored by the stony-faced passersby.

"I need to feel like I'm doing something. Like... if I stop for too long and think about it, I panic. I think *what if it's worse?* You know? What if they start the op, and they find out it's spread to the other one, and they have to take that too? Or that it's spread further, and there's nothing else they can do for me?"

"I think you're getting a bit carried away, son."

"I know! I am!" Tyler chirped. "That's my whole point, boss. It's stupid. But it's just what happens when I get to thinking about it. I can't help it. Why do you think I came back to work on my bloody honeymoon? Sitting around was doing my head in."

"That's a normal response," Logan said.

He spotted a taxi driver getting out of his cab and storming towards the Beamer, so he clicked the button that activated the concealed flashing blue lights. The driver pulled a perfect U-turn and got right back into his car.

"But my point is, boss, being here... Working on something. It helps. It's like... I can't panic when I'm focusing on the case."

Logan grunted. "Since when did you ever focus on a bloody case?"

"But, you know what I mean, though. Right?" Tyler pressed. "Like... whatever else is going on, if you throw yourself into the case, you can shut all that other stuff out."

"Look, son, I get it—" Logan began, but Tyler jumped in before he could offer any further platitudes.

"I feel useless, boss," he said, and there was a rawness to the words that made Logan sit still and take notice. Tyler was looking down into the footwell of the car, his voice just a notch or two above a croak. "You want the real reason I don't want to go? I feel useless. Like... I'm this fragile thing, just there to be looked after. Like suddenly I've got this lump on my bollock that means I'm not capable."

"Were you *ever* capable?" Logan asked, then he flinched. "Sorry, force of habit," he said. "You're not useless. Nobody thinks you're incapable, Tyler."

"You do though, boss. You all do," the DC replied. "I'm getting sent away on the train while you go on your own to talk to some headcase who might've murdered four people. Two of them kids. And I'm supposed to... what? Sit there feeling sorry for myself? Admire the scenery? How is that being useful, boss?"

Logan sighed and stared ahead through the windscreen. There were still a couple of hours of daylight left, but it was on the wane, and Glasgow's red sandstone was looking more grimy by the second.

"I'll be home in plenty of time for the surgery, boss. It's two days away. I'll get on the train first thing tomorrow, no objections. Just... let me stick around tonight, eh? Let me be useful."

"Look... I get it," Logan said. "I do. Believe me, when it comes to throwing yourself into your work to the detriment of everything else in your life, you're talking to the bloody master. But it's the wrong choice. Believe me, I speak from experience."

He puffed out his cheeks and went back to staring ahead. When he continued speaking, there was something distant about him, like his mind was somewhere far away.

"You think it's helping. The job. You tell yourself it's important. Because it *is* important," he said. "You think it's good that it's taking your mind off all that other stuff that's going on, whatever that might be. But it's *right* to think about that other stuff. It's normal to worry, and stress, and shite yourself, and everything else you're going through. That's how you deal with it, Tyler, no' by burying your head in the sand. You face your fears, and you deal with them."

Tyler sat in silence for a few moments, contemplating this. He nodded slowly, like the DCI's words were gradually starting to make sense.

"I see what you're saying, boss. Wise words. Definitely something to think about," Tyler said, then he clipped his seatbelt back into place with a *thunk*.

"What are you doing?" Logan asked.

Tyler grinned. "Train left two minutes ago, boss," he announced. "Looks like you're stuck with me."

"What the fu—?" Logan muttered. His eyes went to the clock on the dash, then to his watch, then to DC Neish. "You fly wee bastard!"

"Good chat, though," Tyler said. "I mean it. I think you make some really good points, boss. Really helped." He clicked his fingers, then pointed to the road ahead. "But we should probably get going if we're going to talk to this Frankie fella, don't you think?"

Logan tutted, shook his head, then fired up the engine. "Aye, well, we've got to find the bastard first. And you'd better get on the phone to explain to Sinead why you'll no' be up the road tonight," he instructed.

He pulled out of the rank, and the taxi behind him immediately surged forward to claim the space.

Logan jabbed a warning finger at the younger detective sitting beside him. "And when you tell her, don't you bloody *dare* try and blame it on me."

CHAPTER THIRTY-ONE

THE EXCITEMENT in the Incident Room was palpable. Jazmin McAllister was a breakthrough, everyone was sure of it. One of Archie's porn starlets, and she'd given birth to a baby the same week that Archie magically acquired one out of thin air. That couldn't be coincidental. There was just no way.

They'd tracked down an address for her via the hospital, and then done some digging. She'd bought a house in Drumnadrochit six months back. Lived alone, according to Council Tax records. They hadn't contacted her yet. Better to turn up and talk to her face to face than spook her with a phone call and turn her into a flight risk.

Dave had found her Facebook profile. It was mostly locked down, but they'd been able to get a good headshot from it, and it now took pride of place on the Big Board.

She was pretty, in an elf-like sort of way, all big eyes and freckles. Boyish, almost, with her short bobbed hair. She had a crooked smile that could've made her unattractive, but which somehow had the opposite effect.

And Christ, she looked young. She was twenty-two, according to what they'd been able to dig up, but Ben would be prepared to bet that she'd still be getting jarred for ID in pubs until she was well into her thirties. Personally, he'd have second thoughts about selling her a lottery ticket without a shifty at her passport or driver's licence.

Still, maybe it was an old picture. Maybe she'd looked much older when she'd started her on-screen career.

God, he hoped so.

"Right, so, searching her name on the internet isn't bringing up any reference to her... acting career?" Ben asked, turning away from the lassie's photograph.

"Nothing, sir," Hamza confirmed. "Presumably, she uses a stage name."

"Aye, that makes sense, I suppose," the DI agreed. "You wouldn't want your real name plastered everywhere if you were getting..." He made some vague hand movements, grasping for an appropriate ending to the sentence.

"Plastered everywhere?" Dave put forward as a possible conclusion, which made Ben's face screw up in displeasure.

"Aye. Well. Whatever it is that goes on in these things. I wouldn't know," he said. "I'm assuming you'd want to keep your real name out of it." He turned to Sinead. "Did we hear back from the Health Visitors yet?"

Sinead checked her notes. "Yeah, someone called... Marion called back. They haven't been around to Jazmin's yet. She was on their worksheet for last week, but she fobbed them off. Said she was going to be taking the baby to see her parents." Sinead glanced around at the others to check they were listening, then turned back to Ben. "Ask me where, sir."

"Where?" Ben obliged.

"Skye. Portree."

Ben, who had been sitting propped on the edge of his desk, stood up. "You're not saying...?"

"They run a guest house," Sinead continued.

"Wait, wait," Hamza interjected. "Jazmin's parents own a guest house in Portree? The same place Archie and his family were staying?" He looked from Sinead to Ben and back again. "Well, do we know if Archie stayed with them?"

"Not yet," Sinead admitted. "I only just heard before we sat down for this."

"We need to get onto them, then," Hamza said. "If Archie and Donna took Jazmin's baby to stay with its grandparents, then that means... That means..." His brow furrowed in concentration for a few moments, before he drew a complete blank. "I don't know what that means, but it means something."

"I say we talk to Jazmin herself before we bring the parents into it," Ben said. "Get her side of the story."

"They might all be together," Sinead pointed out. "Jazmin might be on Skye."

Ben checked his watch. The evening was getting on, but there was still a chunk left of it. "Right, we'll get Uniform up in Drumnadrochit to drive past her house and see if the lights are on. If she's home, Sinead, I want you heading up there tonight. She's likely to respond better to you than to the rest of us. Hamza, Dave, we need to follow up on—"

"Eh, I can't tonight, sir."

Ben's sentence stumbled to a stop. "Sorry?"

"I, eh, I can't," Sinead said. "I need to get Tyler off the train."

"I'm sure Tyler's perfectly capable of getting himself off the train," Ben replied. He thought about this for a moment. "Well, maybe no' *perfectly* capable, but I'm sure he'll figure it out."

Sinead nodded. "Aye. Aye, he will, it's just..." She took a breath, suddenly aware that all eyes in the room were on her. "Tyler and I need to take some time off. Tyler, mostly. But I won't be around for a few days, either. Maybe a bit longer."

Ben gave a half-laugh, like he had just heard a joke that he didn't quite understand, but didn't want to look like an idiot. "Time off?" he said. "I thought the honeymoon had been postponed? You came back in."

"Not... it's not for a honeymoon, sir," Sinead said. She ran both hands up the sides of her face and through her hair. "I should wait until Tyler's here. I shouldn't have said anything."

Ben sat on the desk again, bringing him closer to the DC's height. "Sinead, what is it?" he asked. "What's wrong?"

"It's just, eh..."

Ben indicated Logan's office at the back of the room. "Want to discuss this through there?"

Sinead stole a glance at Hamza. His face was a picture of concern. So much so, in fact, that she felt tears welling up behind her eyes, and a shake creeping into her voice.

"It's fine, sir. It's just..." She cleared her throat. Gave herself a mental slap across the face. Shook her metaphorical shoulders. "It's about Tyler," she announced. Composed. Professional. "I'm afraid we recently got a bit of bad news."

DETECTIVE SUPERINTENDENT GORDON MACKENZIE—BETTER known to polis far and wide as 'The Gozer'—looked up from his computer screen and came dangerously close to jumping all the way out of his skin.

"Fuck!" he yelped, and his distress pleased the man standing on the other side of his desk immensely. "Where did you come from, you creepy big bastard?"

"Hell of a welcome that, Gordon," Logan said. "Nice to see you, too."

"That's Detective Superintendent Mackenzie to the likes of you," the Gozer said. He stood, smiled, and shook the hand of the much larger DCI. "What brings you down this way, Jack? You looking for your old job back?"

"No, I'm looking for yours," Logan replied, which drew a derisory snort from the Detective Superintendent.

"Aye, we both know that's not true. You'd be bloody welcome to it, though." He motioned for Logan to take a seat, then lowered himself into his own. "You're looking well. All that fresh air agreeing with you?"

"It has its moments," Logan said.

"Enjoying the peace and quiet up there?"

It was Logan's turn to be amused. "I wouldn't exactly call it that," he said.

"Keeping busy, then?"

"I'm keeping my hand in, aye," Logan confirmed, then they both lapsed into a slightly uncomfortable silence that involved a lot of nodding and smiling from the senior officer.

"So..." he prompted when the awkwardness became too much to bear. "What does bring you down this way? You here for business or pleasure?"

"The first one," Logan said. "I'm investigating a quadruple

homicide."

"Fucking hell. You are keeping your hand in," the Gozer said. "This the telly guy?"

Logan's eyes narrowed a fraction. Not in suspicion so much as annoyance. The Gozer sat back and smiled.

"I'm a man in the know, Jack," he said. "I was talking to Detective Superintendent Mitchell about it earlier this afternoon. She spoke surprisingly highly of you, in case you're interested."

"No' really," Logan said. "Anyway, I picked up a couple of leads down this way. Thought I'd come down and have a chat with them."

The Gozer interlocked his fingers on a stomach that had grown more ample since Logan had last seen him. His hair, too—once a flat top that had earned him his *Ghostbusters* inspired nickname—had continued its inexorable retreat towards the back of his head.

"And you didn't think to keep me in the loop?" he said, adding a couple of disappointed tuts at the end for good measure.

"This is me keeping you in the loop now," Logan replied.

"And...?" the Gozer prompted.

"And I need a bit of local info," Logan admitted.

"Bingo. There we go. Knew you weren't just here out of courtesy," the senior officer crowed. "I can see right through you, Jack. I'm surprised you're asking for my help, though. You always prided yourself on knowing the local scene better than the rest of us. You were fucking insufferable at times, if I recall."

"Aye, well, things change," Logan said. "I've been away a while, and the guy I'm interested in is a relatively new player in town."

"Well, I'm sure a few of your old team members will be able to assist you," the Gozer said. He raised an eyebrow. "Heather, perhaps? I seem to recall you two being quite... friendly."

Logan bristled. "I'd rather not get bogged down by reunions. They don't know I'm here, and I'd prefer to keep it that way. I just want a bit of information, and ideally an address."

The Gozer gave a shrug that seemed to say, 'Your loss,' then he took a pen from a holder on his desk and rested the point on a wedge of sticky notes. "Right, fire away. Who are you looking for?"

"Frankie Cowan."

The pen started scratching, then stopped almost immediately. The Gozer's head snapped up. "Fuck. Shuggie Cowan's nephew?"

"He's on your radar, then?" Logan asked.

"No. I mean, yes. I mean... he's on there, but he's coated in bloody Teflon. Or... I don't know. Whatever they use on stealth bombers. I don't know. What is it? Magic paint?" He shook his head, visibly annoyed with himself. "The point is, we're aware of him, but we can't get a thing to stick. Not a bloody thing. We've come close once or twice, but he's got a lot of people scared, Jack. Too scared to testify. And he knows it, too. He strides about, all puffed up and smug as fuck, convinced we can't lay a finger on him. And the annoying thing is, he's been right so far. We can't."

"I hear he's taken over his uncle's porn empire," Logan said.

"Oh. Right. Has he?" the Gozer said. His eyes narrowed. He shook his head. "Sorry, porn empire?"

Logan nodded. "Aye. The production company Shuggie had with Archie Sutherland."

"The telly man? Your victim? He was in business with Shuggie Cowan? Making... making pornography?"

"For a few years now, it seems, aye."

"The Neeps and Tatties fella?" asked the Gozer, still not quite believing what he was hearing. "'Where's the haggis?' Him?"

Logan sighed. "Aye, Gordon. Jesus, did you not know this? Archie Sutherland off the telly was a player in the *adult entertainment* industry alongside Shuggie Cowan," he said, slowly and clearly so as to avoid having to go over it again. "When Shuggie retired, his nephew took over his half of the business."

"Bloody hell. I had no idea," the Gozer admitted. "We'll look into that. Maybe there's an angle there that'll let us get the bastard."

"Aye, well I'm wanting first crack at him," Logan said.

"You think he might be tied up in your murders?"

"I do," Logan confirmed.

"He won't talk to you," the Gozer warned. "He's a slippery wee bastard. He won't give you anything useful."

"Leave that to me," Logan said. "All I need from you is one thing."

"And what might that be, Jack?"

Logan leaned on the desk. "A pointer to where I might find the bastard."

CHAPTER THIRTY-TWO

FRANKIE COWAN's address was in the Maryhill part of the city, in one of the big high-rise blocks on Wyndford Road.

The area had been home to the British Army's Highland Light Infantry until the 60s, when the base had been replaced by a council housing scheme. You still heard Wyndford being referred to as 'the barracks' from time to time, although less regularly as the years went by, and 'that bloody shitehole,' had long-since been adopted in its place.

There had been no answer at Frankie's flat when Logan had rung up from the outside intercom. He'd picked a few other flats to call, and had tried a variety of techniques to convince them to buzz him in, from identifying himself as polis to pretending to be a neighbour who'd lost their keys, but with no success. Even the usually reliable method of claiming to be from the fire brigade was met with failure, the residents of this particular block having heard it all before.

"What now, boss?" asked Tyler. He was looking up to the top of the high-rise, bent so far back he was starting to resemble a letter C. "Do we hang around and see if he comes back?"

Logan stepped back from the door, then cast his eye over the area immediately around them. Each of the large Wyndford tower blocks had its own car park, as well as a row of run-down garages with different coloured doors, tucked away around the back.

They'd driven past a basketball court and kids play area on the way in. Logan hadn't been able to get a clear look at their faces, but it had been clear that none of the people hanging around there had been children for a very long time.

"Come on, we'll go for a wander and see if we can spot him," he suggested, shoving his hands in his coat pockets and setting off in the direction of the play area.

DC Neish spent a few more seconds staring up at the block of flats, then hurried to catch up. "Imagine living right at the top of that. Eh, boss?"

"Aye," Logan said.

He waited for the inevitable comment about the lift.

"Imagine the lift was out of order."

"Aye, that'd be rough, right enough," Logan agreed.

"I'm sure it's a cracking view from up there. Not my cup of tea, though." Tyler gave a shudder. "You know me and heights, boss. Did I tell you I once fell off a bridge after nearly getting hit by a train?"

Logan made a sound that was halfway to being a laugh. "You may have mentioned it once or twice, aye."

They walked on, falling into step without noticing. Force of habit. Or a habit of being on the force, maybe. That 'synchronised stepping' was one of the first things you learned on the beat. Nobody ever taught you it, or even mentioned it, but most Uniforms picked it up in the first few days, and those that didn't rarely lasted long.

A couple of cars went roaring past, both of them over ten years old, and both blaring something Logan was led to believe was what passed for music these days. Fortunately, the over-revving of their engines, and the occasional backfired *bang* drowned most of the racket out.

"So, is this Frankie guy our main suspect?" Tyler asked once the cars had gone speeding off again.

"I don't know if I'd call him that, exactly," Logan said. "If Archie stole money from him, then he'd have a motive, aye. But motive isn't everything."

"How would he find him?" Tyler wondered. "I mean, they were pretty much out in the middle of nowhere."

Logan's foot scuffed the ground as he mistimed a step, Tyler's words reminding him of something that had been bothering him all afternoon.

"I've been thinking about that. 'Middle of nowhere.'"

"What about it, boss?"

"That's what Billy Neeps said when we told him about Archie renting a holiday cottage, wasn't it? Something about him not staying out in the middle of nowhere on purpose?"

"Rings a bell, aye," Tyler said. "So what, though?"

"Think about it," Logan prompted. "Think through the conversation."

Tyler fixed his gaze on the pavement ahead of them. His legs swung in time with Logan's as he replayed what he could remember of the interview in his head.

The details were sketchy, though, so he reached into his pocket, took out his notepad, and shot Logan a hopeful look.

"If you must, aye," Logan conceded, then he waited while Tyler flipped through his pages and read through the drunken spider scrawl of his handwriting.

They were approaching the second high-rise block now. Just beyond it, a path led away on the left to the play area. Logan could see half a dozen adult-sized individuals through the gaps in the rusted metal fence, but could make out no more detail than that.

"Oh! I think I've got it, boss!" Tyler announced. "'Middle of nowhere.' Those were his exact words. How did he know that?"

"Well done. And aye, that's what I was wondering. We just said the Highlands. Could've been Inverness. No saying it was out in the wilds."

Tyler folded his notebook shut and returned it to his jacket pocket. "I mean... I suppose he could've guessed," he mused. "Like, if you say someone's staying at a holiday cottage in the Highlands, city folk are probably going to assume it's somewhere remote. They think everywhere north of Stirling's the arse-end of nowhere."

Logan had to concede that point. Up until a couple of years ago, he'd probably have made the very same assumption.

"And how would he find him, boss? Billy, I mean? How would he know where to find Archie, if he was in hiding?"

"I don't know," Logan admitted.

"And, I mean, Billy doesn't strike me as someone capable of... well, much. I can't see him managing to force his way into a house to murder four people, can you?"

"Probably not."

Tyler shot him a sideways look as they plodded along the pavement. "Are you...? Was that you agreeing with everything I just said, boss?"

Logan sucked air in through his teeth. "It's a day full of surprises, right enough," he said, then he nodded towards the start of the path that led to the play area. "Right, here we go. This could be them. Game faces on."

Tyler narrowed his eyes and set his jaw, and somehow managed to look even less intimidating than he had a moment ago.

"Ready when you are, boss," he announced.

Logan rolled his eyes, checked for traffic, then set off towards the path. "Aye, well," he said, as DC Neish broke into a swagger. "Maybe best if I do all the talking."

"Cancer?"

The word hung there in the air—a foul, malevolent bastard of a thing.

DI Forde lowered himself into his chair and gripped the armrests like he was afraid he might fall out.

"Like... *cancer* cancer?" he asked. "Actual cancer?"

"Yeah," Sinead confirmed.

"Of his goolies?"

"Yes. Well, one of them," Sinead clarified. "I mean, they don't fully confirm it until they remove it to do the biopsy, but—"

"So it might not be?" asked Hamza. He looked just as shaken as Ben did. More so, even. "He might not have it?"

Sinead scraped together the most comforting smile she could manage. "They're pretty certain. The doctor—the specialist—he says he'd be very surprised at this stage if it turns out not to be."

"And how serious are we talking?" Ben asked.

"We're not too sure on that, either. First thing is to remove it, then go from there. Initial scans are promising, though."

"Promising how?" asked Dave. "He's still getting a bollock out, isn't he?"

"Promising, in that it doesn't look like it's spread elsewhere," Sinead said. There was a flaw in her voice. A tiny imperfection in the glaze of it. "So far, anyway."

Hamza's hand appeared on her arm. She sniffed back tears, gave it a pat, then stood up. She couldn't suffer their kindness right now. Not if she wanted to hold herself together.

"God. We'll have to tell Jack," Ben said. "He'll have to know."

"He does," Sinead said. "Tyler told him today. That's why he's coming back up the road."

"Oh," said Ben. He gave this some consideration. "I thought he must just be getting on Jack's tits."

Sinead smirked. "Probably a bit of that, too."

"You should have told us earlier," Hamza said. "We could've... I don't know. Helped."

"How?" Sinead asked, then she immediately felt bad for it. "I think he just wanted things to be... normal for as long as they could. Like, if you didn't know, he could pretend it wasn't happening, I suppose."

Ben slapped a hand down on the edge of the desk. "*That's* why he nearly did a runner before the wedding!"

Sinead's head turned slowly in the DI's direction. "Sir?"

"The wedding. When he went AWOL..." Ben began, but the rest of the sentence fell away into silence.

"What do you mean 'went AWOL?'" Sinead asked.

Ben shot a pleading look at Hamza and Dave, but both men just stared back at him in wide-eyed horror. He quietly cleared his throat.

"What I mean is... And, you'll get a laugh at this..." Ben said, stalling to give himself more thinking time. "Is... Oh! Actually, maybe I'm thinking of a different wedding! I think that might be..." He spotted the grin on Sinead's face, then blew out the breath that had been trapped in his chest for the past several seconds. "You evil bitch!" he ejected. "You knew bloody fine!"

"Sorry, sir, couldn't resist," she told him. "Aye, he told me he nearly bottled it. Said Hoon gave him a talking to."

"Probably less of a 'talking to' than a 'swearing at,' but aye, he seemed to get the message across," Ben said. He clapped his hands together. "Right, shocking news like this warrants a nice cup of tea, I reckon. Hamza, do you fancy doing the honours?"

Hamza got to his feet. "I'm sure I can manage, sir, aye," he confirmed.

"Good on you, son," Ben replied. "Then, once you've got that down your neck, grab your coat and head up to talk to Jazmin McAllister, assuming we get word that she's home. What time are we on?"

"Just after seven, sir," Sinead told him.

"Good, plenty of time before the train gets in, then," Ben said. "Until then, you're on the clock. Fair?"

"No complaints here, sir."

"Right, good. Jack said he'd heard that Neeps and Tatties were getting a Hogmanay show on the BBC this year. I want to know if that's true."

"I wouldn't hold my breath for it happening now," Dave chipped in.

"No, but Billy Neeps didn't mention it when he was talking to Jack and Tyler. If it was happening, why didn't he say something? Seems unlikely he wouldn't know he was going to be doing a live New Year's special on the national broadcaster. That's no' the sort of thing that gets sprung on you at the last second. Well, no' outside of a nightmare, anyway."

"I can phone around, see if I can speak to anyone involved in production," Sinead suggested. "Or contracts, maybe. If a deal's been made, there'd be something in writing."

"See what you can dig up," Ben instructed. "Dave, I've got a few jobs for you, too. But let's get the most important one out of the way first."

Dave nodded. "Dig up some takeaway menus?" he asked.

Ben winked and smiled at the man in the wheelchair. "David, my boy, you read my bloody mind."

They all split up to set about their tasks. After gathering up everyone's mugs, Hamza pulled open the door to find a uniformed constable frozen there, hand raised like she was about to knock. She stared at him in mute shock for a few seconds, then stiffly lowered her arm to her side like it was on a rusty hinge.

"Eh... hello?" Hamza said. Somewhere, buried at the back of his mind, a little voice remarked that ooh, weren't police officers getting younger and younger these days? "Can I help you?"

"There's, um, there's... A phone call."

"A phone call?" asked Hamza. "For who?"

"For a..." she quickly checked a scribble on the back of her hand. "DI Forde."

Ben appeared in the doorway behind Hamza. "I'm DI Forde. Who's on the phone?"

"No one, sir."

Ben and Hamza side-eyed each other. "But you just said..." the DI began, before the constable jumped back in.

"Sorry, I meant they're not on the phone *now*. They left a message. For you. Via me." She shook her head, annoyed by her own babbling. "For me to pass on to you, I mean."

Ben smiled patiently. "Who?"

"Oh. Right, the hospital. It's about Moira."

Hamza frowned. "Moira? What, front desk Moira?"

The constable wasn't sure if the question was aimed at her or not, so continued on as if it wasn't. "You've to give her a phone. At the hospital. Sir," she said. "They didn't say what it was about."

"Thank you, Constable. I'll do that," Ben said. "Was that everything?"

"Yes, sir," she said, then she scurried off the moment she was dismissed, cheeks stinging with embarrassment.

Ben could feel Hamza's attempts to make eye contact, but ignored them. "Right, tea run, Detective Sergeant," he said, about-turning and making his way back to the desk. "Dave, find me the number for the Belford Hospital, will you?"

"Front desk?"

"That'll do."

"The hospital? Everything alright, sir?" asked Sinead. Her mobile buzzed, and Tyler's photo filled the screen. She hovered her thumb over the answer button while waiting for the DI's response.

Ben flopped down into his chair, sucked in his bottom lip, then spat it out again. "I don't know," he said, reaching for his desk phone. "But I guess we'll soon find out."

Moira Corson was sitting propped up in bed when the phone was brought to her by one of the nurses.

"Here you go, Moira, pet," the nurse said, passing the cordless handset over. "Just you hang up when you're done."

"I know how a bloody telephone works," Moira retorted.

The nurse rolled her eyes, but laughed it off. She'd gotten a good handle on Moira over the past few days, and had chosen not to take any of her comments personally.

Well, maybe the one about needing to lose weight. That one was harder to shrug off, right enough.

Moira held the mouthpiece of the phone pressed to her shoulder and glared at the nurse until she left. Only then did she put the phone to her ear.

"Hello?"

"Moira?"

"DI Forde, is that you?" she asked. "God, you sound old on the phone. Frail."

"Cheers for that, Moira," Ben replied. "I got a message you wanted to speak to me."

"Well, obviously! Why else would you be phoning, if you didn't get the message?" she asked, then she pressed the phone to her ear and scowled. "Who's that woman shouting in the background?"

"That's just Sinead," Ben replied. "Sounds like there's been a change of plan on something. Was there something the matter? Do you need help with something?"

"No, I do not need help!" Moira spat, offended by the very suggestion. "I'm calling about this silly magazine of yours."

There was a momentary pause from the other end of the line. "The magazine? What about it?"

"There's a celebrity news section," Moira said. "I mean, they say 'celebrity' but I've never heard of half of them. They're either has-beens, or never-weres, if you ask me. Not that you would."

There was a note of exasperation in Ben's response. "Well, I'm sorry to hear they're no' up to your high celebrity standards, Moira, but I'm sort of in the middle of something here. Can this maybe wait until I can get back in...?"

"I didn't ask you to call so I could tell you about the section itself." Moira tutted. "What do you take me for, Detective Inspector? Some needy young thing?"

"Well, no..." Ben admitted.

"There's an article in it. It's about one of those has-beens I mentioned."

She looked down at the magazine spread out on her legs. There, buried way at the bottom of the right-hand page, was a photo of a man with thinning hair, thick glasses, and two malformed turnips for tits.

"And given what you mentioned when you were here before," Moira continued, "I think that it might be important."

CHAPTER THIRTY-THREE

FRANKIE WAS NOT hard to spot. He sat on a swing, arms hooked around the chains as he brazenly skinned up a joint. There was no mistaking him. He was shorter than his uncle, but otherwise, he could've been Shuggie Cowan himself, stepped right out of some time vortex from forty years in the past.

Physically, at least. The mannerisms were all wrong. For as long as Logan had known him, Shuggie had been slow. Composed. Deliberate. Frankie's movements were the opposite of that.

Even seated, every part of him was moving. His feet danced to some mystery rhythm only he could hear. His head jerked from side to side every few seconds, like he had water in both ears and was trying to shake it free.

His face was an animator's showreel of tics, and twitches, and sniffs. Just looking at the bastard was exhausting.

Logan took a moment to size things up before making his move. It didn't take him long. He'd been doing risk assessments on places like these since long before the thought of joining the polis had first entered his head.

There were seven of them in all. Two groups—Frankie and two other men, then three younger guys and a girl in her late teens who seemed to be simultaneously revelling in and getting bored by their attention.

The younger group looked like opportunists, Logan thought.

They'd only jump into a fight if they knew they were guaranteed to win it. A couple of the lads had already spotted Logan, and after some quick calculations of their odds, had quickly looked away.

They'd only be a problem if things went very wrong, or if they thought they could impress the lassie. Given that she was unlikely to be impressed by them getting their teeth handed back to them in a bloody hankie, though, Logan was choosing not to worry about them too much.

Frankie's group was another story. One of them sat on the swing beside him, his stoicism in stark contrast to Frankie's endless fidgeting. He was a solid lump of a man, easily Logan's height and perhaps taller still. He'd caught sight of the detectives as they'd approached along the path, and after a cursory look at Tyler had targeted his gaze on the DCI and hadn't blinked since.

Logan was less worried about the third man. He was about Tyler's age, Tyler's height, and Tyler's build. He perched right on the middle column of a slowly rotating roundabout, his head back so he could look straight up at the spinning sky. He was smiling, but there was a queasiness there, like he might throw up at any moment.

Something else he and DC Neish had in common, then.

"You Frankie?" Logan asked.

Frankie's head gave a sideways jerk, but he didn't shift his attention from the partially rolled spliff. He was at a tricky stage in proceedings, and while the rest of him was in a state of constant movement, his hands were rock solid, his fingers working in harmony as they rolled the *Rizlas* around the buds of grass.

"Who's asking?"

"Let's just say I'm a friend of Uncle Shuggie's," Logan told him.

Frankie's eyes raised from the joint just long enough to take in the two new arrivals. "Naw, you're no'," he said. "Yous are polis. I can smell it off ye."

"I'm that, too," Logan admitted.

He took a step closer, and the man who had been sitting in the swing beside Frankie was suddenly on his feet. He was fast for a big lad. So fast, in fact, that Logan barely saw him move.

"Easy, Budge, man," Frankie said, turning his attention back to his work. He licked the paper and rolled the final part into place, then waved the spliff about like he was showing it off. "You got a light, Mr Polisman?"

Logan shook his head. "No."

"What about your wee pal?" Frankie asked, shifting his attention to Tyler. "You got a light, buddy?"

"Eh, no," Tyler said. His eyes followed the joint. "But, eh, you shouldn't be—"

Logan made a hand gesture, indicating that Tyler should stop talking. For once, the younger officer picked up on a signal and his words fell away into silence.

Frankie grinned. It was a grotesque, twisted thing, like something from a horror movie. "Paco? Gimme a light."

The man on the roundabout jumped to attention at the mention of his name. "Coming, Uncle Frankie!"

He hopped down from his perch, took two steps, then staggered sideways and fell onto the rubberised safety surface that surrounded the park equipment.

"Fuck's sake," Frankie hissed, as Paco vomited loudly on the ground behind him. He patted his own pockets until he found a lighter, then sparked up in full view of the officers. He inhaled deeply, clamped his mouth shut, then gestured for Logan to continue.

"I want to ask you a few questions, Frankie. About Archie Sutherland."

The man on the swing spluttered out a lungful of smoke. "That fucking prick?" he spat. "What about him? Ye know where he is?"

"Do you?" Logan asked.

"No' for want of fucking trying! You know what that fucking rat has done?"

"What would that be?"

Frankie almost replied.

Almost.

"Nothing. Doesn't matter," he said. He took another draw on his joint, let it navigate its way down through his airways, then squeaked a, "Continue," from the corner of his mouth.

Budge, who Logan noted did indeed have a height advantage of two or three inches, was still on his feet. He had made no attempt to close the gap between them, but he held himself like he was ready to move at a moment's notice. Less, perhaps.

The size of him wasn't the issue. Muscle—even that much—was just so much extra weight if you didn't know how to use it. The problem was that everything about this man stated that he *did* know how to use it, and that he'd very much enjoy using it, too.

If the big fella started throwing his weight around, Logan might be able to handle him one-on-one. That would leave Tyler to deal with everyone else, though, and while one of them was currently clinging to the ground and whimpering, danger radiated off the man in the swing. The other group would quickly jump in at that point. Logan could already sense their growing interest, like sharks smelling blood in the water.

He shouldn't have brought Tyler here. Not to someone like this. What had he been thinking?

"I told you to continue," Frankie said. "Archie. What about him?"

"He's dead."

The joint, which had been standing erect at one side of Frankie's mouth, suffered a sudden case of Brewer's Droop.

"What? What do you mean he's dead? How's he dead?"

"Just the normal way. By not being alive," Logan told him. "Him and his family. Wife and her two girls. All dead, Frankie."

"Shitting fuck," Frankie remarked. He sniffed, twitched, then pawed at one ear like a cat with an itch. It was involuntary, Logan thought. Some form of Tourette's, maybe, or just damage caused by a childhood of too much drink and too many Class-A's. "Nae luck, eh?"

"I hear you and he were in business together, Frankie," Logan continued. "I got the impression that things weren't exactly rosy between the pair of you."

"He was a jumped-up fucking nobody who thought he was the big-fucking-I-am, you mean?" Frankie hoiked up a mouthful of phlegm, then gobbed it onto the ground near the DCI's feet. "Because, if so, then aye, you're spot-on, pal. Big-mouthed thieving fucking arsehole, who thought he knew best. And you can get your fucking secretary there to write that down." He grinned and winked at Tyler. "Alright, sweetheart?"

"He stole money from you," Logan said.

Frankie's head jerked. His tongue flicked across his lips and his shoulders twitched up to ear height before dropping back down.

"Who told you that?"

"Lucky guess," Logan said.

"My arse. You found him with it, you mean. That belongs to me, by the way. I can fucking prove it, too."

Logan ignored the unblinking glare of Budge and fixed Frankie with one of his more intense looks. "That's the thing, Frankie. We didn't find it. Whoever killed them took it." He shrugged. "Took it back, maybe."

"Oh aye, here we go. Here we fucking go!" Frankie barked, springing to his feet. He flew at Logan, face knotting itself up in rage like he was losing his temper.

He wasn't completely losing control, though. You could tell by the way he slowed his approach when Logan failed to so much as blink. He stopped a couple of feet from the DCI, right before the height difference made him look *too* ridiculous.

"You saying I did the fat old fucker in?" he demanded. "You got any fucking evidence for that? You got a fucking... what's it called? A fucking warrant to come here talking to me?"

"We don't need a warrant, Frankie. You're loitering in a kiddies' swing park," Logan pointed out.

Frankie looked to Budge for confirmation. The bigger man didn't take his eyes off Logan, yet knew enough about his spliff-smoking companion to nod.

Frankie's mouth pulled into an exaggerated pout, and his eyes screwed shut then popped wide open again.

"Fine. No fucking warrant, then. But you still can't just fucking waltz in here and start saying I killed the bastard."

"Well, I can, but I'm not saying that, Frankie," Logan replied. "Although, I'll give you, the thought had crossed my mind, right enough."

Behind Logan, Tyler anxiously eyed the group of four teenagers. They had moved to position themselves between the detectives and the exit now, and were paying very close attention to the events unfolding before them.

The sharks were circling.

"How'd you fancy coming down to the station with me, Frankie?" Logan asked. "We'll make it quick so your wee pals here will still be out playing when we're done."

"Naw," Frankie said. He took a deep draw on his joint, held it until his lungs were fit for bursting, then blew it into the DCI's face. "Ye're alright. I'm good here."

He raised the spliff to his mouth again. Logan made a grab for it, but a hand even bigger than his own caught him by the wrist and jerked his arm to a stop.

Frankie suffered what seemed to be a whole-body hiccup that burst on his lips like the *brrrrring* of an old-style telephone. "Tip!" His head twitched to the left. "Tip! Uck!" he announced, then he pulled himself together enough to talk some sort of sense. "Aye, best you don't try any fucking funny business, Mr Polisman. Budge here doesn't fucking like it. Do ye, Budge?"

Budge shook his head.

"See? He's a good guy. Knows the fucking score," Frankie patted the much larger man on as close to his shoulder as he could reach. "Hardy bastard. Did one o' the wars, or fucking... something. I don't know, he's no' much of a talker. Knows how to fucking handle himself, though. Knows how to fuck a prick up, put it that way."

"Eh, boss?" Tyler's voice was a low murmur of concern.

Logan yanked his hand from Budge's grip and glanced back to see another group of lads making their way along the path, no doubt drawn by the prospect of a scrap. This lot were in their twenties, Logan guessed. Five of them. Not friendly looking. Not by a longshot.

This was not going well.

"I tell you what I'll do, Frankie," Logan said. His voice a boom of authority. He had to make the gathering crowd behind him believe he was in charge here. Give them a reason to doubt it, and Tyler wouldn't have to worry about his upcoming operation. They'd tear his balls off right here in this swing park. And that would just be for starters. "I'll give you until tomorrow morning to think about it. You mull it over, see if anything useful comes back to you, and we'll discuss it again then."

"How about naw?" Frankie countered. He was right up in

Logan's face now, eyes practically bulging out of their sockets as he tried laying the intimidation on thick.

The urge to knee him in the bollocks then drag him off by the hair was almost overpowering, but Budge was standing ready, the younger man who'd been throwing up on the ground was back on his feet, and the onlookers blocking the path were itching to get involved.

The play area was surrounded by tall fences on all sides. The only way out was along that path, through that crowd.

Normally, he'd front it up. He'd stride through them, shooting them glares that said, "Aye, just you fucking try it, pal."

On a normal day, that would be enough. But, Frankie's crew had tipped the balance of power here. And he had Tyler to think about.

He gritted his teeth. "Right, fine. You win, Frankie. We'll go. For now."

"Says who?" Frankie asked. There was a smile tugging at the side of his mouth. This was amusing him.

"You don't want to do anything stupid," Logan told him. "Right now, there's not a lot I can do you for, minor drug possession offences aside. If things escalate, then that changes. Then, it's open season."

A series of twitches started on the far left of his top lip, then jerked all the way to the opposite end, making his mouth undulate like a rippling wave. His head jerked. His hands spasmed into fists. "Aye, but only if you're able to tell anyone," he said.

There was a laugh from the group behind them. Some whispering. A sound like knuckles being cracked.

Logan heard the shuffle of Tyler's feet and a, "Stay where you are, sir," that was almost convincingly calm.

"Check me oot, getting called fucking 'sir,' an' that!" a teenage voice sniggered. "These two are fucking shiteing theirselves. Check oot the nick o' the wee guy!"

Logan ran the odds. Not good. Very bad, in fact. Control—or the illusion of it, at least—was about to be lost. What happened after that, he could only guess at. It would be nothing good, though. Not from where the detectives were standing, at any rate.

Had it been just him, he'd have stuck the nut in the big lad and then windmilled into the rest of them. He'd still be outnumbered, but seeing their prize asset choking on his own blood would've taken some of the fight out of them before he'd thrown his first punch.

That would be all well and good if he was on his own. He could fight freely that way. You didn't have to think too much when every face and ballsack around you was a target just begging for a fist or the toe of a boot.

As soon as you threw in an ally or someone to be protected, things got more difficult. You had to consider your moves. Coordinate. Keep an eye on them. It cut your effectiveness in half.

So, a headbutt and a punch-up were off the cards, then. Shame. What did that leave?

Not a lot, he realised.

And then, out of nowhere, came the sound of a choir of angels. Technically, it was the wailing of a polis siren, but the effect on Logan's spirits was much the same. Blue lights shone through the early evening gloom. One car, at least, maybe two.

The bastards behind Logan and Tyler immediately bottled it and set off running, falling over each other as they went barrelling up the path. They splintered when they reached the road, all setting off in different directions like they'd been rehearsing for just this eventuality.

They'd come back, of course, as soon as the polis cars went screaming straight past on route to whatever call they were actually responding to.

Logan had no intention of being there when they did.

"You put your thinking cap on for me, Frankie," Logan said, raising his voice to be heard over the approaching sirens. He stepped back, ushering Tyler towards the play area's exit. "And I'll catch you again soon."

LOGAN PULLED AWAY from the tower block before Tyler had managed to clip on his seatbelt. The warning chime reprimanded them as the BMW hung a left at the entrance to the car park, and only shut up when Tyler clunked the belt catch into place.

"Jesus Christ, boss. That was a bit hairy for a minute there," the DC wheezed. It was the first he'd spoken since they'd left the play area, Logan having urged him to keep his mouth shut until they were safely back in the car.

Just as he'd predicted, when the polis cars had gone tearing away, the opportunistic bastards who'd done a runner came crawling back out from inside garages and behind bins. By then, though, Logan was leading the march back to the Beamer, and nobody was brave or stupid enough to give chase.

Logan took a look in the rearview mirror. Frankie stood right up against the fence of the play area, watching the car through the metal railings. They locked eyes for a moment, then a bend in the road broke the connection.

"You shouldn't have been there," Logan muttered.

"Boss?"

"You should've been on that bloody train like I told you to."

"What, and leave you to deal with that on your own? No chance, boss."

"I'd have been better off on my own!" Logan snapped. "I wouldn't have had you to worry about."

Tyler flinched like he'd been physically struck. "No need to worry about me. I'm fine, boss."

"I need to make a phone call," Logan muttered. "But I'm taking you to the hotel first."

"What? But—"

The DCI shot him a dangerous look. "No arguments, Tyler."

Tyler almost snapped back at him, but saw sense just in the nick of time. Going toe to toe with the DCI was never a good idea, especially when tempers were raised.

"It was rough, boss, aye," he said. "But you don't have to worry about me."

"Aye? And what would I have told Sinead, eh? If you'd been stabbed, or had your bloody head stamped on, and wound up in hospital? Or worse? How do you think she'd have taken it?"

Tyler had no answer for that. Or rather, he did, but it wasn't one that would help his case. He sat in silence, watching the city growing denser around them as they headed back towards the centre.

"I know you want to help, son," Logan said, his voice losing some of its edge. "I get it. I do. But enough's enough, eh? Time to step back, and leave this one to the rest of us. You've got yourself and your family to think about."

Tyler dragged his silence out for a while longer, then conceded with a shrug. "Suppose."

"You'll be back fighting fit in no time," Logan assured him. "I'm quietly confident this won't be the last murder case we're given to deal with. There'll be plenty of chances to make a difference."

"Yeah. Suppose that's true," Tyler said. He blew out his cheeks, nodded his head, and subtly touched his troublesome testicle. "Fair enough then, boss. Drop me back at the hotel. Hopefully, they'll have restocked the minibar."

"I'm sure they have," Logan told him. "There's just one problem, son."

Tyler turned to him. "What now?"

Logan's mouth became a thin, tight line. "The bastards in admin have changed our hotel."

"Aye? Don't suppose they're putting us somewhere even nicer?" he asked, then he nodded at the look he received in response. "No, thought not. Still, just for one night, I suppose. For me, anyway. You reckon you'll be down here long?"

Logan sighed. "I have no idea. This whole case, it feels... Off. We're bouncing around all over the place, following a trail that might well lead us nowhere. I feel like we're missing something."

"Aye, well, I had a wee thought while I was standing in that swing park with all those lads behind us," Tyler said. "I thought, if these bastards slit our throats and dump our bodies somewhere, will anyone ever find us?"

"Jesus Christ, son, you went from nought to sixty there."

"Maybe got a bit carried away, right enough. I was starting to panic, if I'm honest. But the point is, it got me thinking about how someone might be able to track us down and find our bodies," Tyler said. "And that gave me an idea..."

CHAPTER THIRTY-FOUR

TWENTY MINUTES LATER, Logan and Tyler had checked in at a Premier Inn that sat tantalisingly across the Clyde from the plusher hotel they'd been in the night before, then headed up to their rooms. They were both on the same floor, and Logan stopped outside Tyler's room for a minute or two, purportedly to discuss dinner plans for the evening, but mostly to make sure the DC was holding up OK.

"I think I'm just going to get an early night, boss," Tyler said, and there was a note of defeat underscoring the words. "I'll give Sinead a ring, then get sorted for the early train in the morning."

Logan agreed that was probably for the best. They exchanged something that was partway between a handshake and a hug, but neither one thing nor the other, then the DCI continued to his own room, dumped his bag inside, then had a thoroughly enjoyable piss that had been building since lunchtime.

That done, he made a phone call. It was short, but about as far from sweet as it was possible to be. It did the job, though, and a key element of a half-formed plan fell into place.

He was heading back down to get himself a bite to eat when the phone had started ringing in his pocket. There were two other people in the lift with him, and when he saw Ben's name flash up on the screen he decided to let it ring until they all stepped out at the ground floor, and he could take the call somewhere more private.

He stepped outside, strode past the huddled grey knot of smokers, and answered with one ring to spare before his answerphone would've kicked in.

"What's the latest?" he asked, his rumbling stomach urging him to skip all the usual niceties.

He jammed a finger in his ear, blocking out the sound of the wind as it gusted along the Clyde and whistled through the gaps of Bell's Bridge. A tumble of words came rushing down the line from a hundred miles north.

"Wait, hold on, slow down," Logan said, and his stomach gave a pitiful whimper of disappointment. Dinner, it knew, would have to wait. "Billy Neeps has *what?*"

———

BILLY NEEPS HAD a quick scan of the shop before he clicked off all the lights. He made a promise into the mobile he had jammed between a cheek and a shoulder that he was on his way, then hung up and shoved the mobile into one of his jacket's many cluttered pockets.

He hummed quietly to himself as he stepped out into the bracing evening air and the rumble of passing traffic, then he pulled the glass door of his shop closed and fished a big bunch of keys from another pocket.

The keys, just as they'd done so many times before, immediately slipped out of his hand and landed on the step. Billy muttered some self-criticism or other below his breath, then his head gave a comical *thonk* on the door when he bent to retrieve the dropped keys.

Still, a dunt to the forehead was better than another pair of ripped trousers. And it was *definitely* better than that time he'd farted in the face of the sandwich shop owner's disabled daughter. That one had taken some explaining.

He stood rubbing his forehead for a few moments, then more carefully retrieved the keys. For about the hundredth time, he contemplated getting one of those extendable keychain things to attach the bunch to one of his belt loops, then he secured the front door.

Grabbing the handle, he gave the door a shake, checking it was locked. You couldn't be too careful. Not round here. Not round anywhere, these days.

Mind you, even if it wasn't locked, the additional security he'd had installed a couple of years back would keep the robbing bastards out.

Billy was just stretching up to pull down the graffiti-stained metal shutter when he caught sight of a reflection in the glass. A man stood there, waiting. A big man, with an unhappy expression.

"William Pinnock," the man said—the voice that had seemed reasonably friendly earlier now much sterner and more official.

Billy swallowed, briefly shut his eyes and whispered a prayer, then turned to face the detective in the big coat.

"Yes?"

"I'm afraid I'm going to have to ask you to come with me, sir," the DCI told him.

"Um... why? What about?"

"I'd like to ask you a few questions, Mr Pinnock," Logan replied. "Regarding the murder of Archie Sutherland, Donna Sutherland, and Donna's two children."

"Wh-what?" Billy stammered. He attempted to laugh it off, but failed dismally and settled into a more sombre approach. "I, um, should I have a solicitor present?"

"That's up to you, Mr Pinnock," Logan replied. "But I would strongly advise that you do."

———

HAMZA SAT outside a semi-detached house in Drumnadrochit, the windows of his car coated with a layer of misty white condensation as he polished off the last of his bag of chips. He'd wanted to get on the road sharp, and so hadn't hung around for the Chinese to be delivered to the Fort William station. Instead, he'd grabbed a poke of chips in Fort Augustus, and dipped into them on the way up the road.

He hadn't counted on the steam factor, though, and had nearly frozen himself to death driving the remaining ten miles of the journey with all four windows wound down and a gale blustering in.

Once the last of the crunchy bits at the bottom of the tray were eaten, he scrunched the paper around it and wiped enough of the condensation from the windscreen so he could check the address. Pitkerrald Road. This was the place, alright.

He got out of the car, snuck his chip bag into the green wheelie bin just inside the garden of the house he'd come to visit, then carried on up the path.

The house seemed pleasant enough. Paintwork could've done with a touch-up, but the windows and doors were new, and the garden—while low maintenance, with lots of gravel and rocks—was well cared for. Cracking spot, too, he thought, looking at the open field directly across the road as he *ding-donged* the doorbell and waited for a response from inside.

The lights were on in the living room, though the blinds had been shut. Uniform had driven past earlier but, as instructed, had kept away. No point scaring the lassie. For all they knew, she was sat in there now rocking her new baby to sleep.

He pressed the bell again, and heard the chime ring out on the other side of the door. While he waited, he took another quick look at her photo to make sure he'd recognise her when she answered. Her big eyes gazed back at him from the screen of his phone, a smile playing across her lips like she was teasing him with something she knew that he didn't.

She was attractive, there were no two ways about it. There would be plenty of men who'd pay good money to see her whipping her kit off, and whatever else she might be willing to do under the beady glare of the cameras.

Hamza definitely felt something stirring as he looked down at those big eyes and freckles, but not that. He had no interest in that sort of thing.

He would've done, once. As a teenager, maybe, and a younger man. But he'd seen the effects of sexual violence up close since then. He'd stood there, a useless great lump of a thing, as women had cried and screamed and demanded to know what they'd done to deserve this. Begged to know why men thought they could do these things. Why they felt they had that right.

They hadn't been women. Not to the men who'd attacked them, anyway. They'd been things. Objects. Items to be used for gratification. To be overpowered. To be *nothing*.

And what was pornography, if not just a slightly more civilised version of that?

He didn't want to watch the lassie currently smiling up from his phone getting her clothes off, and he certainly didn't want to see her doing anything else.

No. He wanted to sit her down and tell her that she didn't have to do this. That there were other options—better options than having some big sweaty bastard grinding away on you under the all-seeing eyes of the internet, anyway.

He wouldn't, of course. That wasn't why he was here. And chances were she'd just tell him to mind his own fucking business, which would be fair enough.

But he'd rung twice now, and she still hadn't come to the door.

And not a sound had emerged from within the house.

Hamza clicked the button that made his phone go dark, then stepped back from the door and took a look at the windows. Lights on downstairs, dark upstairs. The hallway, which he could see through the frosted glass panels of the door, was partially lit by the glow from the living room. It wasn't much, but enough that he'd be able to see anyone moving around in there.

Which he couldn't.

His footsteps crunched on gravel as he approached the front window. The angle of the blinds let him see a foot or two of floor, and not a whole lot else, and a strip of dark green carpet didn't really tell him much about anything.

He returned to the door and knocked this time. "Miss McAllister?" he called. "Jazmin? Do you have a minute?"

He waited, listened, watched through the rippled glass.

Nothing.

Or... something, maybe? In the hall. A figure? Or a coat, perhaps? Something there in the gloom, anyway. Something just beyond the door.

Hamza dropped down onto his haunches and prised open the letterbox. The new fixings were stiff, the metal sharp, and he nearly lost a finger as he stretched what he could of his hand inside and pushed a second hinged bit of metal outwards.

He jumped back, and pain ignited across his knuckles as the skin was scraped off them.

"No, no, no, shit!" he cried, driving a shoulder at the door. Once. Twice. It was a heavy composite thing, the hinges brand new and solid. The door shrugged him off. Ignored him. Laughed in his face.

"What are you doing?" barked a voice from the adjoining garden. A middle-aged man stood there, peering out through a gap in his front door. A woman—presumably his wife—stood behind him, trying to simultaneously see what was going on, and not be seen herself. "Piss off and leave her alone, before I call the police."

"Tell them Detective Sergeant Hamza Khaled needs assistance," Hamza spat back. He grabbed one of the stones from the rockery and took aim at the glass panel that ran up the full height of the door. "And tell them to send an ambulance."

He launched the stone and it connected hard with its target. The outer layer of glass fragmented, but stayed in the frame.

"Don't just stand there!" Hamza ordered. "Go!"

He didn't wait for the neighbours to scramble inside before grabbing a larger rock and swinging it with both hands. He held it this time, driving it against the glass like a hammer.

Bang. Bang. Ban—

The interior pane broke, and the glass spilled inward into the hallway. Thrusting an arm inside, Hamza felt around the door handle, found a key in the lock, and twisted.

He threw the door open, and grabbed at the feet that swung there in front of him, taking the weight off the knotted sheets that were around her neck, hoping that by some miracle he wasn't too late. That somehow, he'd arrived just in the nick of time.

But the colour of her face and hands, and the smell of her bodily fluids knocked any such notions out of him.

With a cry of frustration, he stepped back, surrendering her to the sheets once more. The uppermost railing of the bannister creaked as it took her full weight again. She swung, her body inching left and right less than three feet from the floor.

Her hands were untied. There was no sign of a struggle, besides a toppled kitchen chair she must've stood on, then kicked away.

Down among the fragments of glass, close to where she hung, lay a six-by-four inch rectangle of white paper. Hamza ran back to his car, fished a pair of rubber gloves from the box in his glove compartment, and was heading back up the path when the next-door neighbours emerged, the husband holding the phone like it was some sort of deadly weapon.

"Police or not, you can't just go breaking people's windows," the man said. "You need a whatchamacallit?"

"Warrant," said his wife.

"You need a warrant."

"Did you call it in?" Hamza asked. There was less urgency now, of course. None, almost.

"How are we supposed to know that you're really who you say you are? You could be—"

Hamza reached wearily into his pocket, produced his ID, then all-but shoved it into the couple's faces. "Did you call it in?" he asked again.

The husband looked down at the phone in his hand. "We, eh, we weren't sure if you were... We didn't know what to... Whether to..."

"Forget it." Hamza sighed and swapped the warrant card for the phone in his pocket. "I'll do it. You two go inside. Someone will be in to take a statement."

"A statement?" the wife asked. "About what? Is she alright?" Her eyes went to the door. Fortunately, Hamza had the presence of mind to pull it closed when he'd stepped outside, and her view of the dead girl in the hall was blocked. "She's alright, isn't she? She's not hurt?"

"Just please go inside," Hamza instructed, already swiping to his contacts. "Someone will be in to talk to you soon."

Husband and wife both looked to one another for guidance. Both seemed to be egging the other one, urging them to say something, but neither one rose to the challenge.

Hamza waited until they'd gone inside, then entered the house and made the call to base. Uniform and paramedics were promptly dispatched—five minutes for the backup, he was promised, there was a car nearby.

The ambulance would be a little longer, but there was no rush for that. Not now.

With the call made, he took some digital snaps of the white rectangle on the floor, noted its position, then pulled on the gloves. He brushed away the glass that was partially covering the paper, then carefully turned it over.

The photograph had been taken at the hospital, by the looks of things. In it, Jazmin was propped up in bed, a well-wrapped bundle held awkwardly in her arms, a tiny hand grasping at the fabric of her hospital gown.

She looked tired, and sad, and scared, and a churning mass of other emotions even she likely couldn't have put a name to. There was love there, Hamza thought. Whatever had happened after, there was love there in that photograph.

Pride, maybe. Joy, even. But worry, too. And doubt. And fear. And dread.

It was partly a face he'd seen before. He'd seen it on his wife, and on himself, on the day their daughter had been born. It was a look that spoke of a sudden and overwhelming burden of responsibility. It was a look that said you knew fine well you were going to make a mess of this, that there had been some mistake, that surely no one was actually daft enough to leave you in charge of a tiny human being incapable of fending for itself?

"Aye, joke's over," it seemed to say. "When do the grown-ups come and take it back?"

But here, in this photograph, that look was mixed with something more melancholy. Something bleaker. She was making all the shapes of a smile, curving all the right lines, but none of it was real.

He returned the picture to its spot on the floor. She must've been holding it when she kicked the chair away. It had slipped from her hand, and while it seemed to have landed directly in her eye line, fate and gravity had conspired to place it face down. To hide it from her, in her final moments of life. Whether that was a kindness or a cruelty, only she would have been able to say.

A siren sang from a few streets away. Hamza took one more look at the hanging girl, her hands black, her face a bruise of purple-blue. He whispered an apology for not being there sooner, then he stepped outside into the fresh air and found DI Forde's name in his phone.

CHAPTER THIRTY-FIVE

"WELL, well, well, look what the cat dragged in."

Logan felt everything between his throat and his arse go tight at the sound of the voice that rang through the corridor behind him. He'd hoped to avoid this. Avoid her. No such luck.

"Heather," he acknowledged, turning to face the woman striding purposefully towards him. She'd cut her hair since he'd last seen her. It had always been pulled back into a tight ponytail, but now it was short and styled in a sculpted side-parting. It was a man's haircut, and on other women it might look like some desperate attempt to blend into a mostly male-dominated workplace.

She somehow managed to make it look ironic, though. Like she was taking the piss out of the men who thought themselves better suited for, or just plain better at, the job. *I'm not just taking your place, I'm taking your hair, too*, was the general message here. She wasn't trying to fit in with her male colleagues, she was stamping her authority over them.

"Jack," she replied. She'd locked eyes with him the moment he'd turned, and hadn't yet blinked or looked away. Her eye contact game had always been first class, and he'd seen killers spill their guts just to get her to stop staring them down. "Aren't you meant to be somewhere else?" she asked.

"Ha. Aye. I came down the road yesterday," he explained.

"Not after your old job are you?" she asked, smirking like she was daring him to try. "Because I'm not giving it up."

"I heard you got made DCI," Logan said. "I meant to drop you an email or something, but..."

"Oh, you were going to drop me an email?" she asked, and there was a laugh not far behind it. "That's very official-sounding of you, considering the last thing you dropped for me."

Her eyes flicked very deliberately to his trousers, then refocused their lock on his face.

Logan coughed quietly. "Aye, well... like we both agreed at the time—"

"Mistake. God. Yes. Absolutely. Don't know what we were thinking," she said. "Water under the bridge."

"Aye. Well," Logan said again. He scratched the back of his head, despite it not being remotely itchy, then nodded. "It was good to see you again, Heather. I'd better crack on, though. The Gozer's let me borrow—"

"An interview room. Room two," the other DCI said.

Logan missed a beat. "Eh, aye. That's right. How'd you know?"

"Because I'm sitting in on the interview," Heather told him.

"No." Logan shook his head. "I mean, thanks for the offer, but that won't be necessary."

"Except it *will*. This isn't your patch now, Jack. Our nick, our rules. And, between you and me, I can't wait to see you in action again." She smiled and gestured along the corridor ahead of them. "So... shall we?"

BILLY NEEPS SAT in silence while the introductions were made for the benefit of the recording. Present in the room were DCI Jack Logan, DCI Heather Filson, the suspect William Pinnock, and the suspect's solicitor, Mrs Amilie Maitland, of the legal firm, Maitland & McQuarrie.

Once all that was out of the way, and DCI Filson had locked on her laser-targeted eye-contact, Logan jumped right in with both feet.

"You're a lying bastard, Billy."

"Excuse me. I'd ask that you don't talk to my client like that," the solicitor said, leaning in front of Billy before he could respond. "There's no need for that sort of language. My client is here of his own free will to assist with your enquiries, I'd ask you to remember and respect that."

Logan conceded the point with a nod. The statement had been more for her benefit than for Billy's, anyway. It was a good way of gauging how on-the-ball the lawyers were, and how willing they were to throw themselves into the fray.

This one was keen and confident, which generally made things more difficult.

"You're a lying blighter, Billy," Logan said. He side-eyed the solicitor, who looked unimpressed, but said nothing.

"What? No. How? What did I say?"

"When did you last see Archie?" Logan asked.

Across the table, Billy took a big swig from his plastic cup of water, and managed to spill half of it down the front of his polo shirt. "I, eh, I told you. December last year. When he... when he... When he came in. To the shop—"

"*BZZZZZT!*" Logan slammed his hand down on an imaginary buzzer. "Try again."

Billy's fingertips tapped a tuneless rhythm on the plastic cup, the whirring of his brain practically audible on the other side of the table. "He'd... he'd dropped his phone, you see? And he wanted—"

"I don't believe you, Billy," Logan pressed.

"I... I have receipts! I can show you he came in. I can show you!"

"I'm not doubting he came in then. In fact, after a discussion with a colleague of mine, I'm convinced he *did* come to see you then, and that you did fix his phone for him."

Billy looked up from his cup. His eyes, red from stress and swollen by the lenses of his glasses, blinked twice. He glanced for just a moment at DCI Filson, but the quality and intensity of her eyeballing quickly proved too much.

"What do you mean?" he asked.

Logan smiled. It was not one designed to put the suspect at ease. Quite the opposite. "We'll come back to that, Billy," he said, then he leaned back in his chair and crossed his arms. "It's been niggling me since we came to your shop earlier. Something didn't feel quite right. Felt off. You know what I mean?"

Billy shook his head. "I don't... I'm not sure..."

"Nor was I. There was nothing obviously wrong with anything you said, exactly. But... I don't know. Something just niggled. You ever get that, DCI Filson?"

"Something niggling away?" Heather asked, her gaze still drilling its way through Billy's skull, millimetre by millimetre. "Aye, I've experienced that a few times."

Logan wasted a moment trying to work out if this was some sort of dig at him, but then brushed the thought aside and continued.

"So, it's niggling me all day, but I've no' got time to think about it too much. Too much on. Too much to do," Logan explained. "But then, your name comes up in another context, and I give it some more thought. I run back over it. Tick, tick, tick. What you said. How you said it. Trying to find the niggle. Trying to figure it out."

On the other side of the table, the solicitor made a show of checking her watch. "Is there a point coming here, Detective Chief Inspector?" she asked. "I'm sure we've all got homes we'd like to get to at some point tonight."

Logan ignored her and kept the focus on Billy. "So, two men walk into your shop, identify themselves as polis, then tell you they've got some bad news for you. What's your first reaction, DCI Filson?"

"Concern," Heather said. "I'd be worried about my family. I'd assume something bad had happened."

"Sounds like a reasonable reaction," Logan said. "Would you say it was fair to assume that most people—or even just men in relationships, let's say—would react in a similar way?"

"Far be it from me to second-guess how men may or may not choose to behave in a relationship," Heather said. Another dig, more blatant this time. "But I'd say that was a fair assumption to make, yes."

"You know what Mr Pinnock said? When we came in and told him we were there to give him bad news?" Logan asked. "Mr Pinnock said, 'Oh dear. That's a shame.'"

"Bit weird," Heather remarked.

"That's what I thought," Logan agreed. "Thinking back on it, I mean. I reckon that's where the niggle started. No, 'Is it my wife?' No, 'Oh God, what's happened?' Just, 'Oh dear. That's a shame.'" His chair creaked as he rocked back in it. "Very strange reaction. Very strange."

"Please don't tell me you brought us in here for that," Mrs Maitland said. "If that's all you've got, we're leaving, and you can ask my client again tomorrow if he'd be willing to assist you with—"

"You read many women's magazines, Billy?" Logan asked, cutting the solicitor short.

"Sorry, women's... magazines?"

"Aye. 'Heat.' That's one. 'Bella.' 'Chat.' They've all got names like that," Logan said. "The one I'm most interested in is this one."

He opened a folder and deposited a pristine, near mint condition copy of a glossy tabloid magazine on the table between them.

"For the record, DCI Logan has shown the suspect a copy of 'Love It!' magazine," DCI Filson announced.

"Suspect?" Billy mumbled. "What do...?"

"You ever read this one, Billy?" Logan asked.

Billy considered the magazine over the rim of his glasses, then shook his head. "No. What do you...? No, I've never even heard of it."

"Nor me. But then, we're no' the target audience, I suppose," Logan said. "In fact, I'd say that none of us sitting around this table falls within the target demographic."

Billy flicked glances at the other DCI and the solicitor. "They're women," he said, as if by way of correction.

"Well, aye," Logan conceded. He turned the magazine so it was facing him, and started to flick through the pages. "But, I don't think either of them has the time or the inclination to read about blood-sucking grannies, or dead twins communicating from beyond the grave, or..." He stopped at a double-page spread. "...which D-List Celebrities are currently shagging each other, or fighting in the street, or... Hello!" Logan looked up from the magazine. "You know you're mentioned here, Billy?"

There was a high-pitched squeak from Billy's chair as he leaned closer. "Me?"

"There's a photo of you, and everything," Logan said.

"Must've been a slow news week," Heather remarked.

"You know what it says in the caption, Billy? Under the photo?"

Billy strained as he tried to read upside-down, but Logan picked up the magazine before he could see for himself. "Allow me," the DCI said. "It says, 'Legendary 80s TV funnyman...'" He lowered the magazine again. "That's nice, isn't it? Good start. 'Legendary.'" He returned to reading. "'Legendary 80s TV funnyman, Billy Neeps, of Neeps and Tatties fame, this week welcomed the arrival of his first child, with his wife of over twenty years."

Billy's hand tightened suddenly on his cup, crushing it and launching a splurt of water several centimetres into the air.

"Congratulations, Billy," Logan continued, ignoring the other man's desperate attempts to dry his now sopping wet crotch. He clasped his hands together, and leaned closer across the table. "Why don't you tell us all about your new wee bundle of joy?"

CHAPTER THIRTY-SIX

"Hey. You OK?"

Hamza realised he'd been staring at the front door of Jazmin McAllister's house without blinking for a while now. He'd called in the update to Ben, then—as the SO—had started dishing out orders to the growing army of men and women in polis and paramedic uniforms who'd all come screeching to the scene.

He blinked at the sound of a familiar voice, and jumped in surprise when he found the pathologist, Shona Maguire, standing just a foot or two away, looking like she'd stepped out of a *Hammer House of Horror* film.

Her hair was greasy, lank, and hung down either side of her face like a pair of curtains you'd ideally want to keep shut. There were black circles under her eyes, and while an attempt had been made to wash them off, it had been largely unsuccessful.

If anything, in fact, trying to wash it away had only made it worse. The makeup had run down her cheeks like fat grimy tears, or some sort of malevolent supernatural ooze.

"Bloody hell. Don't tell me you've died, too," Hamza said.

Shona seemed to draw her head into her neck and shot a few embarrassed glances at the Uniforms assembled nearby.

"I do a video call thing. With a friend from uni. We watch a different horror movie together once a month."

"And what, were you making a cameo in this one?"

Shona smiled, taking the jibe on the chin. "We get dressed up. Obviously. It's a whole thing. We were about to watch *The Ring* when the call came through. I, eh, thought it more important to get here quickly than to waste time getting showered." She gestured to her face, her words awkward and hesitant. "It's not... it's not inappropriate, is it?"

"Quite the opposite, I'd say," Hamza assured her. "I'd just be careful they don't end up putting you in the body bag by mistake."

"I'll keep my eyes peeled," Shona said. She followed his gaze to the front door, then studied the lines of his face. She didn't know Hamza overly well, but she could tell by the clench of his jaw and the spacing of his eyebrows that this one had bothered him. "So... you OK?"

"Hmm? Oh. Fine. Aye," he said, giving himself a shake. "It's suicide, I think. I mean, obviously you'll determine that, but I'd be surprised if it wasn't. Young lassie. Early twenties. Just had a baby a couple of weeks back."

Shona winced. "Oh, God. Where's the baby now?" She looked around but found no sign of it. "It's not... it's not still in the house, is it?"

Hamza shook his head. "No."

"So... where is it?"

Hamza turned to her. He smiled. It was a grim, forlorn sort of thing. "That's what we're currently trying to find out."

BILLY NEEPS SLOUCHED in his squeaky chair, his groin soaking from the spilled water, the rest of him merely damp with perspiration.

He'd always been a sweaty man, Logan recalled. They used to make a joke of it, Neeps and Tatties, with Archie relentlessly mocking his comedy partner for his overly-productive sudoriferous glands, and Billy blaming it all on the studio lighting, or the close proximity of the audience.

There were often coloured handkerchiefs involved, if Logan remembered correctly. Sometimes, Archie would 'accidentally' blow his nose in one, and much hilarity would ensue.

It wasn't part of any act now, though, and Billy certainly wasn't seeing the funny side.

"Is it hot in here?" he asked, tugging at the collar of his shirt. He blew upwards from the side of his mouth, cooling his forehead, if only momentarily. "Or is it just me?"

"It's just you," DCI Filson said. It wasn't, of course. They kept the interview rooms warm on purpose, the heater positioned behind the suspect's back.

One way or another, they'd make the bastards sweat.

"You haven't answered my question, Billy. What's the wee one's name?"

Billy side-eyed his solicitor. "Do I have to answer that?"

"You don't have to, no. But unless there's any reason not to, it might hurry all this up."

"Aye, we've all got homes to go to, Billy," Logan said, offering the possibility of this whole ordeal being over at some point.

He left it there, and waited for Billy to fill the conversational void.

"She's, um, we called her Senga."

"*Senga?*" Heather asked. Her tone was so incredulous that it bordered on disgust. She couldn't have sounded more outraged if Billy had announced they'd named the child Colonel Gadaffi. "What is she, one of these babies that are born old and ages backwards?"

"Pretty sure that just happens in the movies, DCI Filson," Logan said.

Heather's tut was audible only to the man beside her. And even then, it took some effort. "Actually, I was thinking of the book."

"So. Senga," Logan prompted, ignoring what he knew to be a jibe from the other DCI. "What made you choose that name?"

"It's my wife's mother's name. Was. She's no longer with us," Billy said. He was saying very little, but he was saying it quickly, as if the words were all lined in his mouth like tiny paratroopers waiting to be deployed. "We—she—my wife, that is—thought it would be a nice thing to do."

"Come back to us in fifteen years and we'll see if wee Senga agrees," Heather said.

"That's assuming you're still around in fifteen years, of course," Logan said, which won a look from Billy that could best be described as 'puzzled horror.'

"I'm sorry?" he asked.

"Sorry, that was very blunt of me," Logan replied. "I'm just saying, you're an older parent. Fifteen years would make you... what? Pushing eighty? Bold choice to be starting a family now."

"How old's your wife?" asked Heather.

"She's... younger than me."

"Don't tell me you don't know how old your wife is," Logan said. "That'll no' win you any brownie points, Billy."

"Will we put him out of his misery?" Heather asked. She tapped her notepad. "See, we looked it up, Billy. She's forty-seven. We can even give you her date of birth, if that'd be useful? Maybe you could write it down for future reference."

The solicitor sighed, mainly for the detectives' benefit. "Could we get to the point?"

"The point is that not a lot of forty-seven-year-old women are having babies," Logan said. "In fact—and we checked this, too —zero forty-seven-year-old women have had babies anywhere in Scotland in the last month."

"We adopted," Billy said. "That's... That's all there is to it. We adopted."

Logan sat back in his chair. "You adopted?"

Billy nodded. There was something mouse-like about the movement. "Yes. We adopted."

Logan groaned. "Well, this is embarrassing," he said. "Here's us checking the hospitals for older mothers giving birth, and they *adopted*, DCI Filson. We didn't bloody think of that, did we?" He crossed his arms over his barrel chest. "Or did we?"

"We did, DCI Logan," Heather confirmed. She shrugged. "Technically, we're still in the process of doing so—turns out there are a *lot* of adoption agencies in the UK."

"And?"

"And nothing so far," Heather replied. She smiled across the table at Billy and picked up her pen. "Actually, if you could tell us the agency you used, it would help us get everything cleared up."

Billy shifted in his seat and tugged anxiously at his wet crotch.

His eyes flitted left and right behind his glasses, like they were searching for a way to break free of his head, and abandon the rest of him to his fate. "I, uh, it's my wife who deals with that sort of... She'd know. If... I mean, if she was here, she'd be able to... to clarify."

"She's not here, though, Billy, is she?" said Logan. "In fact, we don't know where she is. We tried calling your house. We even sent a couple of our most child-friendly uniformed colleagues over to have a chat, but it seems there's nobody home."

"She's, eh..."

"She's where?" Heather urged, giving him no time to think.

"Come on, Billy, where is she?" Logan demanded.

Billy tugged on his collar. Blew on his face. Ran a sleeve across his brow. "She's at her... mum's."

"Her dead mum's you mean?" Logan asked.

"Aye. No. I meant... her sister's!" Billy yelped. "In... Cornwall."

"What's her sister's name?"

"An..drie," Billy said. It started off confidently enough, then rose into something like a question at the end.

"Andrie?" Heather echoed, sounding even more annoyed by this than she had been by 'Senga.'

"She doesn't have a sister. Does she, Billy?" said Logan.

Billy squirmed, like there was something inside him trying to wriggle its way out. The sweat was cascading down his face now, falling as drips from the tip of his nose and the end of his chin.

"She, um, she always... She always wanted a sister," he squeaked, then he launched himself a good six inches into the air when Logan banged a hand down on the table.

"Cut the shite, Billy!" the DCI boomed. "You're no' on the telly now. This isn't a bloody comedy sketch. Four people are dead. A child is missing. I strongly advise that you stop wasting my time and start answering my questions before you make me angry."

"This isn't him angry," Heather added. "This isn't even close."

"But I'm getting there, Billy. I'm headed squarely in that fucking direction," Logan continued, eyeballing him across the table. He inhaled through his nose, closed his eyes, and made a show of trying to calm his temper. "I tell you what I'm going to do," he said, once he'd opened his eyes again. "I'm going to make it easy on you. No hard questions, just yes or no answers. How does that sound?"

Billy looked to his solicitor for help. She sat with a sour look on her face, but offered him nothing.

"Did you kill Archie Sutherland and his family?"

Billy recoiled. "What?"

"Yes or no answers, Mr Pinnock!" Logan said, his voice rising into a shout again. "Archie Sutherland. His wife. Her two daughters. Did you kill them?"

"Of course I didn't kill—"

The *smack* of Logan's hand on the table rolled around the room like thunder. "Yes or no answers!"

"No! No, I didn't. No. God. No!"

Logan dismissed the answer with a scowl. "I don't believe you. Did you take the baby?"

"What?!"

Logan's jaw jutted forwards so his bottom teeth overlapped those on top. He made a grasping motion that balled his fingers into fists, then glowered at the detective beside him. "What bit's he no' getting about 'yes or no answers?'" he seethed.

DCI Filson put a hand on Logan's arm, as if holding him back. "Mr Pinnock, I'm going to level with you," she said. "We've been doing a lot of research this evening. DCI Logan here has a team of detectives working under him, and they've all been focusing their attention, as well as the not insubstantial resources available to them through Police Scotland, on you."

Billy's voice was so high-pitched it would've sent the canine unit into a barking frenzy. "On *me*?"

"What kind of car do you drive, Billy?" Logan asked, taking a conversational left-turn that threw the suspect even deeper into a state of confusion.

"Car?"

"Aye. Car." Logan mimed turning a steering wheel. "*Vroom-vroom.* What kind have you got?"

Billy's expression was utterly vacant, like he'd been trying to decipher a riddle in a foreign language, and something in his brain had gone *pop*.

"I'll tell you, will I?" Logan said. "Kia Rio. Dark blue. Or 'Midnight Saffire' if you want to get arsey about it."

"What's that got to do with anything?" the solicitor asked.

Logan continued to drill his gaze into Billy's skull. "It matches the description of a car seen parked at the house where the Sutherland family was murdered," Logan said. "Which is why we think you killed them, Billy."

"I didn't! I couldn't! I'm not capable of something like... I'm not a violent man!"

Logan sat back. "Well now, Billy," he said. Beside him, DCI Filson removed a printout of a crime report from a folder. "Will we ask Darren Priestley if he agrees?"

CHAPTER THIRTY-SEVEN

TYLER STOOD in front of the room's full-length mirror, a cup of tea in one hand, his phone pressed against his ear by the other. His hair was dishevelled. Or as dishevelled as it was possible to get with all that wax holding it in place.

He leaned in closer to study the red rings under his eyes, then decided that was only likely to make him feel worse, and turned his back on his reflection.

"So... sorry I didn't come up the road," he said. "Are you mad?"

Sinead's voice sounded tinny and faraway through the mobile's earpiece. "No. Not mad," she said. "I'm just glad you finally told him. You've got to do... Sorry, one sec."

Tyler sipped his tea and listened to a muffled conversation with DI Forde. Somewhere else in the office, a desk phone rang.

He turned his attention back to the mirror. He'd taken off his tie and untucked his shirt. The bottom of it was an ordnance survey map of creases and lines. He'd kicked his shoes off, too, and the man in the mirror looked all the smaller for it.

"Sorry, back," Sinead said, once the other conversation ended. "What were you saying?"

"Nothing much," Tyler replied. "I'm getting the early train tomorrow. You still going to be able to pick me up?"

"Eh, aye. I think so. It's all kicked off here, so I just... Dave? Can you get that phone? If it's Hamza, tell him I'll call... Cheers."

"Sounds busy," Tyler said.

"You can say that again."

She told him about Hamza's grim discovery at Jazmin McAllister's. The DS was on his way to Skye now to break the news to her parents—one of the shittiest jobs in a career positively riddled with them.

"Jesus. That's rough," Tyler said. "Is there anything I can do to help from down here?"

Sinead's response didn't make sense at first, until he realised it wasn't directed at him. "Tell her I'll call her back in two minutes."

"You're busy," Tyler said.

"What? No. No, it's fine. Just Shona calling. She's been over the body. Jazmin's, I... What? Yes, sir. It's on my desk. Blue folder."

Tyler waited. The man in the mirror watched him.

"Sorry, Ty, what were you saying?"

"Just asking what I can do to help. How can I make myself useful?"

"Don't be daft. You take it easy," Sinead said. "We're fine here."

"You don't sound fine. You sound rushed off your feet. Just give me something to do. I can help!"

"Rest! Put your feet up!" Sinead insisted. Another phone burst into life in the background. "I have to run. I'll call you later. Love you."

The phone went dead before he could say it back.

"I can be useful," he said again, more quietly this time.

And the man in the mirror mocked him with his silence.

———

MRS MAITLAND, Billy's solicitor, stretched in her seat to see the printout that Heather had produced from the folder.

"Who's Darren Priestley?" she asked.

"Teenage lad. Right mouthy bastard, by all accounts. Bit of a wind-up merchant," Logan explained. "Ended up getting a couple of slaps from his Biology teacher for taking things too far. Didn't he, Billy?"

"That's... That was different," Billy protested. "He was..."

"What? Asking for it?" Heather prompted. "Deserving it?"

"You say you're not a violent man, Billy, and yet this report would say otherwise, would it not?" Logan asked.

"It was... It was a mistake. He kept pushing. I didn't... I reacted badly."

"We know you and Archie were meant to be getting a Hogmanay special, Billy," Logan continued. "Back on the telly. Big payday. That would've been handy with a new baby in the house."

Billy pushed a finger and thumb up under his glasses, wiping the sweat from his eyelids. "That was... Archie was keen, I just... I went along with it for his sake, really."

"Interesting that you say that," Logan continued. "See, we had a chat with the producer. Nice lassie. Younger than my colleague who spoke to her was expecting. Very open and chatty. According to her, the whole idea of the reunion was yours. You pitched it to them, and then you developed it alongside their in-house team."

Billy drained the last few dregs of water from his cup, stalling for time. "I mean... once it was set-up, I got involved with it all, obviously. It made sense at that stage. And, I mean, I had to. Contractually."

"It was your idea from the start, Billy," Heather said. "The producer told us that getting Archie on board was the hard part. You were there from day one. But, you convinced him in the end. Talked him into it."

Logan picked up the story. "And that's when it all fell apart. Isn't it, Billy? They found out about his porn business. The BBC. Found out his dirty wee secret. And they couldn't have that, could they? No' on their Hogmanay flagship. No' another sordid sex scandal. No' so soon after Yewtree. That wouldn't do at all. So they canned it."

"How did that make you feel, Mr Pinnock?" asked Heather, her tone softening, her head cocking to one side. "To get so close to that big comeback, and have it so cruelly snatched away from you? And for something that wasn't even your fault. That must've been a kick in the teeth."

"I'd have been bloody furious," Logan said. "Livid. There's no saying what I'd have done, but I'd have been out for payback, no doubt about it." He sat forward, resting his arms on the table, closing the gap between them. "Is that what you did, Billy? Got a bit of payback? Was he asking for it, like Darren Priestley?"

"No."

Logan pulled a face that suggested he was impressed. "I see you've got the hang of the yes or no answers at last. That's good. But I don't believe you," he said. "See, when my colleague DC Neish and I turned up at your shop earlier, you didn't react in the way I'd expect you to have reacted. Especially knowing now that you had a new baby to worry about. There was no concern that something had happened at home, or that your wife had been involved in an accident, or anything like that. Why was that?"

Billy made a croaky sort of cough, like the words were caught somewhere in his throat.

"You don't have to answer 'yes' or 'no' to that one, Mr Pinnock," Heather told him.

"You don't have to answer at all, Billy," Logan said. "Allow me to do it for you. See, I think you reacted the way you did because you knew why we were there. You knew Archie was dead. And you knew that, whether you were a suspect or not, you'd be questioned. The legendary Neeps and Tatties. How could you not be in the frame somewhere?"

"I didn't kill him," Billy whispered. "I didn't!"

Logan ignored the remark and pressed on. "I spoke to DC Neish about my... I'm not sure 'suspicions' is quite the right word. Concerns, let's say. I told him that I was *concerned* by your reaction. And you know what he said?"

Billy shook his head. "No."

"He asked me how you could possibly have known where Archie was. From what we can gather, he was in hiding. He certainly wasn't broadcasting his location, anyway."

The DCI left a gap there. A few seconds of stifling silence, giving Billy time to stress over what was coming next.

"Except he was doing exactly that. Wasn't he, Billy?" Logan continued. "He *was* broadcasting his location. To you, specifically. Ever since you fixed his phone for him."

Billy said nothing. Not with his words, anyway. His face, however, spoke volumes.

"We've got DC Neish to thank for this, too. He figured it out.

It's a built-in feature, I'm told. *Find My Phone* or something," Logan continued. "You just have to tweak a few settings, and anyone you choose can see your location at any time. All seems a bit creepy to me, but I suppose I can see some upsides." He shrugged. "Few downsides, too, of course, if it ends up getting you and your family killed."

"That's a pretty major drawback, right enough," Heather agreed.

Billy opened his mouth, but Logan silenced him with a raised hand. "Before you say anything, Billy, I want you to know that Archie's phone was handed over to our tech team yesterday, and they've submitted a report this evening."

This was true. They had. Admittedly, it was quite a short report, and one whose focus was almost exclusively on how they had not, as of yet, been able to access it.

"I just want you to keep that in mind before you say anything that might be considered in any way incriminating," Logan added. He gave a smile of encouragement, then crossed his arms and shuffled in closer to the table, like he was waiting to hear a funny story.

Across the table, Billy's mouth was still moving as he started to form the first word of several different potential replies, before abandoning each and every one of them.

"Are we having to go back to the yes or no answers, Billy?" Logan asked. "Fine. Did you share Archie's location when you were fixing his phone?"

Billy shook his head. "It's not like—"

"Yes or no, Billy."

"I mean... Technically? Yes."

Logan kept his face still, fending off the surprise. It had been a stretch, he'd thought. A straw to be grasped at. He hadn't really believed for one minute that it might be true.

Billy was still talking, although he wasn't saying anything of any real note. "But not... I didn't do it for anything... Not because..."

"So, we've established that you knew where to find him," Logan said, shutting him down. "We've established that a car matching the description of yours was spotted at the scene. And we've established that he'd cost you a very lucrative career opportunity that you'd fought very hard to secure, and which could've potentially been life-changing."

"And he concealed those facts from us," Heather added.

"Yes! Very good point, Detective Chief Inspector!" Logan boomed. "And you concealed those facts from us." He sat back and nodded at the solicitor. "You might want to phone home and let them know you're going to be a while," he suggested. "I think we've got a long night ahead of us."

"What about the baby, Mr Pinnock?" Heather asked, her solemn stare not having wavered once. "Wee Senga. Did you take her from Archie after you killed him and his family?"

"I keep telling you, I didn't kill anyone!" Billy sobbed. "And with regards to the tracking thing... It was unrelated to... When he came to the shop, we got to talking about a possible reunion show. He seemed keen. We decided I would pitch it. And I thought... If we were going to be working together..." He grimaced. "Archie was always unpredictable. The number of gigs we did in the early days when he was either late or just didn't show up, you wouldn't believe. He'd be in some other pub somewhere, or at the bookies, or... God. I don't know."

His spectacles had steamed up, his body heat misting the glass. He removed them, pinched the bridge of his nose like he was fighting off a migraine, then unfastened the top button of his shirt.

It really was *very* warm.

"I thought, if we were going to work together, I wanted to be able to find him. I didn't want him doing that to me again. Leaving me holding the can, and looking stupid. It's one thing doing it in a working men's club in Newcastle, it's another when it's the BBC."

"That may have been your original intention, Billy," Logan conceded. "But when everything fell through, it had another purpose, didn't it? It let you find him when he didn't want to be found. And we know you found him. Even if we discount the sighting of your car for the moment."

"You can't prove it was his car," the solicitor pointed out.

"Like I said, we can discount the sighting of the car. The fact is, Billy told us himself he found Archie. Didn't you?"

Across the table, Billy frowned. "What? I didn't... What did I...?"

"You'll have to forgive me for paraphrasing here, Billy," Logan said, producing a small notebook and flipping through the pages. "My colleague, Detective Constable Neish, did the transcribing, and his writing's no' the best. Ah. Here we go. I can actually make this out OK for once. You said that Archie hated holidaying in this country and that he'd never—and I quote—'take himself out there to the middle of nowhere. Not on purpose.'"

He closed the notebook and waited. Heather waited, too. Even his solicitor seemed to be holding her breath.

"What? So what?" Billy asked. "You said he was in Glen Coe."

And there they had it. On tape.

"We didn't, Mr Pinnock," Logan replied. "We told you he was in the Highlands. Nobody ever said anything about Glen Coe."

Billy's cheeks, which had been a skelping shade of red, rapidly lightened until they were almost white. He shook his head and prodded a finger on the tabletop like he was either trying to make a point, or was hunting for the button that would activate an ejector seat.

"No, you did. You said. You must've told me."

"I'm afraid you're mistaken," Logan told him. "All we said was that he was in the Highlands. And that's a big area, Mr Pinnock. Huge. I think we can all agree that you pinpointing the exact spot where Archie and his family were killed would be one hell of a lucky guess."

"One in a million chance, that," Heather agreed.

"Oh, at least. So, how about we cut all this shite, Mr Pinnock," Logan said. He cracked his knuckles, flexed his fingers, then picked up his pen. "And you start telling us the truth?"

CHAPTER THIRTY-EIGHT

HAMZA'S WINDSCREEN wipers *ka-thunked* out a regular beat as he sat in his car across from the guest house. The weather had taken a turn for the worse halfway up the Kyle of Lochalsh road, and by the time he was approaching the Skye bridge, he'd half expected to find it closed due to high winds.

He'd made it over, though, and then made the forty-minute meander north until he'd reached Portree at the opposite end of the island.

It was dark now, and his headlights picked out the carved wooden sign on the garden gate—'The Coorie Doon.'

It was the sort of cottage that popped up on the front of story-books and shortbread tins. It looked like the sort of place where good things happened, where families came together, where love, and laughter, and moments together were shared.

There was a light on downstairs. The flicker of a TV painted pictures behind the grey tartan curtains. Smoke rose like puffs of fluffy white cloud from a squat brick chimney, before swirling away on the wind.

The creaking of the gate was a cheerful two-tone note when Hamza pushed through it. The doorbell's *bing-bong* was a happy one, announcing his arrival to the people inside.

He heard music. Laughter. A shout of, "Coming!"

And then, a woman was there, all warmth and welcome, and smiles for the stranger on her step.

"Mrs McAllister?" Hamza said.

"That's me!" she trilled. "Are you...? Do we have you booked in with us?"

"No, Ma'am. I'm Detective Sergeant Hamza Khaled." He felt the heat of the house escaping past him. "Do you mind if I come inside? There's something we need to discuss."

"Um, yes. Yes, of course," the woman in the hallway said, clearing the way for him to enter.

Hamza nodded his thanks and stepped inside.

And the cold and the rain followed with him.

"I... I CAN'T TELL YOU." Billy Neeps was sitting forward in his chair now, elbows propped on the table, hands supporting the weight of his head. "It'll break her heart. It'll kill her."

"What will, Billy?" Logan asked.

"I didn't hurt anyone. I'd never... Not something like that. I couldn't. When you told me what happened, I just... I don't know." He raised his head just enough to meet Logan's eye. "I cried. Once you'd left. I just lay down on the floor, and I cried. I mean... Archie's one thing. It's bad, obviously. It's horrible... But Donna and the girls? What sort of monster...?"

The two DCIs on the other side of the table said nothing. Billy was finding some sort of flow now, and it was best not to interrupt. Let him talk, see what came out, then pick it all apart. That was how you got the bastards.

"I did know where he was," he admitted. "But not because I was... He phoned me. Out of the blue. I'd been trying to get hold of him, to talk to him about the show being cancelled, but he was dodging my calls. And then, Sunday..." He frowned. "No, Monday. He phones. He's all apologies, says he feels bad, but he says... 'I can make it up to you,' he says."

"Make it up to you how?" DCI Filson prompted.

Tears misted Billy's eyes. He clamped his hands over his

mouth, like he was trying to force back the words that were determined to come.

"Take your time, Billy," Logan said. "We've got all night."

There was a sob, a deep, wet-sounding sniff, then Billy
removed his hands from his mouth and placed them down on the
table, one atop the other.

"There was a girl. One of the... I don't know. *Actresses* from his
films. Something had happened. I think some... I don't know,
partner in the business, or something, had... Well, he'd... Can I say
'sampled the merchandise'? Would that be appropriate?"

"He'd had sexual intercourse with her?" said Heather. The
bluntness of it made Billy flinch.

"Yes. I mean, I think... So Archie told me. I got the impression
it was an unwelcome advance, too."

"He raped her?" asked Logan.

Another flinch from Billy. It shouldn't have been a surprise,
really. The man had built his career on cheeky innuendo. His was a
world where sex was never explicitly mentioned but implied with a
laugh, and a wink, and the occasional *parp* of a bicycle horn.
Talking about rape was unlikely to sit comfortably with him.

"I mean... I don't know. I'm just saying what was implied by
Archie. You'd have to ask the young lady herself."

"Jazmin?"

Billy drew back like the word was dripping with poison. "Um,
yes. Yes, that's her. I never... I didn't meet her, but that was her
name, yes." He squeezed his hands together like he was trying to
stop them clamping over his mouth again. His eyes swam, flicking
from one detective to the other and back again. "Oh, God. She
wants her back, doesn't she? She wants her back?"

"He gave you the baby," Logan realised. "He gave you Jazmin's
baby."

Billy nodded, his tightening throat silencing him more effectively than his hands could ever hope to. He choked, coughed, then
retched so violently his whole body heaved and both DCIs pushed
their chairs back to escape the expected spray of vomit that, fortunately, didn't arrive.

"Sorry," he whimpered. "Sorry, I just... God. It was meant to be
straightforward. God, Louise! It's going to destroy her. We couldn't

have kids. Not of our own. Or... *I* couldn't. And she wanted them so, so much. Always has. But we couldn't adopt. We tried, but... I hit a child. I was a teacher, and I hit a child." He banged a fist on the table. "Darren *fucking* Priestley!"

He did cover his mouth then, practically wedging the hand he'd struck the table with into his mouth as he fought to hold himself together.

"And they wouldn't let us," he whispered through a mouthful of knuckle. "Not after that. Not once they knew. But, she was so desperate. And she was so sad. And... When he phoned. Archie. When he phoned, and when he said what had happened. That young girl. She didn't want the baby. She couldn't deal with it. She needed someone to take care of it. To love it, like their own."

"And Archie thought you fit the bill," Logan prompted.

Billy sniffed, wiped his eyes on his sleeve, then nodded. "I drove up on Wednesday. Louise and I. We both did. I wasn't sure. I thought... I thought we might get into trouble, or... I don't know." The suggestion of a smile changed the shape of his whole face. "And then I saw her. I saw her sitting there in her wee chair. Fast asleep. Wee gloves on to stop her scratching herself. Tiny things, they were."

He closed his eyes, transporting himself back to another time and place, reliving all the details of it.

"And Louise, she made this... this noise. This... I don't know how to describe it. But it was love. That sound. It was love." The smile became a troubled thing, and agitation twitched and furrowed his brow. "There was no harm done," he insisted, the snapping open of his eyes bringing him hurtling back to the here and now. "It was a win-win. The young lady wanted rid, the baby needed a home, and we wanted to provide it. There were no losers in the transaction. Everyone came away happy!"

"Aye, see, you say that, Billy, but Jazmin McAllister was found dead this evening," Logan revealed.

Billy stared. Silent. Mute. Behind his eyes, his brain worked furiously to try to process what he'd just been told.

"What? No. What?"

The words were soft and murmured, like he'd switched into

low power mode while he came to terms with this unexpected turn of events.

"Not... not murdered?" he asked. "An accident?"

"At this stage, we believe she took her own life," Logan replied.

This time, Billy's hands were shaking too badly to find his mouth. "Oh God. Oh God. Oh no, oh God."

"Turns out not everyone came away from the 'transaction' happy after all, Mr Pinnock," DCI Filson said.

On the other side of the table, Billy finally broke all the way. His body convulsed with shock, and sorrow, and shame. He gripped his arms, digging his nails in, and sobbed through gritted teeth, tears, and sweat, and snot glistening all over his face.

"I think we need to take a break there," his solicitor said. "My client is visibly distressed and unable to answer any further questions at the moment."

"One final question, then we'll call it a night," Logan said.

"Detective Chief Inspector—" the solicitor started to protest, but Logan brushed the objection aside.

"Billy. Billy? Look at me."

Billy choked and wheezed and gulped, his whole respiratory system suffering some major malfunction. His eyes met Logan's. They looked feral, like a frightened animal backed into a corner.

"Did you kill Archie and his family?" Logan asked.

The reply came not as a word, but as a shake of the head. Logan regarded him for a moment, eyes narrowed, then gave the solicitor the nod. "Fine," he said. "Let's call it a night."

Heather turned to him in surprise. "What?"

"We'll have someone come and escort Mr Pinnock down to the cells."

"I don't think that will be necessary, do you?" the solicitor asked.

"Well, it's that, or he tells us where his wife has taken the baby," Logan said. He pushed back his chair and stood, his shadow falling over almost the entire table. "I'll leave that decision up to him."

CHAPTER THIRTY-NINE

HEATHER WATCHED in silence as Logan dumped his coat on one of the canteen tables, sidled up to a half-empty vending machine, and secured himself a late dinner of a *Coke Zero* and a *Twix*.

The canteen was empty, as it often was at this time of night, the serving hatch where more substantial meals might be secured having long-since been shuttered for the day.

"You wanting anything?" he asked, glancing back over his shoulder as he waited for the machine to stop whirring and the chocolate bar to drop.

Heather answered with a shake of her head, then crossed her arms and waited for him to return.

"What was that?" she asked.

Logan looked over at the vending machine. "I didn't get a chance to eat anything, so—"

"Not that. In there," the other DCI replied. "Pinnock. We nearly had a confession."

Logan cracked open his can and took a gulp. "We got a confession. They took the baby."

"To the murders. He was about to crack."

"No, he wasn't," Logan said.

"You going soft in your old age?" Heather pressed. "The DCI Logan I knew would've kept at that wee runt until he broke him."

"Seemed pretty broken to me," Logan said.

He set the can on the table and peeled open the wrapper of his chocolate. "Sure you don't want a bit?" he asked, offering out the *Twix*.

Heather smirked. "You offering me a finger, Jack? God, just like old times, eh?" she teased. "But no. I'll pass, thanks."

Logan shrugged. "Suit yourself."

"I could go a drink, though. If you fancy one?"

"There's more *Coke* in the vending machine," Logan said. "No *Irn Bru* left, though, as per bloody usual. Some things never change."

Heather raised an eyebrow. "I meant a real drink. It'd be good to catch up. Properly. Just the two of us."

Logan nodded. "Aye. I know what you meant. But best not, I think," he said.

"No. Right. Yeah. Of course," Heather said. She laughed, but it was a high-pitched chirp of a thing that was so far removed from her normal laugh Logan initially thought she might have stubbed a toe. "Let's keep it professional this time."

"Works for me," Logan said.

Heather tucked her hands into the pockets of her trousers, her thumbs hooked over her belt. "Right, well. Billy, then. You don't think he did it, do you?"

Logan shook his head. "No. I mean, I knew he was tied up in it. I just didn't know how."

"And you believe his story?" Heather asked, the tone of her voice making it clear that she didn't. "You actually believe what he said."

"I think so, aye," Logan said. "I believe it more than I believe him tying up four people and murdering them all."

"He was a Biology teacher," Heather pointed out.

Logan took a bite of his *Twix* and ruminated on the point while he chewed. "And? Are Biology teachers more likely to be murderers? Did I miss that memo somewhere?"

"I had a look at the pathology report. The placement of the wounds. Someone knew where the heart was."

"Oh. That." Logan moved his tongue around inside his mouth, scraping bits of toffee from his teeth. "There's a big difference between knowing where the heart is and being able to plunge a dirty great knife into it."

"I still think we should be treating him as a suspect."

"Aye, well, it's no' your case," Logan said. "He'll tell Uniform where his wife is, if he hasn't already. CID can handle the details. Billy's no' our killer."

"So who is it?" Heather asked.

Logan scrunched up the chocolate bar wrapper. "Don't know yet," he admitted. "But I'm going to talk to Frankie Cowan again in the morning. Put a bit of pressure on. Use the rape angle."

"I'll come with you. You'll need backup," Heather said. "He might look like a wee scrote, but Frankie's not someone you want to mess with."

Logan nodded. "I heard that, right enough," he said. "But I'm sure I'll cope." He pointed to his coat. "Watch that for me, will you? I'm dying for a pish."

He headed off without waiting for an answer, throwing open the door and striding away through corridors so familiar his feet could navigate them all by themselves.

Heather sat on the edge of the table and watched him go. Before today, he hadn't set foot in the building for a good two years, yet he moved like he owned the place. More than that, even. It was like the building—the whole station—was an extension of himself, and if he raised his voice the walls would tremble and shake.

Crossing to the window, Heather checked her reflection in the darkened glass. She drew up her lips and studied her teeth, then ran a hand through her hair, straightened her jacket, and gave herself an appreciative nod.

Looking good.

Good enough, anyway.

There was a buzzing from the table behind her, and her eyes were drawn to Logan's coat. She looked over to the door, saw no sign of him coming back, so fished his phone from his pocket and regarded the picture on-screen with a sort of fascinated curiosity.

A little flashing camera icon told her it was a video call. She gave her hair another quick run-through with a hand, turned the phone to get her from her best angle, then tapped the button to reply.

At first glance, the person who appeared on-screen may have been Alice Cooper. The makeup was spot-on, anyway, although Heather didn't recall Alice Cooper ever looking quite so shocked as the woman calling did.

"Hi!" DCI Filson said. "Can I help you?"

"Um... Hello," the other woman replied in a hesitant Irish accent. "Is... Sorry, is this Jack's phone?"

"It is," Heather confirmed. "Who's calling?"

"It's... Um. Shona. Maguire. Shona Maguire. I'm... a friend."

Heather frowned. "He's never mentioned you," she said. "And... sorry, do you know you've got something going on with your makeup? Is it meant to look like that?"

On-screen, Shona's gaze flitted up to the top left corner of the picture as she checked the overlaid image of herself. She licked a thumb and rubbed furiously at the blurry dark stains under her eyes.

"No. That's not... It was for a movie."

Heather blinked in surprise. "You're an actress?"

"What? No. I'm a pathologist."

"Oh! Right. Gotcha. One of those gothy morbid ones."

"No. Not... I wouldn't say *morbid*, exactly, I just..." Shona stopped talking, took a breath, and tried again. "Is Jack there?"

Heather looked back over her shoulder. "He's actually just gone to the bathroom. We were just having a drink and a bite to eat, then heading off. I can get him to call you back, if you like? Tomorrow would probably be best, though." She smirked. "You know what they say, all work and no play makes Jack a dull boy."

"What?" Shona looked down. Her head shook, but only once. "Um... right. Yeah. Sure. Whatever. Just... if you could tell him I called?"

"I'll be sure to pass the message on," Heather replied. She winked, her smile widening. "Whenever we get a minute."

She gave a little wave, then ended the call with a swipe of her thumb. She hummed quietly to herself as she returned the phone to the pocket she'd taken it from.

A moment later, the door opened and Logan returned, still tucking his shirt back in. "Right, I'd best be getting off," he announced.

"Sure I can't tempt you with that drink?" Heather asked.

"Lovely offer, Heather, but I think we both know that would be a bad idea."

She nodded, although she didn't seem entirely in agreement. But desperation wasn't her style. "I guess we just missed our chance. Eh, Jack?"

"Aye. I guess we did," Logan agreed.

"Our own fault, I suppose. It's what we get for wasting all those years dancing around each other," Heather said. She picked up Logan's coat and handed it over. "Nice working with you again, Detective Chief Inspector."

Logan took the coat and wrestled himself into it. "Same to you, Detective Chief Inspector."

"Come on, then," Heather said. She fixed his collar for him, then ran a hand down his back and let it linger at the base of his spine. "At least let me escort you off the premises."

———

THEY HAD JUST PASSED the Gozer's office when the Detective Superintendent stepped out into the corridor and called after them.

"God, this brings back memories," he said, once they'd doubled back to meet him. "You two. Working your magic in there."

"You were watching?" Logan asked.

"Bits. Couldn't stay for long, but I needed a dose of nostalgia, and that hit the spot." He addressed the next part to Logan, and the way Heather's body language changed suggested she'd taken this as a slight. "You think he's your man, then?" the Gozer asked. "You think he killed them?"

"He doesn't," Heather said, jumping in with the reply.

She put her hands on her hips, making herself appear larger, like she was trying to assert her dominance. This was her patch now, after all. Logan was merely passing through.

"You don't?" the Gozer asked, and Heather chewed at the inside of her bottom lip.

"No. Like DCI Filson said, I don't think Billy's the killer."

"It appears he's got your missing baby, though. I was there for that part."

"Aye. But I think he was telling the truth," Logan replied. "I think the two of them made some sort of deal. The wean was some sort of peace offering."

"You think Archie forced the mother to give the kiddie up? Took it from her?" asked the Detective Superintendent.

Logan had to admit that he didn't know. Not for sure.

"Shuggie Cowan said that Archie was good to the women in his films. Looked after them. If that's true, then it's possible she wanted rid, and he tried to help her. I'm going to have someone talk to some of the other women on the list Cowan gave me, get their thoughts on it. Not a lot to be done on it now, though, either way. No one left to testify or to press charges against."

"There's still Billy and his wife," Heather pointed out. "They're complicit."

Logan shoved his hands deep into his coat pockets. "Aye, well, I'm going to hand that over to your team down here. I'd imagine the grandparents might want to take the baby. Going to be messy, though. If I was you, I'd pass the whole thing on as quickly as I could."

"Like you're doing right now, you mean?"

"Aye. Exactly like that," Logan confirmed. "You can feel free to kick it over to CID, if you like."

"Oh, *can* we?" Heather sniped back. "Thanks for your permission, Detective Chief Inspector."

"Ha!" the Gozer slapped a hand on Logan's shoulder, grinning from ear to ear. "Just like old times, right enough!" He patted the shoulder a couple of times, noted that Logan did not appear to share his amusement, then cleared his throat. "So, you catch up with Shuggie's nephew, then?"

"I did."

"And how is the heir to the Cowan throne?"

"He's a tricky wee bastard," Logan said.

The Gozer shrugged. "I did try to warn you. There's a lot of loyalty to him on that scheme, too."

"So I noticed. Had a big fella with him, too. Bit of a brute."

"Ah, yes. I probably should have mentioned him," the Detective Superintendent admitted. "Brendan 'Budgie' Bowman. No idea where the 'Budgie' bit comes from. Used to be one of Shuggie's. His father and Shuggie go way back. Barry Bowman."

"Christ, aye. I can see the resemblance, now you mention it," Logan said. "Dead now though, isn't he?"

"Yes. Poor old Barry passed peacefully about twelve years back," the Gozer confirmed. "In the boot of a car we fished out of the Clyde."

Logan remembered the case, but just vaguely. He'd been deep in the Mister Whisper investigation at that point, to the exclusion of everything else. "Shuggie's doing?" he asked.

"Oh no. Far from it. A warning to the Cowan clan, if anything. Shuggie went out of his way to make sure the rest of the Bowman family were all well looked after."

Heather snorted. "*Such* a lovely man."

"Yes. A real softy!" the Gozer agreed.

For some reason that he would never be able to put into words, the way the other two officers were talking about the convicted criminal and feared gangster was rubbing Logan up the wrong way. He almost wanted to say something—to stand up for the vindictive old bastard.

He didn't, of course. Doing so would lead to doubts, and funny looks, and questions he couldn't even begin to answer. Questions he didn't *know* how to answer. Not without admitting the terrible truth to himself.

The terrible truth that, despite their years of differences—despite all the many terrible things he knew Cowan had done, and the even longer list he didn't know about—Logan quite liked the old bugger.

Instead of leaping valiantly to Shuggie's defence, he shifted the conversation onto another member of the Cowan family.

"I'm going to go back and talk to Frankie in the morning," he said.

"You taking Heather?" the Detective Superintendent asked.

"He's not 'taking' me anywhere," DCI Filson objected. "I did, however, offer to go with him for support."

"Right. Yes. Sorry, Heather," the Gozer said, awkwardly

scratching his stomach through his shirt. "It's good that you're going. Of your own free will, I mean."

"She isn't," Logan told him. "I'm handling this one on my own."

"What? That's reckless, Jack. They're a dangerous bunch. We've got a local shopkeeper in a coma, and we think Frankie put him there. Can't bloody prove anything, of course. As usual. Can't even tie him to it beyond speculation."

Logan's smile was a thin, solemn sort of thing. It was the sort of smile shared between mourners at a funeral. A gesture, done with the intention of reassuring the other party that things would get better. That things wouldn't always be like this. That brighter futures lay ahead.

"I'll be fine. I've got it in hand," he said. "But I do need one more thing from you though, sir."

The Gozer flinched. "God. He's calling me 'sir.' It must be big." He sighed, bracing himself. "Go on, then. What do you want?"

"A blind eye turned for the next twelve hours or so," Logan replied. He looked from one officer to the other. "And no questions asked."

CHAPTER FORTY

THE FIRST CALL Hamza made when he was back on the road was not to DCI Forde. Instead, as the quaint little Bed & Breakfast grew smaller in the rearview mirror, he dialled home, sat tensed while he listened to the ringing, then let out a shaky breath when his wife's voice came echoing from the speakers.

"Hello?"

Her voice was slurred. Confused.

"Hey. Sorry, were you sleeping?" he asked.

"No. Maybe. I don't... What time is it?"

"It's..." He checked the clock and winced. "Shite. It's half-past eleven."

"Then yes, of course I was bloody sleeping!" Amira replied.

Her voice was gruff, her irritation obvious. She sounded like her mother when she was annoyed. *Exactly* like her mother, in fact. Usually, this would make Hamza fearful for the future. Tonight, though, it filled him full of something else. Hope, maybe. Or gratitude.

"Sorry. I didn't realise it was so late," he said.

Down the line, Amira yawned. "Where are you? Are you coming home?"

"Not tonight, no," Hamza told her. "I'm on Skye."

"What are you doing on Skye?"

"Driving," Hamza said. "I... I had to go and break some news to a victim's parents."

"Oh. Yikes." Amira said, suddenly sounding more awake. "Are you OK?"

"I'm fine."

A lie.

"You don't sound fine."

"I am. Honest," Hamza insisted. The windscreen wipers *whumped* back and forth, battling valiantly against the hammering rain. He passed the graveyard that stood on the outskirts of the town, and his car ploughed on into the dark as he left Portree behind. "I didn't wake Kamila did I?"

"No." Amira yawned again. "No, I don't think so."

"Right. Well, that's good. I'm glad," Hamza said. Another lie. What he wouldn't have given right then to have heard her voice. To hear her smile. "Well, I should let you go. It's late."

"Hamza, you sound upset. Are you sure you're OK?"

"No. Yes. I mean, no, I'm not upset. Honest. I just... I didn't realise the time. If I had, I wouldn't have..." He thought of the couple he'd left in the cottage behind him, their lives forever changed. Forever broken. Their family torn apart.

"Actually, you know what?" Amira said. "I think maybe I do hear Kamila moving about. Do you want me to go see?"

"Eh..." Hamza said, but the rest wouldn't come. Some blockage in his throat stopped the words from emerging.

"Give me a second," Amira said, and this time she sounded nothing like her mother. Quite the opposite. "And I'll put her on."

DI FORDE PUT a hand on Sinead's shoulder, startling her awake. She lunged for her laptop keyboard, stared in confusion at the darkened screen, then looked around the room as if getting her bearings.

It was only then that she spotted Ben smiling down at her, and realised what had happened.

"Sorry, sir. I must've nodded off."

"It's nearly midnight," Ben said. "You should get to the hotel. Get some rest."

Sinead stretched and checked her watch, confirming the time for herself. "God. Yeah." She yawned, then rubbed her eyes with finger and thumb, forcing them to open wider. "Any word from Hamza?"

"He called a few minutes ago," Ben confirmed. "He's been in and spoken to Jazmin's parents. Suffice to say, they didn't take it well."

"No. I can't imagine they would have," Sinead said. "How's Hamza doing? He's had a hell of a night."

"He's... OK, I think. He phoned home and spoke to his wife and the wee one. I think that helped. Or, I don't know, possibly made it worse. You know what it's like."

Sinead nodded. She did. Better, perhaps, than most.

"Did he mention the baby?"

Ben lowered himself onto the edge of a desk. "He did. He reckoned they were shocked. Doesn't think they knew anything about it. They hadn't seen her in months."

"I'm guessing they didn't know about her choice of career?"

"They thought she was working at the school. Teaching Assistant. Hamza decided not to shatter that illusion quite yet. They'd had quite enough bad news for one day."

There was a snore from over by the door. Unlike Sinead, whose forty-winks had been unplanned, Dave had fashioned himself a pillow from a rolled-up jacket, and was fast asleep with his head on the desk.

"He's been like that for the last half-hour," Ben remarked.

Sinead yawned again, the sight of the sleeping Exhibits Officer reminding her how tired she was. "How long was I out for?"

"About the same," Ben said. "I thought the phone ringing might wake you, but you didn't rouse."

"I should check in with Tyler," Sinead muttered. She picked up her phone and glanced at the screen, but found no missed calls or messages.

"He's probably asleep. Jack said he dropped him back at the hotel before bringing Billy Neeps in for questioning."

"Oh. Right."

She checked the phone again, in case she'd missed anything. Tyler was hopeless at being on his own. He got bored of it quickly, and if he'd been in the hotel all night on his own she'd have expected half a dozen texts and missed calls at least.

But there was nothing.

"Billy owned up, by the way," Ben said, and Sinead's body went rigid with shock. "Sorry, not to the murders. To taking the baby. Him and his wife picked her up earlier in the week, he says. It was all arranged through Archie. An off-the-books adoption. He insists Jazmin didn't want the baby, and that they thought they were doing her a favour. He also insists the family was alive and well when he left."

"Anything to back his story up?" Sinead asked.

"A few bits and bobs. Got his car on a couple of ANPR cameras headed up the road on Wednesday. We've got him as far as Tyndrum. His phone history. What's it called? With the satnav?"

"GPS?"

"That, aye. That shows the whole journey, but obviously doesn't tell us what he did while he was at the house. It fits his story, though."

Sinead nodded. "Jazmin's parents. Did they say anything about Archie and his family coming to stay?"

"Hamza didn't want to push too far on it. Don't want them speculating until we know for sure that the baby was Jazmin's, but they confirmed the Sutherlands did stay for a few days. They were very... how did he put it? *Generous* with the wee one. They encouraged Jazmin's parents to hold her a lot while they were there."

Sinead wrinkled her nose. "Bit weird. Rubbing their face in it without them knowing, maybe?"

"I don't think so," Ben said. "I actually think—I hope—maybe they thought they were doing a good thing. Letting the wee one meet her grandparents, and vice versa. I think maybe it was a kindness."

"Or fulfilling a promise to Jazmin, maybe," Sinead suggested.

Ben breathed out slowly through his nose. "I suppose we'll never know for sure," he said. He shook his head. "Sad, sad, sad." He gave a little grunt of effort as he stood up, then tapped his watch. "Right, bedtime. Let's get ourselves back to the hotel and get some kip."

Sinead closed over her laptop, rolled back her chair, and stood up. "What about Hamza?"

"He's going to head straight to the hotel and give me a phone when he's in," Ben said.

The DC jabbed a thumb in Dave's direction. As if on cue, he let out a long, throaty snore. "And what about Sleeping Beauty? Should we wake him?"

"Well..." Ben clapped his hands together loudly, sending the sound racing around the room. There wasn't so much as a flicker from the man in the wheelchair. "I suppose we should at least give it a try."

THE RESTAURANT WAS SHUT when Logan made it back to the hotel, and with no minibar on offer in his room, he had to resort to the second vending machine visit of the evening. There would be plenty of takeaways delivering, but he didn't have the inclination to trawl through menus, nor the patience to wait for the delivery.

And so, a couple of minutes later, he stood in the lift with a bag of crisps in one hand, a plastic bottle of *Irn Bru* in the other, and a cheeky *Milky Way* tucked into his shirt pocket for dessert.

He stopped outside Tyler's room and listened at the door for any sign that the DC was still awake. The TV was off, which he took to be a sign that Tyler was asleep. He could be lying awake reading or something, Logan supposed, but the chances of that were slim. Getting Tyler to read *anything* was akin to getting a cow to walk down stairs.

He had an aversion to silence, too, hence his constant need to fill it by talking endless amounts of shite. If the room was quiet, then that meant he was either out, asleep, or dead.

Logan seriously doubted the DC would've gone out anywhere on his own this late in the day. And, if he was dead, then there was a very good chance that he'd still be dead in the morning, and Logan could deal with it then.

And so, with his *Milky Way* burning a hole in his pocket, Logan headed along the corridor, tapped his keycard against the lock of his door, and headed inside for the night.

TYLER LAY on his back on top of the queen size bed, eyes fixed on the ceiling, fingers fiddling with the more troublesome of his two testicles.

It was bigger, he was sure. The lump. It was the size of a pea now, whereas just a week or so earlier it had felt the size of—he struggled to come up with a suitable comparison—a smaller pea. A *petit pois*, maybe.

Or was it the same size, and his imagination was blowing it up? He had to admit, he was no expert on the lump, having avoided hunting for it even after a succession of doctors had been down there having a good poke around at it.

Aye, he'd had plenty of casual feels of *the general testicle area*, but he'd studiously avoided getting right in for a proper check. Better not to touch it, he'd thought, in case it... what? Burst?

He couldn't explain his exact reasoning for not wanting to feel it, but when he finally had found the growth, his hand shot away like his balls had suddenly started crackling with an electrical charge.

It was an hour later before he'd gone searching again, this time lying in the bath. He'd felt sick when he tracked the lump down that time—a gut-wrenching nausea that had almost made him throw up into the hot, soapy suds.

Although, on reflection, that may have just been him squeezing too hard.

He hadn't gone looking for the lump much after that, and had fallen back on a more idle sort of fiddling. A supportive cupping of the affected bollock here, a comforting wee rub there. Leave the nitty-gritty in-depth examinations to the experts, and he'd handle the bigger picture stuff. The moral support.

He could do with some moral support now.

But, Sinead had sounded so busy. And she'd been stressed enough over the past few weeks, even before his testes had turned cancerous, what with their workload and the wedding organising. Add in juggling her younger brother, throw in a few sleepless nights, and it was a miracle she hadn't had some sort of breakdown days ago.

He wondered if the boss was back yet. Maybe he could offer some support, bounce some ideas around regarding the case, or just reminisce fondly on that time when they nearly had the shit kicked out of them by a load of teenagers in a swing park.

Logan was probably still out. Or probably asleep. Or probably busy. Probably something, anyway.

Tyler exhaled into the darkness. It would be good to talk to someone though, he thought. To hear some voice that wasn't the nagging one in his own head that told him things were going to be much worse than he expected. The one that tutted quietly and muttered under his breath what a shame it was for him. What a loss. *And such a young man, too. Whole life ahead of him.*

Tragic, really.

He'd tried to drown it out with the TV, but even a *Bond* movie on ITV2 hadn't managed to shut it up.

Well, maybe during one of the big action set pieces, but as soon as the plot kicked in the nagging little voice piped up again.

It was a conversation he needed, not a convoluted movie plot. Some reassuring words from someone. It didn't matter if they meant them, or even if they were true. A few comforting lies would do him the power of good.

They had decided not to tell his parents about the operation until it was safely in the rearview mirror. Or rather, he had decided, and Sinead had tried to change his mind. He hadn't wanted to worry them, though. Not until he knew for sure what he was dealing with. His mum would've been frantic, and he couldn't do that to her. Not yet. Not until he had to.

Now, lying here, he wished he'd told them. He wished they'd known from the start, so they'd had time to come up with just the right thing to say. Found the perfect comforting words to say, if such words even existed.

But he couldn't ring them up and inflict it on them now. He'd left it far too late for that.

Who, then? Hamza would be as busy as Sinead. He didn't want to bother Ben with it.

Hoon?

Was he that desperate?

He rolled a testicle between finger and thumb.

Maybe.

Although, when it came to pep talks, the former Detective Superintendent's were a touch more *confrontational* than Tyler was really in the mood for.

Probably not, then.

The ceiling above him was suddenly illuminated by a pale white glow. At first, Tyler didn't understand what was happening. He briefly entertained the idea that he might be dying, but then realised that the light was from his mobile phone on the bedside table.

He reached for it with his left hand, his right continuing with the full once-over of his testicle. There was a message on-screen, and his heart sang.

Hey! U awake? x

Sinead. It was from Sinead.

He shimmied quickly up the bed on his elbows, and was about to start tapping out a reply when a second message came through.

Long day. Busy night. Fell asleep at my desk!

She'd been so tired. She'd been working so hard.

He deleted the response he'd started, and typed out a new message.

Just going to bed. Knackered and got early start. U get some sleep. I'll c u tomorrow. x

He sent the message, then watched the little bouncing dots that told him she was writing a reply.

A moment later, it arrived.

U OK? x

He rattled off a response.

I'm great! But tired. U go sleep x

Then, he added a row of Zs for emphasis.

The reply that came back to him was short but sweet.

Love u x

Love u 2, he replied, then he set the phone down, fixed his gaze on the ceiling, and tried to convince himself that the lump wasn't getting larger.

CHAPTER FORTY-ONE

"Right, you've got a drink? Because the prices they charge on the train are bloody extortionate."

"Got one in here, boss," Tyler confirmed.

He held up the carrier bag of goodies he'd picked up in the *Sainsbury's* just along the road and gave it a jiggle. They'd barely finished breakfast half an hour ago, but the bag was bulging with crisps, chocolate, boiled sweets, a couple of packs of sandwiches, and a twin-pack of cheesecake slices that Tyler had spotted while standing in the queue.

It was, he'd offered in response to the DCI's judgemental look, quite a long train journey.

"And you've got your ticket?"

Tyler patted the front pocket of his shirt. "I do."

"No, you don't. Because you gave it to me to hold when you went for a pee," Logan reminded him.

He held out the ticket, and Tyler took it with a mumbled, "Oh. Aye. Cheers, boss."

It was ten past eight, and Queen Street station was alive with activity as commuters piled off the Edinburgh train, then were replaced by another lot piling on. The platform that the Fort William train sat on was comparatively quiet, but without a ticket for Logan to pass through the gates, the detectives were stuck in the scrum of the main concourse.

Logan waited until Tyler had successfully managed to get his ticket into the shirt pocket he'd previously thought it was in, then asked the question he'd asked three times already that morning.

"You alright, son?"

Tyler laughed. "I'm fine, boss! Quite looking forward to the train, actually. Bit of, you know, peace and quiet and that. I nearly bought a book."

"You *nearly* bought a book?"

"Aye. I mean, I didn't, like, but I nearly did. It'll be that sort of journey, I think."

"The sort of journey where you don't read a book?"

"Where you *might* read a book," Tyler corrected. "Although, obviously, I won't."

"Because you didn't buy one."

"No. But I nearly did."

Logan gestured to the bag. "Maybe you could read the back of your crisp bags. That'll kill a couple of hours."

"I didn't buy *that* many," Tyler said. He opened the bag and looked inside. "Wait. No. Aye, I did." He closed the bag again, then checked the time. "I'd better get going, boss. Anything you want me to do on the train? Since I won't be reading a book." He gave a shrug that was intended to be casual, but was exactly the opposite. "Anything I can, you know, make myself useful with? I'll have time to kill."

"Just you relax," Logan instructed. "Don't worry about the case. You just worry about yourself."

Tyler smiled, but glanced down. "Aye. Right. I'm sure I can manage that OK, boss." He turned to face the train, but continued all the way around until he'd done a full three-sixty. "You going to be alright on your own?"

"I'll be fine, Tyler. Just got a couple of things to deal with, then I'll be heading up the road myself."

Tyler nodded, turned away, then turned back for a second time.

"You're not going to do anything stupid, are you, boss?"

Logan gave a reprimanding tut and a shake of his head. "Come on now, son," he said. "I thought you knew me better than that...?"

FIVE MINUTES LATER, Tyler sat alone on the train, fist buried in his bag of *Quavers,* eyes idling on the empty platform beyond the grubby window.

The train was reasonably quiet, and he'd been lucky enough to find a table seat without anyone else sitting at it. There were a couple of reservation tickets on the seats directly opposite, but they were for the Fort William to Mallaig stretch of the journey, and he'd be off before they got on.

He was facing forward, which was a relief. Trains were one of the few modes of transport that didn't trigger his motion sickness—unless he was facing away from the direction of travel, in which case he'd usually end up spewing for Scotland. Given that the journey was almost four hours long, he hadn't much fancied the idea of that.

Facing forward, though, with a table all to himself? This was living the dream. Better to be making the journey in the daytime, too. It meant he'd get to see some of the scenery—the rolling land-scapes of Rannoch, and Glen Coe, with the deer racing alongside the tracks.

He'd hoped he might be able to get some nice photos, although the film of brown-green muck on the window would likely take the charm off any shots he was able to get.

Still, he'd heard the view on a clear day described as a 'near-religious experience,' and he could certainly do with one of those at the moment, photos or no photos.

He placed another *Quaver* on his tongue and let it fizzle away to nearly nothing. Somewhere, further down the platform, a whistle blew. An engine revved, hydraulics hissed, and Queen Street station started sliding away on the other side of the glass.

Elsewhere in the carriage, above the rumble of the train and the chatter of conversation, a child laughed. It was a hearty giggle, completely unshackled by any thoughts of self-consciousness or embarrassment. Infectious, too. Tyler found himself smiling at the thought of the kid somewhere further along the train car, excited by the adventure that lay ahead.

They were good fun, kids, he thought.

His smile faded. He reached a hand into his crisp packet and found it empty.

A tunnel closed in around him, and he was all swallowed up by the dark.

―――――

FRANKIE COWAN CHEWED SLOWLY and suspiciously, sniffed the bowl he was holding, then offered it across the kitchen table to where his nephew was scraping some black bits off his toast.

"Here. Taste that," he instructed.

Paco's eyes crept to the bowl of cereal that had been slid in his direction.

"Why?"

Frankie's hand twitched, sloshing the cereal around in the bowl. "Just fucking taste it."

"I don't want to," Paco protested. He knew better than to disobey, though, so he took the spoon, scooped up the measliest helping he could, and shoved it into his mouth.

"That milk taste off to you?" Frankie asked.

Paco grimaced. He managed to hold the cereal in a sort of bowl shape he'd made with his tongue long enough to utter, "Yes," then he got up, spat it into the bin, and spent the next few moments dry heaving over the kitchen sink.

"Fuck's sake," Frankie spat. "Budge! Budge! Where are ye, ye big fuckin'—?"

Budge appeared in the kitchen doorway, damp and bare-chested. He had a towel around his waist that *just about* made it all the way, and clenched it with a fist to stop it from falling to the floor.

"When did you get this milk? Yesterday?"

Budge nodded.

"Did ye check the fuckin' date on it?"

Budge shook his head.

"Fuck's sake, man! What do I always tell ye?" He clicked his fingers and pointed at his nephew's back. "Paco."

"'Check the dates,'" Paco replied between retches.

"Check the fuckin' dates," Frankie parroted. He slapped the

back of one hand into the opposite palm. "Every time. These pricks they've got working in the shops these days don't know how to fuckin' rotate stock. I mean, it's no' exactly difficult to pick a thing up, look at the date on that thing, and then work out how long there is left until that date, is it? You don't have to be... what's his name? Him in the wheelchair with the fuckin' robot voice."

"Stephen Hawking," Paco wheezed.

"You don't have to be fuckin' Stephen Hawking to do that, do you?"

Budge shook his head again.

Frankie snatched his spoon back from where Paco had set it down, then rattled it hard against the edge of the table four or five times like a Viking banging a war drum.

"Right, well, someone's gonnae have to run to the shop," he said. An arm spasmed, throwing the spoon to the floor. Nobody passed comment. "Because I'm no' going anywhere the day until I've had my fuckin' *Coco Pops*."

It was right then—right on the *Pops* of *Coco Pops*—that the intercom buzzer rang. Frankie looked first to Paco, then to Budge, but neither man was currently best placed to go and pick up the phone.

"Fuck's sake," he muttered, forcibly pushing the table away and getting to his feet. He went clumping out into the hall just as the buzzer sounded again, and snatched the handset from its cradle. "What?"

There was silence from the other end of the line. Nothing but the faint electronic hum of the intercom, and the distant rumbling of traffic. "Hello? Hello? Who's fuckin'—?"

The door beside him shook as something struck it from the opposite side. *Bang. Bang.*

It flew open on the third impact, before Frankie had even returned the phone to its hook.

"The fu—?" Frankie ejected, and then a man was there in his hallway, all skinhead and scowl.

Frankie swung with a punch, but it was blocked, then a slap *cracked* across his jaw, drawing a disconcertingly high-pitched cry from his lips.

Hands grabbed at him. The world lurched. His back hit the

wall of the corridor outside his flat, and all the air left his body in one big, "Fuck!"

"You mind your language, you cum-chugging walnut-cocked wee fuck," the attacker hissed, and Frankie's nostrils were assaulted by the stench of stale cigarettes and fresh booze.

The stranger was older than Frankie. Quite a lot older. Strong, though, and fast.

It was the look on his face that concerned Frankie most. He'd known enough true, genuine headcases in his time to recognise it. It was a look he'd tried to replicate himself in the mirror many times over the years. He'd come close, but it had been a shadow of the look on this man's face. An artist's impression. This. Here. Now. This was the real deal.

It was the look of a man without an off-switch.

"You alright, Uncle Frankie?" Paco called from the hall.

Frankie's head jerked. He let out a clucking sound at the back of his throat, shouted, "Piss, fuck!" then hissed, "Do I fucking look alright?! Where the fuck's Budge?"

Paco danced from foot to foot. "He's putting pants on."

"Fuck his pants! Tell him to get—"

Another slap struck him, spinning his face to the wall. Open-handed. More humiliating than painful.

But painful, too.

His facial features all spasmed in different directions. He made a clicking sound with his tongue. "Here, watch what you're—"

Another strike. The back of the hand this time.

Then the front, for good measure.

"Will you quit fuckin' slapping me?"

Crack.

"No."

"Everything alright here, gentlemen?"

The voice came from the stairwell on Frankie's left. He turned his head enough to see the big polis bastard from yesterday come plodding up the stairs, both hands in his pockets and a smug-looking smirk on his face.

"The fuck is this?" Frankie demanded, his eyebrows attempting some complex dance.

"You two aren't fighting, are you?" the detective asked. He

tutted and shook his head. "I'm sure whatever the issue is, you can discuss it like reasonable grown men."

"This is fuckin' bullshit! This is a fuckin' stitch-up!" He growled at the man pinning him to the wall. "I'm fuckin' warning you, pal, you'd better fuckin' let me go, or—"

He was jerked away from the wall, then driven so hard against it the rest of his breath was driven out of him in one sour, milky burp.

"Allow me to clarify the fucking situation that you find yourself in, you rectal parasite wi' ideas above its fucking station," the man holding him spat. Literally spat. In his face. "You do not open your fucking mouth to address me unless I specifically instruct you to do so. Is that clear?"

"Who the fuck do you think you're talking—"

The punch, or poke, or whatever it was, was driven hard into one of Frankie's softer parts, right where his stomach met his chest. His lungs, which were already struggling for air, shrivelled inside his ribcage, and all urges to talk were replaced by an overwhelming desire to breathe.

A hulking shape appeared in the doorway of the flat. The detective stepped neatly in front, blocking Budge's path.

"Do me a favour, will you, sir?" he said. "Go back inside and call nine-nine-nine. It appears we've got a hostage situation going on here. Looks like it might turn nasty."

"The fuck you waiting for?" Frankie wheezed. "Nut him."

The detective met Budge's glare with a smile. "I wouldn't," he warned. "Unless you're happy to be hauled into the station looking like that."

The big man glanced down at himself. He was wearing a tight pair of jockey shorts, and not a lot else. He'd wedged his bare feet into a pair of battered old trainers, but hadn't quite managed to tuck the heels in, so they hung off him like flip-flops.

"Best for your sake that you go inside, Mr Bowan," the detective continued. He jabbed a thumb over his shoulder to where Frankie was still being pinned against the wall. "And leave this here stramash to me."

Budge's gaze shifted slowly, moving from the policeman to where Frankie was pinned against the wall.

"Don't. Don't you fuckin' dare!" Frankie warned, twitching violently as the door inched closed.

A moment later, it fastened in place with a click.

"Right, then!" Logan said, turning and rubbing his hands together. "Let's sort this mess out. I'm sure we can talk it over."

"I'm no' goin' to tell you fuckin' nothin'!" Frankie hissed.

"Is that a fact, Francis?" the detective asked. He buried his hands back in his pockets and flicked his gaze upwards. "How about the three of us go put that theory to the test?"

CHAPTER FORTY-TWO

TYLER HAD BEEN RIGHT. The view from up here was something else. You could see for miles in every direction—out beyond the city limits towards Greenock in the west, and east to where the M8 traffic crawled its way to and from Edinburgh.

Up here, you got a sense of Glasgow's scale, how it was growing to consume the smaller towns that had once stood proudly separate, and were now becoming just another suburb with a funny name.

You could see the history of the city, too, watch how the former industrial sites along the Clyde, and the sandstone architecture of the city's original buildings gave way to the metal and glass of the growing financial and IT sector in the West End.

Even the High Street—the oldest road in the city, with its origins stretching back to Medieval times—had evolved into something *new and improved* with a crop of new buildings that, architecturally, could best be described as 'ambitious.'

And the traffic moved through it all, like blood through a network of veins and arteries. People spoke about Glasgow as if it was a place, but Logan knew the truth. Glasgow wasn't a place, it was an *entity*—a schizophrenic living thing with a personality that shifted every minute of every day, and could be transformed completely by the kick of a ball, and the foot you chose to do it with.

Logan gazed out over the living city and breathed in through his nose, enjoying the fresh air. Or fresher air than the stairwell had to offer, at least.

Way up there, you could pretend you were apart from everything going on below. You could tell yourself you weren't part of it. That you'd managed to escape the hive mind.

It was peaceful. Relaxing. Soothing, almost.

Well, for him, anyway.

For Frankie Cowan? Not so much.

"Fuuuuuuuuuck!" Frankie's arms windmilled as he balanced on the edge of the roof, the hand gripping his collar the only thing preventing him from plummeting into the car park that lay a dizzyingly long way below.

The tough-guy act had lasted most of the way up the stairs, then became a bit reedy and desperate-sounding when Hoon had dragged him out onto the top of the building. Now that he was being dangled face-forward over the edge with his feet frantically searching for purchase on the edge of the wall running around the roof, all bravado had upped and left him, leaving him with just his orchestra of twitches, spasms, and tics.

"Please, man! Fuck! Please, don't!"

"Am I dropping him or what?" Hoon asked. He was standing on the wall, too, leaning back a little to anchor Frankie's weight. His closeness to the edge, and the possibility of a sudden plunge to a messy end, didn't seem to bother him.

"No, man! Don't!" Frankie's body shook in big, silent sobs. "Don't fuckin' drop me, please!"

Logan tore his gaze away from the view. "I'm sure this gentleman—whoever he may be—isn't going to drop you, Frankie," he said. "Not if you give him what he wants, anyway."

"What does he want?" Frankie whimpered.

Hoon tightened his grip. "Your eyes!"

Frankie convulsed. "*What*?!"

"Jesus. Calm the fuck down, you teary-eyed wee jeb-end," Hoon spat. "Course I don't want your eyes. The fuck would I do with a pair of human eyes?"

"Necklace, maybe?" Logan suggested.

"No' really my style," Hoon said. "Now, can we hurry this up? My arm's getting tired."

Frankie let out a whimper at that, but tried to stay very still. Unfortunately, his condition made this difficult, and he almost jerked himself right out of Hoon's grip.

"I'd cut that out, if I were you," Hoon advised.

"Piss-piss! Fuck!" Frankie wailed. He shook his head, growled like a dog, then scrunched up his face. "I'm trying. Fuck. Piss!"

Logan joined them at the edge, but stayed down on the flat of the roof. There was no need for them all to be balanced up there on the edge.

Besides, it really was a *very* long drop.

"Information, Frankie. I bet that's what this gentleman is after. Answers to a few questions. Nothing too strenuous."

"Fine! Fine! What? I'll tell you," Frankie babbled. "What do you want to know?"

"Archie Sutherland's family," Logan began. "Did you kill them?"

"No! No, I didn't!"

Logan shrugged. "Right. Drop him."

Hoon jerked his arm, drawing a scream from the squirming wee bastard he was holding.

"No, please, no! I mean it! I mean it! I didn't!"

"He stole money from you," Logan said. "How much?"

"A lot! I don't know! Quarter of a mill, we think!"

Logan breathed in through his teeth. "Ouch. That must've stung. I mean... young man like you, just starting out in life, that's a lot of money. You must've worked hard to build up a nest egg like that." He shrugged. "And yet, you didn't report the theft, Frankie. Why might that be? Someone nicks quarter of a million from me, I'm straight on the phone to the polis. Yet, you didn't do that. Why is that?"

Frankie had no answer to that. None that wouldn't incriminate him in something, anyway.

Logan sniffed and looked out over the city. Blue lights and sirens went tearing through several different streets, but none of them headed this way.

Plenty of time, then.

"Not reporting it tells me one of two things, Frankie. Either you weren't bothered about losing that amount of money, or you decided to take the law into your own hands and get it back yourself," Logan continued. "Now, I'll admit that I don't know you very well, but I'm starting to get a good idea of you, Frankie, and I can't see it being the first one. I don't think you're going to just let a big bag of your money go waltzing out the door without doing something about it."

A seagull *cawed* as it flew up the side of the building and arced past Frankie's face, wings spread wide. Logan wished he could take credit for the convulsion of terror that spasmed through the bastard's whole body, but he'd settle for enjoying the sight of it.

"Now, I know Archie took your money. *You* knew Archie took your money. And now, Archie and his family are all dead, and the money's nowhere to be found," Logan said. "That rings a few alarm bells for me, Frankie. That points a finger or two."

"You can't do this!" Frankie hissed, an acorn of anger growing deep in that quivering jelly of his fear. "You can't fucking do this to me!"

"I'm not doing anything, Frankie. I'm just passing the time until backup arrives, so we can start negotiating with the unnamed gentleman currently holding you hostage. Might as well have a chat while we wait, eh? Makes the time pass more quickly."

"Fuck you!" Frankie cried, and spasms danced across his face.

"You killed them, didn't you?" Logan pressed. "Archie and his family. You murdered them, not just to get your money back, but to send a message. To show what happens to anyone who steals from Frankie Cowan."

"No! No, I didn't!" Frankie protested, desperation flooding back in. "I was fuckin' raging about the money, aye, but I didn't know where he was. I didn't know where to find him."

"Well-connected man like you, Francis? I find that hard to believe," Logan said.

"I fuckin' mean it! I swear tae fuck! I had no idea where he'd fucked off to. We were looking for him—and aye, you want the truth? I'd have murdered the prick if I'd found him—but I didn't. I couldn't. He was totally off the fuckin' radar, man! He'd vanished intae thin air. I didn't lay a finger on him!"

"Unlike Jazmin McAllister, then?" Logan said, and there was a moment of stillness from the man being dangled over the ledge.

"What? What you on about?" Frankie asked.

"She was one of your... what would you call them? *Starlets*?" Logan said. "Pretty wee thing. Short hair. Skinny. Bit boyish, maybe. I'm sure you know the one."

Frankie's tone was suddenly more demanding than pleading. "What about her?"

"You raped her, didn't you, Francis?"

"Fuck off! Did I fuck! Is that what she's saying?"

"That's what I'm saying," Logan replied.

"That's fuckin' bullshit! I never touched her. If that's what she's saying, she's a lying wee slag. I could have her fuckin' charged for that. Defamation of fuckin' character."

"Oh, I wouldn't worry about that," Logan told him. "I think your reputation's already about as low as it can get. A few sexual assault allegations are just the icing on the cake." He drew in a long breath through his nose, held it, then let it out slowly. "She had a baby, you know? Jazmin."

Frankie's head turned sharply, forcing Hoon to adjust his footing. "What? Bollocks. You're lying."

"A girl," Logan said. "A couple of weeks back. Yours, we think. DNA tests will confirm, of course."

There was a scowl on Frankie's face, but the veneer was so thin it was almost see-through. "So? What does that prove?"

"Well, it proves you had sex with her," Logan said. "I'd have thought you'd have understood how that worked at your age."

"I never said I didn't," Frankie retorted.

Logan raised an eyebrow. "You said, and I quote, 'I never touched her.' Impressive trick to get her pregnant without any physical contact. What did you do, throw it at her from a distance?"

"I meant I never fuckin' raped her. She was well up for it," Frankie spat back. Either he was becoming accustomed to hanging over the edge, or his rising temper was making him forget his fear. Whatever the reason, his assortment of nervous tics were subsiding, and that attitude he'd had on him in the park yesterday was racing back to the surface. "Fuckin' gagging for it, she was. For a bit of the big Frankie cock. They're all gagging for it, that lot. I could walk onto any one of the sets for those pornos and have my pick of the minge."

Hoon snorted. "'*Sets.*' Check out Francis Ford fucking Fuckula here with all his fancy movie terminology. The lassies were all getting pumped in the back of taxis or pokey wee hotel rooms, no' on the fucking Warner Brothers studio lot."

"Aye, that's still the fuckin' set, though," Frankie insisted. "And they were all still mad up for a shagging. They love the cock, that lot."

"Jazmin was gay, wasn't she?" Logan said. He was still looking out over the city, worried what he might do if he looked Frankie in the eye. "We researched her a bit. All her videos, they're all with other women. From the conversation one of my colleagues had with her parents, he got the impression that she very much did *not* 'love the cock.' That she had never shown so much as a passing interest in 'the cock,' in fact." Logan gave him as much of a look up and down as he dared. "So, of all the possible cocks on offer, yours would seem like an unlikely one to suddenly develop an urge for."

Frankie hoiked up a wad of snot and spat it down into the car park below. He waited until it had fallen all the way to the ground far below before responding.

"Aye, well, I don't give a fuck what you believe," he said. "She was up for it. She was fuckin' *begging* for it, in fact. All big eyes, an' that. Pleading for me to stick it in her."

He shrugged. A bold move, considering his current predicament.

"And even if I had raped her—which I didn't—what would you do about it? What's the conviction rate for rape these days, Mr Polisman? Two percent? And how many of them are getting their tits out and fingering other birds for guys on the internet to wank over? You think a jury's going to believe a lassie like that? Even if it got that far, which we both know it fuckin' wouldn't. My word against hers. That's all there is."

"She's dead," Logan told him. "Hanged herself."

Frankie ejected something that was dangerously close to a laugh. "Aye well. My word against nobody's then."

"Right, I'm going to drop him," Hoon said, adjusting his grip.

This time, Frankie did laugh. "Are ye fuck, old man," he said.

"You're no' going to do nothing. You think you can come here and... what? Scare a fuckin' confession out of me? Aye, good fuckin' luck. I don't scare easy."

"You were pretty much sobbing your heart out two minutes ago," Logan reminded him.

"Aye, fuck you. See how you like being dangled off a fuckin' roof! You caught me off guard, that's all," Frankie said, and to Logan's annoyance, the bastard did seem to have shrugged off the worst of his panic. "But I know you're no' going to do nothin'. You're polis. You're no' gonnae just drop me."

"Joke's on you, you wee fuck," Hoon said. "I'm not polis."

"No, but he is," Frankie said, nodding in Logan's direction. "And this whole pantomime's a total fuckin' joke. You think you can hang me off a roof and I'll tell you I killed Archie? Nae luck, pal. I didn't do it, and even if I had, I wouldn't say a fuckin' word. And as for some daft lassie getting knocked up then doing away with herself? Fuckin' diddums. No' my problem. And don't even fuckin' think of trying to saddle me with the wean. I'm no' interested."

Logan met Frankie's eye, and forced his hands as far down into his pockets as they would go so they wouldn't try and shove the bastard off the roof before he had a chance to stop them. There was no fear left in those eyes now. None. Just a smug look of victory. Of superiority.

'Is this it?' those eyes asked. 'Is this the best you can do?'

"You've got fuckin' nothing on me. No' for Archie, and no' for that wee slag, either," Frankie spat. "So, either get me down off here or fuckin' drop me. Either way, I'm done talking."

Behind the men, a throat was cleared. Logan and Hoon looked round to find Shuggie Cowan standing a few feet behind them, drowning in an oversized black funeral coat. A now fully-dressed Budge stood a step behind him on his right, while the other one—Paco, was it? Logan hadn't paid him enough attention to be sure—hung a few paces further back on the left, his weight bouncing on the balls of his feet.

"Oh, now you're fucked. Now you're totally fucked!" Frankie cackled. "Alright, Uncle Shuggie? Check oot this pair o' pricks. Think they can fuckin' throw their weight around wi' me."

"Frankie. Jack," Shuggie said, nodding to both in turn. The wrinkles around his eyes stretched a little when he recognised the third man. "Bloody hell. Bob Hoon? Have you not topped yourself yet?"

"No' yet, Shuggie," Hoon said. He yanked Frankie back from the edge and sent him stumbling down onto the roof. "But the day's still young."

"You're looking old, Bob."

"Aye, well, you look like you've just dragged your withered arse out of a fucking hole in the ground," Hoon retorted. "So maybe best no' calling the fucking kettle black, eh?"

Shuggie went through the motions of a laugh without ever really coming close to one. "Fair point, Bob. Eloquently made, as ever," he conceded.

There was a subtle change to his demeanour then—a shifting of gears away from making pleasantries and towards something more business-like.

"I'm afraid you gents are wasting your time with my nephew here," Shuggie said. "He had no involvement in Archie's death."

"See? I fucking telt ye!" Frankie spat, puffing himself up like he was getting ready for a square-go. "I'm gonnae get you two pricks fuckin' fired, or... ex-communicated, or whatever the fuck it is you do."

Logan ignored him, and addressed the older Cowan, instead. "And where did this information come from, Shuggie?" he asked. "What makes you so sure?"

Shuggie tilted his head towards Budge. "Brendan here is an old family friend. He's been bringing me up to date with my nephew's... antics. He tells me that much to Frankie's frustration, he had no idea where Archie and his family were. Says he had no involvement in their deaths."

"And you believe him?" Logan asked.

Shuggie nodded. "I do."

Frankie jabbed a finger at Logan. "See? What did I fuckin' well say?" he seethed. He strutted up to Hoon, teeth bared and flecked with foamy spit. "Check you oot. No' so fuckin' tough now that I've got—"

The hand came out of nowhere, and the *crack* of the slap rang out across the rooftop. Frankie staggered, clutching at his cheek, his face burning red with embarrassment, or rage, or some highly unstable cocktail of the two.

"Oh, you are fucked now, pal! You are royally fucked now!" Frankie said, the words giggling hysterically out of him. He clicked his fingers. "Budge! Fuck this prick up!"

He waited.

Far down below, the city held its breath.

Frankie turned and looked back over his shoulder. "Budge?"

"What are you waiting for?" asked Paco, eyes darting from the big man to Frankie and back again. "Go and help him."

"Brendan doesn't say much," Shuggie said. He reached into his pocket, produced a packet of cigarettes, and drew one out. "He's like his father in that regard. A man of few words." He held a hand out, and Budge passed him a lighter. He lit the cigarette, drew in a lungful, then handed the lighter back. "When you get him talking, though, he says some very interesting things."

Some of that confidence that had swelled Frankie's chest was ebbing away now. "What sort of things?"

Shuggie ignored the question for the moment. "I was coming here to break the news to Frankie about the sad passing of our mutual acquaintance." An eyelid twitched. A hand flexed, then contracted. "Wee Jazzy. Lovely girl. A favourite of Archie's. And mine, actually. Very infectious laugh she had." He smiled at the thought of it. "Do anything for you, too. And, though you wouldn't think it to look at her, a real tough cookie when it came to negotiating her contracts. The other girls, they'd bring her in to make their deals for them. She always managed to get their fees bumped up. Never took a cut, though. Just liked to be helpful."

"Sounds like a fine young woman," Logan said.

"Aye. One of the finest," Shuggie agreed. "So, when I heard what had happened." He flicked his gaze, just briefly, in Budge's direction. "When I heard *everything* that had happened, I knew I had to swing by and have a wee word with my nephew here."

Shuggie took another draw of his cigarette, then dropped it and ground what was left of it beneath the heel of a shoe. He gestured at the detectives, and at the rooftop in general.

"This was a surprise, though, I have to say. This unexpected wee reunion. But, my nephew's right, lads. You say he raped our wee Jazzy, but you don't have any proof. And you won't be able to get proof, either. You know it. He knows it. I know it. We all know it. You can throw your weight around all you like, but there is not a single thing you can do to him."

Logan could see where this was going, even if Shuggie's nephew couldn't.

"Hear that? There's fuck all you can do to me," Frankie sneered.

A hand was placed on his shoulder, courtesy of his uncle. He looked down at it, apparently confused by the suddenness of its appearance, and the pressure it was in the process of applying.

"This is a family matter, Jack," Shuggie said. "Best I don't bother you with the details."

"Aye! You fuckin' tell him, Uncle Shuggie. We're family."

The hand on Frankie's shoulder became a vice on the back of his neck. Shuggie's voice was like the rasping of a rusty saw. "I wasn't talking about you," he said. "Brendan?"

Paco squealed in fright as Budge caught him by the arm. "Hey! What? Uncle Frankie, what's...? What's happening?"

"They took it in turns. These two. They took it in turn to rape her," Shuggie continued.

"Wh-what?" Paco cried. "N-no, no, we didn't. She was—"

"Fuckin' shut up!" Frankie barked, silencing the younger man before he could say anything incriminating.

"Jazzy spoke to one of the other girls. Told her everything. Everything they did. Everything they made her do. How scared she was." Shuggie gritted his teeth, and Frankie squirmed as the grip tightened. "How much they'd hurt her."

Logan took a cautious step forward. "Right, well, in that case we can—"

"She won't testify. Before you start thinking you might be able to build a case. You can't," Shuggie said. "And even if she did, it's still one word against the other. These two against her. You think that's even getting as far as the Procurator Fiscal? Honestly?"

"Maybe we can..." Logan began, but he couldn't keep up the pretence long enough to reach the end of the sentence. There would be no trial, never mind a conviction.

He looked out across the city that had once trembled at the mention of his name. "Mistakes were made, Jack," he admitted. "I was... Christ, naive, I suppose, if you can believe that? You think you can step away, don't you? Move on. Put it all behind you. Forget what we know. What we've done. Who we were. But we can't, can we? It doesn't work like that."

"No," Logan agreed. "It doesn't work like that."

Shuggie's smile was one of grim disappointment. "Aye. Thought as much," he said, then he motioned to the door with a jerk of his head. "Now, I suggest you two get going before our mutual acquaintances in the upper echelons of Police Scotland get wind of what you were doing here."

Logan looked across the faces of the four men standing opposite. "What are you going to do to them?"

Hoon's hand patted him on the shoulder. "Like the man says, Jack. That's a family matter," the former Detective Superintendent urged. "Best you and me don't concern ourselves with the details..."

CHAPTER FORTY-THREE

BEN NURSED a cup of tea as he stood studying the Big Board. It was a collage of information now—photographs, print-outs, and *Post-Its* linked together by lengths of thread and a system of colour coordinated pins.

There were statements, observations, maps, a timeline, and dozens of other scraps of information they'd managed to rustle up between them in the past few days.

And it told them, as far as Ben could gather, nothing.

No. That wasn't true. It told them plenty—just not the thing they wanted to know.

It told them about a girl too ashamed of what she'd done to tell her parents about their grandchild.

It told them about a couple who'd thought they were helping. A child, given away.

A life lost to guilt, and to grief.

It told them all these things, and more.

What it didn't tell them was who'd killed Archie Tatties, his wife, and her two children.

And yet... it was there, he thought. Woven into the web of information somewhere. Waiting to be unravelled.

Hidden, but only just.

"Any ideas?" asked Dave Davidson, the wheels of his chair

squeaking as he rolled himself up. "Because I wouldn't mind getting home for the weekend. Someone's got to feed my fish."

Ben took a sip of his tea. "Nothing jumping out at me yet," he admitted.

"Could we just say 'the butler did it,' do you think?" Dave suggested. "Get it all wrapped up by lunchtime?"

"That would be nice, aye," Ben agreed. "No butler, though."

"Jesus. What sort of Mickey Mouse investigation is this, with no butler?" Dave grumbled. He shrugged. "Well, I'm out of ideas, then."

It was a shame, right enough, the lack of a butler. They were always reliable suspects—ever-present in the background. Part of the furniture, so never really noticed by anyone. They'd see things, though, while they went about their job. They'd notice little details. Spot opportunities. And they'd be so invisible that no bugger would ever suspect them until it was too late.

Aye, a dodgy butler would've been handy about now, right enough. Or a shifty gardener. A shady-looking maid, even.

"DCI Logan's interviewing a possible suspect about now," Ben said, checking his watch. He pointed to a name on the board. "Frankie Cowan. We think he's our best lead at the moment."

Hamza piped up from his desk. "Eh, sorry, sir. Message just came in from the DCI. Frankie's a dead end."

Ben closed his eyes for a moment, then consoled himself with another drink of tea. "Aye, well," he said. "Looks like you'll have to find a babysitter for those fish, after all, Dave."

THEY SAT in Logan's car out by the Dumbarton branch of *Asda*, the glass steaming up with the heat of the *KFC* Hoon had insisted on as "a wee fucking thank you" for his assistance.

It had been a stupid move, the whole thing. Yes, Logan had wanted answers, but the roof was only partly about that. Mostly, it had been about wiping the smug look from Frankie's face. It had been about payback.

Frankie had gone out of his way to humiliate the detectives in the park the day before. He'd largely succeeded, too. That shouldn't have mattered, though. That shouldn't have been what this was about.

"You ever realise you're no' as evolved as you think you are?" Logan asked, staring ahead through the fogged-up glass.

Beside him, Hoon stopped gnawing on a bone long enough to spit out a, "Do I fuck," then he ripped some more chicken flesh off with his teeth and chewed noisily.

Maybe Logan was overthinking it. Back in the day—before his time, granted—that sort of stunt was a weekly occurrence. Got a hard nut you wanted to crack? Dangle him off a roof, or upside-down from a bridge. Lock him somewhere hot in the boot of a car, and leave him to consider the decisions that had brought him there. Find a quiet staircase, and let gravity do the rest.

There was an argument that these methods 'got things done.' And they did. Just not necessarily the right things, and often not even to the right people.

"Stop fucking moping," Hoon said, sucking the grease from the tips of each finger in turn.

"I'm not moping. I just... We shouldn't have left them there like that."

"Aye, we should," Hoon insisted. "Whatever that wee cockhobbit's got coming to him, he's got coming to him. And what the fuck were you going to do about it, anyway? You can't arrest a man for saying he wants to talk to his nephew. Especially no' if that man's Shuggie fucking Cowan."

"We both know what he's capable of, Bob."

"Aye, but you can't charge someone for what they're capable of. Fortunately for yours fucking truly. You can just get them on what they've done." Hoon picked up another piece of chicken, took a bite, then continued with his mouth full. "If your man suddenly vanishes off the face of the fucking Earth, then one, good fucking riddance, and two, you can always tip a wee wink to whoever the fuck's in charge down here now."

"Heather Filson," Logan said, and Hoon almost choked on a piece of crispy chicken batter.

"Seriously? Did you and her no'—"

"Long time ago," Logan said, bringing that avenue of conversation towards a screeching dead end.

Hoon cackled, then returned his attention to his food. "You can't get your tits in a twist about what Shuggie might or might not do to that rapey wee fuck. He might no' even kill him. He might just cut his balls off or something. He did that before, mind? Big Billy No-Balls? Great big fella, wi'—"

"No balls. Aye, I remember," Logan said.

"Speaking of which, did you talk to Boyband yet?"

Logan nodded. "Aye."

"About...?" Hoon whistled through his teeth and looked down at his crotch, which was currently buried beneath a cardboard bucket of fried chicken.

"Aye. About everything," Logan confirmed.

"High fucking time," Hoon said. He plucked a chip from the bucket, dunked it in a little carton of barbecue sauce, then bit the end off it. "No' that I give two fucks, but how's he doing?"

"He's... I don't know. Fine, I suppose. Scared."

Hoon tutted. "Fuck's sake. Scared? Of what? A wee bit of ball cancer?" He caught the look from Logan, and some long-dormant memory rose urgently to the surface. "Shite, Jack. I didn't mean that. I forgot."

Logan waved the apology away. "I think he feels a bit useless. Tyler, I mean."

"Fuck me, more so than usual?"

Logan chuckled. "Aye. He was meant to be off this week. Him and Sinead. But they both came in. I think he wanted to feel like he could still help. Like, despite everything, he could still make a difference."

Hoon chewed in silence. Or chewed without speaking, at least. The chewing action itself made an unreasonable amount of noise.

"Aye," he said, after a sip of his *Pepsi*. "I get that."

"Mind and tell him I *wasn't* asking for him, will you?"

Logan gave a snort. "Aye. I will," he said. "How's the new job going?"

Hoon shrugged. "Was meant to start today, so I'll probably get the fucking sack, thanks to you."

"Sorry. You should've said."

"Nah, just winding you up. Will I fuck," Hoon replied. "The manager there'll no' say anything about it." He held up his pinkie finger and waggled it to suggest he had the man wrapped around that particular digit. "I'll probably get him to pay my fucking travel expenses."

Logan reached into his coat pocket and removed his wallet. "Here, no, I'll—"

"Fucking put that away. Right now," Hoon instructed. He had a chicken drumstick held halfway to his mouth, and a dangerous glint in his eyes. He waited until Logan had pocketed the wallet, then took a bite. "Like you said about Boyband, it's good to be useful sometimes. Even if it is just for dangling wee arseholes off roofs."

"Aye. Well. I shouldn't have done that, and I shouldn't have got you involved," Logan replied.

"Don't fucking stress yourself, Jack. This is the best day out I've had in months," Hoon assured him. "This has been like a fucking day trip to Disneyland." He took another bite of chicken. "Who did it, then?"

Logan blinked. "Did what?"

"Your murders. Archie Tatties and his family. If it's no' Frankie, who was it?"

Logan looked up through the steamy windscreen, as if he could still see the top of the tower block up there somewhere. "It might still be Frankie," he said, but there was very little conviction behind the words.

"Nah," Hoon said, mid-chew. "I'm not feeling it."

"No," Logan agreed. "Nor me. Not now, anyway. How would he have found them?"

"Exactly," said Hoon. "Way up there? Arseholes like Frankie might think they've got connections, but they're worth fuck all anywhere past Clydebank."

"It had to be someone who knew where to find them."

"Like who?"

"Billy Neeps knew. We can place him at the scene. And he had motive."

"There you fucking go, then!" Hoon cried, throwing his chicken leg back into the cardboard tub. "Let's go find that unfunny wee fuck and hang *him* off a roof, then!"

"Tempting," Logan admitted. "But no. I don't think he did it, either. He's mixed up in it, but not like that. Him and his wife made a deal with Archie, but they didn't kill him."

Hoon tutted, and plucked his discarded chicken back out of the box. "Fuck's sake. Who else, then?"

Logan wiped the steam from the side window with the sleeve of his coat, revealing the car park shared by the KFC and the other retail units. He looked out over it, but paid very little attention to the cars, buses, taxis, delivery vans, and trolley-pushing pedestrians who weaved in and out of each other in some clumsy yet elaborate dance.

He'd been blinded all the way through this. Blinkered first by Archie's business income, then the discovery of his close working relationship with Shuggie Cowan, which had, in turn, steered him straight in Frankie's direction.

Each new discovery had taken up room in his head—Billy Neeps and the baby, Jazmin McAllister's suicide, Archie's visit to Skye—so much so that he hadn't stopped to consider the other possibilities. To go back to basics.

Who had the motive, the means, and the opportunity?

Assuming it wasn't Frankie, and taking Billy Neeps out of the equation for the moment, then who did that leave?

Who had the motive?

The Krankies, mainly, if Billy was to be believed.

Christ, that would be a turn-up for the books, wouldn't it?

But no. The geriatric panto stalwarts may well have had their reasons for killing Archie, but he couldn't see them having either the means or the opportunity.

Or, given their age, the energy.

Not them, then.

Fellatio McFudd?

Same again. A motive, maybe, albeit a slim one. But how would the drag act have found them? And would he—or she, depending on the mood of the moment—be capable of murdering a family of four in cold blood? As far as Logan was aware, Ms McFudd had never killed anyone before. This would be a hell of a way to start.

Actually, that was a point.

"It wasn't their first kill," he realised.

Hoon looked up from where he'd been poking through the bones in his tub, hoping to find some more chicken to gnaw on.

"Eh?"

"The killer. You don't go straight to stabbing a whole family to death on your first outing," Logan mused. "I mean, two of them were kids. Wee girls. And it was controlled, too. That's no first-timer."

Someone who'd killed before, then.

Motive, means, opportunity, and experience.

Who did that leave?

Rufus Boyle, the cottage's owner. He knew the family was staying there. Was he capable of murder? Maybe. He had an arrogance about him, and a temper, too. Men like Rufus had a sense of entitlement that allowed them to justify all sorts of things to themselves—sordid affairs, expensive coke habits, shady business deals. The odd bit of wife-beating, maybe.

But murder? Logan wasn't convinced.

Besides, Rufus didn't know about the money, did he? So, the opportunity and the means, in his case, but maybe not the motive.

It could've been random, of course. Just bad luck on the family's part that someone chose that particular day to invade that particular house.

But, no. That didn't feel right, either. Them sitting there with a big bag of stolen money? Hell of a coincidence.

And the house hadn't been ransacked. Given that they were unlikely to keep said big bag of stolen money on display in the living room, it had to be someone who'd targeted them on purpose.

Someone who knew about the money.

Someone who knew where to find them.

Someone who'd killed before, or at least come face to face with death.

A car trundled past the window, and Logan's gaze was drawn to the yellow light on its roof.

"Oh," he said, jerking forward so suddenly that his chest honked the car horn. "Shite!"

CHAPTER FORTY-FOUR

TYLER SHUFFLED out of the station, pulling his case behind him with one hand, and pressing his phone to his ear with the other. A fine drizzle met him as he stepped outside, and he released his grip on the case just long enough to pull his jacket tighter to the back of his neck.

"No, we got in early," he said. "I know. First time for everything. Have you left to pick me up yet? No? Right, just wait there. I'll get a taxi over. No, it's fine. Honest. I want to say cheerio to Hamza and Ben, anyway." He scanned the taxi rank and found just one car waiting. "Put the kettle on. Tea on the train was shite."

He quickly said his goodbyes, then rushed across the road before the woman making her way across the *Morrison's* car park with two big bags of shopping could beat him to the car.

"Alright to chuck this in the boot, mate?" he called to the driver, holding his case up.

The driver's door opened and a man in his mid-to-late thirties stepped out. His head was shaved, but the outline of the stubble suggested he'd have been largely bald even if he hadn't taken the razor to it.

"Morning. Just," the taxi driver said, reaching a hand out for the bag. "I'll take that for you."

"Oh, cheers," Tyler said, handing over the case. He stepped back, making room for the driver to open the boot. It was a large boot, but then it was a large vehicle. A seven-seater. "I could probably have just taken it in the back with me," the DC realised.

"No worries," the driver said. He shoved the case in beside another bag, then quickly closed the boot. "In you get. Might be better up front, in fact. Just had someone with a couple of dogs in the back, and they were both soaking."

Tyler nodded, walked around to the front passenger door, then climbed inside after lifting a glossy brochure that had been sitting on the seat.

"Tesla," he remarked when the driver returned. "Nice. You thinking of getting one?"

"Thinking about it, aye," the driver confirmed.

"Expensive?"

"Not bloody half! Got to treat yourself from time to time, though, right? Besides, fed up of this thing. Too big." He turned the key and started the engine. "I once had a fridge in here, believe it or not. One of them big American ones."

"With the icebox on the front?" Tyler asked.

"That's the one."

"Bloody hell," Tyler remarked. He turned and looked back over his shoulder. "Good size, right enough."

"Said the nun to the bishop!" the driver added, then he winked, clicked his indicator, and pulled away from the rank. "Where we off to?"

"Police station," Tyler said.

The driver did a double-take. "Police station? You with the police?"

"I am, yeah," Tyler confirmed. "Detective Constable."

"Aye? Christ. Well done. I had one of your colleagues in here recently. Day before yesterday." The driver gestured at his face. "Darker-skinned fella. Seemed nice enough, though."

"DS Khaled," Tyler said. "And, aye. He's a good guy."

"Pete. Pete Hill," the driver said. "Me, I mean. My name."

Tyler recognised it from the report. "Ahh. You're the guy who drove... Gotcha. Hello."

"Archie Tatties. *'Where's the Haggis?'* Aye. That was me," Pete confirmed.

"Right. Well, thanks for all your help with the investigation,"

Tyler said.

"Was it?" Pete asked. "Helpful, I mean?"

"It was," Tyler confirmed.

Pete tapped his hands on the wheel, pleased with himself. "Good. Nice to be helpful."

Tyler glanced at him, then out the side window. "Aye."

"Terrible what happened there. Terrible business altogether," Pete continued. He winced. "I mean, you come on holiday for a break. To get away with the wife and kids. And what happens? Some knife-wielding maniac bursts in and kills your whole family. Just... just awful, isn't it? Horrible."

Tyler hesitated, then agreed on auto-pilot. "Aye," he muttered. "Awful."

He looked down at the brochure he still held in his hands.

Expensive cars, Teslas.

Ridiculously so.

"You got someone for it yet?" Pete asked.

Tyler flicked to the back of the brochure, hunting for a price list. When he didn't find one, he placed the glossy sales document on the dashboard. "It's ongoing," he replied.

"Is that police-speak for, 'No,' then?" Pete chuckled. "I'm kidding. I'm kidding. I'm sure you've got it all in hand."

"Hopefully, aye," Tyler said.

He side-eyed the man in the driver's seat.

'A knife-wielding maniac.'

That was what he'd said.

Not 'a maniac.'

Not even 'an armed maniac.'

Knife-wielding.

How the hell had he known that?

Tyler's phone rang in his pocket, startling him. Logan's voice barked at him even before he'd placed the mobile to his ear.

"Tyler. You back in the Fort?"

"I am, boss," the DC confirmed. He stole another look at the driver, then moved the phone to his other ear. "I'm, eh, I'm in a taxi."

"A taxi?"

"Aye. Train got in a bit early, so I told Sinead I'd meet her at the station," Tyler explained. "Funny coincidence, boss, I'm sat right next to the driver who took Archie and his family to Glen Coe. He's literally right beside me now."

"Christ. Don't let the bastard out of your sight!" Logan hissed, dropping his voice. "I think it was him. I think he did it."

Tyler smiled. "Aye, I was just thinking that very same thing boss, as it happens," he said, radiating counterfeit cheerfulness.

"I'll phone ahead. Have someone waiting," Logan told him. "You alright?"

"Hunky-dory, boss," Tyler said.

"I'll call you back."

The line went dead. Tyler looked down at the screen until it went dark, then slipped the phone back into his pocket.

"That the big chief, was it?" Pete asked. They were passing the leisure centre, slowing for the approaching roundabout. "What is he? Detective Inspector?"

"Detective Chief Inspector," Tyler said.

"Detective *Chief* Inspector," Pete said. He whistled quietly. "Big man, is he?"

Tyler frowned. "How do you mean?"

"I mean... is he a big man?" Pete asked. He smiled, but at the same time did not. He took his eyes off the road and fixed them on the DC in the passenger seat. "I thought it was a pretty straightforward question."

"Um, aye. He is," Tyler confirmed. The roundabout was dead ahead now. He braced himself for the swing to the left that would point them in the direction of the station.

"Thought so. Big voice," Pete said. "Fairly carries in a confined space."

The friendly demeanour he'd been projecting prior to the phone call had fallen away. He'd heard everything, Tyler realised. Every bloody word.

Shite.

"I'm going to have to ask you to pull over, Mr Hill," Tyler said.

"What? Why? He told you to head to the station, didn't he? Your boss. That's what he said, wasn't it?"

They reached the roundabout, but didn't take the turning. Instead, horns blared as Pete floored the accelerator, powering the taxi straight over the painted circle in the middle of the junction, and onto the twisting, narrower road that ran alongside the River Nevis.

Thrown back into his seat, it took Tyler a moment to recover enough to bark out an order. "Mr Hill, you're not doing yourself any favours here. Pull over. Now. Before—"

He saw the elbow coming. Not enough to stop it completely, but enough to deflect the worst of it. It caught him on the side of the head instead of the nose, and he was quietly congratulating himself when there was suddenly a hand in his hair, fingers wrapped up tight in his well-tended locks.

Tyler braced his hands on the dash, stopping his face being forcibly introduced to the plastic. He grabbed for the hand holding his head, but it was no longer there. Instead, it *whammed* into his ribcage. Once. Twice.

"Fucking quit that!" he objected, and then the car swung violently to the left, throwing the DC towards the driver.

There were a few panicky moments of punching and slapping. The car rocked and bounced as it barrelled through bushes and snapped saplings under its wheels.

Tyler heard the *click* of his seatbelt being undone, saw a drop into the river racing towards them.

Shit, shit, shit!

Not again!

He fumbled for the belt, grasped at the clasp, saw Pete Hill take his hands off the wheel and cross them over his chest like a vampire in his coffin.

And then came the impact, and the airbags. The scream of crumpling metal. The shout of fear. The water surging up over the glass.

The moment of all-too-welcome pain as his seatbelt tightened across his chest.

He slapped away his deflating airbag and turned to see Pete Hill go scrambling into the back of the car. Tyler lunged, grabbed for a trailing foot, and after a moment's struggle found himself holding a shoe.

The river wasn't deep here. Only the car's front end was

submerged, its back wheels still on the embankment above, but water was flooding into the footwell, soaking Tyler up to the knees.

"It's over, Pete," the DC said, turning in his seat.

An unshod foot flew at him, heel striking the headrest just inches away. Pete clambered up the back seat, pulled up the parcel shelf, then shoved a hand into the boot.

When it returned, it held a small but deadly-looking knife.

But not just a knife, though, Tyler thought.

A murder weapon.

"Don't you fucking dare come after me," Pete hissed, then he tugged on a lever and one of the rearmost seats folded flat against the floor, revealing Tyler's suitcase and a bulging blue holdall. "I mean it. Don't you fucking dare!"

With that, the taxi driver crawled upwards, and the back door raised as if preparing to launch him out of the car.

Pete grabbed the bag. Waved the knife.

And then, he was gone.

Tyler looked out through the shattered windscreen, then down at his partially submerged legs.

This was, he reasoned, just his bloody luck.

They'd catch him, of course. The driver. Now they knew who they were looking for, they'd get him. Sooner or later. No point chasing him. No point in Tyler taking that risk. Not in his condition. Not when Hill was a killer. A killer with a big bag of money he was desperate to hold onto, and a dirty great knife he was willing to use.

Tyler should phone it in. Call the cavalry. Have them handle the search.

He should leave this to someone else.

Tyler gave his problem testicle an apologetic pat.

"Nah," he announced. His seatbelt buckle gave a *clack* as he stabbed down the button that unfastened it. "Bollocks to that!"

SINEAD WAS PACING in the foyer, chewing on a thumbnail, her eyes fixed on the car park at the front door.

"He should be here by now," she said, for the fourth or fifth time. "What's keeping them?"

"Traffic could be bad," Hamza reasoned. He was standing over by the front desk, trying to look busy with paperwork. The last thing they wanted was for the driver to smell a rat and go tearing off before they could catch him.

Yes, they had Uniform on standby around the back of the building, ready to give chase, but a chase meant a risk of injury, or worse. Better to contain the situation here.

"It's not summer. Traffic's fine."

"He'll be OK," Ben promised. The DI was lurking off to the side of the front door, his phone held loosely to his ear. "No, Jack, I was talking to Sinead," he said into the mobile. "No. No sign yet."

Halfway across the foyer, Sinead heard the DCI swear.

"Maybe we should phone him," she suggested. "Just to check up."

"Best to wait," Ben said. "We've got a couple of cars moving to find and follow. They'll report in as soon as they've got eyes on the taxi."

"I should've seen it," Hamza said. "The driver, I mean. I should've clocked it was him."

"Not your fault, son," Ben assured him. "We all should've considered the possibility."

"But I was there with him. I spoke to him. I knew he'd taken the family to the house. He helped with their bags. He told me that himself, so unless he was blind, he'd have known about the money. He said he took his fishing rods in the car. The knife that killed them was used for filleting fish." Hamza wrung his hands. "I should've seen it."

"It's not your fault," Sinead said, her gaze still trained on the door. She tore her eyes away just long enough to check her watch. It was twenty minutes now since Logan's call. Tyler should've been here by now. Long before now, in fact. "Where is he?"

"Eh, excuse me?"

They all turned to find the temporary caretaker of the front desk emerging from the room behind reception. "Just got a call in," she announced, holding up a notepad. "Car in the river up the glen." She looked across their worried faces. "It's a taxi."

"Right!" Ben clapped his hands together and pulled open the door. "What are we standing around here for? Let's get a bloody move on!"

CHAPTER FORTY-FIVE

FUCK, fuck, fuck!

Tyler ran, breath jerking out of him with every step, as he forced his way through a tangle of trees and raced on up a steepening brae.

The incline that was currently threatening to give him a heart attack was near the foot of what was known locally as 'Cow Hill.' Tyler knew the name, but had no idea of the reasoning behind it. Presumably, cattle had been involved at some point, and he had a nagging concern that he might run straight into one of the bastards with the big horns at any moment.

Fortunately, this worry was quickly replaced by a more pressing one, when he caught sight of Pete Hill hobbling through the woodland up ahead, the bag over his shoulder, the knife clutched in his hand.

It was, Tyler realised for the second time in as many minutes, quite a big knife. And, judging by the Post Mortem results he had skimmed through, the attacker had been very accomplished at using it.

He should stop chasing him.

This was too risky.

This was *madness*.

Fuck, fuck, fuck, Tyler thought.

And he ran on up the hill, hot on the heels of a killer.

THE TAXI WAS ABANDONED WHEN they arrived, the passenger door open, the engine compartment well and truly drowned.

Polis vehicles lined the road where the car had gone off, their flashing lights skimming like stones on the surface of the river below.

"Where is he?" Sinead demanded, elbowing through the throng of Uniforms. "Tyler. The people in the car. Where are they?"

"We're not sure yet," a sergeant replied. He indicated the river with a tilt of his head. "No sign of any bodies, but the current could have carried them downstream. We'll need to get a diver in."

Sinead's hand shook all the way to her mouth. "A diver? You don't need... He's not in there! He's not, he isn't!"

"I'm not saying he is," the sergeant said. He was an older man, but new enough to the area that Sinead didn't know his name. "But the passenger door could have been thrown open on impact, so we can't rule it out."

Ben, who had been picking his way down the slope behind Sinead, indicated that the other man should stop talking. "Do what you have to do, Sergeant," he instructed. "Keep us posted."

"Will do, sir," the uniformed officer replied. "Anything turns up, I'll report right away."

"You're not just searching the river, though, are you?" Sinead demanded. "I mean... they could be anywhere. Further up the glen. Over in Claggan. They might have headed back towards the town. Are we even checking that?"

The sergeant looked from her to Ben, then back again. His smile was kind, but patronising. "I'll see what we can do."

Sinead threw her arms in the air as the sergeant made his way back up the slope. "He'll see what they can do? What's that supposed to mean? He should be searching already. We need to look for them. Now."

"I know, I know," Ben said. He put a hand on her arm and held it there. "We'll find him, Sinead. Whatever's happened, wherever he is, we'll find him. He's going to be OK."

Sinead's voice was a whisper of a thing. "What if he's not, though, sir? What if something's happened?"

"It won't. This is Tyler we're talking about. He's like a bloody rubber ball. Gets bounced around all over the place, but always comes back fine."

"But he's not fine. He's not remotely fine," Sinead replied, the words made flat and small to fit past the sob that was blocking her throat. "He's sick. He should be at home, getting ready for the hospital, not chasing a suspected killer! We're not even meant to be here!"

"I know. I know. And he'll be fine. We'll find him," Ben soothed. "Wherever he is, we'll find him."

"Sinead!" Hamza's shout came from up by the car.

Sinead and Ben both looked, then followed his finger to where a figure was stumbling out of the trees on the other side of the road, the lack of a shoe on one foot playing havoc with his gait and balance.

His hands were bound at his back, and as they watched, a second man came striding out of the woods behind the first, a holdall slung over his shoulder, a grin on his face like the cat who'd got the cream.

Tyler stopped when he saw the fleet of polis vehicles assembled at the side of the road.

"Don't know what all the fuss is about," he announced. "I had the whole thing completely under control." He gave Pete Hill a shove, urging him towards Hamza, who had moved to intercept. "Mind if I hand Mr Hill here into your custody, Detective Sergeant?"

Hamza looked the driver up and down. He had clearly fallen at some point. Mud had been involved. A bruise was colouring in an eye socket, and there were thin scratches on his face and neck from where the fingers of branches had clawed at him.

"If you must," Hamza said. He took the taxi driver by one of his zip-tied arms. "I would say it's nice to see you again, Mr Hill, but I'd be lying."

Sinead and Ben had come clambering up the slope to meet them now. Only some cast iron professionalism stopped Sinead either throwing her arms around Tyler and sobbing with relief, or slapping him for being so reckless. She compromised by placing the toe of her shoe on his foot and pressing down firmly but gently.

"Fuck you!" Hill spat. "Fuck all of you! I'll have all your jobs for this. I didn't do anything!"

"Well, you drove me into a river, threatened me with a knife, then ran off with a big bag of money, so we'll maybe start there and see what develops," Tyler suggested. He slapped his hands together, like he was brushing off dust. "Take him away, Detective Sergeant. I want him out of my sight."

Hamza rolled his eyes. "Now you're pushing it," he said, but he did as he was told and steered the limping Hill over to a knot of watching Uniforms.

"Great work, son," Ben said, once the suspect was out of earshot.

"You'll make a real detective of me yet, boss," Tyler said, beating the DI to the punch.

A smile passed between them. "Let's not get ahead of ourselves."

"Aye well, you know me," Tyler said. "Just like to be helpful."

"You were that, alright," Ben replied, then he put a hand on the younger man's shoulder. There was some squeezing, and the cracking of a voice. "Now, you get yourselves up that road, eh? Big day tomorrow."

All of a sudden, from out of nowhere there was something in Tyler's eye. Dirt, maybe. A bit of leaf. He pressed a thumb into it, gave it a rub, then nodded. "Aye. Big day," he agreed, and he looked down to find Sinead's hand slipping into his.

The squeeze became a shake, then a pat, then Ben's hand was withdrawn. "I'll leave you two to it. I suspect there's a bollocking to be dished out." He started to move, then turned back. "Er... no pun intended."

The DCs watched Ben go walking off, already taking out his phone, no doubt to call Logan. Tyler leaned in closer to Sinead and patted the strap of the holdall he had slung across his neck. "Nobody's asked for the big bag of money yet," he whispered. "You think if we keep quiet they'll let us keep it?"

Sinead's look was wholly unamused. In fact, 'unamused' was a good catch-all term to describe her demeanour in general.

"I'm just kidding, like. Obviously, we're not going to keep it," Tyler said. "Besides, there's a big knife in there in an evidence bag. We probably don't want to get caught with that."

Her foot pressed down on his, drawing a little gasp of surprise.

"Ow! What was that for?"

"Did you chase him?" Sinead demanded. She pointed to the car half-submerged in the river. "Did you get out of that car and chase him?"

Tyler looked down at himself. His trousers were a much darker shade from his hips down, and he was standing in a puddle of water.

"No," he said, then he realised there was no way she was buying that, so he switched to damage limitation mode. "It was perfectly safe. I wouldn't have done it if I thought there was a risk of getting hurt."

Sinead studied his face. She eased up on the foot, but only a little. "Aye you would," she said.

Tyler pushed his chest out. "Because I'm a big brave hero?"

"Because you're a bloody idiot," Sinead corrected.

Tyler laughed, and draped an arm around her, pulling her in close. "Hey, you're the one who married me," he said. "So, who's the idiot now?"

She hugged him, and all the flashing lights and hubbub melted away.

They stood like that for a while, alone in a sea of officers. Just the two of them.

"You ready?" she asked him.

Tyler looked to the sky. Breathed it in.

He looked over to where Pete Hill was being forcibly inserted into the back of a polis car. "Aye," he said. "I actually think I am."

Then, with a crafty wee rub of a bollock, he followed his wife to her car.

CHAPTER FORTY-SIX

Moira Corson regarded the device standing propped up on the adjustable table that had been moved into position across her bed.

"What is it?" she asked, squinting at her reflection in the polished glass.

"It's one of them iPad things," Ben told her.

"That's not an iPad," Moira scoffed. "How much did it cost?"

"Never you bloody mind what it cost," Ben said. Then, when she turned her beady eyes on him, he begrudgingly revealed it had set him back a shade under eighty quid.

"Definitely not an iPad, then," Moira said, although she sounded more pleased by this than disappointed. "What's it for?"

Ben folded up the box the tablet had come in, and shoved it into an *Argos* carrier bag. "Well, I'm heading back up the road this afternoon," he told her. "And since I won't be able to get in to see you, I thought I could check in on this. It does video."

Moira regarded the thing with suspicion. "What do you mean?"

"I mean, I'd be able to call you. But with my face," Ben said. "I mean... not with my face. I wouldn't dial the numbers with my... My face would be on the screen, I mean. Talking. It'd be just like I was here."

"And why would I want that?" Moira demanded. "Good

riddance, I say. Bit of peace and quiet's what's been sorely lacking around here lately."

"Ah, quit your moaning, you ungrateful old bastard," Ben muttered, but loudly enough for her to hear every word.

He picked up the tablet, felt around the rim a full five times before he found the power button, then seemed genuinely alarmed when the screen illuminated once he'd pressed it.

"Here we go," he said, like a soldier bracing himself for some imminent battle. He took his glasses from the breast pocket of his shirt and balanced them on his nose. Then, as if to show the tablet he meant business, he rolled up both sleeves. "That's it on now."

"I can see that," Moira said.

They both peered at the screen. "Right. 'Login,' it's saying," Ben remarked. His eyes scanned the display like there might be some sort of clue there somewhere. When he failed to find one, he turned his attention back to the text. "*Login*." He looked hopefully at Moira. "Do you have one of them?"

"How would I have a login for it? You only just took the thing out of the bloody box."

"Aye, right enough." Ben nodded, then turned back to the screen. "Is there a button that says 'no?'" he wondered, giving the display another once over. Then a twice and a thrice over, for luck. "Or 'cancel,' maybe?"

"It just says 'Login.' That's it," Moira pointed out.

"It says on the box it's got a 'voice assistant' in it. Whatever that is. Maybe you talk to it," Ben suggested. He leaned in close enough that his breath fogged the screen. "No," he said in crisp, clear tones. He leaned back like he was worried the tablet might bite him, searched the display for any changes, then tried again, only louder. "No. Cancel."

"It's not doing anything," Moira told him.

"Abort. *Do not log in*," Ben tried.

"It's not doing anything!"

"I can see that, Moira! Stupid bloody thing. Aye, it, I mean, no' you."

"I should think not!"

"Cancel. No. Go back!"

Ben practically shouted the instructions at the screen, but the tablet refused to comply.

Christ, where was Hamza when you needed him?

"You sure you don't have a login?" he asked, shooting Moira a look like she might be deliberately withholding the information. "Because it's saying 'Login.'"

"I can see what it's bloody saying," Moira said. She waved a hand. "It's too complicated."

"The lassie in the shop says it's no' complicated at all," Ben countered.

"And how old was she?"

Ben considered this. "Nineteen? Twenty, maybe?"

"Well, there you go, then!" Moira sighed, letting herself fall back onto the raised head of the bed. "Nothing's complicated when you're nineteen."

Ben straightened and regarded the gadget, his shoulders stooped by disappointment. "I just thought... it'd be good. Wee bit of company for you. Just until you get home. I thought it was a good idea."

"Well, you thought wrong," Moira told him. She sniffed, and darted her eyes to him just fleetingly. "But, I suppose I should thank you for thinking at all."

"Not necessary. I can take it away and get someone to look at it for us," Ben suggested. "Get it set up."

Moira shook her head. "It's not for me. I've got no interest in anyone seeing me like this unless absolutely necessary. Take it away."

"Right. Aye," said Ben. He picked up the tablet, looked into the eyes of the old man reflected in it, then placed it in the *Argos* bag alongside the box. "It was just a thought, as I say. Thought you might appreciate the odd wee blether, but... Aye." He picked up the bag. "I'd best be off, anyway. Good luck, Moira."

He started to move away, then stopped when she spoke. "I mean... Someone's bound to end up dead again soon. Down here, I mean. It's not like you won't be back."

"True," Ben admitted.

Moira shrugged. "And I suppose the odd phone call between now and then would be... tolerable."

Ben felt the muscles in his face twitch, tugging his mouth up at the corners. "Aye," he agreed. "I suppose it would, at that."

———————

ON ANOTHER DAY, at another hospital, DCI Jack Logan was finding the temperature in the mortuary even colder than usual.

"I, eh, I tried calling. Yesterday. Last night. When I got back up the road," Logan said. "But... I don't know if you were out, or..."

"Not out, no," Shona replied. She was standing over by the kettle, the foil lid of a Chicken and Mushroom *Pot Noodle* peeled back in anticipation. "Just busy."

"Oh. Right. Aye. Fair enough," Logan said.

The sound of the kettle was becoming louder as the water rolled to the boil. Logan waited, watching the steam rising to the ceiling, until the switch had clicked and the noise died down.

"I'm just in to see Tyler. He had his op this morning."

Shona kept her back to him as she drowned the noodles in the hot water. "Tell him I'm asking for him."

"Aye. I will do," Logan said. He rocked on his heels, searching for something else to say. Usually, conversation flowed easily between them, but there was something putting itself in the way of that today. "We got our man," he said, settling on a topic. "For the murders, I mean."

Shona drowned the noodles in the water, and shot a thin smile back over her shoulder. "Well done."

"Aye, so that was... good," Logan said. He clicked his fingers, then clapped a hand against a fist. "Anything come up on Jazmin McAllister?"

Shona picked up her *Pot Noodle* and a fork, and began stabbing the contents of one with the other, breaking up the solid carbohydrate block.

"Definitely suicide," she said. "Signs on the body were in keeping, and Geoff was telling me last night that there was nothing in the house to suggest anyone else had been in there recently."

"Geoff? Palmer, you mean?" Logan asked.

"Yeah." Shona jabbed at her noodles. "We met up last night to discuss it."

Logan frowned. "Last night? I thought you said you didn't go out."

"I didn't." More fork stabbing. "He came round to mine."

"Oh. Right." Logan allowed himself a moment to let this sink in. "*Palmer?* Came round? To yours?"

"Yes," Shona said, then some overly-enthusiastic stabbing sprayed hot noodle water up over her hand. She set the pot down on the countertop and sighed. "No. Of course, he didn't. You think I want Geoff Palmer knowing where I live? I mean, he's a nice enough guy—"

"He isn't," Logan countered.

"I phoned you. Facetimed you, actually."

"Did you? When?"

"Night before last," Shona told him. "Some woman answered."

"What woman?"

Shona shrugged. "Don't know. Tall. Short hair. Pretty."

"Heather?"

Shona picked up the fork and the pot, and went back to stabbing. "I don't know. I didn't catch her name."

"Sorry. She didn't tell me you'd called."

There was a shrug from the pathologist. "It's fine. I'm sure you were both busy. No harm done." She smiled, but it was fooling nobody. "Honestly, it's fine. It's not like I waited up until, like, one o'clock in the morning, or anything, in case you called back." She laughed. And stabbed. "I'm not that sad!"

"Heather is the DCI who replaced me down the road," Logan said. "And, aye, cards on the table? We had a thing a few years back. *Several* years back. But that was then. I have no interest in her whatsoever." He shrugged. "I mean, she's well into me, obviously, but you can't blame the lassie for that. She's no' blind."

Shona's stabbing motion switched to a less violent stirring one. "Someone thinks very highly of themselves."

"Well, you did say you'd stayed up until one o'clock waiting for me to call," Logan teased.

"No. I think you'll find I said I *didn't* do that," Shona countered. She tore open the sachet of sauce and poured it over the noodles. "Technically, it was closer to two. But only because *The*

Bourne Ultimatum was on ITV3. I wouldn't have bothered, otherwise."

She stirred in the sauce, and voiced no objections to him moving in closer until he was standing right in front of her.

"I'm sorry she didn't tell me you'd called," Logan said. "If I'd known, I'd have phoned you back."

"It was Facetime," Shona said. "I had this, like, face paint on. It's probably just as well you didn't see me, to be honest. I looked like Brandon Lee in *The Crow*."

"Never seen it," Logan confessed.

Shona dropped her fork into the pot. "OK, not returning my call is one thing, but *that*? Not having seen *The Crow*? That's unforgivable."

"I will do my best to remedy the situation as soon as possible," the DCI promised.

Shona looked down into her pot. The water had worked its magic now, turning the dry, greyish-yellow block into something wetter, and marginally more edible.

"Pretty sure I've got it on DVD," she said. "And there was mention, I seem to recall, of a date..."

Logan chewed his lip thoughtfully and looked past her into the middle distance. "I mean, I'd have to check with Heather," he began, then a jab from the fork made him hold up his hands in surrender. "Kidding! *The Crow* it is, then."

"Tonight?" Shona asked.

"Tonight," Logan confirmed. "I'm looking forward to it."

Shona held his eye, brought the *Pot Noodle* to her mouth, and plugged down a big gulp of the sauce as he watched.

"How about now?" she asked, after smacking her lips together. "Still looking forward to it?"

"Strangely, even more so," Logan confirmed. He checked his watch. "I'd better go see himself. He should be done by now."

"He is, aye," Shona confirmed. "They sent me his bollock twenty minutes ago." She took a slurp of her noodles. "Want to see it?"

"What? No!" Logan yelped. He looked frantically around the room, like a giant cancerous gonad might be lurking somewhere, waiting to pounce. "Why did they send it to you?"

"I do the testing," she explained. "What, you think they pay me to just sit around here waiting for murders to happen? I do have other responsibilities, you know?"

"No, I knew that, I just... Jesus." Logan stole another look around the room. "How is it? The bollock, I mean? Is it...?"

"Don't know yet," Shona said. "At first glance, it looks contained—the cancer, I mean—but I wouldn't like to say for sure. They've just sent me the one, though, so that's a promising sign." She inhaled some more noodles. "Unless they dropped one somewhere."

Logan chuckled. "Unlikely, I'd have thought."

"Sure, just you keep telling yourself that," Shona said, and Logan couldn't quite tell if she was joking or not.

"I'd better shoot off," he said. "Heather'll be expecting me to check in."

"That joke's over," Shona told him, and the way she held her fork told him he should probably comply.

"There was one good thing about seeing her again, though," Logan said. "It made me realise something."

Shona's eyes narrowed. "And what would that be?"

He leaned in. Their lips met. There was no swelling music. No slow zoom. Just the smell of a *Pot Noodle*, and the sense that somewhere nearby, Tyler's testicle was watching on.

"That I should've done that a long time ago," Logan told her.

Then, he turned with the sort of dramatic flounce usually reserved for romantic heroes in historical novels, made it two impressive strides, then accidentally rattled his knee off the edge of a stool, and limped the rest of the way out of the room like Quasimodo.

———

TYLER STARED at the fruit that Logan had deposited on the table by his bed, then laughed so loudly he earned a *shh* from a passing nurse.

"One plum, boss? Helluva generous of you."

"Aye, I thought so," Logan agreed, taking a seat by the bed. "It actually came in a pack of four, but for the purposes of the joke I had to eat the other three."

"Respect, boss. That's dedication to the gag."

"Tell me about it. I don't even like plums," the DCI said. "But, we all have to suffer for our art, I suppose." He looked the man in the bed up and down. "How you feeling?"

Tyler blinked slowly. "Eh... not sure. I know they took one out, but it all feels weirdly heavy. I'm starting to worry the surgeon might've left his watch in, or something."

"Fingers crossed. The money they're on, it might be a Rolex."

"Aye, but it'll be a right pain in the arse to wind it up," Tyler replied.

"Maybe literally, depending on what way it's facing," Logan said. "But misplaced timepieces aside... You're fine, though?"

Tyler nodded. "Aye. I mean... as well as can be expected, boss. And you were right, of course. Had to be done. And whatever else happens—whatever comes out of it—we'll deal with it, you know? Me and Sinead. We'll get through it."

Logan patted him on the arm. "I have no doubt about it," he said. "And well done nabbing Pete Hill. I haven't had a chance to talk to you since then."

"Cheers, boss!" Tyler replied. "To be honest, he basically tripped and whanged his face off a tree, so I didn't have to do that much in the end."

Logan chuckled. "Still. Good collar."

Tyler sat a little higher in the bed at that. "What made you realise it was him?" he asked.

Logan's mouth drew into a thin smile. "A wise man once told me that these things don't always have to be complicated," he said.

"That guy sounds like a genius, if you ask me, boss."

"I was overthinking it. I got distracted by being back in Glasgow, but I should've seen it right away," Logan admitted, completely ignoring the DC's remark and the grin on his face. "He was the only one with the means, motive, and opportunity. Hamza mentioned that Pete had loaded all the bags into the car, so he would've seen the bag of money. He also knew they were staying out in the middle of nowhere, with no car and a patchy phone signal. And he's ex-military. Army medic, it transpires. We looked into him. Bit of a chequered history when he was serving. Not exactly a model soldier."

"And... what? That was it?" Tyler asked. "You didn't have any other evidence on him?"

Logan shook his head. "No. Just a hunch. You're the one who gave us what we need to build the case."

"Really?" Tyler's chest puffed itself up. "Ach, it was nothing, boss."

"And what about you? When did you figure out it was him?" Logan asked. "Did you work through it on the journey up?"

"Eh, not exactly. I fell asleep on the train."

Logan frowned. "How did you know to go for his taxi, then?"

"It was the only one there," Tyler explained. "I didn't figure it out until I was in the car, and he mentioned that the killer had used a knife. We hadn't mentioned that anywhere, so that rang alarm bells. He was looking into buying a Tesla, too, the flash bastard."

Logan sat back in his chair. "Jesus. So... it was just... what? Good bloody fortune?"

Tyler shrugged. "Pretty much, boss, aye." He grinned and waved at someone behind Logan. "Guess I'm just a lucky sort of guy."

Logan turned in his chair to find Sinead and her brother, Harris, waving back from the ward doorway, and carrying a big tub of *Quality Street* and a bottle of *Lucozade*.

"Aye, son." Logan patted Tyler's arm again, then stood up. "I guess you really are."

EPILOGUE

THERE WAS a man on the same side of the street as her. Walking behind, matching her pace. Step for step.

Olivia Maximuke pulled her bag higher on her shoulder, and picked up speed. She was three minutes from her house. Two if she ran. One, if she ditched her school shoes first.

This was Borys' fault. He was meant to pick her up around the corner from school and drive her home. She'd had him pick her up every day since she'd found the note that had been left in her bedroom, its two-word message—'Soon, *malyshka*—just about as thinly-veiled as any threat could ever be.

By the time she'd realised he wasn't going to show up today, the bus had already left, leaving her with no choice but to make the journey home on foot.

She'd spotted the man following her almost immediately, but then, she'd been on the look-out. He was too far away for her to see him in any detail, and the dark jacket he wore with the hood pulled up didn't help matters.

Had she gone straight home, she'd have been there five minutes ago. Instead, she'd taken a less direct route, sticking to the busier roads and thoroughfares where she might usually have followed more secluded shortcuts.

As well as keeping her visible, she'd hoped it might also prove her wrong. Hoped that the man behind her wouldn't follow the same convoluted route. Hoped that he'd turn off somewhere, keep going, walk on by.

He didn't. He wasn't. He was still right there.

She was clutching her mobile in her hand like a weapon. She couldn't call the police, though. For so many reasons, she couldn't call the police.

She tried Borys again. Listened to the same two rings. Heard the same genial-sounding voicemail greeting.

"Can't come to the phone right now. Sorry! Leave a message, and I'll call you back."

"Fuck's sake. Where are you?" she hissed, shooting a look back over her shoulder.

The man was still there. Still walking. Still behind.

"Call me back as soon as you get any of these," Olivia instructed, then she covertly thumbed the hang-up button, but kept the phone to her ear and waved her arms like she was engaged in conversation.

That was what you were meant to do, wasn't it? Make them think you were talking to someone?

Or was that the opposite of what you were meant to do? Did that suggest a lapse in concentration? An opportunity to strike?

Fuck it, she was running.

She waited until she'd rounded a bend in the road, buying herself an extra head start, then she propelled herself forwards into as close to a sprint as she could manage with this bag and that footwear.

Her breathing became laboured almost immediately, her lung-tightening terror cutting short her oxygen supply. Still, she ran, air wheezing in and out, tears bubbling to the surface.

Was he still behind her? Was he running now, too?

Or would he appear ahead somehow, blocking the way to her house, and to the relative safety it offered?

She was a minute away. Maybe less. But she was away from the busy roads now, running along her quiet residential street.

Alone.

She caught the reflection of the pavement behind her in the wing mirror of a parked car, then glanced back to confirm.

He was gone. Vanished.

This only heightened her fear. At least if she could see him, she knew where he was. She could be prepared. Braced.

But now, he could be anywhere. He could've gone behind the houses. He might be running along the paths at the back, closing the gap on her even now.

Panic provided a burst of energy. She picked up speed, her school shoes *clopping* on the hard pavement, her bag trailing along behind her.

The house was dead ahead. No lights on, but that was fine. She had a key. She could get inside, lock the door, arm herself if necessary. She was almost there. Almost home.

Way back at the start of the street, a car turned off the main road. She didn't see it, but she heard the revving of its engine, the squealing of its tyres.

She ran. As fast as she could, she ran.

She was at the gate.

On the path.

At the door.

The key rattled and scraped against the metal.

The engine roared. There was a clatter of metal and plastic hitting a speed bump too fast.

And then, the door was open, and she was tumbling inside, tears streaming, breathing a thing of the past.

She saw the driver of the car. A young guy. Local. Boy racer type. Nobody.

She slammed the door before he'd gone flying past, locked it a half-second later, then jumped back like the whole thing was hot to the touch.

For a moment, she just stood there. In the silent half-dark of her hallway. Alone.

Please, God, let her be alone.

She checked the peephole of the door for any sign of anyone lurking out there, but saw no one. Her head flopped forward until it rested on the wood, and until her breathing returned to some semblance of normal.

It had been nothing. She'd over-reacted. That was all.

Nothing to worry about. Nothing to be scared of.

She turned to face the rest of the house. The day was cooling outside as the evening approached, and various parts of the old building grumbled and groaned about the coming of night.

"Mum?" Olivia called.

No one answered. But then, that wasn't unexpected.

Once, she could've guaranteed that her mother would be at home. Sleeping, probably, or off her face on something.

She'd changed in recent months, though. Got better. She was probably running, or swimming, or picking them up something nice for dinner. She'd be home soon, though.

Olivia was counting down the minutes.

She checked the peephole again, took a look out through the blinds of the living room window, then headed to the kitchen to check the back door.

It was locked, which further slowed her heart rate from its previous record-breaking peak.

She poured herself a glass of water, downed it in a few big gulps, then burped some of her worries away.

This was fine. Everything was fine. She was home. She was safe. Her imagination had gotten the better of her, that was all.

She closed her eyes. Gave herself a moment. Fought back the urge to be sick, which had been growing since she'd realised Borys wasn't turning up.

Just her imagination.

That was all.

Her stomach gurgled, nausea turning quickly to hunger.

It was then that she noticed the photograph.

It had been fixed to the front of the fridge by a smiley-face magnet she hadn't seen before.

It showed her and Borys sitting in the older boy's car, his arm resting on the sill, gold rings glinting in the sunshine.

She looked around the kitchen, grabbed for a knife, then pointed it at the door like she was warding off evil.

When she was sure nobody was about to come springing out, she took the photograph from the fridge and turned it over.

A message was written there, in a shaky script.

'I left you a little something, malyshka.'

The photo slipped from her grasp. The instinct to run flared up again. But where would she go? Where was safer than here?

She found herself shuffling towards the refrigerator, watched as her fingers grasped the plastic handle, held her breath as she pulled.

There was a plate there, on the middle shelf.

A hand sat on top of it on its back, fingers curled in like the legs of a dead spider.

She didn't recognise the hand, but she knew who it belonged to.

The gold rings were a dead giveaway.

Unable to hold it back any longer, Olivia ran to the bin, ejected the contents of her stomach, and became a tightly knotted ball of fear, all alone on the floor of her kitchen.

JOIN THE JD KIRK VIP CLUB

Want access to an exclusive image gallery showing locations from the books? Join the free JD Kirk VIP Club today, and as well as the photo gallery you'll get regular emails containing free short stories, members-only video content, and all the latest news about the world of DCI Jack Logan.

JDKirk.com/VIP

(Did we mention that it's free...?)

HAVE YOU READ?

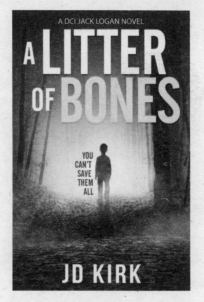

A Litter of Bones

The first book in the million-selling Scottish crime fiction series from bestselling author JD Kirk. Available now.

ABOUT THE AUTHOR

JD Kirk is the author of the million-selling DCI Jack Logan Scottish crime fiction series, set in and around the Highlands.

He also doesn't exist, and is in fact the pen name of award-winning former children's author and comic book writer, Barry Hutchison. Didn't see that coming, did you?

Both JD and Barry live in Fort William, where they share a house, wife, children, and two pets. This is JD's 13th novel. Barry, unfortunately, has long since lost count.